GALWAY GIRL

Feisty Irish gypsy girl, Tamara Redmond is just sixteen when she overhears her parents planning her wedding to the hated Jake Travis. In desperation, she leaves Galway, a place she loves, and stows away with disastrous consequences. She takes refuge in a travelling circus and falls in love with Kit Trevlyn, a trapeze artist. Accused of stealing, she is thrown out. She sleeps rough in Covent Garden where her fears of Jake Travis dominates her waking hours. When he kidnaps her and keeps her captive, Tamara hears a truth, a truth that will change her life and her very existence forever.

GALWAY GIRL

GALWAY GIRL

by

Cathy Mansell

Magna Large Print Books
Long Preston, North Yorkshire,
BD23 4ND, England.

British Library Cataloguing in Publication Data.

Mansell, Cathy
    Galway girl.

    A catalogue record of this book is
    available from the British Library

    ISBN   978-0-7505-4083-4

First published in Great Britain in 2014 by Tirgearr Publishing

Copyright © Cathy Mansell 2014

Cover illustration by arrangement with Tirgearr Publishing

The moral right of the author has been asserted

Published in Large Print 2015 by arrangement with
Tirgearr Publishing

Magna Large Print is an imprint of Library Magna Books Ltd.

Printed and bound in Great Britain by
T.J. (International) Ltd., Cornwall, PL28 8RW

DEDICATION

To my two lovely daughters, Sharon and Samantha, who encourage and support me with each new book I write. I feel blessed to have them around me.

ACKNOWLEDGEMENTS

Romantic Novelists' Association for
their friendship and support.
Just Write group who listened and
critiqued most of *Galway Girl.*
Leicester Writers' Club.
Lutterworth Writers' Group.
Jean Chapman's Tuesday class.
Bead Roberts and Richard Sheehan for editing
and advising on difficult chapters.

My publisher: Kemberlee and Peter Shortland,
without your trust and belief in me
I wouldn't be here.

Christine McPherson: for your
helpful and insightful editing.

Proofreader: Barbara Whary; Cover Artist:
Amanda Stephanie; and all the team
at Tirgearr Publishing.

CHAPTER ONE

1900

The girl lay in the sand dunes, her green cape camouflaged by the tall grasses. Her breath came in gasps. She was lucky to have come this far. The gypsy camp was only a couple of miles behind her. It wasn't far enough, and if her escape failed, she wouldn't live to see her seventeenth birthday.

She could hear the sea lapping the shore, taste the salt spray of the waves lashing the rocks below. Seagulls screeched overhead. Black-horned rams roamed the hilltops. Turf smoke curled from chimneys in the stone cottages in the nearby village. Straining forward, she looked down at the deserted beach. She watched and waited.

The September sun faded and a bitter wind blew in across the bay. She drew her cape tighter around her shoulders when the vessel came into view. The sight of its white sails made her excited. She turned her head as the ship moored alongside the pier and anchored in the bay. She could hear the raucous laughter of the men. They climbed from the vessel and strode towards the beach, their boots crunching the shingle.

They passed by with jute sacks slung across their shoulders. Two bearded and bareheaded, the rest wore caps and rough sea-jackets. She knew they were on their way to the tavern in the village.

The moon was rising over Claddagh; a sight she would never tire of, a place she loved but doubted she would ever see again. Listening to the tide receding, she waited until dark. Then, with one last look at the wild coastline and the misty shapes of the Aran Islands in the distance, she scrambled down the slopes, slipping and sliding in her haste. Her legs stung from nettles, and her bare feet were numb and bleeding. She stepped across the uneven pebbles, her feet squelching the seaweed, her cape billowing, and her red curls tumbling around her shoulders. Making sure no one saw her, she lifted her long skirts and waded through the water. The sea was cold as it rushed over her bruised feet and ankles. Close up, the ship was not as big as she had thought, but it was the only one moored that night.

Without a moment's hesitation, she used her hands and feet to clamber onto the pier. Her feet slipping on the wet stone, she raced along the jetty, only pausing long enough to read the name, *Maryanne*, on the side of the ship. She climbed down onto the deck of the cutter with no idea where it would take her; she had nothing but the clothes she stood up in and a small bundle under her arm. In it, she carried a change of clothes, a hairbrush and a copy of Jonathan Swift's *Gulliver's Travels*, given to her by her grandmother when she first learned to read.

The boat rocked and threw her sideways, her wet skirts clinging to her bare legs. She could quieten a wild stallion, but she knew nothing of boats or the men who worked on them. The ship creaked and groaned as she moved across the wooden deck, leaving wet footprints. Desperate for somewhere to hide and inquisitive about what she might find, she noticed an open hatch. She glanced behind, and then descended the steps. As her eyes became accustomed to the dark, she saw a door with a polished brass plate with the name, Captain Fitzroy. The atmosphere was stuffy; it smelt of tobacco and the stale odour of men.

In the corner of the galley, she noticed a table with a small oil-cooking stove, two saucepans, and several dirty cups. There was no food visible or she would have helped herself. Frightened someone would find her, she pulled the door handle of a cupboard but it wouldn't open. Towards the rear of the boat, she stepped over cables, yards of sail, nets, and clumps of cotton canvas. A line of barrels blocked her way. Behind them, she could just make out several hammocks slung in a row. To the side, there was an enormous earthenware chamber pot with a lid, and a short distance away a barrel containing water, with a tin mug hanging on the side. She drank thirstily. It slipped from her wet hands and made a knocking sound on the side of the barrel.

The shadow of a man appeared on the top step, his bulk filling the entrance. The lamp in his hand swayed from side to side, casting shadows on the floor. Startled, Tamara hid behind one of the barrels.

'Bloody rats again,' the man yelled. 'Did you

13

empty the trap?'

'Flynn did it before he went off,' another man replied.

Her hand covered her mouth. 'God and His Holy Mother save me.' She had not given a thought to the men on watch. 'Sweet Jesus, help me.' Closing her eyes, she pressed her bundle tightly to her bosom. When she looked again, the man had gone.

She could hear the rats scurrying about in the darkness. They were the least of her worries; she was used to them scavenging for food at the gypsy camp. She held her breath and waited until it was quiet again before she climbed back up the steps and crept down the side of the deck. With nowhere to hide, it looked like she might have to find other means of escape, when she saw what looked like the shape of a small boat, protected with tarpaulin and tied down with thick rope, securely fastened to the ship's rail. Her hands shook as she struggled to undo the wet rope, continually looking over her shoulder. It took her ages, but with one last furtive glance behind her, she slipped in underneath the covering. It was dank and fusty.

Crouched down inside the small boat, she hoped she could remain undiscovered; at least, until the ship was out to sea. She was prepared to face anything, even endure the discomforts of being a stowaway, whatever it took to avoid marriage to Jake Travis, the most feared among the Romany people.

She lay still, frightened to move, until she heard

the echo of men's voices and the chugging of a steam tugboat that pulled up close to the ship. The clang of weighty chains, the thud of cargo, and the rumble of barrels being rolled across the deck, made her flinch. Once or twice, her heart almost stopped when heavy boots trampled back and forth close to where she was hidden; so close, she could smell pipe smoke.

'Get these fleeces and hides down below,' a man yelled. The fluff from the fleece irritated her nose and she had to stop herself from sneezing. Finally, she heard the tugboat pull away and the swearing and laughter of the men, then silence. She guessed they had gone below deck to sleep after their fill of ale. Her pulse returned to normal. She stretched her legs. The water lapping the side of the ship felt soothing. In the stillness, she thought she heard a dog yelp, and put it down to the fact that she had not eaten all day and her mind was playing tricks.

She clutched the amulet that hung around her neck with a painting of the moon and stars. She believed it would keep her safe. She longed for the ship to sail and reach its destination, wherever that might be. If she got caught, she would be thrown overboard like trash, with no choice but to swim back to shore.

As the ship sailed out of the harbour, she longed to peek over the side, but quickly changed her mind. She could smell the sea; feel the spray as the wind blew. If she only knew where the *Maryanne* was heading, and, for how long she would have to stay hidden. If it was bound for Australia, she would have to stay hidden for weeks and might die of starvation; she'd be dead on arrival.

A dog barked. So she hadn't imagined it. It growled, gnawed and pulled on the rope that kept her hidden. Her pulse raced. 'Go away!' she murmured. 'Shoo! Shoo!' The barking grew louder. Someone called out, his voice echoed across the deck.

'Goddamnit! Get that dog below before I throw it overboard.' The dog yelped above the flapping of the sails. She tried to imagine the dog's owner. If he liked animals, there was a chance he might show mercy towards her; or, perhaps the dog was on board to deter stowaways.

The current dragged the heavily-laden ship, and the *Maryanne* rushed over the waves. She began to relax and in spite of the cold, she slept. Eventually, the swaying of the ship woke her and she massaged the crick in her neck. Men's feet tread back and forth along the deck, and swear words echoed around her, the wind catching them. Sails flapped wildly; the weather was blowing up a hurricane.

Someone hollered to batten down the hatches. She had never experienced anything like it, and tried to keep the small boat still. Although she had not eaten much, she felt herself retch and muffled the sound with her hand. The small boat began to shift about, her slight body unable to hold it in place. It slid forwards and backwards, banged and crashed against the ship's rails. She could be swept overboard; she knew of men who had died at sea. What if it happened to her? Her life could be over in seconds.

Her head hit the side of the boat. Dear God, the ship was rolling. On her hands and knees, she clung to the amulet in fear of her life.

The swerving action of the vessel made her dizzy. It tossed about like a toy, and waves lashed the canvas covering the little boat. She could hear the clatter of cargo crashing and coming adrift, then sliding across the deck. The wind howled with such force, she clamped her hands over her ears. With each lift and plunge of the ship, she felt so ill she just wanted to die. The rowing boat was partly on its side, with water gushing in underneath. Lightning lit up the deck, flashing on and off like a lighthouse, and she pictured them coming aground, the men abandoning ship, leaving her no choice but to do the same.

When the ship leaned to one side, it threw her sideways, and this time she felt blood on her face. 'Oh, sweet Jesus, save me,' she cried, and retched again. If the dog came back, it was bound to pick up the smell.

How much longer would the storm last? It sounded as if the ship was breaking up. By now, she didn't care if she lived or died. Nerves made her lose control of her bladder, as she clung on for her life.

Then, as suddenly as it had begun, the wind dropped, although waves still rocked the ship. Weak with hunger, she ate the soggy oat biscuits from her pocket. Drenched, uncomfortable, and exhausted from her efforts, she wrapped her arms around herself to try to keep warm. It was quiet on deck apart from the juddering and creaking of

17

the ship.

The sound of heavy boots and a roar to hoist the sail alerted her. A dog barked and grew closer. Claws scratched at the canvas, sharp teeth tugged at the thick rope. She could hear the animal sniffing around where she had crouched in the corner of the boat. Her heart rate quickened. Shivering, her clothes sopping, she slumped to the floor of the boat. What else could she do? The situation was out of her hands. Any minute now, she expected to be man-handled and hauled to her feet like a common criminal.

CHAPTER TWO

Tamara stood with her eyes downcast, her bundle of wet clothes at her feet; she felt sick and couldn't stop shaking. Before her was a stony-faced man, with white hair covering the sides of his face and chin. He wore a heavy waterproof coat and was built like a jailhouse. Two men stood to the side, while two more looked down at her from the top of the mast. She felt their stare penetrate her clothes.

Even the dog, having found its prey, looked up at its master who patted its head. She was fully aware if it had not been for the black and white terrier, she would not have survived the elements another night.

The big man let out a sigh and moved closer. 'You're a gypsy!'

She neither confirmed nor denied it. She knew from experience that most people hated the Roma people, and she wished she had taken the time to remove her coloured bangles and looped earrings.

'What the hell are you doing on my ship?' His voice was husky and powerful. Raising her eyes, she saw anger in his. Her teeth chattered. There was no time to invent a lie and her life depended on her answer.

'Well?'

'Please, sir,' her voice trembled. 'Sure as God is my judge. I ... I had to get away.'

'What are you talking about girl? Why the *Maryanne?*'

'It was the only ship in the harbour last night. I'm sorry, please, sir, don't throw me overboard. I can't swim,' she lied. The men leered at her. She felt nervous and vulnerable, fearful of what might happen to her.

'You'll probably catch your death and save me the bother,' he said. 'We don't carry passengers, especially not women. Do you not realise it is a criminal offence to board a ship without author-isation?' She looked up at his weather-beaten face. 'You'll be reported to the authorities.'

'Ah please, sir, I had no choice. Please, don't report me.' The ship was still rolling and she felt faint. She dropped down onto the deck like a wet blanket, her cloak and skirts heavy and stiff from the salt water. Her hair hung in wet tendrils around her face. She wanted to plead with him further, but with no energy, and looking the way she did, felt bound to fail.

'Do you have any idea where my ship's headed?'

'No sir.' Her voice was barely audible above the creaking of the ship.

One of the men grappling with the tiller shouted. 'We've blown off course, sir.'

'Get her back on course.'

Tamara held onto the rails as the crew shouted and pitched in to help steady the ship and turn her.

Two men were still staring at Tamara. 'Get back to work the lot of you.'

Then the man, she assumed was the captain, pushed his pipe into his mouth, pressed down the tobacco with his thumb, struck a match, and cupped his hands over the lighted flame. When the whiff of tobacco reached her, it reminded her of her grandmother, Lena, who smoked a clay pipe.

Sighing, the captain looked down at her. She felt humiliated sitting on the wet deck, her face in her hands. Whatever he was thinking, Tamara wished he would get on with it. Eventually, he said, 'If you can make it down below, you can use my cabin to dry off and catch a few hours' sleep while I consider what to do with you.' His voice was no longer irate. 'You can wash if we have any water left.'

He handed her a key. Closing his eyes, he shook his head, as if unable to look upon her miserable state any longer. 'Lock the door. I can't be held responsible for the men.'

Inside the captain's cabin, relief flooded her and

20

she muffled her sobs. In spite of his bad temper and obvious annoyance at her presence, the big man's kindness had given her courage. She felt reassured to find he was a humane man. Strewn across the floor were dockets and papers, some of them swimming in water from an overturned water jug. She picked up the oil lamp and placed it back on the table. Then she gathered up the soggy papers.

In spite of the damp and wet, heat radiated from an overhead pipe. Maps and shipping charts hung lopsided on the wall. She could not make head nor tail of them. For now, she was relieved to be inside, away from the elements and the men.

Stripping down to her red petticoat, she laid the wet garments over the back of a chair. She dried her hair on a piece of sacking she found in the corner. A tap on the door startled her. She hesitated before opening it, until she heard his voice.

'Open the door, lass!'

She unlocked the door, holding the sacking in front of her to hide her nakedness.

'I've brought you fresh water and a drop of rum,' he said. 'It'll take the cold out of your bones.' He passed her a tumbler and a small pitcher of water, but he did not attempt to come in.

'Thank you, sir,' was all she could say. She was glad of the fresh water, and although she hated the taste of spirits, she would have drunk anything to get some feeling back into her limbs. She held her nose, threw back her head, and swallowed. It burnt her throat and made her cough, but it warmed her inside.

21

She unwrapped her bundle; everything was soggy. Nevertheless, she washed and then dried herself on a wet towel. Her granny would have called it a lick and a promise, but it was the best she could do. Feeling drowsy, she climbed into the bunk, and pulled the grey blanket up around her.

She wondered why her parents had kept the wedding plans from her. It had been a shock to discover that for years they had been planning and plotting her future. Many a Romany girl would think herself lucky to be marrying Jake Travis. He was a man with money, power and authority, and none of them would have questioned any arrangement. Tamara was not like them; she wanted to find her own husband. Besides, Travis was not a kind man. She had seen it for herself, even if her parents were too blind to see beyond his money. Her eyelids became heavy and she slept.

When she woke, it took a moment to realise where she was. It was early morning. She stepped from the bed, splashed cold water on her face, and got dressed. Her clothes were damp and made her shiver. She wished she could wash the smell of the sea from her hair but, after a vigorous brushing, it looked better. She put her bangles on because she felt naked without them, and tidied the bunk. Making sure she left everything as she had found it, she unlocked the door and went up on deck.

With pains in her stomach, she wondered if she would be given something to eat. It was cold and the sky was smudged with darkened clouds. Two men were scrubbing down the deck, but she could still smell the seawater that seeped through

22

the floorboards. They stopped to stare at her. One of them came over and caught her roughly by the arm. 'If it was up to me, me lovely, you'd be chucked overboard, no questions asked.' His eyes narrowed and she shuddered under his touch.

'Let go of me!' she cried. He raised his hand to hit her, but she stepped back. 'You're just a trouble...' The appearance of the captain silenced him.

'Go below and bring the girl something to eat and drink and be quick about it.'

'Aye, aye, sir.' As the man slithered away, the captain turned towards her.

'When you've eaten, I'd like you to come and see me.' He walked away, calling to the first mate who was operating the helm. She was left wondering if she was to be further humiliated, and if stowing away on his ship was more serious than she had first visualised.

The rice settled her stomach and the cold tea eased her parched throat. She stayed on deck, her few possessions at her feet. The wind swirled around her ankles and she drew her damp cape tighter around her shoulders. Most of the men were below deck, repairing damaged sails and crates. She could tell the captain was a man of principle, nevertheless, she was anxious to know what he wanted to see her about. What concerned her now, was how she was going to persuade him not to report her.

She took a walk down the other side of the deck to get some feeling in her toes. The lifeboat she had hidden in was now on its end, its bottom splintered, loose planks hanging from the sides. It made her all the more aware of how fortunate she had been to survive the storm. A seaman wearing a coarse black jacket was down on one knee driving nails into its sides. He had a grey beard, and the wind blew strips of wispy hair across his face. The terrier was lying next to him, and barked when it saw Tamara. The man smiled across at her and she went over to stroke the animal.

'You're a lucky lass. If you'd a stowed away on McTavish's watch, he'd a let ye starve.' He bent his head and continued to repair the boat. Each lift and thud of the hammer felt like a nail in her coffin, and made her shudder. She had been lucky so far, but she still had to get off this ship. She considered using her womanly wiles to charm the captain into smuggling her off the ship. If that didn't work, she'd have to think of something else.

The sea had turned choppy, and she looked out over the starboard rail. Surrounded by water, she felt defenceless, and wished she was back on land. The cold was turning her toes blue. Her feet no longer throbbed; the salty seawater appeared to have healed her blisters. A fine spray blew upwards, wetting her hair and face. She turned away. She could not put it off any longer. All she could do was pray that the captain was still in a good mood. Her heart pounding, she made her way below.

Placing her bundle at her feet, she stood trembling

24

before him, her hands clasped. The captain sat at his desk, an open ledger in front of him, and glanced up.

'My name's Captain Fitzroy. I'm sure you'd like to know where we're heading.'

'I would indeed, sir.' Pleased that he had bothered to introduce himself, she smiled and relaxed her shoulders.

'If we stay on course, we should arrive in Liverpool within the next few hours, where I'm duty-bound to hand you over to the authorities on the completion of this form.' He held it up in front of her. 'You seem like a nice wee lassie, so make it easy on yourself.'

'I can't write, sir.' She was not going to sign anything.

'I didn't expect you to. What's your name?' He dipped his pen in the inkwell.

'Tamara.' She swallowed. 'What will happen to me?' Fear replaced hope.

'You should have thought of that before you boarded the *Maryanne*.' He cleared his throat. 'Your surname, miss!'

She bit her lip to stem the tears that threatened. 'Err, please sir, do I have to tell you? You see, I, I don't want to be found.'

'Oh, aye.' He put down his pen. 'What have you done?'

Her eyes widened. 'Nothing, sir, nothing at all.'

'And that's a reason to run away?' He laughed.

'You don't understand.' She wiped away a tear. 'I don't want to marry him. I don't love him.'

'You're a gypsy. It is none of my concern. My responsibility is to this ship and the men on it.

Do you understand?'

Dear God, he wasn't going to help her, and his remark sent a stab of fear through her. But she wasn't going to give up. 'I might be a gypsy, sir, but I'll not be bartered for.'

'What's his name, this man you don't want to marry?' He leaned back in his chair and studied her.

She pulled her cloak closer, unable to stop her hands from shaking.

'Come on, out with it, lass. This piece of paper will be completed before we dock. Either way, the English authorities will question you, my gypsy colleen. Let's get one thing straight, lassie. In spite of you being a beautiful young woman, I do not intend to smuggle you off this ship. Is that clear?'

Tamara nodded.

'Either we fill this in here, or I'll leave it to the dockside police, and I can tell you they won't show you any mercy.'

'If I say his name, sir, you'll have no choice but to tell him where I am.'

'Who the devil is he?' He stood up towering over her. 'I won't ask a third...' His voice trailed off as, for a second, he held her gaze. She was not sure what had happened, but he had looked at her as if he knew her, before turning away. He sat down again and massaged his temples.

'Goddamnit, girl! You are the most infuriating...' He got to his feet, took a few paces, stopped, and looked back at her. 'Well?'

'I refuse to involve you.' Frightened of what he might do next, her heartbeat quickened until she thought it would burst.

'You involved me the moment you set foot on my ship.'

'I'll do anything,' she pleaded. 'Please don't report me.'

'It's out of my hands. I have the men to think about.' He walked towards the door and opened it.

'But, sir!'

Ignoring her pleas, his head turned away, he said, 'Go and see Flynn. He's on cleaning duty and will keep you busy until we dock. After that, you will no longer be my concern.'

A deflated expression on her face, her eyes cast down, she walked out and he immediately closed the door behind her.

She placed her head in her hands and wept. All she had done was to make things worse. It was with a heavy step she went to find Flynn, only to discover that he was the mealy-mouthed man she had encountered earlier.

CHAPTER THREE

Tamara approached Flynn cautiously. His smirk left her in no doubt he hated her kind. She swallowed nervously. The men stopped what they were doing and looked up. One man, scrubbing grease from the floor, straightened his back and smacked his lips.

'Ooh, arrah! What 'ave we got 'ere?' Tamara

turned away in an attempt to ignore him, when the black and white Terrier ran towards her. She bent to stroke him and he licked her hand. 'Never mind the bloody dog,' Flynn snarled. 'Ye can start with that!' He pointed towards the smelly chamber pot. They all laughed.

'You don't mean...' Her stomach churned.

'That's right, me lovely,' he said with a broad grin.

'But, what do I do with...'

'You're a gypsy. I'm sure you know.'

The owner of the dog came forward. 'Shut yer filthy mouth, Flynn, or I'll shut it for ye.'

'Come on then, old man.' Flynn balled his fists. 'Think you've got a chance with her yourself, do ye?'

Tamara ran for cover as the two men fought. The dog bared its teeth. It nipped Flynn's ankle, and he kicked out. The dog yelped, and ran to where Tamara crouched behind a barrel. The older man threw a punch, knocking Flynn to the floor. Blood trickled from his nose and he dashed it away with the back of his hand.

'You've been asking for that for a long time, Flynn.'

Flynn got to his feet clenching and unclenching his fists. Eyes flashing, he circled the dog man. The other men gathered round, cheering them on. Tamara clasped her arms over her head. The dog continued to bark until the captain pushed his way through the circle of men, and the two staggered apart.

'Any more of this carry-on and you'll both be detained at the dock,' he shouted.

He ordered the dog man on deck and turned to Flynn. 'Get that chamber pot emptied. It stinks in here. The rest of you, back to work.'

Then he sent Tamara to work in the small galley. The incident with the men had unnerved her, and she wished to be anywhere but on this ship with the likes of Flynn. She scrubbed the galley and washed the tin mugs and plates, all the time glancing over her shoulder in case Flynn came looking for her. When she had finished, her fingers were sore, but the small eating space was grease-free and the utensils sparkled.

That night she slept below deck on a wooden plank and a smelly blanket. A thick piece of tarpaulin slung across an overhead pipe, divided her from the men. She could hear them talking about their families. Flynn was telling dirty jokes and swearing. She trembled beneath the thin grey blanket. Finally, all she could hear were grunts and snores, the sound of rats scurrying across the boards, and the creaking of the ship. She had a lighted oil lamp on a barrel next to her. Frightened to close her eyes, she lay awake.

Her mind gave her no peace. She thought over the days leading up to her running away. Oh God, she had landed herself in terrible trouble. This was all down to her parents. How could they have hurt her like that?

By dawn, her stomach rumbled. She stretched her back and got up. She walked towards the galley where a seaman pushed a tin plate with a measured amount of rice towards her. She ate it where she stood, and then she went on deck as the rest of the men began to stir. The coastline of Liverpool loomed through the mist and gave her a feeling of unease. She walked the deck. The bitter cold made her shiver and she rubbed her hands to stop the tingle in her fingers.

She avoided Flynn and it looked as though the men were busy preparing to go ashore. The captain was busy checking through lists of cargo, so there was no point repeating her plea for mercy. He had done all he intended to do, and she felt grateful to him for at least feeding her and keeping her safe. To be handed over to the authorities as a stowaway, though, terrified her. All she could think of was being marched away and incarcerated in a stinking cell, with no one to bail her out.

A biting wind swept across the deck and she felt frantic to escape whatever fate awaited her. She glanced around for somewhere to hide. Inside the food bunker or one of the water barrels would have been fine, but with the men checking the food store and examining the water levels, she was beginning to despair. She shivered and pulled the sleeves of her dress down over her numb fingers. Her cloak was below, and she couldn't risk going to fetch it for fear of bumping into Flynn.

She looked towards the mast, the sails billowing. Heights had never worried her. If there was the slightest chance of escape, she would risk life and limb. Two seamen were rearranging the sails so there was no escape that way.

The ship approached the dock, and a ripple of

excitement swept through the crew as they worked together to maintain the vessel's speed. After days at sea, Tamara could sense their eagerness to be home with their families. However, she dreaded every pull of the ship.

She looked across at the officials. Their stark uniforms struck terror into her, and her stomach muscles knotted together like a piece of rope. She walked over to where Captain Fitzroy was shouting instructions.

'Please, sir. Won't you change your mind and help me?'

'It's out of my hands. I've said all I'm going to on the subject.' He walked away towards the bow. Tamara moved close to the rails and looked into the dark water below.

A thick rope hung over the side. The men's attention was diverted as a tugboat helped tow the heavy ship into port. Tamara hitched up her skirts and petticoat, tucking the ends into her waistband and, with both feet on the wet rail, she climbed over and curled her legs around the rope. Trying not to look down, she swung back and forth, knocking against the side of the ship. She pulled her body in closer and clung to the ledge, the rivets pressing into the soles of her feet.

'Where's the girl?' It was the captain's voice. There was a shuffling of feet. 'Find her.'

Tamara tensed. The rope was rough on her hands and legs as she struggled to hold it steady. The men were shouting and swearing. She felt a tug on the rope and she looked up. Two seamen were hauling her back up, but she hung on with her feet flat against the rusty hull. A seagull

31

screeched overhead, and began to beat its wings rhythmically above her head. She moved to avoid it and her hair blew across her face. Her foot slipped and she fell backwards into the sea.

The cold water took her breath, and her dress ballooned like a parasol. One minute she was submerged, and the next fighting her way back up. She swam hard. Her chest burned from exertion and fear of the ship's suction pulling her underneath. Gasping, barely able to stay afloat, her heavy skirts were dragging her down. Her strength was at a low ebb, but she did not want to die. When she could no longer feel her legs, she feared the worst and felt herself losing consciousness.

When she came to, someone was lowering her down. Her teeth chattering, she raised her head and looked into the eyes of the dog owner. She turned away, cursing below her breath. She thought she had escaped; been washed up further along the shore. Instead, she was sitting on cold concrete steps leading to the docks. Now, thanks to him, she was looking at years in a cell.

'Sorry, lass, I couldn't let ye drown.' Leaving her there, he walked back towards the wharf, water oozing from his clothes, to join the rest of the men.

A man in police uniform came towards her and dragged her to her feet. She felt wretched and pleaded with him for mercy. He didn't respond, except to prod her in the back and usher her along the dockside towards the officials. Dockers and porters wheeled barrels over cobblestones, and cargo was being loaded and unloaded from ships. She stood before a wharf official, terrified, her head lowered, water dripping from her clothes, seaweed tangled up in her hair. He looked at her as if he had just scraped her off the sole of his boot.

'Take her away. I'll question her later.'

Dejected and humiliated, Tamara found the whole experience so frightening, she couldn't speak. Flynn, a smug grin on his face, stopped unloading and watched along with the rest of the men as the official grabbed her hands and locked weighty manacles around her thin wrists.

When Captain Fitzroy failed to come to her rescue, she felt hopelessly alone and a feeling of doom engulfed her. Her hair covering her face, she was led away, shoved roughly into a wooden shack with a crate of smelly fish, and the door locked behind her.

CHAPTER FOUR

Jake Travis rode from his stud farm in Connemara to the gypsy camp in Galway. The gold rings adorning his fingers and his face as brown as well-tanned leather likened him to a gypsy, but rumour had it his manners were that of an aristocrat. By the time he reached the cluster of caravans and shabby tents of the settlement, his lean chestnut stallion was sweltering in beads of sweat. A barefoot boy ran forward to take his horse.

Some of the women circled a roaring fire; their hair was a tangled mess, their long skirts in tatters, dirt ingrained into their faces. The kids finishing their breakfast of porridge and sweet bread, with snot hanging from their noses, made him want to heave. Tamara was the only reason he ever returned to this stinking fleapit.

She had been ten years old when he found her living with a clan of travellers with no fixed abode. Even then, the girl's beauty had stunned him. Jono, a man of around fifty, claimed to be the girl's father. He was the one the band of gypsies followed.

Jono had not cowered away from him, when he demanded to see the girl. 'She's my daughter, she's not going anywhere.' He'd faced Travis with a knife in his hand. Even when Jake offered him money for the girl, he refused to hand her over.

Finally, Travis had no choice but to offer land to Jono for a minimal rent. It was where he, too, made the hovel his part-time home, just to keep an eye on the little gypsy until she was old enough to become his bride.

In a long riding coat and boots, Travis staggered towards the frightened women, his brown hair braided and sporting a red headband. Driven by power and money ever since he was shunned for stealing the family silver, he knew he could play the gent when he had to, but today he was bent on revenge. He stood before them, legs apart, a tall brute of a man, anger flashing in his cold grey eyes as he questioned each of them about Tamara's disappearance. Mothers drew their children close.

'If any one of you has seen her, or helped her get away, you'll live to regret it.' He used his whip on a barking dog to demonstrate. Heads shook nervously. The injured dog whimpered, a child whinged, the fire crackled, no one spoke.

'Where's Ola and Jono?'

A woman gestured back towards the wagons.

Cursing, he walked on through the camp until he came to a brown wagon. A dog lying underneath scampered. Travis barged inside. Ola was rolling up her bed. She looked older than her fifty years. Loose strands of hair hung around her face, and her eyes widened when she saw him.

'Where's Jono?'

'He's scouring the countryside for Tamara. We've not slept since she disappeared. Where in the name of God can she be?'

'Did she say anything?' He staggered against the table. 'Any clue to where she may have gone?' He swayed. 'For all I know, you could have helped her escape.'

'May God forgive ye! Why would we do that?' Fearful of the anger in his eyes, Ola held her bed mat in front of her.

'Why did she run?' He picked up one of Ola's delicate plates and smashed it on the floor. He swayed forward, crushing the fragments beneath his boots. 'What did you tell her?' He lifted his hand to strike her and she ducked.

'Nothing! She ... she overheard us talking about the wedding, but...'

'You couldn't keep your mouth shut, could you?' He swayed towards her and prodded her on the shoulder. 'Another bloody week and she would have been mine.' He moved away, unhooking a small riding crop hanging on the wall. Ola turned to run, and he brought it down across her back, slicing through her thin cotton blouse. She cried out in pain.

'I'll see she never comes to you. Not after this,' she sobbed.

'You old crone! You dare to threaten me. I could have you thrown in a cell, both of you.' He staggered backwards. 'Don't you realise what you've done? You as good ... as sold ... her to me. So,' he swayed forwards, 'don't ... get high ... and mighty with me. Pray she comes back, or you'll pay ... back every ... last penny with interest, or...' He laughed. 'I'll inform the constabulary, they'll take this serious ... very serious indeed.'

'You wouldn't...' Ola moved further away from him.

'Start praying!' he sneered.

Frightened for Ola, a few gypsies gathered outside, but scattered when Travis stomped down the steps. He stood staring at Tamara's wagon painted red and gold; a house on wheels. It was the same size as her parents', but inside there was a wealth of difference – fitted and furnished with the best money could buy. He recalled how her eyes had danced with delight when she first saw it. She had kept it looking pretty, with flowers in plant pots around the outside.

She was the one he wanted, in spite of her gypsy upbringing. Only one other woman had come near Tamara's innocent beauty. He had come so close to making her his, and if it had not been for ... his eyes narrowed. His temper rose and he stumbled up the red wooden steps, then tore inside, almost taking the small door with painted on flowers from its hinges.

It was clean and tidy. The bed folded into the wall, giving space for a table with matching red chairs beneath a window, draped with floral curtains stitched by her fair hands. He pulled open the hanging wardrobe; her clothes still hung untouched. He tugged open the drawers of the small chest; nothing had been disturbed. He fingered the white petticoat and a sudden longing to see her swamped him. She had taken nothing with her, so she had not gone far. He had to find her. Someone was hiding her and, when he discovered who, he would make sure they never double-crossed him again. He had been humiliated and someone would pay. By God, he would make sure of it.

His resentment raged. He marched through the camp, spouting curses at anyone in his way. He kicked over a gate-legged table, toppling an aluminium bucket of water, and a dog just missed a vicious kick. When he reached his own wagon, he went inside and brought out a lighted lamp, and made his way back. Anger coursing through his veins, he flung the lamp through the door of Tamara's wagon. Caught by the wind, the flames shot upwards, bringing men running from the nearby fields. Ola heard the noise of broken glass and crockery, and rushed outside screaming, spouting curses. Women and children ran out from wagons and tents while others rushed with buckets to the stream. Men, women and children battled to save Tamara's wagon and protect their own belongings.

Later, when all that remained was a charred frame, singed and blackened grass, Jake Travis mounted his stallion and rode through the camp. He stopped and looked at the smouldering remains. 'I'll find her,' he yelled. 'When I do, she'll beg me to marry her.' He rode out of the settlement, leaving behind a cloud of rising dust.

When Jono returned, a smell of burning rubber met him. He quickened his pace and discovered Ola in tears, being comforted by the men and women.

'What's happened here?'

Ola threw her arms wide in despair. 'This,' she sobbed, 'is the result of Travis's revenge. He torched Tamara's wagon. There's no telling what he'll do next.'

'The gobshite! I'll knock his bloody lights out. Where is he?'

'No, Jono.' She tugged at his arm, her eyes pleading.

'He rode out.' One of the men placed a hand on Jono's shoulder 'Best let him cool off. Talk to him when he's sobered up.'

'I hope Tamara never comes back. I'd rather die than see her married to a brute like that.' Thanking the neighbours, he placed an arm around Ola's shoulders and helped her into the wagon. 'Lena would turn in her grave if she could see this, Ola.'

'Thanks be to God, she can't. She'd a swung for him and gotten herself hurt.'

'Aye! She would that.'

'I felt bad keeping the truth from me own mother, Jono.'

'She was old. There was no point upsetting her! Anyways, she's gone now.'

'She'da blamed us for Tamara's disappearance, so she would, and she woulda been right.'

'What's done's done.' Jono opened a cupboard and took out a flagon of poitín, poured a good measure into a tankard, and handed it to Ola. 'Get this down ye. It'll stop ye shaking.'

She swallowed a large amount. 'What do we do now?'

'Did you tell him anything?'

'Not til he used the crop across me back.' Straightening her shoulders, she winced.

'Filthy bog-rat!'

'He weren't no gentleman, that's for sure.'

'He fooled me, Ola. I pray Tamara's in a safe place. With her rare beauty, she'll have men falling at her feet, so she will. And when that excuse for a man comes here again, I'll be ready for him.'

'Don't antagonise him, Jono. That's exactly what he wants. He'd kill ye soon as look at ye. Then what will become of the rest of us?' She shook her head. 'We should never have allowed ourselves to be tempted by that man's money.'

'Maybe we were wrong.' Jono rubbed his hands over his face. 'We needed that money.' He picked up his tankard and poured himself a generous helping. 'I was thinking of Tamara. I thought he'd take care of her, thought she'da wanted for nothing. We won't be around forever.' He sighed. 'You don't think he knows, do ye?'

'I've often wondered the same thing meself.'

She pushed her hair behind her ear. 'No one knows, so who's to tell him?'

Jono nodded and took a good swallow of his drink. 'He wouldn't a loved her for long. I can see that now. She was just a trophy to him, to boast about to his upper crust friends. I shoulda known that Tamara, in spite of her wild ways, would never a been happy with a man like that. I've seen that faraway look in her eyes many a time. We were never going to be enough for her.'

'Oh, Jono, where in the name o' Heaven can she have got to?'

CHAPTER FIVE

Freed from the hut, Tamara was marched to a room along the dock. Her skirts still heavy and wet made her tremble. The room was dark, apart from the skylight overhead. A dock official stood behind a table with some food and heavy shackles. He nodded to the bread and water on the table. She tore into the bread and stuffed piece after piece into her mouth, then drank from the tin mug.

'Right! Get out of those wet clothes and put this on.' He threw her a long gown made of sacking material with rips down the sides. 'Come on, I don't have all day.'

She whipped her wet jumper over her head and he leered at her breasts. 'Jesus, Mary and Joseph, help me.' She pulled the sacking over her head and dropped her heavy skirt to the floor.

'Everything.'

'Please!'

'Everything, I said.'

Her face flushed, she closed her eyes to avoid his glare and dropped her petticoat and drawers. He kicked them to the side. This was her worst nightmare, and she wanted to die.

'I'll have that jewellery, too.' Tamara removed her earrings, bangles and beads from around her neck and handed them over. 'You'll have them back if you ever get out of here,' he laughed. 'Now, put these on.'

She placed her feet into the heavy, brown laced boots, determined not to give him the satisfaction of seeing her cry. Her wrists and ankles shackled, she was shoved along the street to a nearby police station, dragging one foot behind the other, desperate to hide the exposed parts of her body.

Finally, she was led along a stone corridor, and pushed into a dark cell with barred windows. The shackles were removed from her wrists. 'You'll be charged and sentenced in the morning,' the arresting officer said.

The cell was cold and dimly lit, apart from the sliver of light from the high windows. Sawdust covered the floor. The lavatory was a round hole at the end of a wooden bench. She wrinkled her nose at the smell of stale urine.

England was a place she had dreamed of, but never expected she would be locked up or maybe even die here.

'Enjoy the peace while yer can, princess. Tonight,

41

this place'll be crawlin'. So watch the dippers.'

Tamara's distress was such she hadn't noticed the woman slumped on the floor in the corner until she spoke. Pleased to find she wasn't alone, she went over and crouched beside the woman. 'What's a dipper?'

'Pickpockets, yer divvy. Where'd yer spring from? Yer not a Scouser, then?'

Tamara shook her head. 'I've nothing worth stealing.'

'What about that gold ring? Yer managed to hide that from the bugger.' Her laugh was harsh, showing brown uneven teeth. Her skeletal body made it difficult to guess her age. The ring wasn't gold, and being robbed was the least of Tamara's worries.

'How long will I be kept in here?'

'Depends. What yer done?'

'Nothing, apart from stow away on a ship.'

'Hark at her!' The woman laughed. 'Yer like to do it in style. Yer'll get a few years for that, princess.'

'Oh, God!' Tamara placed her hands on her head. 'What'll I do?'

'Ah, dinna fret. Wit' yer lukes, yer won't have to, luv. I was once young and pretty like you. Now luke at me. I ge' chucked in 'ere most nights, for trying to earn a crust.' She looked at Tamara. 'Have yer thought of going on the make? There'd be a tip in it for me, an' all.'

'No. I couldn't do that.' The thought made Tamara shudder. That would be like jumping from the pot into the fire.

'Ah, please yerself. Yer'll soon change yer mind

when yer on yer uppers.' The woman sat forward. 'Gizza bifta? Yer'd better learn the lingo, or yer'll stand out like a sore face. A smoke, have yer got any?'

Tamara shook her head.

'Thought you might have a roll-up tucked away somewhere.'

'Sorry.'

'Just my bloody luck.' The woman shifted onto her side.

Tamara moved away and huddled down on the bench, pulling her knees up under her. The woman's words depressed her, but she was right. What would she do for money if she ever got out? Her hand stuffed in her mouth, she chewed one nail, then another and wondered what was going to happen to her.

The woman in the corner snored, and Tamara could hear mice scratching and gnawing at the wood underneath the bench and men shouting and swearing in the nearby holding cells.

She thought back on all the fine clothes and petticoats she had back home, and wished she had one to cover her nakedness. It was all clear to her now. Money had influenced the local school to take her, alienating her from the other gypsy children who went without an education. Although Travis smiled whenever he saw her, Tamara had despised him on sight, and often wondered why her parents tolerated him in their wagon. Now she knew, and she hated them. Why had they been so pliable? The man was old enough to be her father. The whole business devastated her.

That day she had lost not only her homeland,

but also the parents she had always believed loved her. She wrapped her arms around herself and wept.

Sometime during the night, she felt someone's foot push her off the bench. Too tired to argue, she sat with her back to the wall next to three other women. In the morning, she saw that they were wearing their street clothes; embarrassed, she huddled in the corner. She heard the jangle of keys, and jumped to her feet, brushed the sawdust from her makeshift dress and ran her fingers through her hair.

'Come on, you!' the guard pointed towards her. 'You're wanted in the office.'

'Hey, scuffer! Let me out of 'ere!' one woman yelled.

'Sorry, Queen, it's not your turn yet.' Sneering, he locked the cell.

Tamara followed him down the corridor, her mouth dry, her insides a bundle of nerves. Where was he taking her, and what would her sentence be? She'd had no idea that being a stowaway would land her in so much trouble. She could have caught the cart to Dublin, but there had been no time for that.

The guard swung open the door. 'In you go!' When she hesitated, he prodded her and shut the door behind her.

She was alone in the room. Grey paint peeled from the walls. There was a well-worn table, with various carved out initials and a bundle of papers held together with a dog clip, and two wooden chairs, one behind the desk and another against the wall. A shelf was filled with red and green leather-bound books. It was ten past eight by the clock on the wall. Until that moment, Tamara had had no idea what time it was. As the minutes ticked by and nobody came, she bit her lip, the shackles around her ankles restricting her movements.

The door opened, and a police officer walked in. She looked up, then lowered her gaze at the row of silver buttons down the front of his jacket. He looked important. He dropped a package down inside the door, cleared his throat, and removed his helmet and placed it on the table then walked around her. Fear coursed through her and she gasped, covering the holes in her garment with her hands.

'How did a beautiful young thing like you end up here?' he asked.

Nerves got the better of her, and she blurted out, 'Why can't you sentence me, sir, and get it over with?'

He lifted the chair from against the wall and placed it closer to the desk. 'Sit down.'

Embarrassed by what she was wearing, she obeyed, placing her hands on her lap.

He walked round the desk and sat down, linking his fingers and resting his elbows on the table. Tamara swallowed.

'You've committed a very serious offence, young lady. What have you to say?'

'Sure, I didn't know it was an offence, sir. I just had to get away.'

'Why was that?'

She fidgeted with her hands, but stayed silent.

'And why has this form not been completed? What's your surname?' He unclipped it from the pile.

'I don't have one, sir.'

His laugh was pleasant. 'But everyone has a surname!'

'I don't want anyone to know where I am.'

'Well, if you behave yourself, there'll be no need for them to find out.'

His sigh was deep before he said, 'Your name, miss.'

She hesitated. She would have to make one up. An English name if possible, but for the life of her, she couldn't think of one.

'Perhaps you'd like another spell in the cell while you think about it?'

'O'Connor. My name is Tamara O'Connor, sir.' She reeled it off fast, in case she changed her mind.

'How old are you, Tamara?'

'Almost seventeen, sir.'

'Date of birth.'

'October 1884.'

He filled in the form and pushed it back on the clip. 'Well, now. That wasn't too difficult, was it?' His eyes narrowed. 'Unless, you're already running away from the law, are you?'

'Oh, no, no, sir, it's nothing like that.'

'Well, you're a very fortunate young woman, because Captain Fitzroy has spoken to me on your behalf. According to him, you hadn't fully considered your actions, and worked to pay part of your passage across.'

'Yes, it's the truth, sir. Honest to God! I had no

46

idea I was breaking the law. I won't ever do it again.'

'Stowing away on a ship is a very dangerous and foolhardy thing for a young woman to do, wouldn't you say? What made you do it?'

'My family offered me in marriage to a ... a man I wouldn't give a dog to.'

He laughed. 'Is that all? I've a good mind to return you to Ireland on the next available ship.'

'Oh, please, don't send me back, sir.'

'Who do you know in Liverpool?'

'I've an aunt only a few miles from here. She'll take me in.'

'Do you mean Birkenhead?'

'That's the place.' Another lie, but she was not going to risk being sent back.

He nodded. 'I come from there myself.' Tamara's heart flipped.

'What's the name of the street?'

'I can't read, sir, but I can find my way there all right.'

'Okay, but mark my words, young woman, if you end up back in here you won't be treated with such clemency.'

'Thank you, sir.' She could hardly believe her luck, and wanted to run out of the police station in case he changed his mind. But how could she go out on the streets, dressed in a skimpy gown riddled with holes?

The officer stood up. 'Captain Fitzroy left this for you.' He pointed to the brown paper parcel on the floor. 'Your belongings, left behind on his ship. You can get dressed in here. I'll see you're not disturbed.'

'That's kind of you, sir, thanks.' Her fingers trembled as she untied the parcel. Inside, she found her clothes, hairbrush, and her book – the pages stuck together – wrapped in her green cloak. How kind of the captain to have her clothes dried for her. She felt full of gratitude for his kindness.

She dressed in the long-sleeved brown dress that still smelled of the sea, and brushed her hair. Then she tied her cloak around her shoulders. And, in spite of having nowhere to go and being petrified of sleeping rough, she walked out onto the street, her head held high.

CHAPTER SIX

Tamara stood on the pavement at the corner of Cheapside and Dale Street, with no idea which way to turn. Even if she knew where Birkenhead was, it was the last place she wanted to go. Once word of her disappearance spread around the gypsy communities, there would be a price on her head. She had come this far, there would be no going back.

She walked along narrow lanes towards the shops and alehouses, trying to avoid stepping into steaming horse manure. Barefooted, she had left the heavy brogues in the cell. The tall grey buildings reminded her of Dublin, where she had gone with her father to buy and sell horses. She hated the smoky city smells, and the gassy stink of the drains caught the back of her throat. She missed the fresh air, the rough open landscape, the sea pounding the rocks. She had gone to the shore since she was ten to collect seaweed, nettles, and other ingredients for her grandmother's potions.

The banter of traders drew her towards the docks, and she was surprised to find the streets teeming with people. A young boy, his clothes in tatters, ran between the stalls pinching fruit, while women in posh clothes sauntered along the pavement, some with men in bowler hats, pausing to glance into the milliner's and tailor's shops.

Vendors were offering everything from fresh fruit, vegetables and meat pies. The smell of the pies made her hunger pains worse, and she snatched up a squashed tomato by her feet and crammed it into her mouth. Juice trickled down her chin. Later, she picked up a bruised apple and sat in a shop doorway to eat it. As she chewed her way through the best bits of the fruit, she noticed some of the young working class women were showing cleavage, and sailors carrying white sacks on their shoulders winked at them as they passed by. She felt overdressed in her green cloak. When she had eaten the apple and spat out the pips, she stood up. She would have to find work, and soon. She was not afraid of hard work; she didn't mind getting her hands dirty.

'Mercy, mercy! Spare a copper for the blind.' Tamara looked down at the beggar, his filthy hands outstretched. She hoped to God she wouldn't end up like that, but who would employ her looking as she did, and with so many poor on the streets? She might have to turn to begging, or stealing. It was easy enough once a trader's back was turned.

She trudged on, asking for work at every opportunity, but all she got were cold stares and a shake of heads. The city was busy with all manner of trades to do with the sea, and Tamara went into the Cord Weavers, her fingers crossed. The noise was so bad she had to place her hands over her ears. Men bellowed above the noise. Shelves were stacked with all manner of rope, and women were sitting at benches twisting and braiding thin pieces of twine together. Others sewing fishing and hay nets looked towards her and made signs, as if lip-reading. Men were pulling lengths of heavy cord from the looms. Spotting her, one walked towards her, stepping over coils of heavy rope.

'If yer luking fer werk, there's nowt doing,' he yelled.

Disappointed, she turned away, and outside again her ears popped. There were still other places to try. She pushed her hands deep into the pockets of her cloak. Her fingers touched something round and cold. Her spirits rose when she drew out a silver half crown. She held it up to the light, then placed it between her teeth and kissed it. Thank you, Captain Fitzroy. Tears ran down her cold face, and she hoped one day she would bump into him again and thank him for his kindness.

She bought a meat pie and, breaking it into bite size pieces, ate it where she stood, the juices running down her chin. Her hunger satisfied, she walked on hoping to find cheap lodgings. She passed a shop advertising a room to rent, but the woman said she was looking for long term let. 'Try the lodging house next to the Timber Merchants,' she offered. Tamara thanked her, but when she made enquiries, it was full. The proprietor told her to try the Rose & Crown a couple of streets away.

'It might be suitable,' he glanced down at her, 'if it's just for a night.'

It was lunchtime when she got there. It looked a miserable place and the brown front door was hanging on one hinge. Sighing, she went inside. A customer was holding up the bar. Tamara hesitated until the red-faced publican with a bushy moustache asked her if he could help.

'I'm looking for a room for the night.'

'Always willing to help a lady,' he said. 'It's this way.' She followed him towards the far end of the inn and up the dark narrow stairs to a room on the first floor. The door was open and she looked inside. It smelled of stale beer and was in need of a good clean. The window was so dirty it looked as if it had been painted grey. As she walked further into the room, she saw an oil lamp on the table. A candle, minus the holder, lay on the floor next to a bed that looked as if it was about to collapse.

'The lamp's not werking, so you'll have to make do with a candle. If ye want the room, it's a shilling a night.' He scratched his face. 'Although, you don't look like the usual Judy we get in here.'

'It's just for the one night.' She handed over a shilling, pleased to be off the streets.

51

'That's what they all say.'

'What do you mean?'

Smirking, he walked away, leaving the door swinging on its hinges.

After he had gone, she placed her bundle on the bed and went to look for the lavatory. She walked to the end of the long corridor and followed a handwritten sign down a flight of stairs. Someone was using it, and she waited next to a brown sink with a dripping tap. It was ages before a man staggered out smelling of drink and yanking up his trousers. He glared at Tamara and she hurried inside, bolted the door and pinched her nose before using the wooden seat with a hole.

Outside, she washed her face and hands in the sink and tidied her hair in the mirror, which was dotted with so many brown spots she could just about see her image. Feeling a little fresher, she went back to the room and sat on the bed to think. The springs twanged beneath her and she slid into the middle. With time on her hands, she wished she hadn't left Ireland in such a hurry. There had been no time to say a last prayer at her granny Lena's burial mound. Tamara was sure her granny had played no hand in her parents' plan to marry her off to Jake Travis.

She needed to get out of the room and get some fresh air. Draping her cloak around her shoulders, she pulled the door to behind her. It wouldn't close properly and the bolt was broken.

Downstairs, the proprietor was lifting barrels and jugs of ale onto the counter. The place was dark, the windows too small to allow much light through.

'The door upstairs won't shut.'

'And what would you like me to do about it?'

'Well, I'd like you to fix it before tonight.'

'It'll cost ye.'

'You want me to pay?'

'Nobody shuts their doors here,' he grinned towards another man who was leaning on the bar. 'That would be right unfriendly now.'

The innkeeper didn't look the sort of man who would return her money. If only she hadn't been so hasty. 'Well,' she said. 'If that's your attitude, you won't get many ladies staying here.'

'That's right, Queen,' he smirked. 'We don't get any ladies in here.' With his laughter ringing in her ears, Tamara's face reddened and she fled. God Almighty! He thought she was a whore. Her few possessions were in the room so she was determined to come back. He was not going to diddle her out of a shilling. In spite of having made the wrong choice of inn, it would be much worse if she had to sleep on the street.

Careful not to stray too far, she took note of landmarks. Everywhere appeared strange, but this was her life now. In a shop doorway, a young girl sat shrouded in a grey blanket, a skeletal baby hanging on to her malnourished breast. The girl looked up at Tamara, her young face old and pinched, her eyes pleading. With a shilling and a few coppers left, she pitied the girl and dropped a penny into her hand.

'Blessings of God on ye.' The girl had a strong Irish brogue and it made Tamara all the more determined to find work, anything to keep her

53

from ending up begging on the streets. In these streets, she saw the poverty she had left behind in Ireland.

Tamara feared the gypsy law. They dealt with their own and the police were never involved. She had known of men and boys beaten to an inch of their lives for stealing from their own people. Jake Travis was judge and jury, making sure the punishment fitted the crime. The fact she had turned down his marriage offer would have embittered and angered him, and she felt sure he would make her pay. Other gypsies would shun her. Shamed and hated by their own people was one of the worst curses a gypsy could endure. She knew, too, for the rest of her life she would be looking over her shoulder. In spite of that, she was determined never to go back.

CHAPTER SEVEN

It was late afternoon and getting dark. Unused to the cobbled streets, her feet were sore. She stopped to read billboards about strikes, rubbing her hands together for warmth. A black and white poster pasted on a wall, advertised a benefit concert in the music hall to aid repairs to the church hall. It made her smile when she read an out-of-date billboard advertising cheap trips to the seaside for May 1900.

No one advertised for workers, so she made her way back to the dismal room at the Rose and

Crown, reminding herself that tomorrow was another day. Shops were closing. Two men staggered out from an alehouse and she crossed the street to avoid them. Most of the vendors had cleared away. A woman wrapped in a shawl was putting the last of her apples into her barrow when Tamara stopped and asked if she could buy one.

'Here ye are, me darlin'! You can have two.' Tamara thanked her. She ate one, and put the other one in her pocket to take back to the room. A couple of streets from the inn, stuck to the wall of a brewer's yard, a colourful poster advertising the Mr. Billy Circus caught her eye. The image of a beautiful girl in a red and black costume stood between two white ponies, a ringmaster on one side waving his whip and a laughing clown on the other. A frisson of excitement shot through her. The circus was due to arrive at Stanley Park, on Saturday. That was tomorrow.

Stanley Park, she repeated to fix it in her mind. She would find out where that was. Circuses had fascinated her since she was small. If she could persuade the circus owner to take her on, she could travel with it.

The streetlamps left a yellow pool of light along the cobbled streets. As she approached, the noise of drunken revelry grew louder. It unnerved her; her steps faltered and her heart began to beat faster. She'd heard about the gangs of Liverpool that hung about on street corners robbing and even murdering innocent people. When she lived at home, she had not been allowed out alone at night; none of the gypsy girls were. Here, life was

55

different. Outside the inn, a man was pawing a woman in a doorway.

'Show us yer brass first,' the woman yelled.

From the noise inside, Tamara knew the night would be anything but peaceful. The bar was heaving with drunken men and inebriated women flaunting themselves. A man grabbed Tamara around her waist, lifting her from the floor. She fought him off, kicked him on the shins, and raced towards the stairs. A group of men barred her way and shoved her back towards the first man.

'Leave me be!' she cried, but they only laughed and pushed her from one to the other, until one of the women intervened.

'Lay off her, Tom. She's just a kid.' She linked her arm through two of the men and Tamara escaped.

In the room, her heart thumped and she leaned against the door to catch her breath. Then she pulled the heavy table across it. The room was like an icebox; the noise downstairs and outside on the street, thick with obscenities. The sound of drunken laughter, doors banging and people coming up and down the stairs worried her. She pushed at the dirty window in an attempt to close it, but it was stuck solid. She pulled back the blanket. The bed smelled of stale beer, so she lay on top. The mattress bowed and she rolled into the middle. Sighing, she pulled her cloak over her for warmth and placed her hands over her ears.

As soon as it was light, Tamara rolled up her belongings. It was silent, apart from the drunken snores from the room opposite. She crept along the landing. Downstairs, the place smelled of sour beer. Her foot slipped on the wet floor and she knocked over a table full of dirty pot mugs. She closed her eyes and held her breath, then slid back the bolts at the top and bottom of the door.

In spite of the hour, horses and carts loaded with boxes were on their way to the docks and there was a smell of fresh horse manure. Shop-keepers were rolling up their shutters, and she stopped to ask where Stanley Park was. She discovered it was within easy reach of the docks.

She knew circus owners picked up new artistes on their way through cities. Although she was not an artiste, she was good with horses. Determined to get there, she walked with purpose, stopping only to enquire if she was going in the right direction. Well-to-do people passed by in carriages, the horses' hooves step-dancing on the cobbles. She wondered what it must be like to be rich and ride in a carriage. The people who rode in them looked like they had pucks of money.

When she arrived at the park, a small crowd had gathered, some asking about work. Men drove stakes into the ground to erect the big top that was beginning to resemble a gigantic canvas umbrella. Two more men were placing a white fence around an area. Artistes were jumping through hoops. Others were juggling. Music played. Tamara felt the adrenaline rush through her body just like when she was a child. She pushed through the excited mob until a tattooed, brawny arm barred her.

'You can't go in there, miss!'

'I'd like to see the circus owner.'

'What about?'

'I'm looking for work. I've heard you often take on entertainers.'

'You'd better join the queue. Have you any experience?'

'Well, no but...'

'Clear off and stop wasting our time.'

'I can see into the future and you're wife's just lost a bairn.'

The man looked at her, stunned. He came closer and narrowed his eyes. 'How do you know that?'

Tamara held his gaze. 'I can see the future of some people.'

'Well, if you get in the queue, I'll have a word with Mr. Billy.'

After a short wait, the man with tattoos took her around the back of the big tent to a row of trailers, wooden cages and a number of wagons. Two white ponies with black spots were tethered, grazing on the nearby grass.

'What sort of thing can you do?' the circus owner asked as soon as he saw her. He was free of facial hair, apart from a neat moustache. He perched his bulk on a wooden crate and removed his hat, while two men and a girl bounced and somersaulted on a trampoline next to him. Mr. Billy undid the button of his suit jacket and looked at his pocket watch. 'Well, I haven't got all day, love.'

'I'm good with horses, but I'll try anything.' She smiled, her fingers crossed behind her back.

'I want someone who can perform tonight.

What training do you have?'

'Well, none, but I learn fast.' Her eyelids closed over green almond-shaped eyes, and when she looked up, he was twiddling his thumbs.

'Look, miss, I'd like to help you. Besides, you're an attractive girl and would draw the crowd, but with no circus experience...' He shook his head.

'Please, mister, I'll pick it up in a few days.' Her grandmother had warned her impertinent manner would get her into trouble one day. But she was desperate.

'I doubt that. It takes years. Some of my artistes have trained since they were knee-high.' Smiling, he stood up. 'You're a determined young woman, I'll give you that. If this is some romantic dream of yours, you can forget it. Circus life is hard work. The show goes on, regardless of the mud, rain and cold.'

None of that bothered Tamara; growing up in a gypsy camp had not been easy. The circus was her way of escape, and if she could persuade him to take her on, there was less chance of her ending up on the streets of Liverpool.

'Please, Mr. Billy. I can ride horses, and I can read palms and tell fortunes. I don't mind hard work.'

'Are you a gypsy?'

Although she had removed her beads and bangles, the fact she was a fortuneteller had given her away. The fewer people who knew her background, the better.

'Your origins are of no importance here, but trust is.' He tapped his fingers on the top of his hat. 'Okay, I'll give you the benefit of the doubt.

Don't make me regret it.' A smile spread across Tamara's face. 'I'm a busy man, so if you'd like, take a look round and come back and see me.'

'Thank you.'

Excited, Tamara wandered around the circus. She smiled at the clowns, acrobats and jugglers rehearsing. Two fire-eaters were stuntmen with tattoos, dressed in tiger skin costumes. The ringmaster, Nick – Mr. Billy's son – introduced himself and shook her hand. He gave her a lopsided grin, but Tamara disliked him. Two stunted women with painted-on smiles and a man dressed like an Indian Raj, with a turban on his head, sat on an elephant.

She introduced herself to Princess Zeema, a tightrope walker of about her own age. Zeema's dark skin shone like polished walnut, her long shining hair hung to her waist. As Tamara walked back to where Mr. Billy was giving instructions to the clowns, she felt the ringmaster's fat fingers pinch her bottom. She let out a squeal, and gritted her teeth. She would have to be careful how she handled it, because she needed the job.

Billy chewed the stem of his pipe. 'Let's see what we can find to keep you busy. I'm not at all domesticated, but whenever the tents need repairing, I can stitch better than any woman.'

'Get away with you!' She had never known a man to stitch.

'I'm an ex-seaman, had to repair many a ship's sails.' He smiled. 'Can you cook, read or write, do numbers?'

She followed behind him. 'I can do all of that.' Women did the cooking at home, but it was not her favourite occupation. If that were all he felt her capable of, she would show gratitude.

'Look, I want to help you. I can tell you're down on your luck.'

'I know, and I'm grateful, really I am.'

'It's all I can offer you for the moment. I hope you realise circus folk entertain to survive. The pay is minimal, but you'll be fed and have a roof over your head.' He paused. 'If you behave and show willing...' He glanced down at her clothes and she wished she had something else to change into. 'I'll advance you a small sum, so you may dress yourself.'

This was totally unexpected, and Tamara was lost for words.

'If you're happy, you can start today.'

'Oh thanks, Mr. Billy. It sounds grand.'

'Take a look around, then go and see Nelly. You'll find her in the food tent. Tell her I sent you. She'll tell you what to do.' And he strolled away.

Tamara was standing close to the cages, when the dancing bear stood up and roared. Yes, she murmured. Isn't it wonderful? It was the best feeling she had had since leaving Galway. At least now she had no worries about going back into the city, and a sob caught in her throat. When she turned round, a man with short limbs and an oversized head was staring at her and rubbing his overgrown hands together. It sent shivers through her body.

CHAPTER EIGHT

For the remainder of the day, Tamara couldn't get the strange little man out of her mind. She pitied him and knew what it was like to be an outcast. But something in his eyes made her feel uneasy.

That night, she slept in a wagon shared by Zeema and Nelly, an older woman she had met earlier with pointed features and a broken front tooth. Nelly cooked for the crew of around fifteen people. Tamara's first impression of Zeema had been a pleasant one, but the girl's attitude changed as soon as she realised they would be sharing sleeping arrangements.

'We're overcrowded as it is,' Zeema hissed. 'Where's she gonna sleep?'

Tamara could see the girl's grievance, but sleeping on the floor was no hardship for her. 'Sure, I don't need much room.'

'Bah! Take no notice of her,' the older woman croaked. She opened her closet, removed her black hose and shawl from the top shelf, and placed them at the bottom of the cupboard. 'Ye can put your roll here,' she said, 'as long as ye don't touch nowt 'f mine.'

'Thanks.' Tamara shoved her bundle into the space.

Nelly told her they would start early, and the two women were soon asleep. Although very tired, the excitement of what lay ahead in her new life kept Tamara awake. Nelly's snores reminded her of a kettle coming to the boil.

Each time she looked up at the small window, she imagined she could see the face of the stunted man.

At dawn, she got up and went outside. A cold wind rushed at her face and blew her hair. The camp was peaceful, without a sound. She walked towards the river to bathe before the rest of the camp stirred. Dewdrops sparkled on the long grass and droplets fell from the trees. The unexpected sound of splashing water made her pause. She climbed the grassy bank and hid in the shrubbery. A man was swimming. A dark haired, broad-shouldered man rose from the water, she felt her colour rise.

He was naked.

She backed away, but not before she'd glimpsed his muscular body. Her ablutions forgotten, she hurried back to the trailers. She had no recollection of meeting him yesterday.

She walked towards the horses, inhaling the familiar smell. The animals huffed and swished their tails. 'Hello there, my beauties.' Tamara patted their heads. She missed her own horse and longed to feel the thrill of riding one of these splendid animals. Wondering who their trainer was, she moved on to the elephant enclosure. She hated to see them chained. It was difficult to tell anything by their expression, only through their eyes. They didn't look happy. They kept their backs to her, lifting their massive feet in unison. She read somewhere that elephants walked twenty miles a day in the wild.

The sound of something shifting and falling startled her. At first, she saw no one and walked further along the cages. Then she saw him, the deformed man staring at her from behind a wooden container.

She tensed. 'What is it you want?'

He replied in a foreign language, waving his arms as if he was angry with her. She felt nervous, trapped with no one around. She edged backwards, looking down for something to protect herself with. She picked up a stick and held it out towards him. He yelled at her again. Her heart raced.

'Pablo! What are you doing?'

The little man spun round.

Tamara turned and found herself looking into the reckless blue eyes of the man she had spied swimming in the river. His curly hair wet, a towel was slung around his neck.

'You want to meet the pretty girl, is that it?' He walked towards Pablo. 'Come along, then.' He took his arm and guided the short man forward. 'We can both introduce ourselves. You must be Tamara?' He smiled, offering his hand. 'My name is Kristopher Trevelyan, but everyone here calls me Kit. And this is Pablo.' He placed his arm around him. 'Pablo is one of the clan.'

'I'm pleased to meet you both,' she smiled.

Pablo glanced down, then he looked up and pointed at Tamara. 'Gypsy,' he growled, then ran away on bandy legs.

'I'm sorry. You must take no notice.'

'Oh, I'll try not to.' She was used to name-

64

calling. Still, she hoped Pablo would learn to trust her once he knew her better.

The man's handshake was warm and welcoming. Handsome and six feet tall, he wore a dark blue dressing gown over blue leggings. They stood for a moment regarding each other, then he said, 'You mustn't let Pablo scare you. He's a poor soul.'

'Is he...? I mean...'

'He's harmless, unless he feels threatened. I'm afraid you'll come across a few oddities in the circus.'

'Well, I hope I'm not threatening.' She laughed.

'Not at all. Pablo's Spanish. Doesn't appreciate a pretty girl by the looks of things. I'm glad to say it doesn't apply to the rest of us. Come on, I'll walk you back.'

'What does Pablo do?'

Kit paused by the big top. 'He keeps the horses fed and watered. He's not on show. People would make fun of him.' She saw a hint of sadness in his eyes. 'Mr. Billy found him wandering the streets, and took pity on him; keeps him fed and sheltered, out of the kindness of his heart. Apart from one or two, the company treat him well.'

'That's nice.' She longed to be part of a family again. At the gypsy camp, she had never been alone. There was no room for privacy in the wagons. Children were always running in and out. It was the way of life. 'What do you do, Kit?'

'I'm a trapeze artiste. They call me The Flying Peacock. I also do an act with Zeema.' He smiled. 'We're called The Walk of Death. I've worked for Billy since I was a young boy.'

Tamara eyes widened. 'Really!'

'What about you?' he asked. 'Let me guess. Well, you're not a lion tamer!'

She laughed.

'And you'd be wasted as a clown.'

'You're not even close,' she smiled. 'I'm helping Nelly with the cooking.'

'Oh.' She thought she detected disappointment. 'What brought you to the circus, then?'

She began to fidget with her hands. 'It's a long story, Kit. Look,' she said, 'I'd better go and see what needs cooking for breakfast. It's been nice talking to you.'

'Yes, I'll see you around.'

'You'll find most of what you need in the tent beyond,' Nelly said, taking the clay tobacco pipe from her mouth and pressing more tobacco into the top. The smell made Tamara cough. Many of the gypsies smoked pipes, but she had never liked the smell.

'You'd better make a start,' Nelly said.

'How much will I need to cook? What do you eat for breakfast?'

'Can ye make oatcakes?'

'I'll have a go.'

'Fry a couple dozen eggs with the oatcakes. There's plenty of mash over from last night. You can use that. Bind it with egg. We're still unpacking so you might have to search the food wagon for more provisions.' She chuckled. 'The men around here have healthy appetites. I'll be over in a minute.'

Tamara unpacked flour and oats from the

66

crates inside the tent and went outside to the nearby spinney to gather firewood. Before long, she had a blazing fire going. Breakfast, she soon discovered, was eaten around the fire if the weather was fine, otherwise they ate in the food tent. Making fires was easy for Tamara, something she had done most mornings at the gypsy camp. Rolling up her sleeves, she made the oatcakes, patting and moulding them until they were the right shape and thickness, then dropping them into the pan big enough to take eight at one go. Before long, the appetising smell of the cakes and eggs sizzling brought out the company.

'Mornin' Tamara,' Mr. Billy said, and others followed suit. Some smiled their greeting before sitting round the fire and helping themselves to the food. Kit lifted a plate from the side table and filled it with food. 'I'll take this to Pablo.'

Nelly cut bread as thick as doorsteps and everyone chatted about the evening's show, like one big happy family. Tamara was pleased to be included in their conversation. She had not eaten much in days and she was feeling weak with hunger.

Later, when Kit and the artistes had gone to rehearsals, Tamara was alone with Nelly.

'Ye did a grand job there, girl,' Nelly said. 'I'll give ye a hand with the pots.' They were still putting the stuff away when Billy strolled across to them.

'When you've finished here, can you come over and see me, Tamara?'

'Yes, of course, Mr. Billy,' she said, hoping he had not changed his mind about her working with the circus.

The door to his trailer was ajar and she knocked.
'Come in.'

A mound of dockets covered the table. Mr. Billy relaxed back into his chair, took a drink from his silver hip flask, and returned it to his pocket. 'Can you write?'

She nodded. She could write her own name and other words.

'This wants sorting and put in this here copybook.' He opened the dog-eared book, with pages of ink blobs and squiggles. 'Just put down the name on the docket and cash paid out beside it.' He handed her a bottle of ink and a pen.

She nodded.

'Can you add and subtract?'

'Sort of.'

'It's simple arithmetic. I want to know how much I'm paying for provisions. That kind of thing, can you do that?'

'Yes, Mr. Billy.' Not sure what she had gotten herself into, she decided she would do her best.

He popped his hat back on and left her alone.

She was hopeless with sums, but she was not going to risk telling Mr. Billy. She had been ten before she had any learning in a school, and then she was threatened with expulsion for getting into fights. She wondered why her parents had bothered to send her, as none of the other gypsy children went to school; now she knew it was to impress Jake Travis. In spite of what they had done, she missed them. They were bound to be upset once they discovered her gone. Jake Travis was sure to grill them without mercy.

Tamara sorted the dockets into some semblance of order. The entries in the copybook were messy and she could hardly read the writing. Looking closely at the pages, she realised that most of them were repetitive, with similar entries each month. 2d nails for camel enclosure. £1.4d canvas sheeting – big tent repair. She followed on in the same fashion and hoped she was doing it right.

The jugglers practising outside the window for the evening's performance, distracted her. She envied them. They were like lightning and never once dropped a club. She guessed Kit and Zeema were rehearsing with the other performers in the big top, and she longed to go and watch them.

When she had finished entering all of the dockets, she had ink on her fingers. Reluctant to add up the amounts in case she made a mistake, she left that for Mr. Billy and tidied the desk. She stretched her shoulders and went outside to wash her hands. Voices coming from the big top carried on the wind, and Tamara walked towards it and popped her head round the opening in the canvas. Kit and Zeema were on the tightrope, practising a new act. He was holding her around the waist.

'Now, you try it,' he was saying. 'You can do it!' Zeema flitted nervously from one end of the wire to the other, holding a white parasol. 'That's much better,' he said. 'Remember to slide one foot in front of the other until you feel confident.' Kit climbed the rope ladder towards the horizontal bar, and continued calling out instructions to Zeema. 'Head up, arms balanced.'

Tamara looked on, excited by the danger involved. Kit spotted her, and he beckoned her forward. 'That was good,' he called down to Zeema. 'Carry on. Work on your arms.'

Tamara stood spellbound, hoping that Mr. Billy would not catch her idling. Her eyes flitted right and left, following Kit's movements above her. She wondered how long it would be before she could do that. Rehearsals finished, Kit slid effortlessly down the rope towards her.

'You looked like you enjoyed the act, Tamara.'

'Yes, it was wonderful. I'd love to try that sometime!'

'It's not easy. It takes a lot of hard work and practice.'

'I know,' she nodded.

'You've done it before?'

'No, no. But I want to learn all I can.'

'I'd like to learn more about you, Tamara. Why you came to the circus in the first place.' He picked up his jacket. 'Let's take a stroll.' As they left, Tamara saw the look of disapproval on Zeema's face.

CHAPTER NINE

Tamara was walking around the park when she bumped into Mr. Billy. She hoped he was pleased with the work she had done. He blew cigar smoke into the air and looked down at her. 'Well,

Tamara. I doubt you'll ever make a book-keeper.' He smiled. 'Didn't you learn how to count on the abacus at school?'

'I can't remember, Mr. Billy.'

'Never mind, perhaps you'll improve. In the meantime, go and help Nelly. It's nearly lunch time and I'm getting peckish,' he patted his paunch.

'Yes, Mr. Billy.'

Walking away, she sucked in her breath. If only she had done a better job. She hoped he would not assume she was hopeless at everything.

That afternoon, back at the wagon, when Tamara tried to make conversation, Zeema ignored her. 'What's the matter with you?' Tamara removed her cloak and hung it on the peg by the door.

'Oh, you should ask, little miss innocent. You think that you can waltz in and swipe any man you choose.' Her dark eyes flashed.

Tamara placed her hands on her hips. 'I don't know what you're talking about. Unless going for a walk with Kit is a crime.'

'Of course, you don't.' Zeema turned her back and began to brush her long hair.

'Is he..? I mean, you and he, are you courting?' Although she asked, she dreaded the answer.

'We could be, if you hadn't set your gypsy spell on him.'

'I've done no such thing. I had no idea you had feelings for him. Does he know?'

'None of your business,' she pouted, and continued to give her hair a vigorous brushing.

The high-pitched shrill of Mr. Billy's whistle

alerted them, and they hurried to the big top. It was something he did most afternoons to talk over any hitches before the evening's perform-ance. This left Tamara no more time to make things right with Zeema.

Tamara washed her hair and it dried in tiny ringlets around her face. She ran her hands down the folds of the black dress, bought with the money from Mr. Billy. People were arriving early to get the best seats, and Nick was in charge of arranging them in an orderly line. Tamara was both surprised and delighted when she was in-vited to stand alongside Mr. Billy as he collected the money. It brought colour to her cheeks when young men raised their hats and acknowledged her with a smile. When the queue tailed off, Billy tied up the canvas bag heavy with coins.

'You stay a while longer, just in case there are any stragglers. There's only gallery left at six-pence.'

She nodded, but left alone, she felt vulnerable and worried in case gypsies from round about might see her and word got back to Travis. Jake Travis would be hard to outfox. He would take out a vendetta against her; circulate her name around other gypsy camps. Many would be out looking for her now. Travis had connections with gypsies the world over and she knew how he worked. His first port of call would be Dublin, then Liverpool, so the sooner the circus moved on the better.

She was deep in thought when an urchin, shab-bily dressed with a cheeky grin, came towards her.

''Eh up, miss. Can I have a truepenny ticket?'
'The cheapest is a Joey, luv.'

'Please, miss. I want to see the dancing bear.'
He looked so crestfallen that Tamara glanced
around before lifting the bottom of the canvas 'I
haven't let you in, okay?'

'Ta, miss.' He slipped underneath the tent as
the music struck up and the magic of the circus
began. Minutes later, the place transformed into
a colourful bustling spectacle. Tamara stood in a
dark corner at the back as the clowns in red and
white costumes, threw each other effortlessly
about, leaving the audience in fits of laughter.
The jugglers performed on one side of the ring,
acrobats on the other.

She was amazed at the fast pace of the show.
When Kit and Zeema ran out in matching blue
trousers and boleros and performed on the high
wire, Tamara wished it was her up there with
him. Especially when Kit's hand slipped round
Zeema's waist and he lifted her into the air while
walking the tightrope. She could hear gasps from
the audience.

The highlight was Billy's dancing bear. It lum-
bered into the ring wearing a white ballerina
skirt, and restrained by a thick chain round its
neck. The audience went wild. Halfway through
the act, the bear balanced on one leg, twirling
round several times. Tamara watched, astounded,
until children and then adults threw pieces of
apple and orange into the ring. The bear reared
up, snarled at the crowd, and pawed Billy.

'Please, please don't feed the bear. Stop, please
stop throwing.' Billy raised his hands in a pleading

gesture. The laughing and cheering continued until the ring resembled a rubbish heap. Billy struggled to hold the bear. It reared up, white foam oozing from its mouth. The chain slipped from his grasp and the bear broke free.

People screamed and scrambled over benches. Tamara rushed forward, shouting for everyone to stay calm, but was roughly pushed to the ground. Like a herd of noisy elephants trampling over each other, the place turned into chaos. Tamara couldn't believe a bear could roar so loudly, and her eyes widened when it rose up and ripped the sleeve from Nick's jacket. Kit threw a strap over its head, and he and Billy led it to safety.

Outside, a crowd of hecklers booed and called for their money back until Tamara told them to come back inside, that the bear was under control. People gradually returned to their seats, still talking about the bear and shaking their heads. Just in time, the clowns rushed out, tumbling about, throwing buckets of coloured paper at each other, making children laugh again. Tamara guessed the audience would be talking about the incident for a long time. She sighed and closed her eyes. It made her realise what a dangerous place the circus could be.

CHAPTER TEN

After a breakfast of grilled salted herrings, Billy announced they were moving to Manchester. Tamara sighed with relief. It was all hands on deck while the circus dismantled. As everyone worked together, Zeema was nowhere in sight so Tamara helped Kit to load the canvas, poles, and boxes of nuts, bolts and tools onto a cart. Whenever he was around her, she felt like singing. She had never experienced anything like this feeling before and it made her legs wobbly.

Her father had been strict about boys, making sure no one got close. She had thought he was being over-protective. It all made sense to her now; she was the property of one man and one man only. Well, she wasn't playing along with that. Not while she had breath in her body. Anger welled inside her. If her parents thought that, they hardly knew her.

'When the wagons are loaded, pick up the litter,' Billy called to the crew. 'I'm going ahead to the station.'

It was midday when, as if by magic, the circus disappeared, leaving behind a windswept park. A few people, some of them children, stood in the street waving a fond farewell to the show's performers. Tamara, not willing to take any chances, kept hidden from sight until the animals were safely loaded onto the train.

At their destination, Billy turned the wagons into a large open field. Once the animals were fed and watered, everyone worked methodically to get the canvas tent up and ready for the next day's performance. Tamara was pleased when she was asked to help. It stopped her from thinking about her troubles.

Later that day, Kit was sitting outside his wagon sharpening a piece of wood with his penknife, when Tamara passed by. He beckoned to her. She hesitated, remembering how Zeema had reacted. Enemies were the last thing she needed, but his smile encouraged her and, following her heart, she sat on the step next to him. She saw genuine warmth in his blue eyes and she liked the feeling she got when she was with him. Her feelings for him were growing with each passing day. There was something about him – she wasn't sure what it was – but each time he was around her, she got a funny butterfly feeling in her stomach.

'Have you been avoiding me?'

'Of course not.'

'I'm not married, nor am I walking out with anyone.'

That delighted her, but still she asked, 'What about Zeema?'

'Zeema! She and I are circus partners, nothing more.'

Tamara lowered her eyes. She was about to say he should tell Zeema, when he said, 'Working in the circus, you have to get close in order to build up trust.'

She felt a flush to her face. He folded the blades of his penknife and put it away. 'Billy had a chat with me earlier,' he said. 'He asked me what I thought about you.'

'Has he changed his mind about keeping me on?'

'Don't worry. I told him he'd be mad to let you go.'

'You did? Thank you.' She knitted her fingers. 'Do you think he listened?'

Kit placed his hand on her arm. 'We'll soon see.'

When Tamara was asked to go to Mr. Billy's trailer, she got there quickly enough. It was as untidy as ever, with dockets covering the table. Although she had left it tidy, she could see Mr. Billy worked best surrounded by chaos. He made a space for her, but she remained standing.

'I'm not going to bite,' he said. She perched on the edge of the chair. 'When I took you on, I got the feeling you were running away from something.' Tamara felt the colour rise in her cheeks. Had he found her out? 'But,' he went on, 'that's your business. I couldn't see a young girl like you on the streets.' He smiled and she began to relax. 'Besides, I've always been a sucker for a pretty face.'

'Thanks, Mr. Billy.' She shifted on the chair. 'Are you going to fire me?'

'No I'm not. According to both Nickolas and Kristopher, I need you.' He leaned back in his chair. 'Nickolas reckons you'd make good with the ponies and I'm inclined to agree with him. Therefore, I've decided to give you the opportunity to train as a bareback rider. How do you

77

feel about that?'

'Are you serious, Mr. Billy?' Her shoulders relaxed and a smile brightened her face.

'The question is, are you?'

'Oh, yes, Mr. Billy. I'd love to.'

'Well, then, if you're willing to work hard, and I think you are...'

'I am. Honest, I am.'

'I'm trying out some new acts on the tightrope with Zeema, and that's going well. How is your balance?'

'Fine.'

'Do you think you could stand upright on a horse?'

'I could try, Mr. Billy.'

'Sometimes working hard isn't enough. You need to have an act. Most of the crew can slot in wherever they're needed. When you've not been brought up in the circus, it can take hours of training.'

'I won't let you down.'

'Well, we'll soon know if you've got it in you. Unfortunately, I'm out on business for a few days, but leave it with me and I'll sort something out.'

Tamara wanted to laugh and cry at the same time; she felt overwhelmed. As she turned to leave, she looked down at her dowdy dress.

'Nelly will fix you up with a suitable costume. We're lucky to be supported by our local community, but we could do with one or two more backers, so nothing too extravagant, mind.' He stood up, shot her a smile and extended his hand. 'Welcome to the circus, Princess Tamara.'

This was a dream, and far more than she had ever expected. Things like this never happened to her. She could hardly wait to tell someone – preferably Kit – and maybe then, she might believe it herself.

The sky was grey with a promise of rain, and a sharp breeze blew across the site. Tamara went back to fetch her cape before going to find Kit. His wagon was empty and she went towards the big tent. Instead of Kit, she found Nick. The smile slipped from her face.

Walking towards her, he held out his hand. 'Tamara! You've come to thank me.'

'Thank you? What do you mean?'

'Well, now. If it hadn't been for me, you wouldn't have looked so happy when you entered the tent just now.'

'But ... but I thought Mr. Billy made the decisions round here.'

'Oh, come, come! I'm family. I get to do the hiring and firing.' He smiled sweetly. 'I've been waiting for you. Let's sit over here where we can talk.' He ran his fat fingers down the side of her face. Tamara shuddered, rooted to the spot, disbelief on her face. 'We should get to know each other, seeing as I'll be your trainer.'

Her mouth dropped, and she felt unsure how to cope with the situation. She straightened her shoulders. 'Excuse me if I go and find the others.'

'Not so fast.' He grabbed her around the waist. 'Aren't you to going to thank me first?'

His mouth sought hers, but she wriggled violently in his arms. He gripped her hair and pulled her close. His tongue searched her mouth. When his hand touched her breast, a tremor of revulsion shook through her slender body. She pushed violently against his chest to no avail. She beat her fists against his chest and finally swung her arm, her nail scratching the bottom of his chin. He slackened his grip as his passion cooled, and he released her. Her eyes blazed, her breath came in gasps.

'Stay away from me, or I shall show you how much damage these small hands can do.' With that, she spun on her heel and ran from the tent.

'Gypsy slut,' he called after her.

She picked up a wooden pail and ran towards the river and half-filled it with water. Back at the wagon, she could still smell his sweaty body; the taste of his tongue plundering her mouth made her feel sick. Making sure she locked the door, she stripped to her petticoat and washed herself in the cold water, trying to clean away the memory of the last few minutes.

The tight ball of fear lodged in her throat slowly disappeared, leaving her feeling drained. Everywhere was quiet and Tamara, who had once told the time by the sky, had completely forgotten about supper. She hoped Nelly would forgive her for not arriving to help prepare the meal. Drying herself quickly, she changed into her only change of clothes – a long flowing black skirt and a knitted jersey that laced up the front. How could she work with Nick? He was capable of God knows what. Her hands trembled as she ran her brush through her hair. Her confidence flagging, and with no idea what she should do, she made her entrance to the food tent.

'There you are,' Billy said. 'We were beginning to think you'd left us.'

Nodding across at Mr. Billy, she made her way towards Nelly, who was spooning big floury potatoes into a dish. 'I'm sorry I'm late, Nelly. Shall I take over now? You sit down and have yours.'

'Put these bowls of cabbage on the table before the meat goes cold.'

'Everything all right, Tamara?' Kit asked, as she passed down the long table with the serving bowl. She felt anything but all right, but nodding, she forced a smile. She served the strong man with the tattoos and the twins with the painted-on smiles. When she reached Nick, she doled out his cabbage, slopping some onto the sleeve of his shirt. He glared up at her and Tamara matched his glare with contempt.

If this bull of a man thought he could shame her with insults, he knew nothing at all about this particular gypsy girl.

CHAPTER ELEVEN

In spite of her excitement to train with the ponies, Tamara felt restless. What had happened the previous night with Nick had unnerved her, and left her feeling vulnerable. She was rolling up her mat when Zeema threw her towel over her shoulder and, without a word, stalked out of the wagon.

'Never mind her,' Nelly said. 'What's up? Ye look

81

like a wet rag. I thought ye'd be pleased about training with the ponies.'

'Oh, I am, Nelly. It's just not sunk in yet.'

'Happen ye'll believe it when ye try on one of the costumes.' Nelly went outside and dragged a trunk from underneath the wagon, and Tamara helped her carry it inside. Soon an array of coloured sequined costumes, some old and faded, were scattered across the floor.

'This one is nice, but it's so short, Nelly. It would barely cover my knees. Can't I just ride in my skirt?'

'Nah! You'd have no freedom to move.' She held up a green one-piece elasticised garment. 'This looks about your size. Try it on.'

It was a good fit, and the colour went well with her red hair. The one-piece covered her body and legs, with a matching sequined skirt that came to just above her knees.

'You can't ride barefoot, Tamara. You must wear slippers. You'll find most sizes in here.' She lifted a box onto the table.

Tamara put on a pair of well-worn white slippers, resembling ballet shoes, and tied the ribbons around her ankles. She found them restricting but she would get used to them, if that was what was expected.

'Thanks, Nelly, these are fine.'

'Ye look grand, so you do. This is only a working costume. I'll make ye something special when you're ready to perform in front of an audience.'

Tamara smiled. In spite of her first impression of Nelly, she had soon realised the old woman was a first-class seamstress as well as a good cook.

'Right, when ye've changed we'd better get over to the food tent and start that breakfast.'

The following morning, Tamara was ready to start training. Just after dawn, she put on the green costume, coiled her hair on top of her head with one of Nelly's hair slides, and quietly left the wagon. She carried a torch. A cold wind blew around her ankles, and thoughts of bumping into Nick made her shudder. She was relieved to see no sign of him. Kit was already practising on the trapeze and he slid down the rope towards her. He was wearing black tight-fitting pants and a white sleeveless vest, showing well-toned muscles. Pablo, his eyes cast down when he saw Tamara, was guiding two of the best white ponies into the ring. He tied them up at the side and hurried away.

'Good morning, Tamara. All ready to start, I see.'

She smiled and slipped off her cape. Kit took it from her and hung it up. When she glanced up, he was staring at her. Her face coloured and she placed her hands across her chest. 'Is there something wrong with my costume?'

'No. I'm sorry. It's rude of me to stare, but you look amazing.' His remark made her blush more. He guided her forward. 'Are you nervous?'

'Of the ponies, no.' There was still no sign of Nick and she began to relax.

'Not sure I congratulated you yesterday. You seemed a little preoccupied. You weren't having second thoughts, were you?'

'No. Of course not.' This was not the time to

tell him what had happened with Nick.

'Shall we get started, then?' he said. 'I want to see how the ponies react. They've not had a rider for some time.' He placed his arm around her shoulder and drew her towards the centre of the ring.

She nodded, feeling little flutters of excitement as he unhooked the ponies and brought them to her. She stepped forward, feeling the smooth, silky softness of their well-groomed coats. Kit placed two sugar lumps into her hand. His fingers brushed hers and she felt again a strange fluttering in her stomach. Holding out her hand, palm-side up, the ponies ate and then nudged her for more. 'Well, that's a good start,' he said, and they both laughed.

The ponies ran side by side around the ring as if yoked together, but what made Tamara's heart race was the way Kit moved around, his dark wavy hair brushing his shoulders. Using his whip, he gave the command and the horses came to a smooth halt.

'Ready,' he said. 'You hop up on this one.' He held it steady while she mounted.

'How do you feel?'

'Grand.'

Smiling, he led her forward. She didn't need to be shown how to ride a pony, but she didn't at all mind Kit guiding her round. Then he stood back, gave the command, and the ponies trotted around with Tamara proudly sitting upright. His hands on his hips, he watched her as, without warning, she switched from one horse to the other, bouncing back and forth as if she was playing hopscotch.

Her hair had come loose, flowing out behind her, until Kit gave the command to stop.

'Don't be cross. I got carried away,' she apologised.

'What else can you do?'

She shrugged. 'What do you mean?'

'Well, could you try standing with one foot on each pony? I'm not expecting you can do it straight away. Just want to see what your balance is like. Ready? Look straight ahead.'

After a wobbly start, she stood upright. Then, gently touching her ankle, he asked her to move her feet further back so that they were resting on the pony's hide. 'That's good. Now bend your knees and place your arms above your head. Don't worry,' he said, when she glanced nervously down at him. 'I'll catch you if you fall.'

He guided her round several times and Tamara soon forgot her inhibitions. When he felt she was confident enough, he gave the command and the ponies trotted around and around the ring. Tamara loved every minute of it; she felt as if she was flying.

'You're amazing. Are you sure you've never worked in a circus before?' His hands spanned her waist and he lifted her down. She was close enough to inhale the musky scent of his body as her feet sank into the fresh sawdust.

'I'm sure,' she laughed. 'I'm used to being around horses, that's all.'

'Well, I'm impressed.' He glanced at his watch. 'Let's try that again,' he said. 'This time, try keeping the gap tighter between the ponies.' By the end of the training session, Tamara had enjoyed every second of being with Kit, and was surprised at how quickly the time had gone.

He was helping her on with her cape when Zeema appeared in the opening of the tent. 'Oh,' she said, glancing towards Kit. 'Am I too early?'

'No, we're about finished.' He smiled towards Tamara. 'I'll see you later.'

When Tamara passed through the opening, Zeema glared at her. And Tamara, for the first time, was conscious of the jealousy she evoked in the girl. However, she felt too happy to care.

On her way to the wagon, she bumped into Nick. He paused alongside her and she froze, fearful of what he might do.

'Enjoy it while it lasts,' he sneered.

'Why are you doing this?'

'I think you know why.'

'Never,' she spat. 'I'd rather die! Mr. Billy would be interested to know about your vile suggestion.'

'Ungrateful wench! You need to learn a little respect.' He leaned in closer, his eyes narrowed. 'Don't forget who I am. He'll never believe a little slut like you over me,' he hissed.

'I'm nothing of the sort and you know it.'

He grinned, then walked off, leaving her burning with anger and frustration, wondering whom she could confide in. Was he right? Would anyone believe her?

After all, she was a gypsy and no one took the word of a gypsy.

Tamara finished her outdoor chores and was barely through the door of the wagon, when Zeema rounded on her. 'I was right about you!'

She jabbed her finger into Tamara's shoulder. 'There was never any trouble till you came.'

'What have I done now?' Tamara sat down at the table.

'You giving Nick the eye whilst cosying up to Kit. You disgust me. The circus is no place for the likes of you.'

'You're talking gibberish. Who told you that?' Furious, she stood up and crossed her arms. 'It's not true, none of it. What has Nick been saying?'

'Are you denying it?'

'Yes, of course I am,' Tamara said. 'He had his hands all over me in the tent the other night. I had to fight him off. Are you telling me he's never tried it with you?'

Zeema lowered her eyes and turned her back.

'He has, hasn't he?'

'You're a liar! Now, clear off, I have to get ready.' She swished the curtain across.

Tamara shook her head. 'Well, if he tries it again, I won't let it go. He's not going to slander me. Nobody will.'

Tamara was taking the entrance money – a job she hated, in case someone from the gypsy communities spotted her. She knew gypsies hung around the circus looking for work, and so far, she had been lucky.

Tonight was their last performance in Manchester. The nights were drawing in and gas lamps illuminated the tent. She went inside and passed the takings over to Mr. Billy. He smiled, saying that he was delighted at how she was handling the ponies. Pleased by his comment, she went towards the back and sat down. Nick was smiling and chatting with the spectators, looking dapper in his red coat and tails, top hat and cane. It was difficult to believe he was such a bully around women, and she wondered how much Zeema knew about him.

Early the following morning, Tamara and the rest of the company were packing up, ready to move on. Everyone was eager to help, all except Nick; she guessed he thought that the dismantling of the circus was beneath him. To the rest of the hard working crew, it was as if nothing else mattered. Tamara helped Kit pack away the seating, mostly planks of wood nailed together and flat-packed for transport. This time, the circus was returning to home ground in Covent Garden.

'What part of Ireland are you from, Tamara?'

No one had asked her that since she arrived, not even Mr. Billy. 'Galway, on the West Coast.' She let go of the plank they were carrying so that he could slide it into the wagon. 'My great-grandfather came from Connemara. Is that close to Galway?'

'Yes. It is,' she smiled. 'What's London like?'

'It's like no other city I know. Covent Garden is quite interesting. I'll show you around one afternoon, if you like?'

'Really! I'd like that.' They were still loading when it started to rain. The dedicated crew carried on, and soon everywhere was saturated. Tamara's feet sank into the wet mud as she piled the last of the seats onto the wagon.

Hampered by heavy rain, the journey took

longer. When they got there, the rain had ceased, leaving a foggy mist over the city. It was a shadowy, noisy place, where carriages, carts, wagons and trams blocked the roadway. Angry, impatient drivers waved and bellowed as Mr. Billy heralded the circus's arrival.

Tamara was relieved when the wagons finally pulled onto the common. It looked as grey and colourless as the site they had left in Manchester. Wagons and tents were already stationary on the site. One had 'food wagon' printed across the front, in bold black letters.

In spite of the damp and cold, it was a team effort to get the animals settled, fed and watered, and then the big top erected and ready for the evening performance.

Tamara, tired and wet, her legs splashed with mud, her hair like rats tails, queued with Kit and the rest of the company to take their turn in the washroom where they were given dry clothes to put on. The smell of vegetable broth coming from the food wagon was more than welcome.

That night, she lay awake next to Zeema and recounted her day working with Kit. She felt warm and comfortable just thinking about him. At the same time, the knot in her stomach returned, as thoughts of Jake Travis came back to haunt her.

CHAPTER TWELVE

By morning, ice formed in shallow puddles across the common. Tamara shivered and pulled her cloak tighter around her shoulders, as she side-stepped her way towards the food tent. Yesterday, she had hardly taken in her surroundings, but now the common looked better in daylight. Beyond it, she could see grey and red-slated rooftops, tall buildings and spires. Billy had said the circus would remain on home ground until after Christmas, and she was looking forward to exploring the area around Covent Garden.

Flory, a local woman, came in each day to do the cooking, leaving Tamara free to concentrate on her training, and Nelly to get on with making new costumes for the show.

The performers who lived nearby went home each night after the show. Nick also disappeared, but no one knew where he went. Billy said he was sowing his wild oats. It left Tamara relaxed to walk around the common at night.

When she had been working at the circus six weeks, Billy increased her pay to two shillings a week, including food and lodgings, for which she was grateful. She had been careful how she spent it. She was in need of new undergarments, and material for a new skirt. It felt good to be able to choose her clothes. Her outfits had always been chosen for her in the past, so she had no idea what things cost. Delighted to have money at her disposal – money she had earned – she made her way to Petticoat Lane, where Nelly said she could get anything she wanted at bargain prices.

Tamara was delighted to find such a busy market. Most of the women shoppers, muffled in warm shawls against the November cold, paid her no heed. They wore boots, the toes of which peeped out from underneath their long skirts. Wondering if she could afford to buy herself a pair, she moved further into the market.

Coats and jackets swung from rails too high to reach, and men with long poles unhooked full-length coats for interested customers. She fought her way through to the women's clothing, and scrabbled with a bunch of women to get her hands on the clothes; thrilled when she managed to pull out a white blouse from the bottom of the pile. The woman behind the stall said, 'A tanner to you, luv, you won't buy better new.'

Tamara quickly bought it. She couldn't resist the bargains on offer and succeeded in getting her hands on a couple of long skirts. One of the skirts was a heavy black material and the other in russet. At these prices, she wouldn't need Nelly to run her up a skirt, after all.

'I'll take these,' she said, fishing the shilling from her purse.

On a nearby shoe stall, she tried on several boots, but the cheap leather cut into her ankles. She was about to give up, when the woman next to her, threw down a pair of tan buckskin button boots. 'Too small for me,' she said. Tamara snatched them up and tried them on. They were comfortable and felt good on her feet. 'How much?' she called above the noise of the traders.

'One and a tanner. Take 'em or leave 'em.'

'I'll take them,' she said, handing over the money. Pleased with her purchases, she placed them inside the large canvas bag Nelly had given her, and walked on through the market. She spent a few pennies more before she was ready to go back to the circus.

On the way, she skirted Covent Garden. Then she found herself drawn towards the lively banter of the market and the smell of the tangy oranges and all manner of fruit and vegetables. She sauntered along the stalls, enveloped in a cacophony of mixed voices and sounds as traders tried to outdo each other with their selling ability. Battered fruit lay at her feet and she almost slipped on a wet cabbage leaf. Everywhere, empty fruit baskets were piled high like a leaning tower, waiting for collection. A group of women wearing short capes covering their shoulders and fashionable hats perched on top of their heads, looked down their noses at Tamara as she passed by in her faded green cape. She returned the gesture by sticking out her tongue. Musicians played lively music and she wanted to dance. A man played the harp so sweetly, Tamara dropped a penny in his hat.

Mesmerised by it all, she gazed about her, unaware she was standing in the line of traffic until a man, driving his horse and cart through the middle of the market, hollered at her to get out of the way. She quickly jumped to the side and the cart trundled by. Lifting her skirts, she hurried

92

away, knocking over a barrel of apples in her haste. The trader swore and waved his fist at her. Her face red, she tried to apologise and hurried out of the market.

It was then that she spotted Nick, carrying two shopping baskets. She gasped. She held her bag in front of her and darted behind a tower of fruit baskets next to a cart full of flowers that intoxicated her senses. Nick was not alone. A well-dressed woman, wearing an unhappy expression, walked next to him holding a child in her arms. She assumed the woman, somewhere in her thirties, was his wife. He looked as miserable as the woman did, as they headed towards the fruit stalls. Tamara stayed hidden until they were out of view. Was this woman his estranged wife? Or some other woman?

That night, after the show, Tamara went back to the trailer, picked up her towel and soap and made her way to the shared washing area. As she passed along the animal cages, she heard voices and stopped to listen. At first, she did not recognise who was speaking until the man's voice rose in anger. 'Did you hear what I said, Zeema?'

She recognised it immediately. It was Nick's. She slowed down, hid behind a tree trunk and strained to listen. Zeema ran out from behind one of the cages, Nick close behind her. He grabbed her roughly by the arm and swung her round. 'You'll do as I say. Do you hear? Or you'll be out on your ear.'

She watched Zeema squirm. The girl broke away from him and ran towards the wagons. What was going on with those two? What did Nick want her to do? Tamara stayed hidden until she saw Nick disappear into the night. When she turned round, she was taken aback to see Pablo close behind her. She was surprised that he should be out here at this time.

'Please, miss.' He raised his small arms. 'I not hurt you.' He glanced around furtively. 'Mr. Nick, he bad man. He upset Miss Zeema.'

'Do you know why they were arguing, Pablo?' She relaxed back against one of the water barrels, hoping he would confide in her. 'Tell me what you know.'

'I not know.' He appeared frightened and, shaking his head, he hurried away.

'Don't go, Pablo.' But he had already disappeared between the wagons. Could Nick be mean enough to involve Pablo in his little schemes? In spite of asking herself the question, she knew he would.

Her bath turned out to be anything but relaxing. Was Nick staying on site tonight? She felt the need to share what she had witnessed with Kit the following day. The water had gone cold. She shivered and stepped out of the bath, then wrapped her towel around her. She dried herself quickly, glad that the door had a bolt. For all she knew, Nick could be lurking around outside. Dressed, she wrapped her cloak around her and hurried back towards the wagons.

Zeema was in bed, her face turned towards the window. Tamara called quietly to her, but when she didn't answer, Tamara lay awake trying to figure what it was that Nick wanted Zeema to do.

It wasn't until they were returning from practice the next day that Tamara caught up with Zeema. She ran up behind her as the girl hurried back to the wagon.

'What d'you want?' she said.

'What's going on with you and Nick?'

Zeema's dark eyes fixed on her. 'What's it to you?'

'I overheard him threatening you last night on my way to the washroom.'

'It was nothing! And none of your business, anyway.' Zeema paused outside their wagon and drew her woollen shawl tighter across her chest.

'It didn't sound like nothing. I know what he can be like, Zeema. I saw...' Tamara was about to tell her she had seen him in the market with a woman and baby, when Billy appeared from behind their wagon.

He raised his hat to Zeema. 'Tamara, I want a word.'

Zeema slipped inside the wagon and closed the door. Tamara followed Mr. Billy and struggled to keep step as he strode towards his wagon.

'What is it, Mr. Billy? Is everything all right?'

'You haven't seen Nick this morning, have you?'

'No, Mr. Billy. He didn't turn up for rehearsals.' The older man appeared more anxious each time Nick did one of his disappearing acts. She wondered if she should mention what she had overheard last night, but now might not be the time.

'Come in,' he said, walking up the well-worn steps. He pulled out a chair. 'Sit down. Are you happy training with the ponies?'

'Very much so, Mr. Billy.'

'Good, that's good. Because I think you're almost ready to do a live performance.' He puffed on his cigar.

'Do you mean it, Mr. Billy?'

'Yes, I've been watching you closely and, in spite of my doubts, I believe you're ready.'

Smiling, Tamara nodded.

'One other thing! I've had one of the older wagons spruced up. I don't want to part with it so I kept it as a permanent fixture on the site. I offered it to Nelly some time ago, but due to some silly superstition, she turned it down. And Zeema wants to stay where she is.' He shook his head. 'I know how crammed it is for the three of you. I'd like you to make use of it. The boys will bring it round this afternoon.'

Tamara was stunned. 'Thanks, Mr. Billy. It sounds wonderful.'

'You can fix it up how you like.'

This was more than she had ever expected. A wagon of her own made her feel totally accepted. She had no idea why Nelly was superstitious, but Tamara could not afford to be.

He removed the cigar from his mouth and held it between his fingers, then blew out the smoke. The smell reminded her of her grandmother's clay pipe. 'There's just a tiny favour I'd like you to do for me,' he said. She glanced down at her hands. What kind of favour? Please do not let me to have been wrong about Billy. What would she do if...?

'Hey, don't look so worried. It's nothing you

haven't done before.' He swung his arm round towards the mountain of dockets and tickets piled up on the shelf. 'Look at it! If you have any spare time this afternoon, I'd be grateful.' He placed his cigar down in the ashtray.

The tight ball in her stomach relaxed. 'I'll make time.' Relief swept through her.

'Come back around two o'clock.'

On her way to Mr. Billy's wagon after lunch, she ran into Kit. 'I'm going for a walk. Come with me. I want to ask you something.'

She wanted to go with him, but how could she let Billy down? 'I'm sorry, Kit. I'm working for Mr. Billy.'

He nodded, but she felt torn. If she went with Kit, she was likely to forget the time and her promise to Billy. 'What did you want to ask me?'

'Oh, I'll catch up with you another time.'

Another time seemed like forever, and her heart sank. 'Mr. Billy's bringing one of the older wagons onto the site this afternoon. And he's offered it to me.'

'Well, that's wonderful. Hope it's better than the one he gave me.' He raised his eyebrows.

'Why? What's wrong with it?'

'You can always climb in and take a look.' He smiled and winked.

'Why, Kit Trevelyan, and start tongues wagging?'

'That wouldn't bother me in the slightest,' he said. 'Are you free tomorrow?'

She lowered her eyes. 'Are you asking me on a date?'

'Yes, I guess I am.'

'Okay. I'll keep tomorrow free,' she smiled, walking away. When she glanced over her shoulder, she was aware of him watching the sway of her hips.

CHAPTER THIRTEEN

Tamara watched alongside Billy as the men unharnessed the horse from the wagon. They pushed it along on its large wheels, sliding it into position at the end of a row of wagons. Painted red, it looked pretty, and Tamara wondered whom it had belonged to. Wooden steps led up to the door. It was smaller than most of the wagons, but Tamara didn't mind that.

'Have a look inside,' Billy said. 'See what you think. It might need a woman's touch.' He removed his hat, bent his head, and followed her through the open half door with glazed shutters.

Inside, the original colours had faded and it had a musty smell. She looked upwards. The small skylight in the roof reminded her of her wagon in Ireland. It smelled fusty and a light covering of dust had settled everywhere. She would soon have it looking nice. What delighted her most was that it had been given to her as part of her working arrangement, and not paid for by Jake Travis.

'It's not that bad, is it?' Billy broke into her thoughts.

'Oh, no, Mr. Billy. It's very nice.' She sat next to him on the small bunk covered with a red quilt, and looked about her. An oblong mirror, edged with seashells, hung on the wall and a lamp sat on the small table.

'I've put some oil in the lamp, so it should last you a while.'

'I love it. Thanks, Mr. Billy.'

He nodded. It was spacious, with concealed storage, including a table and a padded bench underneath the window.

'I hope you enjoy living in it,' he said, when he saw her happy face.

'Oh, I will, Mr. Billy. Who did it belong to?'

He sighed, removed his hat, and placed it on the table. She bit her lip, wondering if she should have asked.

'It belonged to Adelaide, my first wife. She was in the theatre before joining the circus, and when we first met, this was her wagon.' He looked pensive. 'She died some years ago in the flu pandemic. Nicholas was only ten.' He sighed. 'Her dying affected him greatly.'

'Oh, I'm sorry, I...' Tamara felt unsure what to say next.

He gave a little laugh and stood up. 'That's life. Well, I'll be off. Let you get settled in.' He looked back at her. 'You can move your belongings in anytime.'

She liked Mr. Billy. He had been kind to her from the day she came looking for work. She felt privileged he had discussed his wife with her. She could tell he had loved her. Why else would he have kept her wagon unused for so long?

She watched him hesitate and look up at the wagon before walking away. Now she knew the reason for Nelly's superstition. Surely, if Adelaide had died in this wagon, Billy would not have kept it. At home, when a gypsy died of a contagious disease, their belongings were burned along with their wagon. She had never understood any of it, and it wasn't going to bother her.

Outside, she picked up some disinfectant and, holding her nose, she poured the pink liquid into a basin with carbolic soap. Then, from the large pot permanently on boil over the fire, she poured water on top and brought it inside. She took the bed covers outside, gave them a good shake, and hung them on the line to air. Then she scrubbed the inside of the wagon. Although it did not restore it to its original colours, it got rid of most of the grime. Curious to know more about Adelaide, Tamara went to find Nelly and collect her things.

Nelly wasn't in the wagon and she had no idea where Zeema was. All that she possessed fitted into a carpet bag. Curious to find out about Adelaide, she went in search of Kit. He was in the big tent, sitting with Zeema, their backs towards her. The sight of him sitting so close, and the way her head lolled against his shoulder, distressed Tamara so much she choked back tears. Fearful of making her feelings known, she ran back to her wagon.

Unable to rid her mind of the image of Kit with Zeema, she left totally confused and distracted for the rest of the evening. So, when Billy asked her to read palms in the little hut next to the long queue that formed outside, she was more than happy to oblige. Concentrating on other people's lives helped her to put her own aside. They were mainly women wanting to know what the future held for them. Some preferred her to read the cards, others were happy to pay a Joey to have their palms read. Tamara made it as amusing as possible, in spite of the tragedies some of the cards revealed to her. She had picked up the skill from her gypsy grandmother, who had told her not to reveal anything too unpleasant, as she had inherited 'the gift' of being a little too accurate.

The last woman had just left the hut, and Tamara was putting the remainder of the money into the canvas bag, when Nick's face appeared around the curtain, startling her. He put her in mind of a magician, appearing and disappearing at will.

'Father wants you to take a look at Sheba, the little white Shetland. She's been limping.'

Tamara stood up. 'I'll go now before the show begins.' She pulled the strings together on the money sack, surprised that Nick had not insulted her with some snide remark.

'I'll take that,' he said. 'Save you carrying it about.' Tamara hesitated, but he reached over and relieved her of the sack. On her way to see the animal, she wondered why she had hesitated. After all, he was the boss's son.

Sheba was indeed limping, in spite of being perfectly fine when she had looked in earlier. In spite of her way with horses, Tamara had to cajole and fuss the pony to get close. She could see she

101

was in pain. When she lifted the pony's hind foot, she noticed a large piece of flint wedged in her shoe. She wondered how that could have got there. It took her a while, but she eventually managed to get it out with a penknife. 'You'll be fine now, girl,' she said, patting the pony before leaving.

She got back to the big top just as the band struck up, and slipped inside the tent. Nick was about to perform. She had to admit that when sober, he was a good ringmaster. 'Ladies and gentlemen, boys and girls.' His delivery to the roll of the drum was spot on. He knew just how to engage an audience, and his scintillating introduction of each artiste never failed to excite spectators. If she did not know better, she would find it hard to believe that underneath his public persona, he was a manipulative bully.

After the show, she avoided Kit. She had thought she knew him, thought he had feelings for her. How wrong she had been. Today proved she knew nothing at all about him. She was sitting drinking cocoa when he came over and sat on the bench next to her. She cupped her hands round the mug.

She wanted to ask him about Zeema, but struggled to form the words. After all, it could have been perfectly innocent, but knowing Zeema, she felt overwhelmed with doubt.

'You're very quiet, Tamara. You haven't changed your mind about our date tomorrow, have you?'

She pushed her plate with the half-eaten biscuit to one side. 'It might not be a good idea, after all.'

'Why?' he frowned. 'I thought it was what you

wanted.' He pressed his elbow on the table and stroked his chin.

'I saw you with Zeema.' She looked up into his blue eyes, and swallowed the lump in her throat.

He raised his eyebrows. 'Oh, Tamara, I'm flattered if that's jealousy I see in those big eyes.'

She blushed. Her growing feelings for Kit had caught her by surprise. Did he feel the same way? She had no idea. The fact that they spent time together and he enjoyed flirting with her was not exactly a sign of real affection.

'We have a date tomorrow afternoon, Tamara, and you can't go back on your word. Trust me.' He smiled and stood up from the table.

'Are you leaving already?' She had expected more, and felt disappointed.

'I want to catch Billy before he goes to bed.' He squeezed her hand. 'You stay and finish your drink. I'll see you tomorrow.'

Nick and Zeema were sitting opposite each other at the far table. When Nick got up to leave, Zeema immediately followed. Tamara wondered what was going on, and more so, what Zeema was up to?

Before going to bed, Tamara slid the bolt across the top of the door. She was not taking any chances with Nick still in camp. She lay in bed looking up at the ceiling, wondering where her life in the circus would take her. Gypsy life was all she had ever known. Their customs had made her who she was. If tomorrow she discovered that Kit was merely a friend to her, it would break her heart. Finally, she slept, until the patter of rain woke her before dawn. It was freezing and she could smell damp. She drew back the curtain and lit the lamp, then swung her feet onto the wet floor. Rain was leaking from the ceiling, forming a dark, sodden patch on the small mat by the side of the bed.

She placed an enamel basin on the floor and heard the rain drip rhythmically as she got dressed. Nelly was right. It was damp, but she was not going to let it bother her. She could always find something to block up the hole. This was circus life and what Billy meant by taking the bumps with the smooth.

She hated these dark mornings, and outside the ground was soggy. Carrying her circus shoes, she pulled her cloak snugly around her and tiptoed around the puddles to arrive at the tent. Inside, she dried her feet in the sawdust. At the sound of raised voices, she paused. Two men were yelling at one another. As she walked further inside, she gasped. Kit had the palms of his hands on Nick's chest, pushing him back. Nick, his face puce, swung his fist at Kit, who ducked, and Nick fell forwards.

'What's going on?'

'It's all right,' Kit said. 'Our friend Nick's just leaving.'

Sneering, Nick tottered to his feet. Tamara had seen him like this before.

'You're drunk,' she said. He wobbled sideways, but managed to keep upright. She glanced at Kit. 'Shall I go for help?'

'No. I'll handle this.' Then, turning to Nick, he said, 'If you don't want your father to hear about this, I suggest you leave now.'

Nick smirked, removed a whiskey bottle from his pocket, and held it aloft. 'Oh, you'd like that, wouldn't you, Kristopher? Have the little gypsy all to yourself.' He drank the remainder of the liquid and threw the bottle aside.

Tamara wanted to wipe the grin from his red face and hang the consequences, but Kit beat her to it. Holding Nick by the collar of his red jacket, he hauled him towards the entrance, pushing him outside into the rain. 'Now, go somewhere and sober up before any of the others see you.'

The incident with the two men bothered her. 'What was that all about?'

'It was nothing. I'm sorry you had to witness it.' His face tense, he walked into the ring. 'He's wasted enough of our time already.' Kit called Pablo to bring on the ponies. Gradually, jugglers, clowns, acrobats and then Zeema came into the tent and began practising their acts.

Tamara couldn't concentrate, and each time she looked across at Zeema, jealousy consumed her. The cosy picture of her head resting on Kit's shoulder was eating away at Tamara. If it were not for her growing feelings for Kit, she was not at all certain that the circus was where she wanted to be.

CHAPTER FOURTEEN

That afternoon, Tamara put Zeema to the back of her mind as she prepared for her date with Kit. She washed her hair and, regardless of the cold, she put on her best white blouse, pulling it down to reveal her slender shoulders and just the right amount of cleavage to make him look. Then she sat by the small window where she could watch Kit arrive.

He was on time. He wore a short dark jacket, white shirt, tight-fitting trousers and knee-high riding boots. He walked between two reddish-brown horses and stopped opposite her wagon to wait for her. He had said nothing about going riding, and she certainly wasn't dressed for it, but the idea excited her. She admired everything about him, knowing he could not see her. She watched the way the wind blew his wavy shoulder-length black hair; noticed the glint of his gold watch and the dark hairs on his arm, as he stretched up to steady one of the horses. She could have stayed where she was, looking through the window at his handsome face, but the horses whinnied and scraped their hooves on the ground, forcing her to abandon her post. She felt guilty to have spied on him again, and she quickly opened the door. Smiling, he came over and mounted the steps, his earlier encounter with Nick apparently forgotten. She was aware of his eyes scanning her bare shoulders and she gave him a beguiling smile, determined to win him back from the beautiful Zeema.

'You look beautiful.' He coughed to clear his throat.

'Are we going riding?'

'Billy reckons this pair of 'osses need exercising. They eat more oats than a nobleman's 'unter.' He laughed.

'Billy's probably right.' She placed her hands on her hips, increasing the swell of her breasts beneath her thin blouse, and swayed from side to side. 'When was this arranged?'

'Last night.'

'Where are we going?' She tossed her newly-washed hair.

'Hampstead Heath. You'll have to wrap up in something warm.'

'Do you think I should change?' She continued to tease him, running her hands down the length of her shapely body. She had on a long dark skirt that fell to just above her ankles, showing the tips of her second-hand boots.

He smiled. 'Well, I wouldn't want you to catch cold.'

'Just give me a minute.' With a mischievous grin, she unhooked her jacket, scarf and gloves from behind the door. Before Kit could say a word she was astride the lean chestnut mare, her skirt pulled up to her knees. 'Come on then. What are we waiting for?'

'Hang on. Slow down.' Laughing loudly, he followed her out of the common and along the busy cobbled streets. He could see she was heading for trouble when pedestrians ran for cover.

'Bloody 'ell!' one man yelled.

Laughing, Tamara kept going until a police officer raised his hand and stopped her. He asked her to dismount. Her hair blew in front of her face as she stood close to the animal, controlling it only with her voice and the piece of rope looped loosely around its neck.

'What's this, young woman? Riding a horse like that through the busy London streets is a dangerous pastime.' He sighed. 'What have you to say for yourself?' Onlookers gathered to watch the commotion, and Tamara, embarrassed by the attention, bit her lip and realised her stupidity. Thoughts of ending up in another cell flashed across her mind, and she closed her eyes and prayed. When she opened them, Kit was by her side.

'Sorry about that, Officer,' he said. 'The horse bolted.'

'Aye. Is that so?' The police officer narrowed his eyes, looking at them both. 'I'll overlook it this time.' He lifted the flap of his breast pocket to put away his notebook. 'Now, be off, the both of you, before I change my mind.'

Leading the horses one apiece, they walked on. 'I can see I'm going to have to tame you, Tamara,' Kit murmured.

'I doubt anyone could ever do that, but I don't mind you trying. Seriously, I'm sorry, and thanks, Kit.'

'Are you thanking me for telling the officer a lie or for coming to your rescue?'

'Both, really! It's been so long since I was able

to ride like that, and I just couldn't control the urge.'

'How old were you when you started riding, Tamara?'

'Three years old.'

'What else don't I know about you?'

'A gypsy's life is hardly an exciting one.' It was too soon, she thought, to start telling him about her past, and she didn't want reminding of any of it. As they moved away from the city, she asked, 'Is it safe to ride the rest of the way?'

'Yes, but just a slow trot. We've a couple more miles yet.' They rode side-by-side, keeping pace with one another. Each time she glanced up, Kit was looking at her. They both laughed. Before long, they were heading onto Hampstead Heath where wide open spaces with green fields and tall trees stretched before them, leaving behind the busy streets, steeples and domes. In spite of the cold, Tamara felt a sense of freedom that she had not experienced for some time. The wind was in their hair as they rode hard, skirting curved footpaths with clumps of gorse and hedgerows of dog rose and blackberry brambles that reminded her of home. Suddenly she was back in Galway, galloping over grassy banks, jumping over posts, and leaving hoof prints in the wet sandy beaches.

They slowed to a halt by a flower girl wearing a shawl that covered her head and shoulders. She was carrying a basket of lavender and roses.

'Buy a rose for the pretty lady, sir?'

Kit placed some coins into her hand and she handed him a red rose. He dismounted. 'Let's stop here a while, Tamara.' After securing the horses to a nearby oak tree to graze, Kit and Tamara sat on a wooden bench opposite. He was still holding the red rose, twirling it between his finger and thumb. She was beginning to wonder what he intended to do with it, when he sidled closer to her, undid the button of her jacket, and slipped the stem of the rose into the buttonhole.

'Thank you. It's beautiful.' She lowered her head to sniff its scent.

'You, too, are beautiful, Tamara. I've wanted to say that for a long time.'

She felt herself blush, and pushed back her windswept hair, her heart pounding. She longed to tell him how she felt, but there was still that business with Zeema he had not yet explained. An elderly man and woman hurried past arm-in-arm, their collars turned up against the cold. A young couple was running to keep pace with their dog straining at the leash.

'We mustn't sit here too long,' he said. 'I can't have you catching cold.' He drew the collar of her coat up around her neck, and she wondered what it would be like to slip her arm through his. She glanced up at the determined angle of his chin, his face flushed after his ride. This was their first time together away from the circus, and she felt tongue-tied. All she could think about was Zeema with her head on his shoulder. If only he would say something, it would help clear the fuzz going on inside her head. She was aware of the side-glances he was giving her every few seconds.

'Tell me about yourself, Tamara. Is your mother very beautiful?' She had never thought of her mother in that way; she was just her ma. 'Have

110

you any brothers or sisters?'

Suddenly, she found her tongue. 'No, none. I've always envied other kids who had. And there were always plenty of them around the gypsy camp.'

'Were you lonely?'

'Not in the least. I always knew I would travel; not just as a traveller, you know. I wanted to explore parts of the world for myself, get away from the stifling confines of living with my parents.' She left out the fact that she had been a stowaway, and had spent a night in a Liverpool cell.

Kit nodded. 'I never knew my parents. They died when I was quite young.'

'I'm sorry.'

'Oh, you don't miss what you don't remember, but I often wonder what it would have been like.'

She discovered that he was born in Covent Garden, both his brothers had fought and died in the Boer War. His grandfather came from Connemara, a place he told her he hoped to see one day. She learned about his strict regime in keeping his muscles toned and his ambitions to become a circus owner himself one day.

However, when he took hold of her hand, entwining his fingers with hers, she felt a quiver of excitement. 'You don't mind me taking liberties, do you?'

'Well, that depends.' She lowered her head. 'You took liberties with Zeema. You said you would tell me about that.' There was no sarcasm in her voice.

A frown wrinkled his forehead and he let go of her hand. Tamara's heart sank and she inwardly

111

rained down curses upon herself for spoiling the moment.

He stood up and glanced at his watch, then up at the rolling grey clouds. Then he took long strides towards the horses. Stunned, Tamara felt tears gathering in her eyes. 'What have I said? What's wrong?'

He untied the horses and handed her the rope. 'It's not you, Tamara.' He took a deep breath. 'It seems a shame to spend what time we have together talking about Zeema and Nick, because that's what it was all about. But I guess you've left me no choice.' They walked the horses towards the pond, where the animals drank. 'There's an inn not far from here. We can talk there. I'll tell you what you want to know.'

Soon they were sitting opposite each other, a drink in front of them. Tamara's was a fizzy soda. The tiny bubbles tickled her nose as she sipped. Kit lifted his glass to his mouth, leaving a creamy line of foam across his upper lip. Tamara could not resist reaching over to remove it with her finger. Kit took hold of her hand and kissed it.

'What you saw with Zeema was nothing. She's like a sister to me. She asked my advice on whether she should take another chance with Nick.'

'What?'

'I gave her my advice for what it's worth. I doubt she'll heed me, though. Daft as it sounds, she's in love with him.'

'Oh, poor Zeema.'

'You mustn't say anything, Tamara.' He sighed.

'Do you understand?'

She nodded. She had little experience of men herself, but she could see right through Nick. The inn was empty apart from two other people and they were far enough away not to overhear.

'Nick walked out with her when she first came to the circus, but he cooled off about a year ago.'

'Is he married?'

'Why do you ask?'

'I saw him in the market recently with a woman and a baby.'

'A baby!' He leaned his elbow on the table. 'I don't know about any baby. He did marry, but he left his wife some time ago.'

'So it might be his wife, I saw him with.'

Kit shrugged. 'He's a complex character. Married or not won't stop a man like Nick.'

'Does Zeema know?'

He nodded.

'And she's still...'

Kit shrugged.

'Kit, I saw them together. He was shouting at her.'

'When was this?'

'Just a few nights ago,' she continued. 'When I asked her, she denied it.'

'Did you hear what he was saying to her?'

'No, but Pablo saw them, too. Poor little man looked frightened to death.' She took another sip of her drink. 'Why were you and Nick fighting?'

'He was drunk and boasting about his women. I wanted him out of the tent.' He swallowed the rest of his drink. Tamara still had half of hers left. 'Would you like another drink?'

She shook her head. Kit pushed his glass aside and reached for her hand again. 'We've spent enough time talking about the obnoxious Nick. I want to know more about you. The first time we spoke, I thought you were a Liverpudlian.'

'That doesn't surprise me,' she laughed. 'Most of them talk Irish, anyway. I've lived in Galway all my life. Have you ever been there?'

'No, but what's Connemara like?'

'It's beautiful all year round. I went there with my father to buy a horse and sell our old nag.'

'Well, is it as beautiful as they say?' He was staring intently at her.

'Did anyone ever tell you it was rude to stare?' she joked.

He blinked as if coming out of a trance. 'I can't help it. You've completely hypnotised me.'

Tossing her head, she removed her hand and giggled. 'Connemara is beautiful. Towering rugged mountains; lakes that always appear blue; deserted beaches that reach out to the Atlantic Ocean.'

He took her hand again. 'You must miss it.'

'I miss the landscape and the sea, but that's all.'

She was glowing with happiness. For the first time in her life, she had met someone she truly loved. Yet, she could not tell him everything.

'What made you join the circus?'

She lowered her eyes. 'I had nowhere else to go.'

'Why was that?'

'I wanted to see the world; some of it, anyway.' She stood up. 'Isn't it time we were getting back?'

He followed her outside and untied the horses.

114

'You know, I've never met anyone like you,' he said, helping her to mount. 'I don't care why you joined the circus, but I'm glad you did.'

CHAPTER FIFTEEN

Tamara and Kit strolled hand-in-hand towards the stables. They heard whispers of endearment. Pablo came up behind them, placed a finger over his lips and, with his other hand, gesticulated towards an empty stable. Then he ran away.

They guessed who it was immediately. Zeema and Nick were kissing and canoodling, thinking they were safe from prying eyes. When they saw Kit and Tamara, they pulled apart, as if scalded.

'How dare you spy on me?' Nick backed into the corner. With a defiant gleam in his eye, he plucked a cigarette from a packet and hung it loosely from the corner of his mouth. Zeema looked from Kit to Tamara, a look of annoyance on her face.

'*Spying on you!*' Kit stood in front of Nick. 'You're not that important. My only concern is for Zeema.'

'Oh, forever the hero. She doesn't need you. She's got me.'

Kit turned to Zeema. 'Are you all right, Zeema?'

She nodded. Nick shifted, lit the cigarette drew in the smoke and popped it back into his mouth. 'So, you see, you can go now and leave us alone.'

'Put that cigarette out! You're upsetting the animals.' Tamara went into the next stable to quieten the mare.

Zeema hurried from the stables in tears, but Nick did not attempt to follow her.

'When did you get to tell me what to do, gypsy whore?' he snarled.

Kit squared up to him, but Tamara ran between them. 'His cruel words can't hurt me,' she said, wafting the smoke away from her face.

He gave a snort of amusement. 'I'm top dog round here, and don't either of you forget it.'

'You're a no-good drunk!' Kit said, his fists curling and uncurling. 'And if it wasn't for the respect I have for your father, you'd never get away with this. I'd have you slung out of the circus before you give it a bad name.'

Tamara tugged at his arm and led him outside. 'He's not worth it, Kit. Neither of them are.'

Tamara was in the little hut, telling fortunes. The queue grew longer each night and it took her all her time to see everyone before the start of the show. But at least she felt useful, and she was sure Mr. Billy must be pleased with the money she was making.

It was mostly single women who flocked to have their palms read. They were only interested in hearing one thing from Tamara: that they would meet a tall dark stranger, and be married within the year. The occasional boyfriend popped in discreetly, wanting to know if his girl had cheated on him. Tamara had to bite her lip to stop herself from giggling at how some men mistrusted their sweethearts.

At times, Tamara could see much more than a

cloud on the horizon but she had learned from her grandmother never to upset people by telling them the whole truth. So today, when a young mother in the family way asked to have her palm read, Tamara had to hide her distress. She saw nothing but darkness, and she knew something terrible was about to befall the unfortunate woman.

Smiling, she asked the woman. 'Is this your first?'

'No. I've two more 'f the little pests at 'ome,' she said, patting her tummy.

Tamara swallowed the lump in her throat, took a deep breath and said, 'I see a long life to your family. You are due some luck soon and your husband will find work.'

'Gor blimey I could do with some 'f that, an' all,' the woman said, handing over her penny.

'You keep it.' Tamara held back the curtain and, when the woman had gone, she popped a penny of her own money into the bag. When Nick collected the money again, she handed it over without hesitation.

The next day, Billy was in a foul mood, biting the heads off everyone.

'I reckon he's fed up to the teeth of Nick wandering off whenever he feels like it,' Kit told Tamara. 'He disappeared again halfway through the show last night, and Billy had to stand in. He wants me to go and look for him.'

'He's proper fed up and I don't blame him. I can't see my dad putting up with that sort of thing.' Tamara hooked her arm through Kit's as they walked towards the food tent. 'You must get

117

cheesed off searching Covent Garden for him.'

'I do it for Billy. He deserves better. The sooner I get off, the quicker I'll be back.' She was about to say she would come with him, when Billy walked towards them.

'Haven't you gone yet?'

'I'm on my way.' He touched Tamara's arm and walked away.

She had never heard Billy speak to Kit in such an offhanded way. After all, it was hardly Kit's fault that his wayward son had no respect for anyone's feelings apart from his own.

'I need a word with you, miss.'

She did not like his tone and wondered what she had done to displease him. He walked off, leaving her to follow him. He stopped outside his trailer, removed his hat, and ran the palm of his hand over his head, flattening wisps of his grey hair. In spite of the cold, he sat down heavily on the chair outside.

'What is it? What's wrong, Mr. Billy? Is it..?' She was about to say Nick, but quickly realised it was none of her business.

'Well, I hope you'll have the answer, young lady. I sincerely hope I am mistaken. And don't insult me by lying.'

Tamara clasped and unclasped her hands, then pulled her shawl around her. 'What do you mean? I wouldn't lie to you, Mr. Billy.'

'The other night, the takings were down, and they were down again last night. Once I can understand, but twice,' he shook his head, 'I get suspicious.'

Tamara had no idea what to think. She frowned.

'I don't know anything about it, Mr. Billy.'

'You take a couple of guineas in the hut each evening, give or take the odd copper. I saw the crowd tonight. Yet, there were only ten coppers in the canvas bag.'

She pushed her hands through her hair. 'I passed the money over to Nick, didn't he..?' she paused, careful not to accuse him. She rubbed her hands over her arms against the cold.

'Are you saying that my own son took the money?'

'No, of course not. Look, Mr. Billy, I don't know.' She bit her bottom lip. 'All I know is that the sack was full. I counted every shilling that went inside.' She kicked at the hard frosty ground. 'I didn't steal it. I gave it to Nick.'

'What do you suppose happened to it, then?'

'I don't know.' She kicked the ground again, hurting her toe. She tried to recall the first time she had handed the money to Nick.

'Nicholas has no need to take money, he has more than enough. I don't believe you. Nicholas is not here to speak for himself, so I'll defer throwing you out of this circus until he returns.' She saw disappointment on his face and his eyes narrowed. 'I trusted you, against my better judgement. I should have listened to my son, he said you were trouble from the word go.'

Tamara's mouth opened to speak, but she could see it was useless. Billy would not have a word said against his son.

She dropped to her knees on the cold ground. 'I didn't steal from you, Mr. Billy. Honest to God!' She turned her head away to hide her tears. By

119

now, the rest of the company had gathered, and were standing close by, listening to every word. Nelly came across and placed her arm around her shoulder.

'What's all this about, Bill?' The older woman glanced up at Mr. Billy, now standing in the doorway of his wagon.

'There's money missing, quite a bit.'

Tamara stood up and turned towards the crowd. 'Of course, I'm a gypsy. It's what you all expect, isn't it?'

Her outburst did nothing to relieve the situation.

Billy waved his arms. 'Get out of my sight, you thieving little brat.'

'Steady on, Bill,' Nelly croaked. 'She's surely innocent until proven guilty.'

'She can stay the night, but not in my wagon. And, if my instincts prove right, I want her off this site tomorrow.'

Nelly took the sobbing Tamara to her wagon and made a strong pot of tea. Zeema sat on her bed with hardly a word to say either way on Tamara's behalf.

'I've never seen Bill in such a state.' Nelly handed Tamara a mug with the hot drink. 'It is so unlike him.'

'I never took the money, Nelly. I handed it over to Nick. I don't know what happened to it after that.'

'What's that supposed to mean?' Zeema asked.

'Well, you should know Nick's character better than anyone,' Tamara retorted.

'Now don't you two start,' Nelly intervened. 'It

will all be sorted by this evening. Kit will find Nick and we'll get to the bottom of it.'

The last time Tamara had felt like this was when she'd been hauled before the officials at Liverpool docks. Only this time, she was innocent. This was Nick's final revenge to get rid of her because she refused to lie down with him. Well, damn him to hell. Somehow she would prove she did not take that money.

By morning, there was still no sign of Kit. Tamara felt like an outcast. She was aware of whispers as she tried to eat her oats. Her throat tightened. Nelly was the only one who spoke to her. 'The show had to be cancelled last night, and Billy's none too pleased.' She patted Tamara on the shoulder. 'They'll be back soon and we'll get at the truth.'

Everything had changed overnight, and there was no way of clearing her name unless Nick owned up. She walked around the site, feeling like a spare piece of furniture, blanked by everyone she passed. In spite of Mr. Billy saying she wasn't to sleep in the wagon, she went back and, to pass the time, she cleaned every inch of it until it sparkled. No one came over to speak to her. What was keeping Kit? She had never known him to be away this long.

By the afternoon, when he still had not returned, Tamara feared that something had happened to him. Without him, her life here would be unbearable. Her eyes red from crying, she packed her bags and then sat on the steps with her head in her hands. Her mind swung back and

121

forth like a pendulum, logic one minute and despair the next. Embarrassed and humiliated, tears welled in her eyes. With nothing to do but wait, the minutes dragged into hours. Back inside the wagon, she lay down on top of the bunk until she heard someone knocking on her door.

Kit! Her heart somersaulted and she hurried to open it. Shock registered on her face when, to her horror, Pablo stood before her, flanked by two clowns and two of the jugglers. Zeema stood a little way off, a smirk on her face.

'What is it?'

'You, bad person. You go!' Pablo said. 'You upset Mr. Billy. You go!'

Tamara felt sick to her stomach. They were an angry mob, determined to run her out of the circus. These people had known each other for a long time, and it was obvious they would stick together; she felt powerless against them.

'Does Mr. Billy know you're here, threatening me like this?'

One of the clowns said, 'You've got half an hour to get out.'

Tamara shut the door and stood with her back to it for a few moments. She could hardly believe what had just happened. Well, she would not stay here another minute. Her hands shaking, she put the rest of her things into the carpetbag she had bought second-hand at the market. She had a little money left from her wages, but it was not much, and she wished now that she had not spent so much on a new dress the week before.

She wrapped her cloak around her shoulders, choking back tears. If Kit turned up now and saw

122

her humiliation, she would die of embarrassment.

Glancing around what had been her cosy little home one last time, Tamara straightened her shoulders and left the wagon. Some of the artistes came out to watch. Their glare said all she needed to know. Fear gripped her insides and she walked away from the circus. It was the only place she had felt safe since leaving home, so what was she to do now, with nowhere to turn? What frightened her most was that she had nowhere safe to sleep.

CHAPTER SIXTEEN

Fog closed in around Kit as he searched Nick's old haunts. He scoured the dingy courtyards where, on more than one previous occasion, he had found the boss's son with a prostitute, drunk as a duke. Tonight, though, he appeared to have disappeared from Covent Garden.

His drinking had worsened of late, and Kit felt sorry for Billy. A man of great principle who loved the circus he had built up over many years, Billy would have to make a stand with Nick. He could be too soft-hearted and had spoiled Nick since the loss of his wife.

Kit sat down on a wooden crate at the side of a pub. What was he doing here?

He could think of better things to be doing. Nick was twenty, two years younger than him. He had helped him out of many scrapes when they were little, but Kit didn't want to be his body-guard forever. He did it for Billy. How could he forget how Billy had saved him from the work-house when he was just five? He would always be grateful to him.

Sick of the sight of grotty public houses, Kit decided he had had enough. Billy would be disappointed if he returned without his precious Nick, but this time the other man had outfoxed him.

Feeling cold and miserable, the fog obscuring his view, Kit walked along the pavement, his head bent to his chest and his shoulders slumped. A door opened a short distance in front of him and he could see the figure of a man coming out onto the footpath. A woman with a baby clinging to her chest came to the door, but Kit couldn't see her face. Then the man yelled back at her, his voice muffled.

Unsure who it was through the fog, Kit reached the door just as the woman slammed it shut. He followed at a distance until the man, unsteady on his feet, paused and leaned against a window. 'Nick!' Kit ran to catch him up.

'Don't tire of babysitting for the old man?'

'Respect was never your strong point, was it? Does Zeema know you're seeing another woman?'

'S'none yer business.'

'It is when you upset people I'm fond of.'

'Is zat so? Well, I'm not going back. I need a drink.' He staggered along a few steps.

Kit took his arm. 'I think you've had enough, don't you?'

Shrugging Kit aside, Nick glared into his face.

124

'Need another drink.'

Kit gripped his arm. 'I'm not going back without you.'

Nick shrugged him off again, but Kit threw his arm across Nick's shoulders and pinned him against the wall. 'You've wasted enough of my time, you useless piece of shit.'

Nick lashed out in his inebriated state, yelling abuse until Kit wrestled him to the ground. Above them, a window opened and a chamber pot emptied over the pair. They continued to roll around on the pavement, until a small crowd gathered. A few minutes later, a police constable pulled them apart. 'Right! You can explain yourselves down at the clink.'

After a spell in a cell, Kit and Nick made their way back to the circus in silence. Kit promised himself that this was the last time he would get into trouble on Nick's behalf. Mr. Billy was going to have to stand his ground with Nick, or the circus would go under. It was a pity that he could not see any wrong in his son. Billy was used to compromising, but Kit was sorry he had to.

As soon as they got back, Nick tried to sneak off towards his wagon. But Kit grabbed him roughly by his collar. 'No you don't. You're coming with me now.'

'Tell my father, I'll see him later.'

'Face up to your father like a man.' Kit pushed him towards the boss's trailer. Billy and some of the artistes walked towards them, but there was no sign of Tamara.

Billy rounded on Nick. 'Bloody hell fire. Look

at the state of you. You're disgusting! My wagon, now!'

Kit looked across at Tamara's wagon, her lamp not yet lit. He was looking forward to seeing her. Nelly touched his arm while the others, their heads lowered, walked away.

'Get cleaned up, Kit,' she said quietly, 'I need a word.'

Kit picked up his boots and threw them at the wall. Then he sat on his bunk, his head in his hands. Frustration wound him up like a coil. He did not know who he was most angry with – Nick, or Billy for sending him to look for Nick when he could have been here and maybe stopped Tamara from leaving. He refused to believe that she had taken the money, and had said as much to Nelly and the same to Billy when he visited him later. In spite of the older man's belief that a gypsy could never be trusted, and quoting his second wife as an example, Kit had seen the other side of Tamara. She was nothing if not honest and good.

No woman had ever had this effect on him. He recalled Tamara's hair, the colour of it, the way it lay in little curls around her forehead. He had watched her many times when she walked through the compound. The sway of her hips, her small waist, and the way her breasts pushed out the front of her blouse. She was a terrible temptation and he'd had to hold back from kissing her full lips more than once already.

What reason did she have to steal, especially now, when she was about to become a horse rider in the show? He recalled their ride out together when he had told her how he felt. He had gained the impression that she felt the same. So why had she left without a word? How far could she have gone? She could be anywhere by now, and as far as he knew, she had no relatives in London. He wasn't going to give up on her. He would find her and bring her back.

CHAPTER SEVENTEEN

Jake Travis travelled the west of Ireland in search of Tamara, without success. Now he was back, his mood no better than when he had left two months earlier. The sound of his white stallion's hooves plundering the ground alerted the settlement. Hens scratching in the dirt scattered. Ola and Jono ran outside, anxiety etched on their faces. As if possessed, Travis rode onto the gypsy site. Jono pulled Ola to safety, then he turned to the circle of gypsies behind him.

'Keep out of this. It's between him and me.'

Travis pulled to a halt in front of them, and Ola cried, 'Is there any news? Have you found her, have you found Tamara?'

Travis threw his right leg over the horse, hitting its head with his boot. The stallion foamed at the mouth and, in spite of the bitter wind that blew in from across the fields, the animal was drenched in sweat. It limped towards a young gypsy boy.

Jono stood, legs apart, facing him. 'For God sake's, man, if you know anything, tell us!'

'No one's seen hide nor hair of her. Some say she drowned herself in the sea.'

Ola gasped, and placed her hand over her mouth.

'What do you think, old woman? Would she do something like that?'

Ola sobbed, her whole body shook.

'No,' Jono said. 'She'd never do anything like that. Her plans went beyond marrying the likes of you!'

The slash across his back was sharp and it brought Jono to his knees. Ola cried out, and knelt down next to him. Jono staggered to his feet and head-butted Travis. Women screamed as the two men fought like wild animals. Travis gripped Jono's hair, pulling the thin strands from the roots. Then he punched him hard in the chest, making Jono double over.

'If I find out you're keeping anything from me, old man, you're as good as dead. And that goes for the rest of you.' Travis gasped for breath, straightened up, and wiped the blood from his nose before stomping off.

'God's curse on ye!' Ola called after him.

The loud gunshot in the early hours, woke the settlement. Shortly afterwards, Travis rode out of the camp. He rode hard over the land that belonged to him. It still gave him enormous pleasure to recall how he had built up his empire. His only brother had shunned him once he had won the hand of Lady Greystones. After their wedding, the marriage had proved fruitless. Travis had been in love with the Lady himself, until his brother

128

enticed her away. It was Travis's intention to marry the gypsy girl and show his barren brother how to make babies. He had been obsessed with Tamara ever since he had clapped eyes on her, camped out by the side of the road with a cluster of travelling gypsies. She had been ten years old at the time, but he knew who she was. He had been searching a long time. Now, after waiting years to marry her, she had run out on him. He wasn't about to let her go now, not until he found the spiteful wench and settled a score with her.

Travis stabled his horse close to the railway station, and purchased a ticket to Dublin, where he bought a passage on the boat to Liverpool. While he waited for the ship to sail, he took a walk along the docks. He passed a couple of jolly sailors who tipped their hats to him, but he didn't reciprocate. He had hated seamen of any calibre ever since his father had tried to force him to join a naval ship, and said it would make a man of him. He had run away, taking the family silver with him. It had enabled him to buy up most of the land he now owned.

Before he went on board ship, he bought a tin of loose tobacco and cigarette papers. A cigarette could buy information. He believed someone had helped Tamara to escape; she had not done this alone. The little gypsy had caused him grief as well as money, and he was furious.

Travis arrived in Liverpool, where he planned to stay for a couple of nights. In spite of drinking on the boat, his throat felt parched and he stopped at the first alehouse on the Dock Road. Inside, he sidled up to the bar, careful not to place his elbows on the damp, sticky surface.

The bartender, with a whimsical moustache, threw a tray cloth over his shoulder. 'We don't often get the likes of you in here, sir. What can I get ye?'

'Beer, and be quick about it.'

The barman poured his drink and passed it to Travis, who swallowed it quickly and asked for another.

'I'll have yer money up front, if ye don't mind, and I'll ask ye to keep a civil tongue in your head.'

Travis took out a two-shilling piece and slammed it on the counter. 'Keep the change,' he said. Then he picked up his drink and settled down on the wooden bench with his back to the window. Two young men were sitting at a nearby table, empty tankards in front of them and looking like they had spent their last penny. A few working class men in caps, dock men hoping for work when a boat came in, were drinking there in spite of the early hour. They glanced over at him. He was wearing a dark blue coat, pale brown breeches and heavy riding boots. Travis was past caring how he looked; he had his reasons for being here. The men began to snigger. If they were spoiling for a fight, he was the man to give them one. He was burning up to knock seven bells out of someone, and he wasn't fussy who it was. The bartender, appearing to sense the tension, came across the room.

'Look, I don't mind taking yer money, but who are ye and what are ye after?'

130

'Have you seen a gypsy girl in here recently?'

'Are you kiddin'?' the bartender laughed. 'Bloody gypsies. I never let them through the door.' He paused. 'Besides, we only get the usual type down the docks at night.' He laughed. 'You're a bit early if that's what you're looking for.'

'This girl is seventeen and very beautiful. Goes by the name of Tamara. Are you sure you've not heard anyone mention a woman like that?'

'Naw.' The man shook his head and went back behind the bar.

Travis threw down a silver coin and the barman snatched it up. 'Get me another drink.'

'Feeling flush, mister?' One of the men sniggered into the dregs of his tankard.

Travis didn't answer.

'Ye better watch ye pocket on the streets, so.'

'What part of the country do ye hail from then?' laughed the other.

Travis glared over at them. 'Where I'm from is none of your business,' he said sharply, 'but if you can give me the information I want, you could earn yourselves a few shillings.'

They stood up, picked up their empty tankards and stumbled across the room, plonking themselves down next to Travis. He plied them with more drink.

'Kind of ye, I'm sure.'

Travis was aware of their eyes settling on his gold rings, quite forgetting that he had meant to remove them while walking down this particular part of Liverpool. 'Where'd ye say ye were from, mister?'

'I'm asking the questions, understand!'

131

The two eyed each other. 'Aye, aye we do, don't we, Mick?'

'I'm looking for a girl.'

The two tittered again. 'Aren't we all!'

'She's a gypsy, a beautiful girl with bright red hair. Have you seen anyone like that in the last couple of months?'

One shook his head and the other elbowed him in the ribs. 'What would bring 'er round 'ere, sir?'

Travis slid his eyes round the pub. 'Desperation, I guess.'

'I need time to make enquiries for ye, sir.'

'Why? You think you might know something, someone whom you've heard talking about a gypsy girl?' He took a note from his wallet and waved it in front of them.

'Aye!' both men said. Travis knew they were playing him along, but the colour of money was enough to make them comb the haunts of Liverpool in the hopes of bringing back some information that would satisfy him. Travis was willing to take that chance. They were itching for another drink, but Travis did not intend to spend any more money without some return. He glanced up at the clock behind the bar, scraped back his chair, and stood up.

'You've got four hours. I'll be back and, if you've got anything worth listening to, I'll make it worth your while.' When he got to the door, he turned his head over his shoulder. 'Don't bother me unless it's the right girl.'

He walked away, knowing that the other men in there, in spite of being half-cocked, had heard the whole conversation. The more that knew about

132

his search for Tamara the better.

He made his way past the many dock taverns, surprised at how young the girls were who accosted him for sex. Most of them were only children. That was not what he wanted, and was one of the reasons he had waited for Tamara to grow up first before arranging to marry her. Now he felt cheated, angry and embittered. The little minx was sure to be somewhere around here, and someone might remember her asking for work. A far as he knew, she had no money of her own, but that would not have stopped her stealing to get what she wanted.

He tried two more inns without success. The police might know something, but he hated authority and he would have to be desperate before he would go crawling to them. They were hardly likely to give him any information, but he knew how to wheedle it out of them if he had to. Even the police had a weakness when it came to money.

As he walked past a building site, a woman who looked like she could do with a good feed tottered towards him. If Tamara had sunk into this kind of thing, this woman might know something. As he drew alongside her, the woman smiled up at him, showing brown uneven teeth. Her fair hair was limp and unkempt, and she pulled her thin black coat across her shabby dress.

'What's a handsome gentleman like yourself doing in these parts, sir?'

Travis, who couldn't resist flattery, smiled. 'Is there somewhere we can talk?'

'Sure, mister.' Her eyes brightened. 'You look

133

like the sort of gentleman who'd pay a girl well for her time.' She led the way down the side of the building to a narrow passageway that smelt like a sewer. He shook out a handkerchief and placed it over his mouth. The woman stood with her back to the wall and held out her sooty palm. 'Like me money first.'

'I don't know if you can help me yet,' he mumbled.

'If you don't want...' She paused, her eyes furtive as she edged away from him. 'What do ye want?'

'Information.'

'And I want paying for me time, mister.'

He placed a silver coin into her outstretched hand. She clenched her fist over the money and pushed it down the front of her dress.

'Have you seen a girl about seventeen, with hair as red as fire and eyes the shape of almonds?' He could see the woman frown, and her shoulders stiffen. 'There's more where that came from, if you can lead me to where I might find her.'

'Fiery red 'air, ye say.'

'Look, stop wasting my time. Have you seen her or not?'

'Might a done.' She buttoned her coat and stood up straight. 'I need a bifta. Otherwise I can't think.'

Travis opened a tin of tobacco and offered it to her. She pinched the dry leaves between her finger and thumb, placed it onto the cigarette paper, and rolled it up. He struck a match and held it against the cigarette. She drew in the nicotine a couple of times and blew out the smoke. 'She was Irish. A

134

real innocent, from what I could tell,' she cackled.

Travis grabbed hold of her roughly, shaking her skeletal frame. 'Where is she?'

The woman shrugged him off. 'Ger off me. The last time I saw her, she was locked in a cell. She's looking at a few long years for what she's done.'

'And what's that?'

'I can't remember. Now gis me money.'

Travis withdrew another coin from his pocket and threw it at the woman. As she scrambled to pick it up, Travis hurried on his way.

'I hopes ye don't find 'er, ye bleedin' bastard.'

CHAPTER EIGHTEEN

After trudging lonely roads and dark alleyways in utter despair, Tamara rested in a doorway. Two men approached her. 'Hello, me darlin',' one said.

'Want to earn a shillin' or two?' the other said, touching her hair. She cringed away, then lashed out at them until they fled, calling her a mad lunatic. She was mad; mad with frustration and disappointment. Selling her body was the last thing on her mind. She moved on, passing an old beggar woman who pleaded with her for money. A shudder ran through her body as she hurried away from the city, with its eerie shapes and shadows. She needed to find somewhere out of the cold, a safe place to lay her head. She could sort things out better in the daylight.

The fog had thickened and she had walked for ages before she realised she was going in the direction of Hampstead. She had gone this way with Kit when they went riding on Hampstead Heath. If only he was here with her now. Why hadn't he come back? If he had, she felt sure she would not be in this frightening situation. She passed through Golders Green until she came to a grassy patch. It started to rain and she ran for shelter under a tree, shivering in her damp clothes. By now, she could hardly feel her hands and her feet ached. In the darkness, she saw what looked like a deserted farmhouse and her spirits lifted. She climbed over a wooden fence for a better look and started to walk towards it.

As she drew nearer, she could see smoke curling from the chimney stack. She pictured a log fire and warming herself in front of it. A rickety cart, draped in canvas, reminded her of her almost perilous journey on the *Maryanne*, and she thought of climbing into the cart for the night. Then she noticed the barn door ajar and ran towards it, her heart thumping. Inside, she sniffed the smell of leather harnesses hanging on a hook inside the door, but she saw no sign of a horse. In the semi-darkness, she could make out empty sacks, boxes, and crates piled one on top of the other.

Squeezing in past them, she climbed the wooden ladder to the hayloft, panting from fear and exertion. Her presence disturbed the pigeons in the rafters and they fluttered and cooed. She took little notice when a rat scuttled past her. She removed her wet cloak and lay down on the dry hay. In spite of her tiredness, she could not relax in case someone discovered her. Exhausted, her mind mulled over what had happened earlier that day. It seemed unbelievable to her that she was running away again. Now she longed for daylight in the hope that whoever inhabited the house was a kind woman who would give her something to eat. Eventually, her eyes closed and sleep overtook her.

She awoke, her throat parched and her lips dry, to the sound of someone digging outside towards the back of the barn. She could hear the clunk of a spade slicing through the hard ground and clumps of clay falling on something solid. For a second she thought she was back home listening to the sound of her father, Jono, digging vegetables for the day's meal. She brushed straw from her hair and clothes, pulled on her cloak, and went outside.

She watched from a safe distance. The man was stocky and middle-aged. Wisps of grey hair fell down underneath his flat-topped hat. He was wearing a long dark raincoat and heavy, toe-capped boots. One foot resting on the side of the spade, he paused. Tamara moved closer, swallowing her fear. The man swung round as if sensing her behind him and raised the heavy spade. She gasped, stretching her hands above her head. When he saw Tamara, he lowered the scoop and pushed it into the soil.

'Bloody hell fire. Where did you come from?'

'Please, sir, I'm lost and I've walked a long way. Can I have a drink of water, my lips are parched?'

He moved closer, peering at her in the semi-darkness. 'Well, I'll be bound. What are you doing on my property?' The bottoms of his trousers tied with string and his boots caked in mud, he looked like a scarecrow.

'I mean no harm, sir. I'm looking for work.'

'Well, you're in the wrong place. I suggest you scarper back to where you came from.'

Tamara, willing herself not to faint, asked. 'Can you tell me where I am?'

'Finchley's a couple of miles that way.' He pointed towards the track then turned back to what he was doing. 'I've vegetables to get to market and you're holding me up,' he sniffed.

'Can I have a drink of water before I go?'

'Over there.' He pointed to an oblong concrete water trough. 'And then I want you gone.'

Tamara rushed towards it, broke through the coating of ice, cupped her hands in the freezing water and drank. Her hands stung from the cold, but she drank until she had quenched her thirst. She splashed water on her face and it made her gasp. However, she did not intend to go anywhere, as she could see the man needed help. He was tugging up cabbages by the roots, and he had dug up a tonne of potatoes and they all needed to be loaded into something.

'Look, mister, I could help you if you could spare a little food,' she said, holding her stomach.

He glared round at her. 'I ain't had a woman round here in years and I don't need one now. Besides, you're too fin. What could a slip of a girl like you do?'

'I know about growing vegetables. I can do anything. Give us a chance, please.'

'Oh, all right,' he muttered. 'You'll find a wedge o' cheese and a cut o' bread on the kitchen table. You'd better be quick. I want these spuds sacked and loaded onto the cart. You'll find sacks in the barn.'

An hour later, when the vegetables were packed and loaded onto the cart, the man said, 'The name's Tom Murray. What do you call yourself?'

'Tamara,' she smiled.

'You done well! But you better scarper now. I'll get Jimmy from his stable, get him harnessed up and be off.'

'I'll get him.'

'No. He won't come to just anyone.'

Tamara took a carrot from the sack and, within minutes, the horse was not only eating out of her hand, but also harnessed between the shafts of the cart. Tom Murray nodded. 'Aye, you might be useful to me, after all. How would you like to help me set up the stall this morning?'

'I'd love to,' she said, climbing onto the wagon beside him.

As the cart moved out of the yard, the wheels bumped over the hard frosty ground. Tamara shivered, cupped her hands, and blew into them. 'Here ye are,' he said, handing her a pair of gloves much too big for her, but she thanked him and pushed her hands inside them. 'There's an old blanket in the back, you can wrap it round your knees.'

She did not need telling twice. The man had a piece of sacking around his shoulders and a per-manent drip on the tip of his nose. 'I'll tell you what,' he said. 'If you can help me sell extra produce today, I'll give ye a shilling. I can't afford no more.'

'Thank you, that sounds grand.'

'You're not a Londoner?'

She did not answer immediately. Then she said, 'I'm from over the water.'

'Aye, I could tell that, and you're obviously running from something or someone. It's none 'f my business, but if I find out you're telling pokies, or catch you stealing from me...'

'I won't,' she said, feeling her anger return when she thought of how she had been accused of stealing back at the circus. She wondered if Kit, too, believed her to be a thief.

As daylight dawned, Tamara sighed audibly when she saw that they were travelling back the way she had trudged the night before. 'Which market are you headed for?'

'Covent Garden, where else?' He glanced across at her. 'If you're in any trouble there, you'd better get down now.'

'No, of course I'm not, I just wondered, that's all.' With the circus so close, there was the likelihood of her bumping into Flory as she shopped for vegetables and fruit, not to mention Nick. What could she do? She had to make a living and take her opportunities as they came along.

When they arrived at the market, Tamara was surprised at how busy it was; mainly traders unloading. The smell of the fresh fruit made her mouth water and her stomach rumble again. The streets in and around the market were congested with carts and the costermongers had arrived in immense numbers. It was a noisy, crazy place where stallholders were setting up lines of stalls selling all kinds of things. Women sat on the steps around the church selling flowers, and she could smell the scent of violets as she passed by. Boxes of oranges, sacks of nuts, crates of grapes, pears and bright red apples were piled up everywhere.

Tamara had never seen anything quite like it. It was exciting and she felt part of it all when they finally arrived through the congestion to Tom Murray's stall. Without hesitation, she began setting out the stall with the potatoes, swede, carrots, onions and cabbages, underneath a sign that read in bold capitals, T. E. MURRAY. Then she stood back to admire her display. There was so much produce that she felt they would never sell it all. Tom handed her a long white apron that covered her feet. She did not care what she looked like.

'You're new,' the woman in the next stall said. Christmas tinsel decorated the edges of her stall. 'Where'd you pluck her from, Tom?'

Tom Murray shook his head and continued to unload his wagon.

Tamara smiled, and the woman turned away and began to rearrange her fresh fruit. Tamara loaded Tom's stall and, before she knew it, she found herself replenishing the stall from the stack of cabbages, cauliflower and swede that Mr. Murray had piled up against the wall. Tom brought out crates and baskets to the buzz of camaraderie all around them. Tamara could see that it was not his intention to join in any of the banter. He lay the empty crates down next to the stall and dropped more carrots and onions into them.

By midday, some of the traders had wandered off to nearby alehouses. Tamara was beginning to wilt, and when Tom brought her over a meat pie and a tankard of ale, she ate and drank eagerly. By afternoon the walls and columns surrounding the market were stacked high with empty baskets, and scattered fruit and vegetables choked the narrow passageways. The majority of stalls were looking festive, and people walked by with armfuls of holly. The idea of gathering up a few sprigs of holly to decorate the stall crossed her mind. Would Mr. Murray approve? She guessed not.

Towards the end of the day, Mr. Murray told her to put the remainder of the produce into boxes, and together they took them into the storeroom at the back of the stall. That also had his name over the door. Outside, urchins ran amongst the stalls, salvaging what they could and stuffing it into sacks.

With so much going on, Tamara hardly thought about Kit. She didn't have a minute to speak to the woman on the stall next to her, until they were packing away. The rosy-faced, able-bodied woman leaned across to Tamara. 'That miserable old skinflint won't pay ye much.'

Tamara smiled. 'It's better than walking the streets,' she replied.

'Aye, he can be a changeable buggar.' It was obvious that the two had a love-hate relationship. 'If he's picked ye up, he'll expect you to do his bidding.'

Tamara ignored the remark and continued to

clear the stall. 'Might see you tomorrow,' she said, and followed Tom into the storeroom.

'Do ye think you could kip down in here for tonight?'

Nodding, she glanced around her. A large weighing scale dominated the store. An outdated calendar hung lopsided on the wall, boxes of produce littered the floor, and she tried to imagine where she could sit, never mind lie down. Anything was better than the street, she thought. 'Thank you. It'll be fine.'

'There's an old sofa in the room above. It's only temporary mind.'

Feeling a little better at that, she asked. 'Don't you want me to help you dig up the vegetables in the morning?'

'I'll manage. I reckon ye did well today, girl,' he said, and handed her a shilling. 'Are ye a good riser?'

She nodded.

'Right then. Get the stall set up at 4am. Start with what's in here. I'll arrive as soon as I can with fresh produce. Do ye think you can do that?'

'Sure, I can. But, is there somewhere I can wash and…?'

'Oh, aye, there's a tap and the lav's outside.'

'Does this door lock?' She went over and turned the knob.

'I'll leave a key. You've no need to let anyone know you're here. Keep the lamp low. Enough light comes through from the street. There's ruffians out there who'd rob the eyes out the back 'f your 'ead.'

CHAPTER NINETEEN

Travis had hated the police ever since they'd arrested him for stealing when he was nineteen. But they hadn't been able to prove anything.

It went against the grain for him to be calling on them for help now. He paced impatiently as he waited to see someone. Time was of the essence and if he did not catch up with Tamara soon, God only knew what might happen to her, the stupid wench. What experience did she have outside of the gypsy camp? Once he found her, she would plead with him to take her home. Had she forgotten that he had the power to evict her family off his land? For the measly sum, they paid him, he had planned to cut all ties with them once he had married her.

'So, what can I do for you?' Travis swung round and faced the sergeant now standing behind the counter.

'What do you know about a young gypsy girl? I believe she was held in a cell here. Can you tell me what happened to her?'

The sergeant sighed. Travis leaned his elbow on the counter. 'Well? Is she still here? You can release her and I'll take her off your hands.' He straightened up and spread his legs out in front of him.

'Given that I have no idea who it is you're talking about, I...'

144

'Tamara Redmond.'

'Might I ask your interest in this particular girl? Are you her father?'

Travis drew in breath and almost spat the word. 'No, I'm bloody not.' He placed the palms of his hands on the counter. 'Now where is she?'

'Let me warn you that bullying won't get you anywhere. Fill in the form on that table over there and come back in a few days.'

'A few days! I don't have the time.'

'Neither do I. It's up to you. Now clear off, my good fellow, otherwise your enquiry won't be dealt with and we'll be none the wiser, will we?'

Furious, Travis snatched up the sheet of paper from the desk and filled in what he knew, including Tamara's age. Then he signed his name and slammed it down on the counter. 'What about that ledger, don't you keep the names of offenders in there? How many women have come in here in the last two months?'

'We don't give out that kind of information, sir. Now, as I've said...'

'I'll be back tomorrow and I want answers. I know she's been here.'

When he returned the following morning, the same sergeant was standing behind the counter.

'You again! I have no information and even if I had, I couldn't divulge anything about this young woman.'

Travis exploded. 'Bollocks. You old fart. You must know something. Tell me?'

'Your attitude won't help you, sir.'

'This is my business. It has nothing to do with the law.'

'You can leave quietly, or I can have you locked in a cell. It's up to you.'

Travis shrugged and adjusted his jacket. 'Damn you! I'll find her.' A furious expression on his face, he stormed out.

Later that day, still smarting from his treatment by the police, Travis felt in need of relaxation and a drink to calm his nerves before his visit to one of his favourite brothels.

His mind focused, Travis made his way to the gypsy camp in Birkenhead. It was the most likely place for her to go if she was in trouble. A ragged gypsy youth alerted the camp of his arrival, and Travis was welcomed with a gush of hospitality, something he had come to expect on such visits.

That evening, as they gathered round the open fire, he questioned them about Tamara. He told them about her disappearance from the gypsy camp in Galway and that anyone with information which resulted in finding her would have a month's free rent. He described her, stressing her exceptional beauty, with red hair and a temper to match.

'Have you seen anyone like that in the last few weeks?'

The gypsies began to whisper amongst themselves. 'You won't fool me, mind!' Travis stated, knowing how their minds worked when it came to making a bit of brass.

One of the gypsy men said, 'We'd remember someone like that. But give us time to think.'

A small youth, rolling marbles on the frozen ground, looked up. 'Sir, I saw a woman like that.'

146

Everyone glanced towards him. Travis jumped up from his crouched position, where he was prodding the flames of the campfire with a stick. He grabbed the boy roughly by his shoulders.

'You had better not be fibbin', boy.'

'It might not ha' been her, sir, but she had red 'air and she turned a blind eye and let me into the circus.'

'The circus! Well, I'll be damned. Are you sure about this, boy?'

The boy nodded.

'What circus?'

One of the men moved closer. 'Leave him be, Jake. He can't read.'

'Come with me and show me where you saw this woman.'

He demanded their best mare and, jumping onto its back, he hauled the boy by the scruff of his neck up in front of him, and rode out of the camp.

It was getting dark when they came to what the boy thought might be the spot, but there was no circus. In its place, they found a grassy patch inhabited by a group of young boys, smoking clay pipes, some tricking about. They ran when they saw Travis approach.

'Is this the spot, boy? Don't lie to me!'

The boy nodded. 'I think so, sir.'

The proprietor of the newspaper shop on the corner was just pulling down the shutters.

'Go in there.' Travis propelled the boy towards the shop. 'Ask the shopkeeper what he knows about the circus. If he asks you why you want to know, tell him you want to join it.'

147

The boy ran to do his bidding. When he returned, he told Travis what the man had said. Travis nodded. 'Umm, a travelling circus from London, eh?' Interesting, he thought, very interesting indeed. A few enquiries should soon locate this Mr. Billy.

He turned towards the boy. 'That's it, boy. You can go back now.' He handed back the mare, and slipped a Joey into the boy's hand.

CHAPTER TWENTY

A cold draught blew in underneath the door and the wind whistled through the cracks in the window frame. It kept her awake until she got up and plugged the gaps with dusty potato sacks, then tried to sleep. She piled boxes and crates around the sofa to keep out the draught. With only her cloak for warmth, she lay on the fusty sofa, broken springs digging into her flesh, while life still went on outside.

She could hear shouts coming from the labyrinth of murky alleyways, and the rumble of wagons never ceased. Then later, the clip-clop of horses and the rumble of carriages over cobbles on their way home from the Opera House. She had seen posters advertising Caruso and the great Irish tenor, John McCormack, and wondered what it would be like to see them live on stage. The squabble of coachmen and linkboys kept her awake. Turning onto her side, she tried to block out the noise.

She thought of Kit, pictured his face and that look she had taken for love in his eyes the last time they were together. How did he feel when he returned to the circus and found her gone? She missed Kit and the friendships she had made at the circus before the money went missing. Finally, sleep overtook her.

She woke at 3:30am. Her grandmother used to say that she had a built-in clock. By 4am, Tamara was outside setting up the stall. It was dark, apart from the lamps some stall holders had lit to see their way. The ground where she stood glittered with frost and, in spite of the fruit and vegetable market being undercover, she could see her breath in front of her. She was wearing two dresses, a long white apron and gloves, but the cold made her shiver.

'Here, have a swig o' this. Tamara, ain't it? I'm Mary.' The woman next to her handed over a flagon. Tamara sipped from it gratefully. 'Not too much, mind. We can't have ye fallin' asleep. Old Tom would never forgive me,' she laughed.

Tamara thanked her and passed it back. A drop of the hard stuff, as they called it back in Ireland, was just what she needed to get the blood circulating. Her fingers were almost dropping off with the cold. As she became accustomed to the sounds that vibrated all around her and the constant chatter of the market traders, she began to feel part of it all. Some of the stalls had hanging lanterns, making the place festive. Others were selling holly, ivy, and Christmas fare. Tamara wished she could make her stall look a bit more festive, but then, she thought, it was not for her to decide.

Determined to sell more produce, she called out to passers-by, 'Come and get your fresh vegetables. The best potatoes, freshly dug this morning. Roll up, roll up!' Her voice mingled with the banter that went on around her, but the stall was so busy that Mr. Murray had to return home for more vegetables. At the end of the working day, Tom was so impressed with her efforts that he gave her two shillings and an old blanket, reminding her that the sleeping arrangements were only temporary.

After two weeks, the ache in the lower part of her back was killing her, but she had managed to save a few shillings. Sleeping in the storeroom was starting to get her down until she discovered that she was not the only one scraping a living in the market. She had witnessed poor families surviving on bowls of vegetables and meat bones. She knew what it felt like to be hungry, and she was grateful to Mary, who brought her a bowl of hot broth every day to fill her belly.

One morning, early, Tamara was humming softly to herself while piling more cauliflowers onto the stall alongside the cabbages. She stood back to admire her display, but decided that it needed a bit of colour to attract the customers. She emptied the basket of carrots into the centre and arranged them neatly between the green hearts of the cabbages and white cauliflower, when she heard a familiar voice bantering with a stallholder.

Flory walked past without a word of greeting until Tamara called out to her, 'Flory, wait! It's me, Tamara.'

Flory paused without looking round. 'I don't have any cotter with thieves,' she said.

'Shush, will ye? Do you want to get me the sack? I never stole anything. Honest to God.'

Flory turned round and walked back to her. 'And I should believe you, should I?'

'Believe what you like. I'm innocent.' She placed her hands on her hips, a determined expression on her face. 'The missing money had nothing to do with me.' Luckily, for Tamara, Mary had gone to fill her flagon.

'If you're so innocent, why'd ye run? Why didn't ye stay and prove it?'

'What chance was I given, eh? Tell me that.'

Customers approached and Tamara turned her mind to dealing with them.

'Happen ye couldn't,' Flory murmured, then walked along the line of stalls, picking at the fruit and choosing her vegetables from another stall. Tamara took a deep breath and swallowed her frustration. Did Kit think she was guilty, too? Flory's words kept going round in her head. Perhaps she should have fought to stay until Kit returned.

Tom Murray arrived late. 'What's this?' he asked, pointing to the pile of cabbages against the wall. 'I hope you've not been idling.'

'Course not, Mr. Murray. Cabbage may not be on the menu today, but look at how many cauliflowers I've sold.'

'Get those carrots into a basket and shift these cabbages onto the stall now!' he yelled. She had been looking forward to the ten minutes break he allowed her most mornings. However, seeing the mood he was in, she set to. 'They had better go today, girl, I've got another load to go in the store-room for tomorrow.'

His attitude did not surprise her. She had realised after a few days of working with him that he could be a contrary old devil who cared about no one, and kept himself to himself. He paid her wages and she intended to stick it out until something better came along. When she handed over the takings at the end of the day, she had taken no less than the previous day but he made no comment.

Tamara was on a well-earned break, with only enough time for a bite to eat and a quick banter with the traders. She spoke to a couple of women whom Mr. Murray said might be able to help her find a room to rent. Shaking their head, one of them pursed her lips. 'You'd be hard pressed to ge' a room to yourself, darlin'. Most 'ouses round 'ere are overcrowded ... but if I ge' wind of anything...'

Tamara thanked her. This was going to be harder than she'd first thought. Sighing, she turned away and was making her way through the square, back to the stall, when she saw him. Her heart flipped. He was standing with his back against a column, his shoulders stretched as if searching for someone, a frown marring his handsome looks. Her heart beat faster, and she felt a warm flush to her face. 'Jesus, Kit!'

Seeing him like that made her feel giddy. She longed to talk to him, feel his arms around her again, but how could she bear to have him accuse her as Flory had done? If she carried on the same path, she would have to walk straight past him. She looked away, turned round, and walked through the middle of the market taking the long way back. Mr. Murray would be furious if she was late. She pushed her way between porters wheeling boxes of oranges, sacks of nuts, boxes of grapes, winter pears and apples, in her effort to get away. The smells made her feel hungry again, in spite of having drunk a mug of tea and eaten a couple of buns.

Above the banter, someone called her name, leaving her no option but to turn round. There was no mistaking the piercing blue eyes. She was face-to-face with the man she loved. He held her gaze.

'Is there somewhere we can talk?' he said.

Thinking she knew what was coming next, she said, 'If you've come to make me feel guilty for something I didn't do, you can save your breath.' She turned to go as tears sprung in her eyes.

He reached out and placed his hand lightly on her arm. His touch sent a shiver of excitement through her. 'Hang on a second.'

She struggled free of his grasp. 'Look, I've got to get back.'

'What time do you finish?'

'Quite late.'

'I'll be back. Meet me tonight at eleven at the entrance to the Floral Hall.'

She hesitated.

'Please.' He smiled. Her spirits rose and, biting her bottom lip, she nodded her reply.

Mr. Murray yelled at her for being late back, but it didn't bother her. She was too happy to let anything upset her for the rest of the day.

CHAPTER TWENTY-ONE

Tamara made a special effort getting ready, brushing her hair until it shone. She changed her dress, then spat on her brown boots and polished them with a piece of sacking. She hoped Kit would believe her once she told him her side of the story. But if she noticed the slightest hesitation of doubt, it would break her heart and she would never see him again, in spite of how she felt.

Making the best of her appearance without a mirror, she was ready to leave. Her heart did a somersault. She wrapped her green cloak around her, locked the storeroom, and made her way through the market. It was still active with poor families scavenging for what they could find between the stalls. The voices and laughter of the well-to-do returning from the theatre had re-placed the buzz and excitement of traders that existed during the day.

When she arrived, Kit was standing by the flower market, as prostitutes paraded themselves outside the Opera House, some lurking in the doorway. Tamara watched them, some not very old, and thought to herself, there by the grace of God go I.

Kit was hiding a small Christmas posy of winter

flowers behind his back. He came towards her, dressed in a black winter coat and riding boots. 'These are for you,' he said.

Bringing the blue violets to her nose, she closed her eyes and inhaled their fragrance. 'They're beautiful!' Was this a sign that he believed her to be innocent? Oh, she hoped so.

'Let's go somewhere we can talk. I'm afraid it will have to be an ale house.'

She nodded, feeling the chill of the winter night. He placed a protective arm around her and they walked away, mingling in with the crowd until they could escape down a side street.

'It might be a bit rowdy, but I've bribed the landlord to let us have a quiet table towards the back of the room.'

She felt safe with Kit as he ushered her into the inn. Most of the revellers were drunk, some celebrating Christmas a week early and took no notice of them.

They sat down, and Tamara again drew in the scent of the flowers before placing them on the small mantle shelf next to them.

'What would you like?'

'Could I have a port, please?'

'I never knew you liked port.'

'There's lots of things you don't know about me.' She smiled.

'It would seem so.' When Kit returned, he was carrying a large glass of port and a pint of ale. He placed the drink down in front of her, then sat down and lifted his glass to his lips.

Up until now, Tamara had said little. Her emotions were high and she still did not know why he

155

wanted to see her. If the posy was anything to go by, she hoped he was on her side. The last time they had been together, he had given her the impression that he cared. Whatever reason he was here, she knew that seeing him again, she would never be able to forget him.

He reached across the table and touched her arm. 'Why didn't you leave me a note? I had no way of knowing, no idea where you'd gone until Flory mentioned she'd seen you.'

'I'm sorry. I had no choice. I waited as long as I dared to before ... before they forced me out. I saw hate in their eyes, Kit. I was frightened. I walked the streets, sheltered in doorways until I came across a barn belonging to Mr. Murray, not far from Finchley. I persuaded him to take me on and I owe him my life.'

'Oh, Tamara, I'm so sorry. I tried to get back, but by the time I found Nick, it was late. He was with a woman, probably the same one you saw him with. He was despicable, showed no respect for his father, so we fought. We both ended up in a cell. I heard about the missing money when I got back. With no idea where you'd gone, I clung to the hope that you would come back.'

'How could I?' Tears welled in her eyes. 'I'd been shamed, had fingers pointed at me. Even a gypsy has her pride, you know.' Talking about it brought back her feelings of anger and she gripped the table.

'I can understand how you feel, but,' he sighed, 'you can't leave things like that.' He sipped his drink.

'I was afraid you'd believe Mr. Billy.'

He shook his head, and this time he took hold of her hand. 'No, I didn't. I told him and said that you had no reason to take the money.' He tilted her chin. 'How have you managed?'

'Okay, I suppose. At least I'm off the street.'

'I want you to come back with me. I have my own theory as to who the culprit is, but I can't prove anything without you there. You must come back and clear your name.'

'I can't go back there.'

'You must!'

'Why should they believe me now?'

'You're going to make them.'

She smiled up at him. 'It's so good to see you, Kit.' He leaned across the small table and placed a light kiss on her lips. They stayed long enough for another drink before Kit walked her back to the storeroom.

When Tamara unlocked the door and Kit stepped in behind her, his face clouded in a frown. 'You can't be serious? What kind of an employer leaves you to sleep in a place like this?'

'It's not that bad,' she said. 'It's only temporary.'

'I know you were desperate, Tamara, but this is unbelievable. Promise me you'll tell Murray that you're leaving.'

He ran his fingers down the side of her face. Then he pulled her towards him and kissed her. His kiss was soft and warm and, although it only lasted a few seconds, Tamara felt as if the world had stopped as the musky smell of him washed over her. She drew back breathless.

'I'll be waiting for you at the same place tomorrow night. I'll bring one of the horses and we'll ride back to the circus together.'

'All right, I'll be there.' He kissed her again, and this time she responded, feeling the passion that was building up between them.

CHAPTER TWENTY-TWO

When Kit left, Tamara placed her fingers to her lips;, she felt woozy from the drink and could not remember ever being this happy. With a little more persuading, she might have gone back with Kit tonight. Outside, she found an old jam jar next to some crates. A spider stirred inside, and she gently turned it upside down to let it escape.

She filled the glass with water from the tap and took it inside. Then she placed the posy, the red ribbon still attached, into the jar and took it upstairs. Having Kit on her side made all the difference to her, and she fell into a deep sleep.

Later, a noise startled her and she cried out as if in a dream. A face loomed before her, one she could not recognise. Before she could react to what was happening, someone placed a hand-kerchief over her mouth and nose. It had a pungent, sweet smell and she tried to resist breathing it in. Unable to fight back, her strength drained away until she felt nothing more.

When Tamara finally came to, she found herself in strange surroundings. She felt sick and her head was fuzzy and grainy. There was an unpleasant taste in her mouth. She retched into a bowl by the side of the bed. It was as if whoever had brought her here knew she would need it. Someone had tried to poison her, she felt sure of it. However, she could not focus her mind.

She threw back the white sheets on the four-poster bed and stepped out onto the deep pile carpet, astonished to find she was wearing a low-cut, silk, oyster nightgown. She couldn't remember anything. How in the name of God had she got here? Her legs went from under her and she fell to the floor.

The next thing she knew a young girl in her twenties, dressed in black and white as if she was a maidservant, was helping her back into bed. Embarrassed, Tamara pulled the sheet up to her chin.

'Where the hell am I?'

The girl inclined her head. She had dark eyes and brown skin. 'My job to see you eat ... get well, miss. Please, you eat breakfast now.' She carried across a tray with fruit, tea and toast.

Why was she calling her miss? 'What is this place?'

'I'm sorry, miss. You've been ill and need to rest.'

'Ill! Rest! What are you talking about?'

The woman ignored her and busied herself fluffing up the bed pillows. Her frustration rising, Tamara picked up one of the pillows and threw it at the woman. 'I've got to get out of here. What time is it? I have to get to work.' She glanced around the room. 'Where are my clothes?'

Completely ignoring Tamara's pleas, the woman said, 'I be back shortly for tray and help you dress.' Then she left, shutting the door behind her.

This was a nightmare, and she would wake up in a minute. In spite of pinching her arm until it left a mark, her mystifying ordeal continued. What rubbish was the girl talking? She sounded like one of the Spanish gypsies Tamara had come across last year in Dublin. She had to get to the market. Mr. Murray would be livid with her.

The clock on the mantelpiece struck eight-thirty. Tamara got up, knocking over the tray and spilling the tea. It made a brown stain on the white sheets. The room was richly furnished and spacious, with a polished round table with two velvet-upholstered chairs, but she couldn't find a stitch to put on. Frantically, she pulled on the doors of the wardrobe and tugged at the drawers, but none of them opened. She rattled the door handle. It, too, was locked. She went across to the window and glanced out. She was at least three storeys up. She could see the streetlamps and cobbles below, and hear church bells, carts and traffic rumbling past.

She was not far from the market, she thought, as she turned back into the room with its high ceiling and chandeliers. A feeling of desperation gripped her. She sat down on the bed and sank into the soft mattress, thinking back to the previous night. Someone must have entered the storeroom, but she'd never heard a thing. Had she forgotten to lock the door after Kit left? Everything still felt fuzzy as she tried to make sense of it all.

160

Anger, mingled with fear, welled up inside her. She had to get away. How, she had no idea. With no clothes, she could hardly run out into the street. She had to try. She didn't want to miss seeing Kit. When the girl came back in for the tray, she would make a run for it. It was her only hope. Until then, all she could do was wait.

Tamara was sitting on the bed, the sheet securely wrapped around her, when a key turned in the lock and the maidservant walked in. 'Oh, I see you are ready for your bath, miss,' she said, smiling as she walked towards the bed. Tamara wasted no time and fled through the open door. 'Miss, come back.'

The corridor was empty and she glanced in both directions before dashing down the stairs. She was halfway down when she came face-to-face with Jake Travis. Tamara froze as she looked up into his cold grey eyes. He looked every inch a gentleman; his hair cut short, his locks neatly shaven, and wearing a suit and tie. Tamara gripped the balustrade and her legs turned to jelly. She had hoped that by running away, she could outfox him. How wrong she had been.

He picked her up as if she was a child and carried her back upstairs. 'Did you think I wouldn't find you?' he hissed. Then, smiling towards the young servant, he nodded for her to leave.

'Let me out of here, you beast! Thanks to you, I've lost my job. And where are my things?' Tamara yelled. Lashing out, she fought him like a tigress.

Travis had no choice but to release his grip on her, and he flung her roughly onto the bed. She screamed out, hoping that someone would come to her aid, when Travis placed his hand over her mouth. She thought he was going to drug her again and she bit down hard until she drew blood.

'You will pay for that, you vixen,' he said, sucking the blood from his finger. 'Now you listen to me. No one is going to help you. That goes for circus boy, too. I saw you with him last night. Well, you can kiss him goodbye, because you'll never see him again.'

'You despicable creature,' she spat. 'I've always hated you. No matter what you do, you won't make me love you.'

'We'll see about that,' he sneered. He sat on the side of the bed, and Tamara stiffened. 'You'll do exactly as you're told and, if you cause me any more trouble, Jono and Ola will find themselves off my land. The choice is yours.'

His cold eyes bore into her. 'If you're looking for someone to blame, you can blame them.'

Tamara stifled a sob; she had blamed them every day since she ran away, but she could never hate them, not in the way she hated this man. She gripped the sheet tighter around her.

He laughed and stood up. 'All in good time.' He walked across to the wardrobe and unlocked it. Tamara stayed where she was, hoping he would take out something she could put on. What she saw was a wedding gown hanging alongside quality dresses and outfits. Dear God, he was going to force her to marry him. Never. Not even if her life depended upon it.

Travis did not speak. He selected a lavender gown with a low neckline and slipped it from its hanger. Then he opened one of the drawers, which overflowed with fine lingerie. Taking the dress across the room, he placed it over the back of the chaise longue. 'I'll be back around seven this evening. Be dressed and ready. We're going out.'

Tamara looked at him aghast. 'I'll not wear such trash. Where are my clothes? I'm leaving here right now.'

'You won't need them. Your old life's behind you now.' He walked towards the door. 'Things will be different from now on.'

'What are you talking about? What is this place?'

'This place, my dear, is a hotel; soon to be a high class whorehouse.' Then he left, leaving a wide-eyed Tamara staring at the closed door.

CHAPTER TWENTY-THREE

Tamara sat in a daze, scarcely able to comprehend what had happened. The maidservant returned with lunch. Any desire to eat had left Tamara, and the girl gave her no more than a cursory glance as she changed the bed sheets. Travis had obviously won her trust, but she was the only person Tamara could plead with for help.

When she had finished sheeting the bed, the servant glanced down at the untouched food. 'Mr. Travis, he say you must eat, miss.'

'Mr. Travis can go to hell, and can you stop calling me miss! Whatever he's told you, I'm just a gypsy,' she spat. Wringing her hands, she went across to the window and glanced out. Life was in full swing, people hurrying towards the market with no idea that she was being held captive. She turned back into the room. 'Can't you at least tell me how long he plans to keep me here?' Tamara cajoled.

'Sorry.' She shook her head. 'I not know.'

Tamara tried being friendly. 'What's your name?'

'Sophia,' she smiled.

'Why are you working for him?'

'Mr. Travis, he ask me to come look after you.'

'I don't need looking after. He kidnapped me. He is keeping me here against my will. Don't you understand? You could help me to get away,' Tamara pleaded.

'I'm sorry. Mr. Travis, he tell me you're ill, miss. He say you be like this. He concern for you. You need food and rest.'

Tamara could feel every muscle in her body tighten. 'You believe him, you stupid woman.' She gripped the girl's arm. 'He's lying. I'm fine. I have a job to go to.' Then she released her hold, her voice softening. 'Help me, please. Where are my clothes?'

'Mr. Travis had me burn them,' she said, and began to fidget with the collar of her uniform.

'Not my cape! Did you burn that, too?' She wiped her tears with the back of her hand.

'There was no cape, miss.'

'Well, help me find something to put on.' She crossed the room and rummaged through the drawers, scattering the floor with colourful lacy underwear until she found something modest enough to wear. She pulled open the doors of the wardrobe, tugging at the dresses. They were all evening gowns. Some were glittered with sequins. If she turned up for work in one of these, Mr. Murray would have her arrested. She slipped a negligee from the hanger and wrapped it around her. Sophia looked on, a frightened expression in her eyes, and then she quickly gathered up the lingerie and placed it back in the chest of drawers.

'Are there no other clothes, apart from these?'

The girl shook her head.

'You must have something that would fit me?'

The girl's eyes widened. 'I ... I don't have, only uniform.' Tamara did not believe her.

'Is there anyone else in the building?'

She shook her head. 'Not open for business yet. Mr. Travis is expecting Madam Lilly to take over in the New Year.' She walked towards the door and turned her head over her shoulder. 'You sleep now.' Tamara saw an opportunity and rushed towards the door. The girl reached it first and stood in front of Tamara, spreading her arms.

'Get out of my way.' Tamara pulled the maid's cap, gripping her hair tightly so that her head went backwards. She opened the door, leaving the girl flustered, panting for breath and straightening her cap. Tamara found herself confronted by a well-built man in a black suit, standing sentry-like on the landing.

'I wouldn't try that, young lady, because you'll

165

find another like me on the front door.' Tamara's heart sank. Her shoulders sagged and, muttering a curse, she went back into the room.

Sophia hurried past her onto the landing, saying she would be back later with her medicine. Tamara kicked the door shut and heard the lock turn on the other side.

Tamara's stomach rumbled, and in spite of her frustration, she ate the poached eggs on crispy bread with fruit put before her. She declined to drink the cloudy water, and poured it down the lavatory. She still felt drowsy from whatever had been in her drink earlier.

Unable to solve any of her immediate problems, she fell back on the soft pillows. The echo of voices and the sound of horses, their hooves making a loud noise on the cobbles, brought her to the window. She glanced down. Travis was handing over two horses to a man who was placing the reluctant colts into the back of a cart. She saw the man tender a roll of notes. The bulk of Travis's money came from buying and selling horses, but now he could add prostitution.

She wandered around the room aimlessly, not knowing when he would put in an appearance. If he was determined to marry her, he may already have bought a licence. She was not sure if marriages took place during Christmas, but he would keep her prisoner until it happened. Sighing, she turned up the wick on the table lamp and sat down, thinking of ways to soften his black heart. She considered the possibility of throwing herself at his mercy, confessing how she had felt at being deceived about the whole marriage thing.

When Sophia returned, Tamara asked her to bring her hot water. The girl appeared delighted. Later, she eased herself into the luxury soap-scented tub Sophia had prepared for her, and took a long soak. She scrubbed herself from the top of her red hair to the soles of her feet. However, she refused to let the girl help her dress.

Left alone, Tamara pulled on the dress Travis had left out for her. It was a perfect fit and she wondered how he knew her size. She also refused to have her hair piled on top of her head like a cone, preferring to let it fall loosely around her. It covered her bare shoulders, but she felt uncomfortable showing the tops of her breasts. Finally, she slipped her feet into white fluffy slippers by the side of the bed, and sat in one of the red leather-backed armchairs. She was planning what she would say to Travis when the mantle clock chimed nine, an hour after the time he said he would be back.

Kit would be making his way to meet her tonight with no way of knowing where she was. She regretted her decision not to tell Kit about Travis. If Jake Travis were to rape her – because she would never give herself to him willingly – Kit would be lost to her forever.

Well, she was not going to end her life tied to Travis; she would play him at his own game, charm him with false promises to get him to release her. The hands on the clock moved slowly, and she could feel her heart beating in the silent room. As she pondered her situation, she felt her fury rise. Travis wanted to humiliate her by keep-

167

ing her guessing as to his intentions, imprisoning her in a future whorehouse and getting her to dress like one.

Thinking about it made her furious. She paced the room like a caged animal, damned Travis for his treatment of her, then tore the dress from her body and threw it across the room. She pulled the sheet from the bed and wrapped it around her. To be ordered to dress in a certain way was not in her nature, neither was it to be told how she should look and wear her hair. She did not intend to start now.

The fact that no one knew she was here apart from Sophia made her jittery, and if Kit failed to find her, she was doomed to spend the rest of her life beholden to Jake Travis. She could not let that happen. Then a sudden thought struck her. She slipped the silk pillowcase from the pillow, carried a chair across the room and placed it in front of the window. On tiptoe, she could just about reach the opening at the top. She pushed her arm through the gap, the pillowcase dangling from her fingers, and yelled as loud as she could.

'Help me, please! Someone help me.'

A few people walking by gave her a curious glare before moving on. The streetlamps that lined the cobbled streets were bright. Young girls paraded along the pavement, stopping occasionally to pose provocatively as men approached them. No one offered to help. Tamara kept on calling until she was hoarse. Finally, two men in caps, with scarves wrapped round their necks, stopped, raised their heads and looked up. She repeated her plea, waving the pillowcase, until one man shouted, 'I'd love to come up and help ye love, but I can't afford it.'

The two strode away arm-in-arm with two women on the street. Tamara could hear their raucous laughter and felt her face redden. Her hopes dwindling, she rattled the doorknob and was surprised when it opened. The big man was still on duty and he acknowledged her with a warning glare.

'Have pity,' she said. 'I shouldn't be here.' She bit down hard on her bottom lip to stem her distress. She felt his eyes piercing hers, and for a split second, it appeared he might relent. Then he cleared his throat, straightened his shoulders, and looked away.

'It's more than me life's worth.' He gripped her arm and hurried her back inside the room, locking the door behind her. Tamara found the loneliness intolerable. The prison cell in Liverpool, had at least been bearable because she had someone to talk to. To defeat Jake Travis would be hard, as he had no scruples; he was a man very few refused. With nothing else to do but wait for him to return, she went back to bed and cried until she slept.

CHAPTER TWENTY-FOUR

When Kit arrived at the market, there was an eerie quiet about the place, which was deserted apart from the poor searching for scraps. He had passed a few of them already and dropped some coins into their begging bowls. Frost covered the pavements and he glanced up at the laden sky, pulled the collar of his warm woollen jacket around his neck and his hat down over his ears. Kit stood at the spot not too close to the Opera House, where whores paraded themselves.

When he had stood for half an hour with no sign of Tamara, he began to feel the cold penetrate through his clothes and he stamped his feet to try and keep warm. It was so unlike Tamara to be this late. He had read about the epidemic of typhoid sweeping Europe, and the possibility that she could be ill struck him. He had been appalled when he'd seen the conditions she was living in, and tonight he was looking forward to taking her back with him to the circus where he could look after her.

His watch said one minute to eleven. He began walking towards the fruit and vegetable market, annoyed that he hadn't done so sooner. Church bells rang out the hour. He met few, apart from a couple of drunks arguing. It was a common sight at night around these parts and worsened around Christmas time. He could hear the sound of horses' hooves, and carriages echoed in the surrounding streets close to the Opera House.

When he arrived at the storeroom, he knocked several times, and called out her name. He pushed at the door. It was locked. He called again, before going around the back. The door swung open and he hurried inside, still calling her name. A cold shiver ran through his body and he took the narrow staircase two at a time. The window was broken and he had no idea if it had always been like that, but it felt colder up here than it did outside. The glow from the market streetlamp shone into the room; he could see a rickety sofa and guessed that was where she slept. Her green cloak was lying on the floor. He wondered where she could be. Only last night she had seemed reconciled to returning to the circus with him to clear her name, and he wondered what had changed her mind?

He racked his brain to think of where she might have gone without her cloak on such a freezing cold night. He ran his hand across his forehead. What had started as an exciting evening had turned into a frightful mystery. Now he did not know what to think. Should he alert the police, or wait and see if she turned up. He waited a while longer then he went back outside. His gait slow, he made his way back to the floral market with still no sign of Tamara, then went back to where he had stabled the chestnut mare and returned to the circus.

Kit's thoughts were constantly on Tamara. She had completely turned his head. That was what

171

Nelly had told him, and he knew it was true. He had never felt this way about any woman before. He longed to see her, gaze upon her lovely face. Nelly noticed his misery and drew him aside.

'What's up with ye, lad? You look like you've lost a Joey and found a farthing. Are ye still mooning over that gypsy girl?'

'She didn't turn up last night, Nelly.'

'Well, there ye are then,' she said. 'She's guilty. Why else would she have run? Forget about her is my advice. Have ye never noticed how sweet Zeema is on ye?'

He was fond of Zeema, and Nelly was like a mother to him, so he didn't want to upset her. 'Zeema's a lovely girl, Nelly,' he replied. 'She's just not the one for me.'

'Bah, rubbish,' Nelly said, shaking her head.

When Billy asked Kit if he would mind giving a hand to shift one of the wagons, he was glad of the distraction.

'I want to make room for a larger wagon to accommodate two new clowns who are arriving after Christmas. Besides,' Mr. Billy said, 'it's a sad reminder of broken trust.'

Kit made no comment, realising he was asking him to shift Tamara's wagon. 'There's a space next to the lions' cage, but make sure you cover it well.'

When Kit had secured the wagon, he could not resist looking inside. With Tamara's clothes and personal belongings gone, there was no trace left of her. The small dressing table had come away from the wall during the move. When Kit hunkered down to secure it, he found a hessian moneybag taped to the back.

His heart flipped and he sat down on the floor, staring at the bag of coins in his hand.

CHAPTER TWENTY-FIVE

The following morning, Travis was in the room before Tamara was awake. He was sitting on a ladder-backed chair facing her, his legs crossed, dressed as if he had just been out riding. A rare smile swept across his face. If things had gone to plan, she would have been his wife and she would have wanted for nothing. In his own way, he still desired her, but he would never let her see his emotional side, not until she agreed to be his. He wanted her to come to him willingly. It might take time, but he was sure she would come to realise it was the only way to free herself from a life of poverty.

Tamara woke with a start, and sat up. Quickly glancing about her, she pulled the sheets up around her neck. How long had he sat there looking at her sleeping?

'What do you want?'

Travis gave her a lazy, amused smile, his grey eyes glinting wickedly. 'I hear you were calling for help last night. But it will do you no good because no one comes in here uninvited.'

'How much longer are you planning on keeping me here?' She struggled to keep her tone gracious in spite of the rage flaring inside her.

'Oh, how proper you sound, just like a convent-bred schoolgirl,' he mocked. 'But I know differently.'

'What do you mean?' She sat forward.

'I know circus boy was in the store room with you. I saw you kissing.' His eyes narrowed. 'Have you lain with him?'

'How dare you spy on me. You're not my keeper.'

'Oh, don't be too sure of that, my little Tamara. I don't intend to let you escape me a second time.'

'Let me out of here,' she cried. She scrambled from the bed, taking the sheet with her. 'I hate you. Keep away from me or I'll scream the place down.'

He laughed. 'You look even more bewitching when you're angry. If you continue to thwart me, it will give me pleasure to tie you up.'

'Urr!' She kicked out at him. 'You monster!'

'You may say what you like, my dear Tamara, but I think it's time I tasted what I've bought, don't you?' Before she could think of an answer, his arms were tight around her, crushing her against him. His mouth was on hers. Startled, she fought him as if she was fighting the devil himself, and managed a well-aimed blow that caught him across the nose before he trapped her hands in a tight grip. 'Oh, no, you're not going to claw me this time, my little wildcat.'

Then, swinging her up into his arms, he carried her across the room and through a connecting door that led to his bed chamber and threw her onto the bed. She feared he was going to rape her, and there was nowhere to run.

174

He walked back towards her and sat on the bed. Tamara closed her eyes, inched her way up against the oak bed head, and wrapped her arms around herself. If only she had gone back to the circus with Kit that night, none of this would be happening. She could feel Travis's eyes penetrate her body. She opened her eyes. He was watching her closely.

'Please let me go, Jake,' she begged. 'It don't need to be like this. Please, please let me go.' She hated having to plead with him. Her green eyes filled with tears.

'Ah, Tamara, do not distress yourself. I don't want to hurt you.' She turned her face away. 'Soon you will see I can be nice.' She knew that to be true. She had witnessed his courteous manner whenever he approached her at the gypsy camp, but she had also seen his brutality towards anyone who crossed him. He stroked her cheek. Frightened, she drew back.

There was a rap on the dividing door. He sighed and stood up. 'Yes, who is it?'

He picked up his robe from the bottom of the bed and threw it towards her. 'Put this on.'

Encasing herself in the large robe, Tamara rolled off his bed and stood facing him, her eyes full of hate, when Sophia walked in.

'Sorry I disturb you, Mr. Travis. I left meal as you ask on table in other room.' She glanced at Tamara then towards the large open fireplace with smouldering embers. 'Should I mend fire, Mr. Travis?' A low fire burned in the hearth.

'No, leave it.'

The girl curtsied and left them alone. Tamara

stomped her way back into the other room. Travis followed.

'You've no need to keep me prisoner,' she spat.

Ignoring her, he lifted the lid and ladled soup into two bowls. 'Sit down,' he demanded.

'I'm not hungry.' He pulled out a chair and bid her sit, placing a napkin across her knee.

'Now eat,' he demanded.

Despite her hunger, she couldn't eat a bite. She would die rather than have him touch her and she wanted to wipe the satisfied smirk from his ugly face. He lowered his head and began to eat his mushroom soup, soaking it up with bread.

'You can protest all you like, but you'll stay here until I can obtain a marriage licence.' He laughed. 'I told Sophia that you were my mistress.'

Tamara jumped up, her eyes wide, her hair dishevelled around her face. She raised her hand to hit him, but he caught it and forced her to sit down.

'We will discuss all that tonight, my dear Tamara. Now eat your soup.'

She pushed it away spilling soup on the white tablecloth. She stood up again and crossed to the window, then turned to face him. 'It's Christmas Eve. I want to go out. I need some decent clothes and fresh air.'

'Unfortunately, my dear, I can't let you out until later. Try to be patient. I have urgent business with Madame Lilly Morgan, whom you will meet in due course. She has agreed to run this place for me. She will be away tomorrow for a few days and you, Tamara, will be spending Christmas with me.'

She moved towards the chaise longue and ran her hand across the gilded edge. If he took her out, there was a chance she could escape. She could draw attention to the fact that he had kidnapped her. 'If you intend to keep me here until you come back, can you at least get me something to read?'

'Of course,' he said, getting to his feet and wiping his mouth with a serviette. 'I'd forgotten you can read. I'll ask Sophia to bring you a daily newspaper.'

Taking her arm, he walked her back through the dividing doors. He removed his jacket and threw it across the chair. Then he began to undress in front of her, changing out of his riding britches into a business suit. Tamara felt embarrassed and covered her eyes, but he only laughed. 'After tonight there will be no need for shyness, everything will be all right. Sophia will come in and help you to dress.'

'What do you mean help me? I don't want her bloody help.'

'I suggest you do as she says, because tonight my little dove, you and I are going to a Christmas Eve ball. I want you looking your best, and tonight, married or not, you will sleep in my bed.'

CHAPTER TWENTY-SIX

Tamara watched Travis leave and get into a waiting carriage.

As if sensing her watching, he glanced up at her window. His cold eyes sent shivers through her body. She turned away and hurried back into his room, kicking his discarded clothes underneath his bed just as Sophia came in. Tamara heard her placing the dirty dishes along with the untouched soup onto a tray. 'I reheat soup, miss?' she called.

'Please yourself. I won't eat it.'

The girl shook her head. 'I back soon to prepare bath.'

Tamara came through the dividing door and it was all she could do to stop herself slapping the woman's face. Gritting her teeth, she dug her nails into the palms of her hands. 'What sort of an eejit are you?' she yelled. 'Can't you see what he's doing?' The girl continued to walk towards the door as if she had not heard. 'Go to hell!' Tamara threw a hairbrush, narrowly missing the servant, as the door closed and she heard the key turn in the lock.

'Holy Mother, help me get out of here.'

Travis's window looked out across rooftops, courts and alleyways. She could see a flat roof a good way below her. She just had to get the window open. First, she pulled on Travis's brown corduroy trousers, threw the white cotton shirt

178

on over her nightgown and shrugged her arms into his jacket. It came down to her knees. Untying the cord that held back the curtains, she drew it around her waist to keep the trousers from falling down, and turned up the bottoms. Barefooted, she stood on the windowsill, pulling and tugging at the clasp until the tips of her fingers were sore and the skin tore away, making them bleed. Gasping from the exertion, she muttered a curse and glanced around for something heavy, her eyes settling on a brass candlestick holder.

The bodyguards were bound to hear the glass break, but she was past caring. Covering her face with her arm, she hit the glass panel as hard as she could. It smashed and splintered, falling with a loud crash onto the flat roof below. Before she could act, the door burst open and one of the guards was upon her. The candle holder still in her hand, she hit out at him with such force that he staggered and fell sideways. It was enough time for her to squeeze her slim frame through the broken window, barely feeling the pain of the jagged glass as it cut into her leg.

A large hand gripped her ankle, clearly intent on bringing her down. Struggling to balance, she wrenched herself free, and her right hand reached out for the drain pipe.

'Get after her,' was the last thing Tamara heard as she clambered down the waste pipe, cutting her feet on the sharp edges, expletives hissing from her lips. She landed safely on the flat roof.

She could hear distant bells and the hum of the city below her. Her heart beating in her ears and

179

with no thought of danger, she jumped the rest of the way and landed awkwardly on the concrete yard, twisting her ankle. Ignoring the pain, she ran through alleys and courtyards until she reached Leicester Square. It was dark and she had no idea where she would go. She glanced down the street, white with frost. It was empty apart from two girls hanging around on the corner close to the Empire Theatre. Taking a deep breath, she hurried on as fast as she could, in spite of bleeding feet and the pain in her ankle, towards St. Martin's Place. These men would be upon her soon and think nothing of killing her to save their own necks. Music blared out from alehouses, and men and women spilled out onto the pavement, singing Good King Wenceslas. People stood about in clusters enjoying the fact that it was Christmas Eve. Laughing, they stared at Tamara, her eyes crazy with fear. 'The mad house is the other way, love.'

She darted down an alley. Shadows leapt out at her from every corner. In pain and frightened for her life, she stumbled across a couple who were canoodling in the narrow passageway. 'Bugger off!' the man yelled, and a dog barked, baring its teeth and forcing her to quicken her pace in spite of the pain.

In the empty market square, she glanced around. 'Oh, Kit,' she cried. 'Where are you?' Warm tears ran down her cold face.

She heard heavy footsteps and hid behind a pile of empty baskets. Trembling, she bit her lip to stem her tears. She could smell the fruit and vegetables left behind, some squashed underfoot.

She held her breath. Then she spotted the two bodyguards running across Henrietta Street. She hobbled from her hiding place, wincing through sharp jolts of pain. Her ankle swollen, her feet bruised and bleeding, she crossed the cobbles towards Maiden Lane. Parishioners were going inside a church, their collars up against the bitter cold. She hoped this would be a safe place to hide for a short while. She bent her head and sidled into the porch. She had lost the feeling in her fingers, and her frozen feet numbed the pain in her ankle.

Dressed in men's clothes which were far too big for her, she knew she looked odd. She followed the people down the steps and, as the door opened, the hymn 'Silent Night, Holy Night', drifted towards her. People stared at her, but she was past caring what they thought. She hobbled inside and sat in a pew at the back, biting her lip to stop herself crying out in pain. Aware that she was bareheaded as well as shoeless, there was nothing she could do about it.

She tried to recall happier times when she had gone to midnight mass with her parents and grandmother on Christmas Eve. Now here she was in some strange church, with people who looked down on her as if she was the muck off their shoes. Her only consolation was that she would be safe and warm for at least an hour while the service lasted, then she would have to go outside again in the knowledge that the two men might still be out there searching for her. Tamara prayed for renewed strength, while all around her people stared and whispered.

When the service finished, the aroma of incense lingered in her nostrils, dousing the homely smell of polished pews and the whiff of candles burning at the shrine of St Teresa, the little flower. People mingled to wish each other seasonal greetings, but no one came and shook her hand, and she overheard whispers of 'dirty filthy wench'. Tamara lowered her head and tried to ignore the cruel jibes as the pain in her ankle intensified.

When the church emptied and the altar boys extinguished the last of the burning candles, Tamara knew she would have to leave. A priest in a black cassock walked down the aisle. He had a short white beard and hardly any hair. He stopped next to the pew where Tamara sat. She held her breath, unsure what his reaction might be. Would he call her a gypsy and have her thrown out. He was holding a bunch of keys.

'Why are you still here, child? I'm about to lock up.' He beckoned her to leave. Tamara hobbled to her feet, wincing with pain. He glanced down at her strange attire and saw blood running down her leg. 'Are you hurt?'

'It's just a scratch, Father, but I've twisted my ankle and I'd be grateful for a flagon of water.'

'Come with me.' He led her towards the vestry. An altar boy was still putting the vestments away when the priest handed him the key to the presbytery and asked him to bring Tamara fresh water and something to eat.

'Now,' he said. 'Sit here and rest a while, and you can tell me how you came to be in this situation on Christmas Eve of all nights.'

Tamara hated lying to a priest, so she told him the truth, that she had run away from a man who had kidnapped her two days ago. The priest was astounded.

The altar server returned and handed Tamara a tumbler of water, then put a plate with a slice of bread on the table next to her.

Tamara thanked him, took a long drink of ice cold water, then bit off a small piece of bread.

'Look, child, you had better come into the house. My housekeeper will take care of you, at least for tonight. What is your name?'

'Tamara, Father. Tamara Redmond.'

'Good.' The priest instructed the head altar boy to lock up and turn out the lights, as he proceeded to help Tamara limp painfully through the church and into the house. 'I'm Father Malone, by the way, and this is the Church of Corpus Christi. My housekeeper is Miss O'Keefe.'

In the kitchen, the housekeeper gave her a suspicious glare when the priest explained that Tamara would be staying for the night. 'Father Malone!' she exclaimed. 'Do you think that's wise? You don't know who she is, or what...'

'It's all right, Miss O'Keefe. Christmas is a time of goodwill and we must not forget those less fortunate than ourselves.'

The woman shrugged.

'This young woman has been hurt. Would you be so kind as to see to her injuries and make sure you put on enough fare? We have someone joining us on Christmas Day.' He smiled warmly towards Tamara. 'Sit here, my child, and put your foot up onto this stool. You will need to rest it and

183

we'll see how it is tomorrow.'

'Thank you.' Tamara was relieved to sit down again. She could feel the warmth from the fireplace in spite of the dying embers. The house was an extension of the church; it smelled of polish, and a clock ticked on the mantelshelf. Statues of Mary and Joseph were on either side of the mantelpiece, above which hung a black crucifix.

Tamara rolled up the trouser leg. Congealed blood had stuck to her leg from her knee to her ankle, and Miss O'Keefe cleaned the cut on Tamara's leg with iodine as if she was cleaning a stain from the cooker, making her wince.

'You might need a stitch in that,' she said, just as the priest came back in.

'Well, I'll bid you goodnight, Father,' the house-keeper said.

'Before you retire, Miss O'Keefe, would you look and see what is left over from the Christmas jumble sale. You might find some clothes to fit Miss Redmond, preferably something warm, and a nightgown.'

The plastered smile slipped from her face. She stood up and walked from the kitchen, and the glare over her shoulder, left Tamara in no doubt what her feelings were.

CHAPTER TWENTY-SEVEN

When Jake Travis returned, he found the two bodyguards hunkered down in the large hallway with their heads in their hands. He stood, legs akimbo, looking down at them.

'What's up?'

'She's gone, sir, Mr. Travis.'

'What do you mean *gone?*' Travis took the stairs two at a time and burst into the room. The men came up behind him. Turning on them, he exploded with rage. 'How the devil did she get out?' he yelled. In spite of their muscular build, Travis towered over them.

'She broke the window, in there.' One of the men pointed towards Travis's quarters.

'You pair of incompetent fools. You let her escape!' he roared. 'You were being paid to watch her, not fall asleep on the job. You're sacked. Get out of my sight.'

'We want paying,' one of them said.

'I'll give you paying. Get out, before I smash your bloody heads together.' The two slunk away. 'It's Christmas, Mr. Travis.'

'Don't give me that sentimental rubbish.' He paced the room. 'Fluttered her eyelashes at you, did she?'

'No, it wasn't like that. You gotta 'ear us out. There was nothing we could do.'

'Get out!' he yelled. 'If I set eyes on either of

185

you again, I'll kill you.'

'You won't get away with diddling us. We want what we're owed.'

Travis picked up the ornate clock and threw it at them. It made a loud clatter as it hit the wall, and fell to the floor in a hundred pieces. Sophia came from the kitchen as the two men ran down the stairs. They brushed past her muttering, 'Bloody lunatic!' and slammed the front door behind them.

When Sophia reached the landing, she knocked and entered the room. Taking small, tentative steps into the centre of the room, she crossed her arms in front of her.

'Well, what do you want?' Travis was sitting in a high-backed chair, his feet outstretched, an angry expression on his face.

'I ... I...'

'What? You were supposed to keep your eye on her. If you had any hand in this, you can go, too.'

'No, no, Mr. Travis. I not know. I saw her minutes before. Men ran outside to stop her, but she too fast. They follow, I follow, too, but got lost in market. Men stay out long time looking.'

'She'll very likely catch her death. What did she have on?'

'She wear your trouser and jacket.' Sophia lowered her gaze.

'You left them lying about, you stupid woman?'

'I sorry, Mr. Travis. I not see any clothes.'

He smirked, as if imagining Tamara dressed in his oversized jacket. 'Well, she can't have gone far, can she?'

'I not know, Mr. Travis. We did our best.'

'Your best. You think that's your best?' He clenched his right fist and hit it against the palm of his other hand. Sophia stepped back. 'Those two morons won't be back. You can join them, since you've done yourself out of a job.'

Tears welled in the young woman's eyes. 'I not want to leave.'

'There nothing for you to do until Lil arrives in the New Year.'

'Please, Mr. Travis. I look after you and house. Need money for family.'

'Oh, stay if you want,' he yelled. He could always find some use for the little Spanish maiden. 'Get someone in to repair that window. Tell them it's urgent. I don't care if it's Christmas.'

'Yes, straight away, Mr. Travis.' The girl curtsied and left.

Each time he thought about Tamara running around the streets of London dressed in his clothes, it made him smile. The girl had some guts. Leaving her without clothes had not hindered her escape. But if she thought that she could outsmart him, she was in for a shock.

He stomped downstairs, shrugged his arms into his heavy coat and went out. He questioned everyone he met, from St. Martin's to the market-place. He went into every alehouse he came across. He questioned the whores hanging around street corners, but no one had seen anyone matching Tamara's description. Drunk with rage, he downed another beer and grilled the proprietor in another rowdy den before he gave up, furious that the girl had managed, so far, to give him the slip.

He was due to attend a high-class function with

187

Tamara tonight. Swearing under his breath, he went back to get ready. When he was dressed for the evening ahead, he paused to look at himself in the mirror. He adjusted his stiff white collar and sprayed on some cologne. There was no doubt in his mind that Tamara would come crawling back. However, tonight, he was going to enjoy himself, with or without the little gypsy girl.

Tamara woke late on Christmas morning, surprised to have slept. Since Travis had kidnapped her, she had only had snatches of disturbed sleep. She felt safe and relaxed for the first time in days, and she stretched her full length until her toes touched the bottom of the single bed before she pulled back the warm covers and got out of bed. The swelling on her foot had gone down some, and when she stood up her ankle was less painful. The cold compress the housekeeper had reluctantly made and asked her to keep on for a couple of hours had made a difference.

It felt strange to have spent the night in the priest's house, hiding from men who would cut her throat as soon as look at her. She tried not to think about Travis, or to imagine his foul temper once he discovered her gone. Where she would go from here, she had no idea. If only she could get word to Kit. Now she feared she would never see him again.

She washed in the bowl of water that had been left for her, and dried herself on the towel. Then she dressed in the undergarments the housekeeper had given her, which were all too big. The long, wide drawers came down well below her knees, but she was grateful for them nevertheless. Then she slipped the blue woollen dress over her head. She liked the full skirt with long sleeves and a white silk collar. The black shoes were too big, in spite of her slightly swollen foot, and kept slipping off her feet. Finally, she discarded them and went downstairs barefooted.

The house was silent apart from the ticking of the clock on a shelf in the kitchen, and she wondered what Kit was doing today. If only she could have got word to him. A smell of goose roasting in the cooking pot over the range made her mouth water.

The breakfast table was set for one, with two large cuts of bread and butter on a plate, next to a pot of tea. She took off the tea cosy and lifted the lid. It looked like it had been stewed for some time.

A cabbage, some carrots and several potatoes were lying on a small worktable, and she decided that after she had eaten she would prepare the vegetables and try to be helpful. The housekeeper was probably in church hearing Christmas Day mass, and Tamara hesitated about whether she should go. However, until last night she had not attended church since her grandmother had died, and it did not feel right for her to go now just because she was here. Her stomach rumbled and deciding that the tea must be for her, she sat down and tucked in.

She was looking forward to having Christmas dinner at the presbytery, thankful she did not have to spend another day with Jake Travis. She was finishing her second cup of cold tea, when the housekeeper came into the kitchen.

'Thank you for the food and the clothes, Miss O'Keefe.'

The woman made no reply.

'I was beginning to think I was all alone,' Tamara said cheerfully.

'Not likely. I've met your type before,' the woman said, drawing her thin lips together.

'I'm not a thief,' she said. All her life she had been accused of doing things she hadn't done, just because she was a gypsy, and she was beginning to tire of it. However, she held her tongue. The housekeeper turned her back and began to peel the potatoes.

'Can I help?' Tamara asked, trying to put the insult to the back of her mind. It was Christmas Day and she did not want to make an enemy of Miss O'Keefe. It was written all over the woman's face that she had an intense dislike of anyone who was likely to invade her territory.

She glared at Tamara in the same loathsome way that Flynn had done on the ship.

'The best way you can help is to go back to where you came from.'

This woman was not going to let her in and Tamara could see there was no point in trying to befriend her. Her spirits low, she limped back upstairs. The housekeeper did not want her around. She would have to leave, forego the Christmas dinner. She had hid her small savings in the sofa at the warehouse, but how was she going to get them? Before her kidnap, she recalled seeing a poster advertising a steamship service from Portsmouth to Cork. Her small stash might be enough for the train fare, but the likelihood of Tom Murray taking her back or allowing her near the place, was slim. She had let him down. The only other option was for her to pour out her heart to Father Malone, tell him everything, in the hope that he would show her mercy. If Miss O'Keefe had any say in it, though, she would see her starve.

She packed the clothes the housekeeper had given her back into the bag and went downstairs. She avoided the kitchen and slipped out the presbytery door and into the church. She sat on a bench in the vestry, next to where the altar boys were hanging up their black cassocks and white surplices, and waited for the priest. She could see him through the half open door as he chatted and smiled with parishioners, then he genuflected in front of the altar and walked towards the vestry.

Tamara stood up. 'Good morning, Father Malone.' He paused next to her, a puzzled expression on his face. She could smell the incense on his vestments.

'Are you not going to mass, my child, on Christmas Day of all days?'

'I'm sorry, Father. I ... just... Can I talk to you for a minute?'

'Yes, I'm sure I can spare a few minutes before my next mass, but I thought if you couldn't attend mass you'd at least be helping Miss O'Keefe with the Christmas dinner.' She lowered her head, feeling a flush to her face. She had disappointed him, and he had been so good to take her in last night when no one else had showed her any kindness.

'I'm sorry, Father, I'm not staying.'

191

CHAPTER TWENTY-EIGHT

'Hold on!' Father Malone said, and disappeared into a side room. She could hear him wishing the altar boys a happy and holy Christmas. When he returned, he was wearing his black cassock with buttons down the front. He sat on a wooden chair and invited her to sit opposite him, as if he was about to hear her confession.

'What's all this about?' He glanced down at the bag by her side. 'Have you got someplace to go, child?'

'No. I, I don't know, Father.' Overwhelmed by the situation she found herself in, her eyes filled and tears cascaded down her face.

'There now. There's nothing so bad it can't be fixed.'

If only that were true, she thought. The priest was the only one she could possibly confide in. 'Can you hear my confession, Father?' she asked, knowing that whatever she told him would remain between the two of them.

He stood up, went to a drawer, and took out a purple stole. Then he closed the door that led into the vestry and sat down again. Kissing the stole, he placed it against his forehead, and finally over his shoulder. 'Make the sign of the cross, my child.'

In the quiet of the small church room, she told the priest everything that had happened to her since she ran away from Galway at the end of the summer. With the telling of each piece of the story, Tamara felt the weight gradually lift from her shoulders until she arrived at the part where Jake Travis had kidnapped her. She had told no one about Travis, not even Kit. Father Malone listened, showing no shock at anything she told him.

'Is there anything that you've done to encourage this man that you would like to confess?'

'No. Nothing, Father.'

'As a penance for past sins, say three Hail Marys and one Our Father. Now I absolve you from all your sins. Please tell God you are sorry.' Then he blessed her with the sign of the cross, removed the stole from around his shoulders, kissed it, and put it away. He remained standing, and Tamara wasn't sure whether to kneel down there and then to say her penance, so she got to her feet.

'I'm sorry you've had to suffer at the hands of this man, and bear in mind it could get a lot worse. You must tell the police everything you've told me. He could still find you, and God only knows what his intentions are.'

Tamara shook her head. 'He has friends in the police. It would be his word against mine, Father. I could end up in a cell again. I couldn't bear it.' A sob caught in her throat.

'This man can't be allowed to threaten you.' He fingered his short white beard.

'I'll go back to Ireland.' She swallowed. 'I have a little money hidden in Tom Murray's warehouse. I was thinking of going over there to get it.'

193

'You'll be walking right into danger by doing that. Try to think sensibly, child.'

'I'm sorry. What can I do? I can't stay here forever!'

The priest ran his hand across his brow. 'I just might have the answer.' He took a couple of steps across the room then he turned to face her. 'Will your gypsy clan accept you back?'

'No.' She sighed. 'That's how it is, Father. Once you leave, you become an outcast. I'd rather not go there.'

'If I was to help you, it would be on condition that you return to your parents.'

'I'm not sure that they...'

'It's the only way. They're your parents. You must make peace with them.'

If she refused, where could she turn? The Salvation Army was known to help people, but that would mean going outside. The priest was right, she couldn't take the risk.

Father Malone glanced at the clock. 'Look, we better go across before Miss O'Keefe starts imagining all sorts.' He smiled. 'Come, it's Christmas Day. Tomorrow we'll discuss this again. I know someone who might be willing to help.'

The housekeeper was lifting the goose from the pot when Father Malone said, 'Can you set another place, please? Miss Redmond is staying. Can you give me a few minutes before serving up, Miss O'Keefe?'

'As you wish Father Malone,' the housekeeper replied, lifting the lid from the large saucepan and prodding the potatoes with force. Tamara

194

noticed the look of disappointment on the woman's face. She was obviously looking forward to dinner alone with the priest, or perhaps the woman couldn't bear to have her sit at the table with them. She hoped that she would show a little charity towards her, at least until the Christmas meal was over. And if Father Malone was to help her, she would be on her way in a few days.

Miss O'Keefe handed her a knife and fork and asked her to sit at the table, but not to touch anything, as she had spent a lot of time making the table look nice. Tamara did as she was asked and said nothing. She was upset at not being allowed to help. It was as if the woman thought she had a contagious disease.

Father Malone appeared at the table with a smile and Tamara reciprocated.

'Now, doesn't this look lovely?' he said. The housekeeper's face brightened as she placed his dinner before him, all set out on the plate.

'I hope ye won't find the goose too dry, Father.'

'Well, it looks good to me. Before we partake of this wonderful food, we must thank the Lord.' The two women lowered their heads while the priest said grace.

Tamara couldn't remember when food smelt this good, and she couldn't wait to taste it. She appreciated Miss O'Keefe's efforts to be civil during the meal, passing a plate with slices of succulent goose and telling her to help herself to vegetables. Father Malone got up and went towards the cabinet in the corner of the room. He brought out a bottle of sherry and poured them each a small glass. He asked Tamara what she had been doing this time last year.

'A group of us got together for Christmas dinner. Afterwards, the men played cards while the rest of us danced round the campfire and played music, singing well into the night. It was wonderful and it was my grandmother's last Christmas. She died shortly afterwards.' Her eyes saddened.

'You're a gypsy then,' the housekeeper said, as if confirming what she already knew.

'We are all God's children, Miss O'Keefe.'

'Well, of course, Father.' She stood up. 'I'll just go and get the Christmas pudding.'

That afternoon, Father Malone encouraged Tamara to write a letter to her parents. She wasn't happy about it and had no idea what to say to them. Miss O'Keefe went off to visit her family and Father Malone retired to his room for an afternoon nap.

Tamara had never had cause to write a letter before, and certainly not to her parents. Staring into space for a long time, she finally started to write the words, 'Ma and Da, I miss you'. She crossed that through and made doodling circles on the paper. There were so many things she wanted to say. So much had happened in the months since she had run away. She didn't want their sympathy; besides, they would still blame her.

She scrunched up the sheet and began again. What could she say? Father Malone had suggested she should start by apologising, but she didn't feel that she had done anything wrong. They had been the cause of all her problems.

Anger flared inside her, thinking about what they had done. If she was to let her true feelings spill out, they would undoubtedly forbid her to come anywhere near the gypsy camp again. They would expect her to be sorry for running away, but in spite of all she had been through, she wasn't sorry.

The other gypsies would ostracise her, especially the young women, who would see Travis as something of a catch because of his money. Well, they were welcome to him. After deliberating for an hour, she said briefly all that she wanted to. When Father Malone came downstairs, she asked him to look over it. He made a few suggestions and corrected her spelling. The letter read:

Dear Ma and Da,
I'm sorry I went away angry with you, but you left me no choice. I'm coming home. We have to talk. Keep this to yourselves, 'cause if Jake Travis finds out where I am, you might never see me again.
Love Tamara

She didn't want to say she loved them, but Father Malone said it would help them to accept her back. So she complied.

'Thanks, Father.'

'I'll get Miss O'Keefe to post it after Christmas. You must not be seen outside, and keep away from the window. Anything you need, you can ask Miss O'Keefe to get it for you.' She nodded. His smile reassured her. 'Now if you'll excuse me, I have a sermon to prepare.'

197

Later that evening, when Miss O'Keefe hadn't returned, Tamara started to prepare supper for the priest. She sliced some bread and had taken the boiled ham out of the cupboard, when Miss O'Keefe came back all of a fluster. On hearing her voice, Father Malone came out of the drawing room holding his prayer book.

'What is it? Has something happened?' He placed his hand on the housekeeper's elbow and guided her into the kitchen. Her face was as white as paper.

He pulled out a chair. 'Sit down.'

'There's a man outside, demanding to know if I've seen a girl with red hair dressed in men's clothes.' She paused for breath. 'Grabbed me arm, he did. Put the heart cross ways in me.'

Father Malone glanced at Tamara then back at Miss O'Keefe. 'What did you say?'

'God forgive me, Father. I told him I hadn't seen any girl.'

'Is there any tea left in the pot, Miss Redmond?'

Tamara poured boiling water into the pot, and felt fear again creep into her heart. 'What did he look like?' she asked.

'He was a big brute of a man with a posh accent.'

Tamara's hand shook as she poured the tea.

'Does that sound like him?'

'That's him, Father.' Tamara placed the tea down in front of the housekeeper.

'Did you lock and bolt the presbytery door as you came in?'

'Yes,' the housekeeper said, spooning three heaped sugars into her tea and stirring it.

'I'm sorry to have been the cause of this,'

Tamara said. Father Malone appeared to ponder, as the housekeeper took a few sips of her tea. Tamara took plates from the cupboard. 'Would you like me to carry on with the supper?'

'No, I'm perfectly fine now, thanks.' Miss O'Keefe stood up, removed her hat and placed it on the table, then she threw her coat across the back of the chair and took her place next to the kitchen sink.

The priest stood up. 'We normally get market people calling once they resume work. And of course, someone might be sick and need anointing, or indeed need to arrange a funeral. So, for the next couple of days, no one but me answers the door, is that clear?'

Both women nodded.

CHAPTER TWENTY-NINE

Father Malone went about his pastoral duties, leaving Tamara alone with the housekeeper. Each time she heard a knock on the presbytery door, she tensed, bit her lip and waited with baited breath until the caller gave up and went away. Time dragged with nothing to do. If only the woman would let her help around the place. Anyone would think she owned the house.

When the priest returned that afternoon, Miss O'Keefe got ready to leave. 'Is there anything special you'd like me to get for dinner, Father?'

'Whatever you think will be fine, thanks.' He

199

handed her Tamara's letter to post. 'Don't take any unnecessary risks.'

'Oh, I won't, Father,' she said, picking up her shopping bags.

Tamara felt bad to be the cause of disrupting their lives and she did not know what to do to show her appreciation. The priest picked up his post. 'Will you be all right on your own? I've some correspondence to see to.'

She nodded. As grateful as she was for the priest's help, all she wanted was to be free to live her own life. Travis would hunt her down no matter where she went, but returning to Ireland was not where she wanted to go. Leaving there had almost cost her her life.

She missed Kit so much and thinking about him weighed her down with sadness. How would he ever find her now? She felt like weeping. If only she could stay in Covent Garden, see Kit whenever he had time off from the circus. Thinking of what might happen once she returned to Galway terrified her. The gypsies would hound her out and she was not sure if her parents would help her. With no other choice on offer, though, it was her only escape route.

Later, when Tamara knocked and popped her head around the door of the study, the priest was reading a letter. He placed it down on the desk and looked up.

'I've brought you a cup of tea and a biscuit, Father.'

'Thank you. Is Miss O'Keefe back yet?'

Tamara shook her head.

'Sit down a moment.' She perched on the edge

of the chair. 'You remember me saying I knew someone who might be able to help?'

She nodded.

'Well, I had a word with the very person; a parishioner by the name of Mr. Ivan Brooks, and he's agreed to take you by cart to Portsmouth. He runs a small knitwear factory not far from here. It won't be very comfortable and you'll have to stay undercover in the cart.' He took a sip of tea.

Tamara sighed, remembering the last time she'd gone undercover and the terrible consequences.

'Mr. Brooks,' the priest continued, 'has a delivery to make in Guildford. When you get to Portsmouth, get on the ship for Cork. Because it's Christmas, there are no scheduled sailings until Saturday morning. It will take many hours to get there. So can you be ready when he comes to pick you up at midnight tonight?'

'Tonight!'

'The sooner you can get away, the better. I'll give you enough money for the steamer and train fare.'

'Father, I don't know what to say.' She didn't want to sound ungrateful, but the idea put fear into her heart. 'I'll pay back every farthing.'

An hour later, Tamara was pleased when Miss O'Keefe returned unscathed just as the priest came downstairs with a battered suitcase. 'Would this be any good to you?' he asked, holding it up. 'It needs a bit of a polish and might be better than carrying a paper bag.'

'I'll give it a rub down for ye,' Miss O'Keefe offered. It was the first kind word she had spoken to Tamara. After a good dust and polish with her best beeswax furniture polish, the case looked as good as new.

'Grand. Thank you. I'll take it upstairs and sort out what I need to take with me.'

It was getting dark, so she struck a match and lit the candle by the bed. Sorting through the clothes the housekeeper had given her, she noticed that some were of good quality. The people who had thrown these away must have money to burn, she thought. She tried on the black twill trumpet-skirt that brushed the floor and a fashionable white frilly blouse with long sleeves and a high collar. They were a good fit.

In another bag, she pulled out a woman's full-length coat with high shoulders and wide sleeves. It buttoned down one side. She placed the skirt and blouse, an oversized jersey, and the coat, over the chair to put on later. Then she placed the rest of her stuff into the case, closed it and lay down on her bed, her hands clasped in front of her.

Since she had stowed away on Captain Fitzroy's ship, her life had not been an easy one. As long as Jake Travis pursued her, it wasn't going to get any easier. If it had not been for him, she might have stayed with Kit in London. It gave her another reason to hate the man.

A knock on the bedroom door made her jump and she swung her legs out of bed and opened it.

'Father Malone's had to go out on a sick call,' Miss O'Keefe said. 'But he'll be back shortly.'

Tamara nodded.

'Would you like some tea? You've a while to wait yet.'

Tamara blew out the candle and followed her downstairs. While they waited for the kettle to boil, the housekeeper handed her a pair of boots. 'Try these on. They're about your size.'

Tamara ran her fingers over the fine buckskin leather. 'But these have never been worn.' Unable to believe her luck, she slipped off the black shoes. Then she crossed one leg over the other and pulled on one of the boots. It went on without effort. She fastened the small buttons at the side. Then she tried the other one, and stood up. 'They're lovely. Thanks, Miss O'Keefe.'

'Well, don't thank me,' the woman said. 'Some kind parishioner handed them in for our next jumble sale.' Steam billowed from the spout of the kettle and she went to make the tea, bringing it to the table on a tray with buttered homemade scones, just as Father Malone walked through the presbytery door and slid the bolt across behind him.

'My, it's cold out there.' He rubbed his hands together, removed his black overcoat and hat and hung them on the coat stand. 'It looks like I've arrived in time,' he said, glancing down at the scones. 'Well, my child, are you all set?'

'I think so, Father. Thanks for arranging everything.'

He waved his hand. 'Glad to be of help. There was no sign of anyone hanging about outside as I came in.' He leaned back in the chair. 'I doubt he knows for sure where you are. But just the same, keep vigilant until you're well out of London.'

They sat drinking tea in companionable silence, then the priest said, 'I'll wait up until Mr. Brooks arrives. You just make sure you have everything ready. Any delay could attract attention.'

'I'll go and get ready and bring my case down.' She stood up and glanced down at her feet. 'Thanks for the boots, Miss O'Keefe. They're really lovely.'

'Indeed they are,' the priest said. 'Well may you wear them, child.'

The housekeeper beamed and began to clear away the crockery. Tamara noticed how approachable she looked when she smiled.

Tamara sat in the drawing room; the trundle of carts and carriages and noise outside in the street had gathered momentum. Folk would be coming out of the theatre and the Opera House, she thought. The last few days had been tense and she hoped that whatever sick plan Travis had in his crazy head, it would not interfere with her escape to Portsmouth. Each time she thought about Kit, she got a strange feeling in her stomach, the same ache she'd experienced when her grandmother died, and she stifled a sob.

By the time they heard the sound of cartwheels pulling to a halt on the cobbles outside the presbytery, her eyes were beginning to droop. She picked up her case and followed Father Malone to the door. Her heart thumped inside her chest. She felt lonely and sad to be going off with a complete stranger, and all she could do was trust the priest.

'We won't delay, miss,' the man said, taking the case from her. 'I hope you've got warm clothes on, it's perishing out there.'

He was wearing a long tweed overcoat with a fur collar, heavy brown boots, and a cloth cap with ear flaps that fastened underneath his chin. Tamara swallowed nervously and glanced towards Father Malone. His smile reassured her and she hurried outside. Brooks rolled back the green canvas. The cart was full of boxes. Tamara got in and lay down on a rug, pushing her case up against the boxes.

'As soon as we're clear of London, you can sit up here alongside me,' Mr. Brooks said, then rolled the canvas over her, securing it to the sides of the cart and leaving just enough gaps for her to breathe.

He gave a quick wave to Father Malone, climbed up behind the horse – a strong built Shire – and they began to move out along the cobbled streets.

Under the cover, Tamara gave way to tears. 'Goodbye, Kit,' she whispered. 'I may never see you again, but I'll never forget you.'

CHAPTER THIRTY

Tamara woke up feeling cold. The cart had stopped, and from underneath the canvas she could hear angry voices. She stayed as still as she could, hardly daring to breathe. There was no panic in Mr. Brooks's voice as he spoke to the men who were shouting, but she couldn't make out what they were arguing about.

She tensed. Could it be the two burly men that had chased her through Covent Garden? Praying, she closed her eyes and whispered, 'God, help us!' She felt the cart move to the side and horses' hooves galloping away, and let out a long sigh of relief.

'Easy now, old boy,' Mr. Brooks said aloud to the horse. 'Giddy up.' And the horse moved forwards.

She felt the bumps as the cart rolled over an uneven surface, the wheels dipping into large pot holes, rocking her sideways. She could hear the mooing of cows and wondered if they were in open countryside. She felt panicky underneath the canvas. It brought back too many bad memories, and she wished she hadn't agreed to the idea. She longed to sit up and see the countryside around her.

After being cooped up for days with Jake Travis, and again at Father Malone's, she longed to breathe some fresh air into her lungs. But the cart rolled on for some time and Mr. Brooks sang little ditties, which he later told her shortened the journey with only Dobie to talk to. The cart finally came to a halt and Tamara hoped they were in Portsmouth.

'I'll have you out in a minute.' Mr. Brooks lowered the back of the cart and helped her out. Her limbs felt stiff and she wiggled her toes inside her boots to get feeling back into them. 'You'll be all right in a minute after you've walked around for a bit.'

They were outside a depot. 'Where are we, Mr. Brooks?'

'This is Guildford. I've a couple of deliveries to make and I'm picking up some grain and flour for the missus. She likes to shop here when she comes wi' me.'

Tamara glanced around. Apart from the horse shit that littered the street, it was a tidy little town. Cleaner than some places she had seen, there were no poor people begging on the street, although she could see the poor house and she guessed that people had troubles no matter where they lived.

Mr. Brooks was checking his paperwork when she asked, 'What was all that about, back there?'

'Oh, that. Sorry if it worried you.' He removed a few heavy boxes from the cart. 'Two men on horseback were arguing with one another on the quickest route into London.' He shook his head. 'Couple o' roughnecks, if you ask me.' He stood the boxes on the ground and began to unload the rest of the boxes.

Tamara glanced back the way they had come, just in case anyone had followed them. She felt jittery out in the open like this.

'If you'd like to feed Dobie, you'll find his oats and some hay in a sack underneath the cart,' said Mr. Brooks, and went inside the depot. Delighted to have something to do, Tamara hooked on the nose-bag and fed the horse.

When Mr. Brooks came back, he removed the nose-bag and led the horse to the water trough at the far end of the street to let him drink.

'How far is it now, Mr. Brooks?'

'We're almost half way. And you don't need to keep calling me Mr. Brooks. Me name's Ivan.' He whipped off his glove and shook her hand. 'If we're lucky, we'll make Portsmouth sometime this afternoon. In the meantime, I know a small inn on the Portsmouth road where we can get a fresh pot of tea. I'm sure you're parched like meself.'

Tamara was relieved to hear that, for she was beginning to feel rumblings in her stomach.

But when the horse lifted his tail, Tamara jumped onto the pavement just in time.

'My word, Dobie,' Ivan said. 'You'll canter the rest of the way after that.'

Tamara laughed, feeling more relaxed. The smell of the steaming manure rose into the air.

'If you get up onto the cart, love, we'll get rolling.'

Tamara enjoyed riding up front with Ivan. Before long, they were moving away from Guildford on the road to Portsmouth. Ivan handed her a rug which she placed over her knees. He glanced up at the grey overcast sky and pulled his coat collar closer around his neck. They chatted freely about the state of the country, including Ireland, and about the situation the country would find itself in should the old Queen die now. Ivan told her that people had no confidence in Edward as their next King.

'Is the Queen very ill?'

'I'm afraid so.'

Tamara found it interesting as she couldn't spare a penny every day to buy a newspaper, and missed most of the country's news. Ivan asked her nothing about her reasons for fleeing to Ireland. Instead, he said, 'I gather you're not planning on coming back to London, Tamara?'

'I don't really want to leave,' she replied.

'I wasn't prying, love. Only, you seem a nice young woman, someone that might get along with Beth, my wife. I run a small hand knitting business with my good lady wife, on Charing Cross Road. The missus, she does most of the knitting, but we're hoping to expand the business with a new knitting machine.' He smiled. 'Can you knit, Tamara?'

'Yes, I can. My grandmother taught me when I was quite young. Nothing fancy, though.'

'Look, if you do come back in the next few weeks or so, come and see me. My wife could do with some help, although she won't admit to it.'

He pulled up at the side of the road, wrote his address on a piece of paper and handed it to her.

'Thank you. That's very kind of you.' She folded the paper up small and pushed it inside her glove. The further they travelled, the more Tamara's heart ached to be leaving Kit behind. She straightened her shoulders and tried to stay positive.

Ivan steered the horse towards the inn on the side of the roadway. 'Here we are. I'm sure you'll be glad of a stop here, love.'

Tamara nodded.

They arrived in Portsmouth on Friday evening, later than expected and as it was getting dark. A police officer stood on either side of the gate leading into the city and docks. Ivan stabled Dobie near the docks to be fed, watered, and have a well earned rest before the return journey.

Ivan carried her case and they walked towards

the town. It was a lively, noisy and busy place, especially down by the docks where cargo was being unloaded and porters pushed heavy trolleys piled high with crates and sacks towards the waiting ships. A Navy ship was in dock, and officers and men in sailor suits walked along the pier. She envied them their freedom.

As much as she had enjoyed Ivan's company, she wished he wouldn't hang around. She wanted to dodge going on board the steamer, and stay here to find work.

'I suppose you need to be getting back,' she said optimistically.

'Oh, I'm afraid I need a kip first. I usually sleep in the back of the cart. But I'll find somewhere more comfortable for you. I know a respectable board and lodgings used by waiting passengers. First, I'll come with you while you purchase your ticket.' He glanced around for the ticket office.

Tamara looked behind her. Across the street, a man resembling Jake Travis stood with his back towards her, in conversation with a police officer. She felt the blood drain from her face and her whole body shook.

'It'll be over there where that queue is. What's the matter, love?' Ivan said. 'You look like you've seen a ghost.' He placed his hand on her elbow.

She couldn't speak. How could she tell him that the man she was fleeing from was across the street, looking for her. 'You've not eaten enough,' Ivan said, and picked up her case.

Tamara slipped her arm through his and gripped tightly, moving her body close and placing her

210

head on his shoulder. 'I'm so sorry to take such liberties.' Ivan's face puckered and he coughed to clear his throat. 'I'm sorry,' Tamara whispered. 'Can we go somewhere quickly before I make a complete eejit of myself?'

Ivan patted her hand and they walked further up the street. 'I'll take you to the guest house. You can get something to eat there and rest. It's not far. Then I'll go back later and buy your ticket.'

Tamara went along with whatever Ivan suggested. She couldn't get away fast enough. The lodging house was a grey two storey building. The woman on the desk booked her in, and Ivan asked if she could have something light to eat.

'At this time of the evening?' the woman glowered. Then she looked at Tamara. 'Well, she looks like she could do with something. I might be able to rustle up some soup. Ye can sit in the kitchen.'

'I'm guessing that show of affection earlier was not for my benefit,' Ivan said.

'I'm sorry to have embarrassed you. There's someone out there that I really don't want to see.' She lowered her eyes.

'You'll be all right here, just make sure you keep your room locked,' Ivan said. 'I might be a while queuing, so I'll leave your ticket at the desk.' Smiling, he left her to rest.

Tamara told the woman not to trouble herself about food, that she was tired and needed to get her head down. Once inside her room, she turned the key in the lock and looked out across the pier. A feeling of apprehension gripped her.

Was Travis still skirting around out there looking for her? Or worse still, could he be in this very guest house? Overwhelmed with insecurities, she placed her face in her hands and wept.

CHAPTER THIRTY-ONE

Kit had hated every day of the holiday, his mind was full of questions he couldn't find answers to. Since discovering the money in Tamara's wagon, he had said nothing to anyone. He needed time to think things through. If Tamara had taken the money, why hadn't she taken it with her?

There was no way Billy would give her the benefit of the doubt. Kit decided to wait a bit longer before confronting Billy about his find. He still had strong feelings for Tamara and he didn't want to contemplate that she would do such a thing.

After his early morning exercises, Kit rushed through rehearsals and went down to Covent Garden to see Tom Murray, who was the only link he had left with Tamara. He found Murray muttering curses as he refilled the stall with cabbages.

'Excuse me,' Kit said. 'You had a girl working for you before Christmas. Do you know where she is now?'

'No, I don't. And if you ask me, I should ha' known better than to employ a gypsy.' He turned his back, and went into the storeroom and returned with a basket full of carrots.

'Look, you're in me way. Are ye buying? If not, clear off.'

'I believe something's happened to her and I'm not going until I find out what.'

'So ye think I know, do ye? Well, I bleedin' don't,' Murray snarled.

'You must know something. Anything that might help me find her?' Kit, anxious to get some answers, followed Murray closely as he arranged his vegetable stall.

'No. I bloody well don't.'

The woman in the next stall leant across to listen in on their conversation. 'Ye all right there, Tom?'

'I told ye afore to keep your bleedin' nose out of my business.'

'Please yourself. I'm not surprised the girl left. Ye miserable sod,' the woman said, turning her back to serve a customer.

'When you saw her last, did she say anything about going away?' Kit continued.

'What are ye implying? I've not seen her for days. She just scarpered.'

'Can I look upstairs?'

Murray glared at Kit. 'You'll find nothing up there, and afore ye start getting any ideas, I don't want the coppers round here.'

Kit took the narrow stairs two at a time and looked around the small derelict room. It looked as though it hadn't been used in years. He got the distinctive smell of carbolic soap. Tamara's green cape was lying on the floor where he had first seen it next to the shabby

213

sofa with springs protruding the cushions. He picked up her cape and fingered the soft velvet before holding it to his nose, recalling the last time he had seen her wear it, the night he had kissed her and she had promised to meet him the following night.

He knew how much her cape meant to her. Why had she left without it? Her hairbrush, rouge and a bar of soap, lay on the wooden floor next to the sofa. He pulled a long curly red hair from the brush and wound it round his little finger. Should he take her belongings with him, or leave them here, in the hope that she might return? He wasn't sure if Tom Murray knew any more than he did himself. Wherever she'd gone, she had done so in a hurry. Something didn't ring true about this whole business and it unsettled him.

He placed the cape over his arm, put the hairbrush and rouge into his pocket, and went back downstairs. Murray had his back to him serving a customer. Rather than have any more cotter with the man, Kit strode away from the market vowing to find Tamara if it was the last thing he ever did.

CHAPTER THIRTY-TWO

The next morning, Tamara followed the passengers towards the pier, nervously looking over her shoulder. There was no sign of Travis. If he was on board, he would travel first class then wait until they arrived in Cork before confronting her. She knew how his mind worked.

She spotted Ivan standing on the cart, waving to her from the docks. She forced a smile and waved back. Carrying her case, and a one way ticket, she crossed the wooden bridge towards the steamer. It wasn't where she wanted to be, and her stomach lurched.

She stayed on deck and watched the steamer move slowly out of Portsmouth harbour, saddened to be leaving England. Returning home with no idea what awaited her, was daunting. She was tense and frightened to let her guard down in case any moment the face she hated would loom up in front of her. This was going to be the longest journey of her life.

Tears gathered in her eyes as she made her way below deck and joined the other steerage passengers.

When the boat anchored in Cork harbour, Tamara's heart pounded. She disembarked with hundreds of passengers, fatigued after her ocean travel. Each time she heard a man's voice, she

215

expected to see Travis, but to her relief there was no sign of him. Had she imagined seeing him the previous night? Confused and tired, she made enquiries at the railway station, but there were no trains running to Galway, so she purchased a ticket to Limerick.

A few hours later, she was on the road that would eventually take her home. She hadn't gone far when the heavens opened and, with nowhere to shelter, she walked close to the stone walls. As the rain soaked through her outer clothing, she felt it penetrate through to her skin. She felt like throwing her suitcase in a ditch, but she needed the few clothes she had brought with her, so she plodded on.

She arrived in Galway just as dawn was creeping across the horizon. When she saw the familiar cluster of caravans and tents on such a cold miserable wet morning, she paused to look, surprised at the way it made her feel. In truth, she had missed it, but living here again without Kit would feel like part of her was missing.

In spite of knowing the gypsy code of conduct, she couldn't bear the thought of her parents rejecting her. Would they treat her differently? It was five in the morning and the camp was shrouded in mist. She hoped to avoid the accusing glares of some who would take pleasure in watching her humiliate herself by returning to where she was no longer welcome.

She was so tired that she could barely put one foot in front of the other. One of the camp dogs ran towards her wagging its tail, but thankfully it didn't bark.

As she drew closer, she could just make out a square patch of grass where her wagon had once stood. It made her gasp. It had completely disappeared, a sure sign that she was not welcome. She was about to turn away when she heard a hissing sound behind her. Fear gripped her and she turned round to find herself face-to-face with her father, Jono.

In spite of her wet clothes, he drew her to him. 'Tamara, thank God!' he murmured, and quickly ushered her inside their wagon.

Ola woke to the sound of whispers and she sat up, rubbing the sleep from her eyes. Her long hair was plaited down her back. 'Who's there? Is that you, Jono?'

'Shush,' he said, putting a match to the lamp. Ola's eyes widened. 'Glory b' to God! Is it really you, Tamara?'

'Yes, it is, Ma.'

Ola opened her arms, then she drew back. 'Look at ye. You're soppin' wet. And what are ye wearin'? These are the clothes of a Giorga. Why are you dressed like one o' them?'

'Travis had all my clothes burned.'

'Did he buy ye these?'

'No, Ma.'

Jono passed them both a tin mug of cold tea. 'Drink this and speak easy now. Some won't be happy to see you back.'

'I don't care about any of them,' Tamara spat. 'I've come to see you, and to make my peace with you.'

'We're okay, lambkins, but if anyone sees ye, we'll all be mud.' Ola drew back the covers. 'Let me get dressed and I'll make ye something to eat. And get out 'f that wet coat. You must be starved after your journey.' She threw on a long shift dress and rolled up their bed mat, then handed Tamara a warm shawl and wrapped it round her shivering body. 'There's so much I want to know. Why in the name of the Almighty did you have to run away from us, Tamara?'

'Did you really expect me to stay and marry Jake Travis? He's a rogue and old enough to be my father.'

'We're sorry, Alana.'

'Look, there's no time for that now,' Jono said.

Ola busied herself and made a pot of porridge over the primus stove. They sat round the small table talking in whispers while Tamara tucked into the delicious oats and brown sugar. She told them briefly all that had happened to her since she fled, her emotions spilling over in the retelling.

Jono stood up, running his fingers through his thinning hair. 'The dirty filthy blighter!'

'Quiet, Jono. The less they know round here, the better,' Ola warned.

'I'll effin kill 'im. I should 'ave done it years ago. If only the others would stand with me against him. They're too bloody scared, even though they know he's the devil in disguise.' He sighed. 'Look, Tamara, you can't stay here. When we heard you were coming back, we arranged for you to live with your Granny Lena's sister, Meg. The devil has never shown any interest in her or her plot, and I doubt he will now. I told her that Travis burned your wagon so she agreed that you

218

could stay, as long as you do the chores.'

'But, she talks Gaelic, Da. I won't understand a word she says.'

'You've no choice,' Ola said. 'Humour her. The less you tell her, the less chance of her blabbing off to anyone.'

'But it's miles away, and I'm jaded.'

'Aye, it is that. But, that's the way of it, Tamara. We'll take the old cart. And in spite of how ye feel, we must away before the camp begins to stir.'

'Pull that shawl up over your head. If anyone is about they'll think it's Jono and me off to the early fish market,' said Ola. 'Leave that case; I'll bring it when I can.' Pulling her close, Ola embraced Tamara and a sob caught in her throat.

'Don't start,' Jono said. 'Come on now, we must away.'

Tamara followed Jono outside to where the mare was tethered to a makeshift cart. He beckoned her to hurry and once she was in the cart, he covered her with an old blanket. It smelled of rotten vegetables and she wrinkled her nose. Her life in the gypsy community was over and she was sick of hiding. Tiredness befuddled her brain, and she wondered if her life would ever be normal again.

Tamara had not been a regular visitor to Meg's. As a child, she always thought the woman was a witch and hid behind her grandmother's skirts whenever she was forced to visit. She remembered her much as she saw her now, crouched over the hearth, dressed in black, her hands dirty

219

and blackened from smuts, her old face lined. Megs greeted them in Gaelic.

'*Conús atá tú?*'

'*Ana mhaith, gur amaith agát*,' Jono replied. '*Agus tú fein?*'

Meg assured them she was fine, while at the same time using her hands to put turf on the fire. Sparks flew up the wide chimney. Tamara looked at Meg and wished she hadn't let her father talk her into coming.

Meg turned to look at Tamara. 'Aah, the *Babsheen! Suí síos.*'

Tamara sat down next to her father on the wooden bench by the fireside and leaned her head back. The cold from the stone floor penetrated her boots. Candles on either side of the mantle cast shadows on whitewashed stone walls, black with soot. A crucifix hung on one side and a cracked mirror on the other.

Meg and Jono chatted on. Tamara, her eyelids heavy, soon bored of it all. She couldn't understand a word of the Gaelic they were speaking. Finally, her father stood to take his leave.

'I'll let ye get to your bed,' he said, looking at Tamara. 'I'll be back in a few days when I know it's safe.'

Tamara was so tired she would have slept anywhere, and willingly helped Meg to make up a bed for her on the wooden settle.

Tamara knew what was expected of her, and she was first up. She made porridge and got on with the chores while Meg slept. Outside, the landscape was shrouded in mist and a bitter wind blew across from the sea. No one ever came down here and she guessed that was one of the reasons her father had chosen Meg's as a safe place to hide. But how long did he expect her to stay here?

For the first few days, Meg refused to answer Tamara unless she spoke in Gaelic. Tamara knew few Irish words, only those picked up from her parents on the occasions they greeted others who spoke in the Gaelic tongue. She had no interest in learning the Irish language; she had more important things on her mind, her head still full of feelings for Kit.

Desperate to talk to someone, she found herself talking to the hens as she gathered in the eggs. Her days were spent digging potatoes on the bleak hillside at the back of Meg's cottage. Once a week, Meg took the produce into Galway city to sell, bringing back any post and fresh fish from the market, leaving Tamara to do the washing. She was pegging it out on the clothes line strung between two hedgerows, when she spotted her parents coming down the narrow track towards the cottage.

Overjoyed, she ran to meet them and ushered them inside. She hooked the black kettle with its long spout over the fire, and set the table with cups and plates and whatever bread she could find. The cupboards were almost bare and it would be ages yet before Meg got back with the provisions. But she needn't have worried, because her mother had brought some homemade cakes to have with their tea.

'I've brought your case,' Jono said, placing it in

the corner. 'Well, how's it been?'

'Terrible, Da. I'm going out of my mind. I want to go back to England.'

'Don't talk rubbish,' Ola said.

'Ye won't be safe,' Jono added. 'He won't give up!'

'I know that. But I'm done with hiding.'

'Look, Tamara. We just want to make up for the mess we've made. I know it's not easy living here with old Meg, but what's the alternative?' Jono asked.

'Me mind's made up, Da. I'm not going to let him run my life anymore.'

'We knew this would happen once you tasted living elsewhere.' He sighed. 'You're not like the rest of us.'

'What do ye mean, Da?'

Jono put down his cup and stood up, his chair making a scratching noise on the stone floor. He sat down again, knitting his fingers, then looked across at Tamara.

'What ails ye, Da? Why can't you sit easy? Has Travis come back?'

'No. There's no sign of the bog-rat.'

'Holy St. Bridget, tell her, Jono, before Meg gets back.' Ola sniffed and lifted the hem of her apron to wipe a drip from her nose.

'Tell me what?' Tamara swallowed her fear.

He shifted and pulled his chair closer to the table. 'We covered things up before, and look where it got us.'

Tamara felt her face pale. Surely they weren't going to insist she marry that vile man. She got to her feet and went and stood next to her father,

her hands on her hips. 'If you're going to ask me to marry that man, or any other man, I won't.'

Jono glanced across at his wife, then he lowered his head. 'That's the last thing we want. There's no easy way to say this, and I suppose we should have told you before.'

'For the love o' God, Da!'

'We're not your parents, Tamara.'

CHAPTER THIRTY-THREE

The ticking clock on the mantelpiece appeared louder. The shock of what she had just heard made her tremble and she sat down to steady herself.

'What … what are you saying, Da?'

She glanced at Ola. 'Ma, is … is it true?'

'We're still your Ma and Da. After your reaction to Jake Travis, we decided no more secrets,' Ola said.

'I don't understand. If you're not my Ma and Da, then who is?' With so much going on in her life already, this was the last thing she had expected to hear. Anger flushed her face and she glared at their tearful faces. 'Why didn't you tell me years ago?'

'We had no reason to, but the way things are going, we thought you might hear it from someone else,' Ola sniffed.

'Jake Travis, you mean?'

'It's possible. Who knows what that man knows?

223

It would account for the way he's humiliated us.'

'Who else knows I'm a stray, then?' Tears gathered in her eyes. Agitated, she paced back and forth.

'No one knew, apart from Lena,' Jono said. 'We were never in one place for long, always on the move. The night we found you, we were travelling along Spiddal Road towards the village. It was lashing rain and we could hardly see for the mist. We stopped overnight by the roadside.' He sighed. 'It wasn't until early the following morning that I looked outside and found you wrapped in a shawl and a rubber sheet under the steps of the wagon. Years later, when Travis offered us land for a reasonable rent, we took it.'

'He appeared genuine,' Ola said.

'And we needed somewhere permanent to bring you up,' Jono said. 'So when we moved onto Travis's land, no one was any the wiser.'

Tamara sat down. This all seemed like a bad dream.

'I had recently lost a baby and you were a gift from the Gods,' Ola added.

Jono swallowed. 'You've always been our little princess.' He reached out to her but she shrugged him off.

'You let me live a lie. Does Meg know?'

'No. I told you, no one knew apart from your Granny Lena. You couldn't have coped with knowing before, Tamara.'

'And I'm expected to cope with it now?' she snapped. 'Do you know who my real mother is? Or are you keeping that from me, too?'

'We don't know who she is. You've always been

my baby,' Ola cried.

'This hasn't been easy for us,' Jono said.

'You haven't exactly made things easy for me, have you? It's because of you I'm in this God forsaken place with a woman who talks Gaelic most of the time. And now you tell me I don't belong.' Tamara jumped up. 'Why should I believe you?'

Ola reached out to comfort her, but Tamara turned her back. 'Go away and leave me alone.'

'Perhaps you'd better read this then.' Jono held out a faded white envelope. 'It was pinned to your shawl when we found you.'

She heard them pull away, the crunch of cart wheels rolling over the rough ground until the sound grew fainter. Shocked and numb, she sat down and cried. Tears of anger at what she had been told, and regret that she'd come back. She couldn't stop shaking. The letter still clasped between her finger and thumb, she finally opened it like it was precious parchment. She could feel the quality of the paper that after seventeen years had yellowed around the edges. The letter was written in a good hand. No address, but dated the month of her birthday, October 1884.

My precious baby girl,
For months leading up to your birth, my mind was in turmoil. If I keep you, it will cause heartache for so many people. I'm left with only one option that breaks my heart. I'm writing this letter in private just days after your birth, and it's breaking my heart. To part with you so soon after giving birth, is a cruel blow. If

225

there was any way of keeping you, believe me, I would.

I've sinned against God and my husband. In spite of my reasons for doing so, may God forgive me, and I hope one day you will, too. Your father is a good man, with the sea in his blood, and if I'd had the chance to christen you, I would have named you Maryanne.

I wish you a good and happy life.
Goodbye my precious, Maryanne.
Your mother,
Catherine

Tamara read the letter three times, wiping tears from her eyes. Then, folding it, she placed it back inside the envelope and uncontrollably wept.

When Tamara awoke, the news that Ola and Jono were not her parents flooded her brain. She got dressed and looked into the cracked mirror; her eyes were swollen and red, and she wished she had never come back to Galway. Flour, salt and buttermilk – provisions Meg had brought back – were still on the table along with the fish. They were still cold, and she put them into a dish.

Meg would expect her to gut the fish ready for their tea. But Tamara couldn't think straight. The cottage was freezing, the water in the wooden pail frozen. She cracked the ice with the heel of her boot and poured the icy water into the black kettle. She made a fire in the hearth and placed turf on top.

Meg's heavy snores came from the bedroom, and Tamara hoped she would sleep a while

226

longer. She cut herself a wedge of bread and drank some buttermilk from the can. It too, had bits of ice in. Only now did she recall the times she had felt different while she was growing up – other gypsy children making fun of her white skin; Ola telling her to take no notice, that they were jealous of her looks. The taunts had made her feel the odd one out and distracted her from learning.

Last night she had stripped herself of the gypsy bangles and removed the big looped earrings that she vowed never to wear again. She wrapped them in old sacking and placed them inside her case. She planned to sell them the first chance she got.

Loneliness cloaked her. With no idea who she was and no way of discovering who her mother was, she felt totally bereft.

The bedroom door was ajar and she looked in. A strong smell of poítin wrinkled her nose. Meg's snoring rocked the small bedstead and an empty pitcher lay on the table next to her. Tamara didn't blame her. Living alone in this God forsaken place was enough to drive anyone to drink.

Tamara pulled her coat on and ventured outside. The fog was dense across the fields. The hens clucked, but stayed huddled inside the wooden hut, and Tamara scooped up a couple of eggs. Doubts about who she was overshadowed everything.

She looked out across the dry stone walls that boxed the individual plots of land, and the biting wind cut across her face. Time appeared to stand still. She could hear the rams and sheep.

Shrouded in mist, they looked like ghosts moving slowly across the land. In the distance seagulls squawked, and she pictured them fighting for food along the beach, turning over seaweed with their beaks in hopes of a morsel. She loved the sea, but today she could neither see nor hear the rolling surf hissing in, covering the small sandy beach below them.

She turned and hurried back inside. What had her mother's life been like? Where had she given birth to her? Tamara's head ached with unanswered questions.

She thought about Kit, their lives so far apart. Would she ever see him again? If only Meg would speak English, she might confide in her and persuade her to help her get away. It was worth a try. She had nothing to fear from the gypsies now, and Jake Travis could go to hell. She had her life to live and she wasn't going to waste any more of it.

It was midday when Meg came into the room. Tamara's plans would only work with Meg's help. She knew Meg had money she made from the produce she grew. Tamara had seen her stash it away underneath her thin mattress. Thinking of ways to placate the old woman, she warmed her porridge and placed it on the table in front of her. No matter what time Meg got up, she insisted on porridge.

Tamara sat opposite her, ignoring Meg's look that said to get on with the chores.

'Can't you talk to me in English, Meg?'

'If ye'd gone to the local scoil like other gypsy

childer, ye'd a learnt your Gaelic.'

'Well, I'm sorry I didn't.'

Meg supped the porridge from the bowl and wiped her hand across her mouth.

'I want to get the train to Dublin, but I have no money.' Tamara pressed her back into her chair and waited for Meg's reaction.

'God and his Holy Mother, why?'

'I want to find work, take lodgings there.'

Meg's eyes narrowed to slits and she placed her boney elbows on the table. 'What do ye mane? Are ye forgettin' why yer're here? That blighter will stop at nothing. If ye'd not run away in the first place, all this would ha' been sorted.'

Tamara sighed and folded her arms. 'So, if I'd married that scoundrel, everyone would have had an easy life, is that it? Well, I'm sorry I disappointed you.'

'It's only a matter of time before he comes up here.'

'Well, surely I should go.'

'Ye've no need to go. I've got a shotgun.'

That didn't surprise her. Most isolated farms kept one in case of raids. Tamara leaned in close. 'Did you never want to get away, Meg, see what's on the other side of the ocean?'

'The world's the same wherever ye go, *mavourneen*.' She opened a small tin, pinched the snuff between finger and thumb, and sniffed it up her nostrils. Spilling fragments of the powdery substance down her front, she wiped her nose with the back of her hand. Tamara held her head in her hands. Her grandmother used to take snuff, too. What it was supposed to do, she had no idea.

Tamara folded and unfolded her arms as the old woman kept her in suspense. 'Will you help me or not?'

'You're a strange one, not at all like the rest of the gypsy clan. Gypsy women never work outside the home. Why aren't you happy with that?'

'I want to do things my way.'

Meg chewed a crust of bread. 'What've ye done with your trinkets?'

'They're with the rest of my stuff.'

'Taken agen them, have ye?'

Tamara shrugged. God only knew what this crafty old woman would wheedle out of her if she didn't get away. If Meg wouldn't help her, she would have no choice but to wait two weeks for the cart. Whatever happened, she wasn't staying here.

'How much do ye need?'

The question jolted Tamara. She swallowed nervously. 'Fare to Dublin and lodgings when I get there.'

Meg scraped back her chair and went into the bedroom. Through the open door, Tamara saw her lift her mattress and take out a pouch heavy with coins.

'The train, is it?' She came back and sat down again. 'Why can't ye wait for the cart? You're aiming high, missy. I hope you know what you're doing.'

'I'll be fine.'

'Two guineas should cover it then.' Meg reached up to the mantle for paper, ink and a quill. She wrote down the amount including interest. Then she wrote it out again and asked Tamara to sign

230

each copy.

'What for?'

'You want the money, don't ye?' Tamara nodded. 'It manes I loan ye two guineas and you pay me back two guineas and four shillin' besides.'

Tamara was taken aback, but had no choice but to agree. Meg counted the money out into her hand. 'I won't be chated mind, so ye better not forget what ye owe me.'

'I won't.'

'Before I give ye leave with my money,' Meg said, 'ye must clear it with Ola and Jono, the ones who brought ye into the world.'

CHAPTER THIRTY-FOUR

In Covent Garden, Jake Travis sipped his beer while reading the *London Herald*. The headlines made sad reading for Londoners. All around him, words of condolences were being passed from one individual to another. Travis read the news with indifference. He finished his drink, folded his paper, and decided to go somewhere less dismal. Outside, the paper boy called: 'Read all about it! Old Queen dies!'

Travis returned to his hotel, where work was underway to turn the premises into a high-class brothel. After a quick word with the foreman, Travis went to his room and settled into his armchair to finish reading the newspaper. He checked the *Herald* every day since Tamara's escape, and found nothing to link her to any crimes, petty or otherwise, committed around the London area.

Dressed as she was, she would have steered clear of crowded places. No one appeared to have seen her; even money hadn't loosened their tongues. Would she have gone to Ireland? The gypsies would shun her, so he had to assume she was still in London, scatting about, stealing to keep food in her belly. London was a dangerous place with nowhere to go. He must find her before she became second-hand goods.

He stood up and stretched his legs. This room had bad memories and he wished he'd played things differently with Tamara. He walked across to the window, and looked down onto the cobbled courtyard. How she had managed to climb down there was still a mystery to him. He shook his head. It took courage, and it was a stark reminder of how much she hated him.

When he found her, he'd show her how nice he could be, wine and dine her at the best restaurants. And sooner, rather than later, otherwise she could well present him with another man's bastard. Until then, he had more than enough beauties to amuse him whenever he wanted. In fact, several refined young ladies had been brought to his attention. He felt disappointed that not one of them had Tamara's spirit. Most of them were correct, identically curled, and had not much rattling around in their empty heads.

Sighing, he pulled his thoughts back to more important matters. He read Lilly Morgan's letter again. In it, she made clear she would only work for him if the price was right. He had drawn up a contract readily agreeing to her demands, and felt lucky to have secured someone with Lilly's experience. He could always change her mind to see things his way once he had a chance to wine and dine her. He'd heard she was a hard taskmaster; well then, they had something in common. She was arriving this evening and he was looking forward to meeting her very much indeed.

Travis had expected a shrivelled-up violet, but instead he found himself greeting a dignified woman who had looked after her appearance. In spite of face powder and rouge that gave her face a warm glow, he could see the neat one-inch scar on her left cheek.

Travis dropped her luggage in the hall.

'It was so kind of you to collect me, Jake.'

'My pleasure!'

Lilly removed her dark blue, fur-lined cloak and gloves, and handed them to Travis. She wore a blue velvet, full-length walking suit, with swirls of embroidery along the hem, cuffs, and along the edge of the long jacket and lapels. Her wide-brimmed hat, festooned in white feathers, covered one side of her face.

'I'd like to freshen up first,' she said, 'then take a look around.'

'Of course.' He nodded to Sophia, who was waiting in the doorway and came forward. 'Sophia will show you to your room.'

Travis followed behind, carrying the heavy cases,

and noting the elegant gait of the older woman. Oh yes, he had made a good choice.

Later, when Travis accompanied Lilly around the premises, she had removed her hat. Her perfect coiffure hairstyle, plaited in a circle around the top of her head, resembled a halo.

'A well proportioned property, Jake, good-sized rooms and windows that let in plenty of light.' She smiled. 'It's so difficult to obtain a good property to let in the middle of London.'

'I'm glad you approve.' He smiled.

She walked in front of him along the wide corridor. She paused and glanced over her shoulder. 'The whole place needs modernising.'

'Of course. I'll leave the colour scheme to you, but there will be a budget.'

'Just the one small lift, is it?' She placed her hand on the lift door, opened it, and looked inside.

'Just enough room for two persons,' Jake said. 'May I call you Lilly?'

'You may, for now.'

Travis frowned. 'Are you still considering?'

'That depends.' She continued to walk back down. 'I have one or two clauses I would like added to my contract. I assume you have one drawn up?' She inclined her head. 'Shall we go downstairs and discuss terms?'

That afternoon, sitting in his room, Jake Travis was still reeling from Lilly Morgan's directness. This business of a contract had left him wondering what he was getting into. One of Lilly's conditions was that once the business was up and

running, she would accept six monthly incre-
ments to her salary, depending on how well the
business was doing. And she wanted no interference from him on what she deemed necessary
for the welfare of herself and her girls.

She was not what he had expected at all. And
he was not used to anyone, least of all a woman,
laying down terms of business to him. In need of
a whiskey, he refrained from pouring one; he
needed to keep his wits about him for the evening
ahead.

Later, dressed in a white silk shirt, satin waistcoat with matching cravat and dark striped suit,
he glanced at his reflection then sprayed on a
musky fragrance. He slicked back his hair, picked
up his coat, hat and gloves, and went downstairs
to wait for Lilly.

At the exclusive English restaurant in Soho, the
waiter directed them to a secluded corner table.
Travis removed his outer garments and, together
with Lilly's white stole, handed them to the
waiter. After perusing the wine list, Jake asked for
a good house wine agreeable to her; it was not yet
the time to be ordering champagne. This woman
had him at an awkward disadvantage. He wished
now that he had interviewed others, but Lilly
Morgan had come highly recommended by a
trusted friend.

A slow smile crossed his face when he glanced
across at his dinner partner. Her appearance
was in total contrast to the businessperson he
had met earlier. Her smile charmed and
delighted him, and she appeared to be in a
frivolous mood. She wore a black velvet gown

with a pearl necklace and matching dangling earrings, her fair hair loose around her shoulders. Jake found himself staring at the lovely picture she made. Her white breasts swelled above the darkness of her gown.

He spoke with careful politeness, only once allowing his eyes to fall below the top of her head.

'Of course,' she said, 'you may find my conditions unusual, Jake.' Then she added, 'I intend to make your business the best for miles around.' She sipped her wine.

'That's the least I'd expect, Lilly.' He took a fair gulp of his drink, feeling the amber liquid burn his throat. 'I didn't think we'd be discussing business tonight, Lilly.'

'Of course,' she smiled. 'But, it does make pleasant conversation, don't you agree?'

Their food arrived and as they tucked into the finest cuisine of roast rack of lamb, fresh green vegetables, and mouth-watering baby carrots, Lilly said, 'I'll place some advertisements tomorrow.'

Jake speared a baby carrot. 'I have to leave tomorrow, so I can safely leave things in your capable hands.' He popped the carrot into his mouth and pulled a card from his inside pocket. 'You can reach me here if you need me.'

She studied the card. 'You're going to Ireland?'

He nodded. He was expecting a shipment of brood mares, a pack of gypsy horses, and a young black stallion, as well as a purebred Arabian pony he had bought as a special wedding gift for Tamara.

Lilly pushed vegetables onto her fork. 'Have you

thought of a suitable name for the new venture?'
Before he could answer, she suggested, 'How
about The Pleasure House?'

CHAPTER THIRTY-FIVE

Tamara arrived in Dublin carrying all she owned
in a small suitcase. She found life fast in comparison to Galway, where everyone dallied. Here,
they went about their business as if they hadn't a
moment to lose. She had to charge across Sackville Street for fear of a tram running her down.

She wore boots, a warm coat, and a navy
bowler hat trimmed with white ribbon, her red
hair bunched up underneath. Her future now in
her own hands, she was keen to erase all traces of
her gypsy life.

She bought the *Evening Herald* from the newspaper carrier on the corner, and was saddened to
read of the death of Queen Victoria. She scanned
the list of rooms to let. After careful enquiries,
she found herself walking down Hardwicke
Street to a lodging house with a vacant sign in
the window.

She stopped outside and looked up at the red
brick three-storey house with its lace curtains. It
was mid-morning and two women huddled in
shawls chatted over the railing while small
children played around their feet. They turned
their heads to look at Tamara. She stepped up to
the brown Georgian door with a skylight, took a

deep breath, and knocked. The door opened at the first knock and a thin woman in her fifties, with a long angular face and wearing a long white apron, stood before her. 'Can I help you, dear?'

Tamara pointed to the newspaper advert. 'I'm here about the room.'

'Oh, dearie me! I'd clean forgot. Come in, won't you?' She opened the door wider and Tamara stepped into the hall. It was stark and felt colder than outside. 'I'll take you up in a minute. Have you come far?'

'Galway.'

'Sure, I could tell. Ah sure, it makes a change from the Dublin brogue. It's two shillin' and I only do breakfast on Sunday mornings,' she sniffed. 'If you only want the room, it's a shillin' and six-pence.'

Sighing, Tamara dropped her case at her feet.

'Now you sit here a minute while I finish seeing to one of me lodgers. I won't be a tick.'

She hurried away towards the back of the house. Tamara perched on the basket chair, glancing around at the green paint peeling from the walls and the threadbare carpets, and hoped she had not run from one bad situation into another.

The woman, who called herself Mrs. Kennedy, explained to Tamara where to find the lavatory and the water tap outside in the yard. Tamara nodded and followed her up the stairs to the top of the house. The room was small; hardly enough space to swing a rabbit, but the single bed along the wall looked okay next to a tallboy with a

mirror on top. There was a small table underneath the window with an enamel bowl for washing.

'Oh,' the woman laughed, 'I forgot to ask your
name, love.'

'Maryanne.' It felt nice to say her proper name
and she liked it.

The woman frowned. 'Well, Maryanne, you'll
have to supply your own soap, and wash your
own bedding before you leave. How long do you
want the room for?'

Tamara hesitated. 'Can I let you know later,
when I've tried for work?'

'Ye can, but ye still have to pay me for now.
Well, do you want it?'

'Yes, sure it's grand.' In spite of the smell of
damp that permeated the room, Tamara handed
over the money.

'And a week up front,' the woman interjected.
Tamara had not expected to have to hand over
three shillings before she had a job. 'Here's the
key to the door. I'll not charge ye for that, although some would. You can lock it if you want,
although ye've no worries on that score.' She
sniffed again. 'I only have dacent folk in my
house, clerks and the like. You look like a smart
girl yourself. What kind of work are you looking
for?'

'Shop work,' she said, off the top of her head.

'Well, I'll want paying either way.' She turned
the ring on her finger. 'I'm a widow woman and
I won't be messed about.'

Tamara nodded.

Alone in the room, Tamara shook her head.

This one was as tight as old Meg was. Too tired to think of anything but sleep, she removed her hat and coat, undid the laces of her boots to ease them off her feet, and flopped down on top of the bed.

She woke several hours later shivering, got underneath the covers, and went back to sleep.

Tamara woke refreshed. Through her window, she could see out over rooftops and the dome of a church. The damp fusty smell made her cough and, in spite of the cold, she opened the bottom half of the window. She picked up the ceramic jug and went downstairs, filled it with cold water and brought it back up to the room.

With no hairbrush, she gave her hair a vigorous shake before pinning it up as neatly as she could, and put on her hat. She shrugged her arms into her coat and glanced in the mirror. She wished she had a little rouge or lipstick to rub into her pale cheeks, but she would have to do for now. Then she left her lodgings to search for work and find something to eat, before she died of hunger.

Not far from Hardwicke Street, she came across a church in Gardiner Street. It was some place to go out of the cold. Tamara found the inside was similar to many of the churches in Galway, with statues of Mary, St. Joseph and the Sacred Heart, and a beautiful painting of St. Frances. Candles burned brightly in front of each statue and women in headscarves muttered in prayer. Tamara placed a penny into the box and lit a candle in front of St. Joseph's statue. She prayed for Catherine, the mother she hoped to meet one day, and for Kit. How she missed him. They knew so little about each other. How would they ever find each other? It brought a tear to her eye. If only she'd gone back to the circus with Kit when he had asked her to.

Regrets were pointless. She must get on with the situation she found herself in and earn some money. Genuflecting, she left the church.

Tamara had no luck at any of the big stores. They all said they same thing, retail experience was what they were looking for. With no prospects, she would have to lower her sights, maybe try for work on a street stall. She certainly wouldn't turn her nose up at anything she was offered.

It was lunch time and, although she had stopped earlier at the Pillar cafe and bought herself a plate of colcannon and sausages, and buttered brown bread washed down with a pot of Lipton's tea, she felt hungry again. Her adrenaline was drained but she couldn't afford to eat again today. It had cost her an arm and a leg and she was counting the cost already.

It was growing dark when she picked up a copy of the evening paper, determined to find work before returning to her lodgings. She huddled in a doorway to read the job vacancies. In the small ads, she read an advertisement for a picker, whatever that meant, in a tailor's off Dorset Street. Pleased to find it was only a short walk from Sackville Street, she arrived outside the single storey building, and found a scratched and dusty brown door with a small window on the right. She guessed it might have been a shop once.

Taking a deep breath, she knocked. The door opened straight onto the pavement, to the clatter of sewing machines. Her heart sank. She had never used one in her life. 'I've come about the picking job.'

The woman looked her up and down. Then she turned back into the dismal room with its low ceiling where three other women sat, their feet working the treadle. 'She's come about the picking job.' They all laughed.

Tamara had no idea what was funny and felt her face redden until a potbellied man with a tuft of grey hair on his big head pushed in front of the woman. 'I'll see to this one,' he said, smiling appreciatively at Tamara. 'Come in, come in. I'm Mr. Stapleton. So, have ye done this kind of work before?'

She nodded and stepped inside. She could hardly admit to never having set foot inside a factory in her life. The smell of dust and oil made her cough. The floor was littered with men's heavy overcoats and she stepped carefully so as not to stand on anything.

Stapleton turned to a young girl sitting on the floor. 'Get them bloody coats finished and off the floor, or you'll be going home with no wages on Friday,' he bellowed.

Tamara sighed. The rattle of four machinists in such a small room hurt her ears.

'This way,' he said and she followed him into a small untidy office with a rolled-top desk, the drawer hanging open to reveal a half empty bottle of whiskey. A newspaper lay open on a table alongside the window, beside ledgers and

242

bits of paper.

'I'll give ye one and thrupence a week until I see how fast you can work.'

Tamara bit her bottom lip. 'I was hoping for a bit more,' she said. 'I need the money.' She regretted the admission when she noticed the way he looked at her, sweat breaking out on his fat face.

'Well, now. Yer such a pretty girl, an' all. I'll stretch to another thrupence, but ye'll work fer it, I can assure ye.'

'When can I start?'

'Be here tomorrow morning at seven sharp.'

Tamara nodded and found her own way out.

CHAPTER THIRTY-SIX

After a week of working at the tailor's, Tamara found the workers as coarse and bad-mannered as their boss. One of them, a tubby fresh-faced woman, delighted in making Rosie cry and whispering about Tamara. Tamara had gritted her teeth. Fear of losing her job kept her from retaliating.

She left for work at the same time each morning and gave herself enough time to arrive before Stapleton stood in the doorway, checking his pocket watch. Tamara soon realised he was just the sort who would dock wages for a minute's lateness. The work was back-breaking, sitting on the cold floor with their backs to the wall, picking the tightly-tacked threads from the garments.

When Tamara asked him for scissors, he glared at her. 'Bloody hell. Use yer fingers. It's what I pay ye for.'

This morning, her breath clouded in front of her as she walked along Sackville Street, dreading the day ahead. The room was dark and stuffy, and it was impossible to see the stitches on the dark coats. Three of the machinists wore glasses, which was no surprise. How they could sew in a straight line in semi-darkness was a mystery, but then no one checked what they had done.

This morning, before going inside the dark den, Tamara took a deep breath to remind herself that it was only for a short time. Rosie arrived just behind her and hung her thin shabby coat on a nail behind the door. She nudged Tamara, casting her eyes towards the huge pile of garments halfway up the wall. 'They must have got here at six,' Tamara murmured.

'Get that tea made and 'urry up about it,' a woman yelled.

Rosie rolled her eyes. They were a miserable bunch, Tamara thought, and treated Rosie like a servant.

'You start picking, I'll make the tea.' Tamara took the copper kettle outside and filled it. Then she placed it on the primus stove. Lining up the mugs, she could hear the older women bitching about Rosie.

'Ye've got the new one skivvying for ye now, have ye?' The women laughed over the noise of the machines. Rosie didn't reply. Tamara wanted to lace their tea with something bitter; arsenic

244

came to mind. With no idea whether or not they took sugar, she spooned six sugars into each of the four mugs. She and Rosie weren't allowed one until eleven.

She placed the mugs down beside each machinist, careful not to spill tea on the garments, and walked away. None of them smiled or thanked her, and she sat down next to Rosie and began to pick the stitching from the labels of the coats, a nonchalant expression on her face.

'What the bloody 'ell...' The red-faced woman stood up. 'The silly bitch put sugar in this, a full bag, by the taste of it.'

'Oh, sorry! I had no idea,' Tamara said, and carried on working. The other three women cupped their hands around their mugs and began to sip their tea. Then they began to pull faces.

'There's a list pinned to the wall. The culchie can't read,' the fat woman sneered.

Tamara couldn't hold back. She flew at the woman, pulled her hair from its bun and pushed her to the floor, knocking the breath out of her. The others hooped and hollered as the pair rolled around on top of the garments, Tamara's arms and legs flaying in all directions.

Rosie hunkered down in the corner, her hands covering her head, when Mr. Stapleton walked in. He stood staring a while at the two women, as if enjoying the spectacle before separating them. Tamara, her curly hair now resembling a bird's nest, brushed herself down while the other woman – her hair bedraggled and hanging down her back – sidled towards her machine. Tamara stood still, her hands by her side.

'I'm not going to ask what this brawl is about,' Mr. Stapleton huffed. 'Knowing you women, it could be any number of things. Get back on those bleedin' machines, and no tea break.'

He beckoned to Tamara. Her pulse still racing, she followed him into the pokey office with her head bowed. She felt ashamed of her behaviour, but no one was going to get away with calling her an illiterate culchie.

Stapleton sighed and loosened the jacket that bulged across his fat bulk. 'As I said, I don't want to know what that was all about. You're a spirited young woman, but if this happens again, I'll sack you.'

'I'm sorry. It won't happen again,' she said.

'Well, we'll see.' He paused, and Tamara glanced up. She didn't like the way he was looking at her. 'Unless,' he went on, 'you were to work in here with me. Less chance of bother out there.'

She glanced around at the small messy office, with little space between the desk and the table. 'Doing what?'

'What you're doing now, and you can clean this place up at the same time. What do you say?'

'You want me to clean as well as help Rosie? Will there be more money in it?'

'You're a canny one if ever there was one.' He shook his head. 'Two bob, how's that? You can sweep the sewing room and clean the lav.' How could she refuse? An extra nine pence a week would get her back to London quicker.

'You'll pull your weight with the picking, mind? Is it a deal, then?'

Tamara hesitated. The thought of working with him made her skin crawl. But one shilling and six pence? She had already gone through half of Meg's money, in spite of buying only essentials.

Stapleton looked at his watch on the end of a silver chain. 'Well. Is it a deal?'

'Will you get them out there to stop tormenting Rosie?'

He leaned back, and she felt his gaze running down the contours of her body. She knew his type would do anything she asked if he thought he could have her. After her experiences with Flynn and Jake Travis, she knew full well the ways of men. This eejit was no different.

He sighed. 'Okay! I'll try. Now get those coats and bring them in here.'

That evening, Tamara arrived back at her lodgings later than usual. Mrs. Kennedy shook her head. 'You know, that boss of yours is getting cheap labour out 'f you.'

Tamara hung her coat up in the hall and turned round. 'What do you mean?'

'Sure, I thought he was short changing ye and had a word with a friend 'f mine. She works in the tailoring business, south 'f here.' She folded her arms. 'She's a seamstress and knows all the rates. The women there get three shilling for what you're doing and better conditions, too.'

'Really! He only pays Rosie a shilling.'

'The mean devil. What are ye going to do about it?'

Tamara sat down on the hall chair. 'I had a fall-out with one of the women and he's asked me to

247

do my work in his office as well as do the cleaning for two shillings.'

'Well, if ye have any sense, ye'll ask him for more money.'

'Oh, I will,' she said, running upstairs.

That night, Tamara lay in bed thinking. She wondered where her mother Catherine was now and if she would ever get to meet her. Her father was a seaman, that much she knew. A good man, her mother had said in her letter. Apart from Jono, she had only met two good men. One, she had admired and respected until he openly accused her of stealing his money; the other, she would love forever.

Before she fell asleep, she made up her mind to ask Stapleton for the going rate of three shillings a week. He might say no. However, she had a good idea what his answer would be. She was playing with fire, but all she could think about was getting back to London.

CHAPTER THIRTY-SEVEN

Kit found it hard to concentrate since Tamara's disappearance. He had tormented himself for weeks trying to find her, and finally he had to admit that perhaps she did not want him to. Eight weeks without a word was evidence enough. However, his love for her hadn't waned, and clouded everything, even his obligation to Billy.

Billy had been like a father to Kit most of his life; he'd cared for him, taught him everything he knew. When Billy remarried after the death of his first wife, Adelaide, Kit had been old enough to live his own life, but Billy still kept a watchful eye over him.

Kit knew only too well how Billy's mind worked, and the money turning up in Tamara's wagon would not convince him of her innocence. Someone would have to have planted it there. But who? It would be difficult to prove. To enter someone's wagon uninvited was a sackable offence.

Kit waited until late evening when he knew Billy would be relaxing with a whiskey before bedtime. As he rapped the circus boss's door, a whiff of tobacco smoke drifted through the open window.

'It's Kit. Can I come in?'

'Of course, boy.' Billy sat upright. 'Nothing wrong is there?'

Kit scratched his forehead and sat on the bench seat next to Billy.

The older man opened a box of cigars and offered one to Kit. 'Try one, lad?'

Kit shook his head. Billy leant forward, lifted the globe from the oil lamp and held his cigar to the flame. Smoke swirled above his head. 'What's on your mind?'

'I know you've taken against Tamara and I'm here to try and change your mind.'

The older man frowned. 'I have a feeling I'm not going to like this.'

Clearing his throat, Kit removed the small sack

of money from his pocket. 'Is this the money that went missing?'

Billy took the bag and emptied the coins onto the table. Then he looked at Kit. 'Where've ye found this?'

'In the wagon you asked me to move.'

'I knew it. The thieving gypsy.' He placed his cigar in the tray and puckered his lips.

'How can you say that? If she stole the money, why didn't she take it with her? I hoped she would come back and clear up the misunderstanding. I knew you'd react like this. It's the reason I hung on to the money.'

Billy's fist came down on the table, making the coins skip. 'Now you listen to me, young feller. There's been no misunderstanding. Do you hear me?'

Kit straightened his shoulders. 'I hear you. But you're wrong. If Tamara is a thief, as you say, she'd have come back to collect it.'

'Oh, there's still time. She'll be back.' Billy collected up the coins and placed them back in the bag.

'I refuse to believe that.' Kit got to his feet.

'Well, you're a fool.'

'That may well be, but I'll not judge her until I hear it from her own lips.'

'And how, pray do you intend to do that?'

'I don't know. But I intend to find her.'

'Well, we're on the road again soon. So, think on, Kit. I've already signed you up for the next six weeks.'

Kit sighed and looked at Billy. 'You're wrong about Tamara, and I intend to find her.'

'If you insist on this foolish whim,' Billy said, 'you'll be the cause of this circus being off the road for the foreseeable future. And all because of a gypsy girl who couldn't be trusted.'

CHAPTER THIRTY-EIGHT

Travis arrived back at his farm in Connemara in plenty of time to oversee the delivery of his brood mares. The two black stallions and the Arabian pony were due in a couple of days. He stayed overnight at the farm, but he couldn't sleep.

It gave him plenty of time to reassess his life. At forty-six, he could not remember a time when he had not despised his older sibling. Bruce had squandered his inheritance, then had had the good fortune to marry money – a woman Jake himself had desired and wanted. After years of struggle to accumulate his own wealth, Travis would rather leave it to a nunnery than see his brother get his hands on it. He would make sure that never happened.

Too young to remember his mother, Jake recalled a succession of nannies and a father with little time to spend with his sons. Even now, he still remembered the harsh punishments meted out by his father whenever he disobeyed, while Bruce could do no wrong.

Jake regretted messing things up with Tamara. He had taken his frustrations out on her, but he was still convinced that one way or another his

251

arrangement would work. She had run away from him twice. This time, when he found her, he would show her a more caring side; anything to further his plan.

The following morning, he left instructions with O'Leary, the head stable man. 'I'll be back tomorrow to oversee the delivery of the stallions.'

'Fair enough, Mr. Travis.'

Mounting his horse, Travis rode off in the direction of Galway, intent on reaching the gypsy camp by noon. He was keen to discover if Jono and Ola had had contact with Tamara, while at the same time collect two months' rent. These gypsies were proving more trouble to him than they were worth. If he couldn't have Tamara as his bride, there was no reason to allow them to continue renting his land.

He liked to surprise them by arriving when they least expected him; he enjoyed seeing the fear on their faces. It was still light as he approached the camp, and the women and kids ran to hide. The rest cowered with guilty expressions on their filthy faces. The only one who had ever stood up to him was Jono, and if the older man had no news regarding Tamara, Jake would hold him responsible for the eviction of his clan.

Ola was outside washing clothes in a round galvanized tub, rubbing the clothes up and down on a wooden scrubbing board. She glanced up and then called to Jono, who was loading his cart with pieces of piping and scrap metal ready to take out the following morning. He came to her side.

'It's you, is it?' Jono said. 'A dirty bog rat can't

stay hidden for long.' Jono took a few deep breaths and found it difficult to conceal his feelings of rage at what Tamara had told him.

Travis dismounted and led his horse to a post and secured it.

'I'm going to ask you a question, Jono. Think carefully before giving me the wrong answer.' He could see fear in Ola's eyes. 'You're forgetting your manners, Ola. Aren't you going to invite me in?'

She hesitated, dried her hands on her apron, then the two men followed her inside. Travis could tell by the woman's body language that she knew something. She busied herself pouring him a drink of poitín, and one for her husband. Her fingers trembled as she passed the drinks.

Travis swallowed his. 'Now, tip up the rent. I hope you've got it all. I'm not a charity.'

Jono unlocked a box he kept underneath the cupboard, took out a canvas bag, and handed it to Travis, who threw it in the air and caught it. 'It feels light, are you sure it's all here?'

'Count it if you want.'

'Now, to the other reason I'm here. Where is she?' He made himself comfortable, placing his muddy boots up on Ola's cushions. He observed restraint from Jono, and Ola wringing her hands.

'You've been away two months. Are you telling me you haven't found Tamara?' Jono said through gritted teeth. He took a swig of his drink.

'I did, but she escaped me again. This is the only place she can be. Now where is she?' He stood up, towering over them.

'We haven't seen her in weeks, and when we do,

253

you won't get within an inch of her again.' He opened the door. 'Now go on, get out! We have to work for our livin'.'

'You're lying!' Travis bellowed. 'Where are you hiding her?' He grabbed the jug of poitín, and poured himself a generous helping. Then he pushed the door and slammed it shut, almost taking it off its hinges. 'Now think on this. *No Tamara! No tenancy!* You'll be responsible for all those poor beggars being evicted off my land?' His cold eyes glared at Ola, who had started preparing rabbit stew in the corner of the wagon. 'If you refuse to cooperate, I'll force you off my land.'

Jono faced him. 'Go on. Do your worst, Travis. There's other land.'

'I think you'll find my name is on it.' With an amused smile, he staggered over to Ola. 'I know you've heard from her. And one way or another, I'm not leaving until you tell me where she is.'

As the drink took hold, Travis became more abusive. 'Is there nothing to eat in this God forsaken place? Have some of that slop sent over to my wagon. I'm going for a lie down and when I come back, I want answers.' He stood up, his large bulk swaying as he stomped out.

Travis ate the rabbit stew the young gypsy boy brought to him, with a thick wedge of oat bread. It tasted good, and afterwards tiredness overtook him. He woke a couple of times with stomach cramp and slept late. When he finally woke, he dragged himself out of the bed and glanced at his watch.

'Hell's fire.' He pulled on his boots. There was no time now to intimidate Ola and Jono again. He must get back to the farm. He trusted no one, and liked to oversee the horses before accepting and signing for them. As he rode out, he noticed the surprised look on Jono's face.

'Don't worry. I'll be back,' Travis yelled. 'And wherever you're hiding Tamara, I'll find her.'

As he rode away, he had already convinced himself that they knew something. Ola had given it away by not enquiring about her daughter as soon as he rode in. Oh yes, they had been in touch with her, alright.

He rode his horse along the windswept beach, kicked its belly with his stirrups, then raced the stallion along the deserted strand. It felt good to breathe in the sea breeze after the confines of London. The horse reared up and whinnied, forcing him to ride at a slower pace. The blustery wind blew around his head, making him wish he had not had his long hair cut short.

He shivered and pulled his collar up around his neck, when a sudden dizziness made him sway and he gripped the reins to stop himself toppling from his horse. Lack of proper food, he guessed. The rabbit stew the gypsy boy had brought to his wagon had given him the runs during the night. The little shit must have poisoned him. His energy waned, but he kept on along the narrow lanes, feeling a growing exhaustion, until he spotted the light from the tavern up ahead.

Anxious to reach it, he spurred the horse on. Perhaps a tankard of ale would settle his stomach. He tethered his horse, leaving it to drink from the trough. A dim light flickered through the window. He knew the place well, but he hadn't drunk here in years. He pushed open the door to the smell of tobacco smoke and spilled ale.

A hushed silence descended as soon as he stepped across the threshold. One of the locals was singing a ballad in Gaelic. A dog peed on the sawdust floor, whimpered, and crawled underneath a table.

Travis removed his heavy coat and hung it up on a hook. A couple of anglers and three locals having a drink at the bar stopped talking and gave him a sideways glance, but made no attempt to speak to him. Then they took their drinks and moved to the far corner of the room. Travis smiled. They would have had their fill of gossip about his runaway bride.

'Sure 'tis a bitter wind that blows out there the day, sir. What can I get ye, Mr. Travis?' the bartender asked.

'Ale, and be quick about it.' Travis slumped down at a table and placed his head in his hands. The bartender brought over a full tankard and put it down next to him.

'The missus and I were sorry to hear that the wedding was called off,' the barman said. 'A fine fellow like yourself could have your pick o' women.'

Travis supped his drink. 'Leave me be, can't you?' Didn't these people have anything better to gossip about?

Seeing the mood he was in, the barman glanced across at his wife and went back behind the bar. His wife went across to Travis. 'You know, you don't look too grand. Would you like to lie down in the back for a while?'

He didn't answer and she left him alone.

The drink gave him the trots. Staggering to his feet, he headed outside to the lavatory. The cold cut through him and he was glad he was wearing one of his thick jerseys. When he came back, he could not stop himself shivering.

'Ye've caught a chill, Mr. Travis,' the woman said. 'You need to rest.' She picked up his coat and directed him into their small living room behind the bar. Travis felt too ill to protest.

'Ye'll be all right in here.' She sat him down in an armchair in front of the open turf fire. 'I'll see you're not disturbed.' She placed a rug over his knees and his coat on top, and went back to the bar, closing the door behind her.

Travis leaned back and closed his eyes. He no longer felt dizzy, just cold. This was a huge embarrassment to him. He had never been sick a day in his life, but right now he felt so tired he would have slept on the stone floor. He regretted eating the rabbit stew and, when he got back to the camp, he would string the kid up by his feet. His eyes grew heavy and he slept.

He woke when the woman came back into the room. 'How ye feelin', sir? Would ye like something to eat now?'

'No,' he waved his hand. 'I'm fine.' He got to his feet, flexed his broad shoulders, and placed a sovereign into the woman's hand. 'Keep the change.'

'Thanks, sir.'

'What time is it?'

'It's late, sir. The bar's closed. You've been asleep for hours.'

'Why didn't you wake me? You *stupid* woman!' He put his hand to his head. This was a nightmare. 'I've missed an important delivery.' He shrugged into his overcoat and pulled the collar up around his neck.

'I'm sorry. If I'd known, I'd have woken ye.'

He swore and made for the door.

'Ye don't remember me, do ye?'

Travis took a deep breath. If she was propositioning him, he didn't have the inclination. He shook his head. Then he glanced back over his shoulder. She was folding the blanket and placing it over the back of the chair. He narrowed his eyes. 'Should I?'

'Well, it's been a long time.'

He was in no mood for guessing games.

'I'm married now, sir, but you would have known me when I was Myra, Myra Kelly. Mean anything to ye now?'

Her husband, who was spreading fresh sawdust across the floor, paused to look up. 'Ye don't want all that raking up again, love.'

'Hang on! You ... you were Catherine's maid.' How could he not have realised?

'Like I said, it's been a long time.'

'I hope you've kept your side of the bargain, woman?'

'I've never told a livin' soul, sir.' She glanced towards her husband, who was wiping down the bar. 'Exceptin' me 'usband, like.'

'Good. It's got to stay that way for a while longer.' He sat down again, his energy waning.

'Have you set eyes on Tamara recently?'

'Well, not this long while.' She sat down opposite him, her elbow on the table. 'Don't you think the girl might be interested in knowing who she is?'

'No. I don't.'

She began to fidget with her hands, twisting her ring around her thin finger. 'Look, sir. I was sworn to secrecy seventeen years ago. You're a man of means and what you and your brother paid me at the time was a pittance.'

Travis glared at her. 'So, you want more money, is that it?' He sat forward and gripped her arm. 'You know where she is, don't you?'

'Let go of me.'

The woman's husband came over and glared at Travis. 'Lay a finger on my wife again and you'll rue the day, mister. I don't care who ye are. That beautiful young girl has a right to know the truth.'

Travis reached out and gripped him around the throat. 'Why? What do you know? Have you seen her?'

The bartender struggled to speak and lashed out with his fists.

'Let him go or I'll break my silence!' the woman screamed. Travis released the man and stood up, his eyes wide and bloodshot.

'Threatening me won't shut my mouth,' the bartender croaked, massaging his neck. 'And if it hadn't been for my wife's trust, that girl would have known who she was a long time ago. Now, unless you make it worth our while, I can't guarantee keeping silent.'

Travis threw three sovereigns on the table. The

bartender glanced towards his wife. 'Make it five,' he said, still kneading his throat.

Desperate to keep Tamara's parentage from her until his plans were in place, Travis complied. Then he leaned in close. 'Betray me, and I'll have this business closed down.'

'You're as mean as your brother ever was,' the woman said. 'He would have killed that infant if the mistress hadn't instructed me what to do.'

'Cross me and you'll both find out which of us is the meanest.' Travis scrambled unsteadily to his feet and made for the door. 'Now open up and let me out of here,' he growled.

CHAPTER THIRTY-NINE

Back in Dublin, Tamara started work half an hour earlier to do the cleaning before the others arrived. It was a thankless job and no one took any notice. Within minutes of the women starting up the machines, the place resembled a scrap yard, with bits of material and dust flying everywhere.

She left the lavvy until last. It made her heave, and each morning she tied a piece of waste material across her mouth and nose before tackling it. She cleared Stapleton's office of empty whiskey bottles and discarded newspapers before starting work, knowing that the next day he would return to his slovenly ways. She didn't care as long as he paid her.

That morning, Tamara shrugged him off when he leaned over her shoulder as she unpicked the tacking, but he took no notice. His attitude infuriated her. 'Would you like to do the job yourself, Mr. Stapleton?'

'Well, of course not. I was just checking the batch number.'

'In that case, you can ask, and please don't sit so close.'

Smiling, he sat back in his chair. 'You're a smart girl. How would you like to come with me to collect the wages?'

She turned towards him, a frown on her face. She didn't expect to be working here much longer, but to get out in the fresh air was enticing. She shrugged, feigning disinterest. Her laid-back attitude appeared to surprise him. 'I thought you'd like to get out for a bit.'

'Well, of course I would, but why?'

'We could go together to the bank. One day I might trust you to go on your own.'

'Okay! Grand.'

'Good. We'll try it on Friday.' He lit his pipe and the smell of tobacco filled the small space. It made her cough, but he took no notice.

Anything was better than sitting in this smoke-filled cubbyhole with him. Time dragged, and when the machines went quiet for lunch, she went out and sat with Rosie.

'How ye getting on?' Rosie asked, unwrapping a jam sandwich.

'All right, but I hate being in there with him leering at me all the time.' Tamara munched a beef-dripping sandwich Mrs. Kennedy had made for her the night before.

'He gives me the creeps,' Rosie whispered. 'I hate going in there on me own, so I do.'

'I need the job and the extra money he pays me to do the cleaning.'

'How long will ye have to stay working in there?' She inclined her head towards the door.

'Not long.' Tamara was already counting the days. 'I'm leaving as soon as I have enough money, but keep it to yourself.'

'I'll miss ye.'

The other women sniggered and whispered amongst themselves. Then one said, 'Ye'd better watch that old fart. The married ones are the worst.'

On Friday, Stapleton took Tamara with him to the bank. She enjoyed the walk and the fresh air, in spite of the fine rain that fell, wetting her curls. It was the first time she had been inside a bank and she felt important, in spite of the surprised stares from the bank clerks. She stood next to Stapleton at the counter while he waited for the money in the usual currency from his bank account.

'Certainly, sir, I won't keep you a moment while I count it out.'

'This young lady may come in from time to time to pick the money up. I'll give her a written note to that effect.' Stapleton smiled at the cashier.

The bank clerk smiled at Tamara. It made her feel important and reminded her of the last time she had been trusted with money. Stapleton placed the money inside the brown leather shoulder bag, careful to pull the zip across.

Tamara had learned there was always a price to pay with men like Stapleton, a price she was not prepared to pay. She was saving herself for Kit, and thinking about him made her sad. It seemed like a lifetime since she had felt his kiss on her lips, and she longed to feel the thrill of that again. She hoped he still felt the same. The thought that he might have taken up with Zeema unsettled her.

When they got back, there was a Friday buzz in the sewing room. 'Don't forget I worked an extra half hour last week,' one of the women voiced.

'You'll get that next week,' Stapleton said, and ushered Tamara inside and closed the door. He pulled open the drawer and took a swig of whiskey, then he pushed two chairs together. 'You can sit here next to me and watch how it's done.'

'What about..?' She pointed to the pile of coats on the floor.

'Leave them for a minute.' He emptied out the money, leaning across Tamara, rubbing against her breast as he did so. She moved her chair away. He divided the money into the different coinage, ticked off each name, and passed the money – mostly coins – into her palm for her to place into the small brown packages. He held onto her hand as he did so. Tamara pulled her hand away and clicked her tongue.

She could hardly wait to be finished, but her boss appeared to linger, recounting the money when it wasn't necessary. He belched a gust of whiskey into her face. Tamara felt bile rise in her throat and, excusing herself, she rushed outside to the lavvy. When she returned, he had bagged it all up, apart from a few small coins. He placed hers down on the desk and went outside to distribute the wages. Tamara checked hers and then placed it inside her coat pocket.

It was ten minutes to lunchtime and, in order to keep occupied, Tamara gathered up the stained tea mugs and placed them into the washing-up bowl on the table.

'Leave that.' He placed his hand on her bottom.

'Get off.' She swept it away.

'You and me, we make a good team. If you're nice to me, I can offer you anything your little heart desires.' His fat belly pressed against her hip.

She pushed past him to the corner of the room, but he continued to harass her, backing her into a corner as he touched her breast.

'Get off me, you pervert.'

'Oh, don't be like that. We get on all right, don't we?'

'Where did you get that idea from?'

As he grabbed her around the waist, she lashed out at his fat body, aiming a kick that left him moaning and holding himself. He lost his balance and fell backwards, hitting his head on the corner of the desk. For a second Tamara panicked, thinking she might have killed him. But then he stirred, swearing profusely, unable to pull his fat bulk upright.

She made no effort to help him until two of the women rushed in. They glared at her and then down at Stapleton. One of them rushed to help him, but he shrugged her off and struggled to his feet.

Tamara was pulling on her coat.

'Hold on, you little tart,' he shouted.

Tamara turned and looked at him with disgust. 'You report me, and I'll tell your wife what you did.' She threw open the door. 'That man in there is a pervert.'

Rosie came towards her. 'Where are you going?'

'I'm leaving. Something you should do, too.' And she walked away, knowing she would never return.

CHAPTER FORTY

A few days later, Tamara was back in Covent Garden, knocking on the presbytery door of Corpus Christi. She tried to block out thoughts of Jake Travis. If he threatened her, or tried to abduct her again, she would leave word with Father Malone to inform the police. She had an ally in the priest, so she did not feel completely alone. The sour-faced housekeeper opened it.

'Oh. It's you, is it? It's true what they say about a bad coin.' She sighed. 'Well, ye'd better come inside then.'

Tamara ignored the unwelcome greeting. 'Is Father Malone at home?'

'He's in church.' She closed the door behind them. 'If you're planning on waiting,' she pointed her towards the parlour. 'I'll let you know when he can see you.' Her tone was cutting. A cup of tea would have been welcome, but Tamara guessed the woman was in no mood to show her any hospitality.

The room was as tidy as ever, and she ran her hand along the tops of the freshly polished chairs before settling in the armchair. Tired after the journey, her eyelids drooped and she could not help drifting off to sleep.

She woke as soon as Father Malone popped his head around the door. Her hair had fallen across her face and she hooked a curly strand behind her ear and sat upright.

'Hello,' he said, and shook her hand. 'It's nice to see you again.' He smiled.

'Hello, Father Malone.'

'What brings you back so soon?'

'It's two months, Father.' She opened her handbag and took out an envelope. 'I'm returning the money you loaned me. If it hadn't been for you, God knows what would have become of me.'

'I never expected the money back, child. I'd like you to hang on to it until you get settled.'

'No, please take it, Father.' She smiled and placed it into his hand.

'Look, you must be famished. I'll ask Miss O'Keefe to make us a pot of tea. Then you can tell me all about your travels. I'm free for the remainder of the morning.'

Over tea and fresh muffins, Tamara spoke privately to Father Malone. She told him everything that had happened from the moment she arrived back

266

in Galway, and of her shock discovery. He shook his head, dismay on his face.

'Keeping secrets never does anyone any good. All the same, credit must go to your gypsy parents. They did a grand job bringing you up. I've no doubt you'll want to find out where your real mother is, Tamara?'

'Oh, I'd love to, Father, after I find out if Kit still loves me.'

'Well, I guess you'll need to go to the circus, as he has no way of knowing where you are.' He sat back in his chair. 'Besides, you need to clear your name. I'll come along with you, if it will help.'

'Thanks, Father, but that won't be necessary.' She was not going anywhere near the circus until she had a job and somewhere to stay. It felt good to unburden herself to someone she trusted. She stood up. 'Thanks for the tea and cakes.' She placed her hand on her tummy. 'I feel quite full. Can I leave my case here, while I go over and see Tom Murray?'

'Well, sure you can. But you will still need to be vigilant. There's no telling where Jake Travis is hiding.'

'Oh, I will, Father. Besides, I'm not frightened anymore. I don't know why. But since I discovered who I am, I feel different. More in control, if that makes sense.'

'Well, you best stay here the night until you sort yourself out.'

'I'd be grateful. Thanks, Father.' He walked with her to the door. 'I wouldn't advise working on the market again.' He shook his head. 'Leave yourself open to all kinds of prey.'

'Oh, I'm not. Anyway, Murray wouldn't take me back. I just want to pick up my cloak.' She smiled. 'It has sentimental value. My grandmother gave it to me on my sixteenth birthday.'

'Well, your belongings will be safe here. God bless you, child,' he said, opening the presbytery door.

Tom Murray was busy unloading sacks of potatoes and didn't stop to listen, or even look up at Tamara as she tried to apologise for letting him down. He grunted and then told her he had no interest in her explanations. 'Well, if you won't listen to the truth, do you mind if I go upstairs and collect my belongings?'

'What belongings would that be then?' He stood in front of the storeroom, blocking her path. 'There's nothing belonging to you here.'

'Why? What have you done with them?' She had hidden the money she had saved for a room inside the ripped horsehair cushion of the sofa.

'There's nothing up there I tell ye. Now clear off, you're trespassing.'

'No.' She shook her head. 'I insist on taking a look.' She pushed past him and ran up the wooden stairs as Murray's voice echoed up the stairs behind her. A lump formed in her throat when she saw the room from where Jake Travis had kidnapped her. The broken window and the musty sofa were still surrounded with boxes and crates. There was nothing belonging to her in the room.

She rummaged deep inside the cushions, pulling the stuffing out with her hands until she found her money, but she found no trace of her belongings anywhere.

When she came back down, he said, 'Satisfied now, are ye? I've a good mind to call the coppers.' He emptied a basket of cabbages onto his stall, the roots still covered in soil.

'Have you thrown my things away?'

Tom Murray turned to look at her. 'I've not been up them stairs in years.' He paused. 'Some young circus feller came looking for ye. He was the last one up there.' He hauled sacks of potatoes from his cart. 'Now, leave me be, will ye?'

'Did he say he'd be back?'

'No. And he needn't bother.' He turned his back on her to serve a customer and Tamara walked away, her mind full of questions. The fact that Kit had come looking for her made her heart skip. If he didn't care, would he have done that? Oh, she hoped she was not building herself up for a fall, because in her heart, she knew she would never feel this way about anyone else.

CHAPTER FORTY-ONE

Travis arrived too late to oversee the remainder of the horses, but found them all in good condition and bedded down in the stables. Yes, he had a good man in O'Leary and should have trusted him, given him some credit.

The following morning, he woke to bright sunshine and felt refreshed after a surprisingly good night's sleep. While he ate a hearty breakfast of eggs and bacon served up by his housekeeper, he pondered on the previous day's events. He had no idea that Catherine's maid and her money-grabbing husband still lived in Ireland, or he would have paid them a visit sooner; much sooner. How long would they hold their tongues? He had to find Tamara and explain things to her. He was desperate to marry her now, take her with him to Spain and flaunt her in front of his brother.

He pulled on his black Wellington boots and went outside to the yard. In spite of the late February sunshine, there was a nip in the air. He buttoned his yard jacket across his ample chest and stood with his hands on his hips. He glanced at the workers busy in the yard and the field. He inhaled the farm smells that he loved, even the heap of horse manure outside the barn door already turning into fertiliser.

A great deal of work went on here, and he employed only the best; men he could trust to keep the place going while he was away. He walked down past the stables where two young men were grooming the mares, while another was mucking out the stables.

'Where's O'Leary?' Travis asked.

'Down in the bottom barn, sir.'

O'Leary was shoeing one of the stallions, tapping nails into the new shoe while a stable lad took a firm hold of the reins. The large barn was spotless, the stone floor still wet, when Travis walked in.

'I thought I'd be back in time yesterday,

O'Leary. You did well.'

O'Leary paused, nodded, and then carried on shoeing the horse.

'I have to go back into Galway tomorrow. I'll only be gone a day. Keep an eye on things here.'

'Aye, I will that, Mr. Travis. Ride carefully now.' He laughed. 'These stallions are getting through some shoes.'

Travis liked O'Leary. He wasn't a busybody. He did the job he was paid to do. As Travis turned to leave, his foot slipped from beneath him. He muttered a few expletives and splayed his hands to prevent himself falling backwards. But he fell forwards onto an upturned rake. The horses whinnied and O'Leary dropped the hammer and ran to him. Travis's hand was already stuck fast on the sharp points of the rake. Yelling a curse, he bit down hard on his bottom lip, making it bleed.

'Holy shit,' O'Leary said, and helped him into an upright position. 'I'm sorry, sir. Grit your teeth. I've got to free your hand quickly.'

Travis winced as O'Leary, as gently and as quickly as he could, eased the hand from the implement, then threw the rake aside. Two deep holes were clearly visible on the palm of Travis's right hand, blood flowing profusely from the wounds. O'Leary untied his neckerchief and wrapped it tightly around the hand. 'I'll help ye back to the house, sir. You'll need to have that looked at.'

Travis shoved him aside. 'Don't fuss. I'm fine, man.' He kicked over a bucket of water. 'Get this mess cleared up.'

Travis slept soundly after smoking opium, and in the morning, he repeated the dose. He felt little pain. His hand wrapped in a white bandage, he ate a bowl of porridge oats and read the day's newspaper.

Later that morning, a letter arrived from Lilly. All was going well at the brothel and business was good, she told him. It took him several attempts to write a reply and he cursed with annoyance. His hand stiff and sore, he only managed to scribble a few important instructions. Sealing the sparsely written note into an envelope, he left it for his housekeeper to post.

Exhausted after his ordeal, he sat back, his mind wild with thoughts of Tamara. He still believed Jono and Ola knew more than they were letting on. These gypsies could be devious. In spite of what he knew about Tamara's parentage, he had never divulged any of it to Jono and Ola. Had they known how he was connected, Jono would have taken a shotgun to him.

It was time he was getting back to Galway. Jono had had enough time to consider his options. Jake hadn't forgiven them for letting Tamara go, and he still believed that had they kept their mouths shut, they would be married now. She would be here with him, expecting the heir to his estate. Instead, she was wandering the country unchaperoned. Now it was payback time, and if he didn't get answers, he would not hesitate to carry out his threat to turn the whole flea-ridden lot of them off his land.

He arrived, feeling groggy, to the hostile stares of the gypsies. He felt cold; colder than he had ever felt. Some of the men walked towards him armed with pick axes. His hand throbbed and pain fogged his brain. The faces before him turned into caricatures of leprechauns with beards, as if he was having a bad dream. He rubbed his eyes and massaged his stiff, painful neck. Then, unable to stop himself falling, he toppled from his horse.

'He's drunk as a skunk,' someone said.

'Fetch Jono,' another said.

The last thing Jake remembered was being half-carried, half dragged, through the encampment.

'What is it?' Jono called, running towards them.

'It's Travis. What should we do with him?'

Ola said, 'Put him in his trailer. Let him sleep it off.'

Once they managed to get him inside, sweat was trickling from his brow. Voices echoed around him. He felt powerless.

'He's burning up,' Ola said, opening the window. In spite of her dislike for the man, she undid his heavy coat and unwound the scarf from around his neck. 'The dressing on his hand wants changing, but I'm damned if I'm going to do it.'

'Is he going to peg out?' someone asked.

'Do us all a favour,' one of the women added.

Jono stood looking down at Travis, feeling nothing except disgust at his treatment of Tamara. He had done nothing to make their life at the camp easy, only thwarted them at every turn. 'Come on, Ola. Leave him to get on with it.'

273

When Travis had not shown his face for days, one of the gypsy boys who took him food and water came running for Jono. As Jono and Ola arrived, Travis screamed out in pain, and his face went into spasms. Startled, Jono looked at Ola.

'What is it, Jono?'

'He's not drunk.' He turned to the frightened faces staring in at the door. 'Mother of God! Get the God-damned doctor!' he yelled. 'He's got lockjaw!'

Travis was aware of muffled voices around his bed. He felt stiff all over. Someone raised his head and offered him water and a couple of aspirin. A grey curtain surrounded his bed and two people – a male and female in white coats – were looking at notes. Travis licked his dry lips. 'Where the devil, am I?' He could smell lavender and someone leant over to soothe his brow.

'You're in a Dublin hospital, Mr. Travis. Some men from the country brought you in.'

'What the bloody hell is wrong with me? How long will I have to stay here?' he gasped, his breath laboured, his heart beating rapidly.

'We're doing tests.' She placed a jug of water by his bed. 'Don't distress yourself, sir. We'll know more in a day or so.'

Feeling as though he had run a mile, he fell back onto the pillow. The nurse drew back the depressing curtains. Travis could see a line of beds similar to camp beds on either side of the room. Men lay motionless, attended by a nurse wearing a rubber apron. One patient sat up reading the

274

newspaper, while two walked up the ward chatting. The long sash windows were open and the place smelt of something resembling carbolic soap. The nurse with the protective apron went to the large white sink and scrubbed her hands. If this was a contagious ward, then why was he here? He had only hurt his hand.

He must have slept again, because the next time he woke, he was able to draw himself up in bed. It was then that he was aware of it. What was this hole in the middle of his bed? Christ! Was he incapable of getting himself to the lavatory? He glanced down at his hand. It looked inflamed and puffy under the clean dressing, but he couldn't remember it being changed. The pain was back and he longed for a puff of opium. He was wearing a long gown, and when he swung his feet out onto the cold floor, his head swam.

'Nurse,' he called. The young nurse came running. 'I need my clothes. I have to get out of here.' If the cursed gypsies had arranged to have him sent here, thinking he was going to snuff it, they could think again.

'Come on now, Mr. Travis. You're in no condition to leave the hospital.' She swung his legs back underneath the blanket, and he felt too weak to protest. 'I'll bring you something light to eat and then doctor wants to ask you a few questions.' She tucked in the bed covers and patted the bed before leaving him.

His head felt woozy as if he had drunk too much wine. He closed his eyes. Why did they want to question him? He ran his hand over his face, feeling the start of stubble on his face, chin

275

and upper lip. His face still twitched, and at times the aches in the muscles of his back made it difficult for him to lie comfortably. Besides, you could hardly call this a bed, and he could hardly wait to get back to his own comforts. He had never been ill, and the last thing he wanted was for Jono to visit him here. For anyone to see him in such a vulnerable state would be the worst thing he could imagine.

It was late evening when the doctor finally got round to see him. By then, he was running a temperature, and each time the nurse helped him to drink water, he found it difficult to swallow. The doctor stood aside while the nurse undid the bandage.

'Try to relax, Mr. Travis,' she said, and moved aside.

The doctor in the buttoned-up white coat pinched his bearded chin and picked up the clipboard lying at the bottom of the bed. 'Well now, Mr. Travis. How are you feeling?'

'Bloody awful!' Travis croaked, his breathing erratic. 'What are you going to do about it?'

'We're doing all we can.' He glanced at the hand swollen to double its size, and placed a clean piece of lint over the injury. 'I'll get the nurse to prepare a poultice. See if we can draw some of the pus from that wound.'

Travis glared at him. 'Never mind my bloody hand. It's only a scratch and will heal in time. What are you doing about the twitching in my jaw and the terrible pain in my back muscles?'

The doctor sighed. 'We'll know more tomorrow, Mr. Travis. Are you managing to sleep?'

Travis sighed. 'What do you think?'

'Nurse will give you something to help with that, and I'll look in on you again tomorrow.'

With no energy to argue, Travis's head fell back onto the pillow. Although reluctant to admit it, he had his suspicions; he had seen the truth in the doctor's eyes. He felt feverish. His mouth felt dry, his limbs sore, and movement was proving painful, so he tried to keep still. He hated being at the mercy of the white coat brigade. They were all witch doctors who knew nothing, and he was not going to die in any God-damned Dublin hospital.

CHAPTER FORTY-TWO

Tamara rose early to avoid Miss O'Keefe. Father Malone was already in church for early morning mass, and she left a sealed note on the desk in his study. After helping herself to some oats, she gathered up her belongings and left the vicarage.

The morning was dull but dry. With Ivan Brooks address in her pocket, she crossed the market, avoiding Tom Murray's stall. Traders were setting up for the day, as trucks and horse-drawn carts queued to get through the narrow alleyways. She missed the jolly banter of working here, but she had plenty to occupy her mind as she hurried along.

Clutching her case in one hand and her bundle

underneath her arm, she walked through the narrow streets towards Floral and Garrick Street, recalling how terrified she had been when she had run through these streets at Christmas. God only knew where Travis was now. He was as elusive as the Scarlet Pimpernel. At home, no one ever knew when he would turn up.

Now she knew the truth about her birthright, she felt stronger, and Travis no longer held her in fear. She crossed over St. Martins and a shudder ran through her body when she saw again the building – now a brothel – where Travis had kept her prisoner. Fine laced curtains hung on the windows and the words 'Pleasure House' were written in bold letters on the wall above the entrance. Had she not jumped from the building that night, risking life and limb, she might well be one of those women who sold their bodies for money to line Travis's pockets. She quickened her gait and could not get away from the area fast enough.

She arrived on Charing Cross Road out of breath. Her arm ached and she placed her heavy case down on the pavement and flexed her arm, then rearranged her bundle under her other arm before continuing. Many of the shops still had the shutters down; others were hanging their wares above the shop doorways. Apart from a few horse-drawn omnibuses and carts, the street had not yet come to life.

Ivan had said they started work at eight o'clock, and she wondered if it was a bit early to be calling, but he hadn't mentioned anything about living above a shop. The shop numbers were now in the hundreds and appeared to go on forever. At last, she came to a shop with the number over the door. It had the word 'Pawnbrokers' written in white enamel paint across the window, and above her head hung three brass balls.

She sighed. She knew only too well what that symbolised. Her grandmother had pawned her wedding ring on a number of occasions, back in Galway. Tamara peered in through the small glass window. Old watches, rings, and brooches were set out in rows. She glanced again at the number above the door. This didn't look anything like a knitting manufacturer. Could she have the wrong street? She did not know what to think and went inside the shop to enquire.

The bell jangled and a man came forward. He lifted his spectacles from his breast pocket and placed them on the bridge of his nose. He peered at her, a smile on his face. She guessed he had seen her looking through the window and thought she had come in to buy something. 'Can I help? You're sure to find something you like.' He began to unlock the mahogany cabinet below the high counter.

Tamara cleared her throat. 'I've not come in to buy anything. 'I'm looking for Mr. and Mrs. Ivan Brooks.' The smile slipped from his face, and Tamara said, 'I'm sorry to bother you. I'm clearly in the wrong place.'

'In there.' He gestured towards the brown door towards the back of the shop.

'In future, use the side entrance.'

She nodded, then frowning, she walked towards the rear of the shop, straightened her shoulders and rapped on the door. A short, stout woman wearing a white apron, her hair in a neat chignon, opened it. Her smile was pleasant and Tamara relaxed. Before she could speak, the woman said, 'You must be Tamara. My husband's description of you is so apt. Am I right?'

Smiling, Tamara nodded, delighted by her welcome.

'Come in, my dear.' The woman stood back and Tamara struggled in with her bundle and her case. Heavy green curtains hung from a brass rod on the other side of the door, and the woman pulled them across, giving the room a cosy feel. 'Sit down, dear. Have you walked far?'

'Just from Maiden Lane.'

'Well then. I'll bring you a cup of tea. I'm sure you could do with one.' She smiled. 'Ivan will be pleased to see you. He's just finishing his breakfast.'

Tamara felt embarrassed to have disturbed them so early, but a cup of tea sounded lovely.

'Thanks, Mrs. Brooks.'

Skeins of wool, mostly dark shades of brown, grey and black, were stacked in a corner of the large room. Boxes of patterns were on the floor, and knitting needles of every size lined the sideboard, where a brass ornate clock ticked. Collarless knitted garments hung along the dado rail around the room, and hand-knitting lay on the sofa. This was obviously where Mrs. Brooks sat to knit.

Balls of wool in pastel and dark shades were in baskets ready for use, and Tamara wondered if the new knitting machine that Ivan had talked about had arrived yet. The room had oil lamps with fancy globes giving plenty of light in the windowless room, quite a contrast from the dismal little shop out front.

She had just finished her tea when Ivan put his head around the door.

'Hello, Tamara. It's nice to see you again.' He came into the room and warmly shook her hand. 'How did it go? Your visit back home, I mean.'

'Oh, it was fine, thanks. I'm sorry to have disturbed your breakfast.'

'Oh, nonsense!' He glanced down at her luggage. 'You've only just got back then?'

'I've spent the night at the vicarage.'

'So, you have nowhere to stay yet?'

She shook her head.

He sat down. 'It's a bit costly along here. Your best bet is to try back towards the market, where a room is more affordable.'

She felt disappointed. She'd hoped he would offer her a job and then she could think about a room later; a very cheap one, by the weight of her purse.

'Look, let me show you round first,' he said. 'I'm still trying to come to grips with the new knitting machine.' He took her through to another room with two tall sash windows with oilcloth blinds and heavy plush curtains. Pink floral wallpaper covered the walls. Samples of knitted squares lay on a mahogany table next to a sewing machine. Tamara was surprised at the spacious rooms.

She could hear the excitement in Ivan's voice as he showed her how the knitting machine worked.

A long piece of knitting resembling the back of a jumper was hanging from the machine. To Tamara, the machine looked like a smaller version of a church organ with Ivan sitting in front of it, his feet riding up and down on the wooden pedals. Large cones twirled like dancers, and hooked needles bobbed up and down as the garment grew.

'I've never seen anything like it.' She leaned forward to feel the tightness of the stitches. It was much neater than any knitting she had ever done. 'What about the colour, Ivan?'

'Oh, that. I take them to the factory to be dyed navy or brown.' He took his foot off the pedal. 'There's just one problem. This machine can't knit collars and cuffs. I need another smaller machine to do that, but in the meantime, this is where you come in.'

She looked at him, her eyes wide.

'You still want a job?'

'Oh, yes, yes I do.'

'Good. As you probably guessed, Beth is busy with household chores, so if you can knit the collars and cuffs – from a pattern, of course – Beth will show you what to do. It will help her a lot. She still likes to knit whole garments by hand for certain clients.' He was checking the pegs and loading more yarn through the carriage, and Tamara looked on, thinking how complicated the whole process was. 'This particular knitting machine is called a hand flat frame and can sew 500 stitches per minute. Isn't that incredible? Beth tells me I'm like a child with a new toy.' He laughed. 'I've had a few disasters, mind, broken a

282

few hooked needles, but I'm getting there.'

It was a long time since Tamara had done any knitting, and she hoped Ivan would not regret taking her on when the collars ended up full of holes.

'Don't look so worried, Tamara. You'll soon get the hang of things.'

'Yes, I'm looking forward to it. Thank you.'

'I'm sure you have things to do. If you have no luck finding a room around the market, you could try the other side of Charing Cross. Come back and let us know how you get on.' He smiled. 'I'll see you out.'

With very little money in her purse, she would need more than luck to find a room at the right price. 'Can I leave my things here? That's if they're not in the way?'

'I'll put them in the cupboard under the stairs.' He paused. 'If you need an advance, you know to get you started...'

'An advance? I don't understand.'

'I could let you have a week's wages in advance and then you will have to wait two weeks before I pay you again. It's just a thought.'

'A very kind one. Thanks, Ivan. Sure, that would be grand.'

CHAPTER FORTY-THREE

Tamara went back out through the side door, thus avoiding the angry glare of the pawnbroker. The traffic was practically at a standstill along Charing Cross Road. Omnibuses and horse traffic, drivers perched high, almost made it impossible to see the far side of the street. She made her way along the pavement busy with people, glad to have left her heavy luggage behind. Street odours mingled with the fragrant smells drifting from the open shop doorways.

She made a few enquiries along the way, but they were, as Ivan had said, too expensive. If it was possible, she wanted to avoid living anywhere close to St. Martin's Lane with its bad memories. She avoided the narrow streets and alleyways with the noise and bustle of the marketplace and, taking her life in her hands, she weaved a path between the traffic and finally managed to cross the street where she hoped to find affordable lodgings.

A hole had burrowed through the sole of her right boot where a blister was smarting, so she could not believe her luck when she came across a bed sitting room to rent on Moor Street. The property owner was happy to take one week's rent in advance, as opposed to the usual two weeks, others were asking. The house was small, with only one other lodger – an elderly man who lived downstairs – and she had the small upstairs room to herself. According to the owner, the man did not like to be disturbed except when she called for the weekly rent. The house was quiet, but Tamara was getting used to being on her own. Pleased to have a job and a room so quickly, she could hardly wait to go and find Kit.

Along the pavement, the mixed aromas of various foods coming from inside the shop and the smell of newly-baked bread reminded her that she had not eaten. She stopped the muffin man with a tray of fresh cakes and bought one.

Ivan was pleased to hear she had found somewhere within walking distance. 'You must have brought a smidgen of Irish luck back with you, Tamara, to have found somewhere so soon.'

'I'd like to think so.' She smiled and picked up her case and other belongings.

'See you tomorrow then,' Ivan said. Beth came into the room. 'Can you come just after eight, dear? I'll have everything ready.'

'Thank you, both,' she said, taking her leave.

She had hoped to go and see Kit, but Ivan had been so kind, she would have felt bad asking to start work a day later. But she could not settle until she had seen Kit and discovered if he still had feelings for her. Two months was a long time. He might well have forgotten her, tired of waiting, or found someone else. The sooner she went to see him, the better. As things stood, she would have to wait until Saturday and it couldn't come soon enough.

Tamara enjoyed working for Ivan and Beth. They

made her feel so welcome, and needed. Beth was patient with her as she relearned how to knit, finally knitting a perfect square with only a couple of dropped stitches which Beth showed her how to reclaim. She felt comfortable and at ease in Beth's company, and was encouraged to make tea in their kitchen whenever she felt the need. They knew little about her private life, for which she was grateful. It meant she didn't have to tell them about Jake Travis or make up any lies.

One evening in the week, Beth invited her to stay for a meal. She enjoyed a warming rabbit stew and baked apple tart. Tamara had not tasted anything so delicious in a long time. She thought back to the drudgery when she worked at the tailor's shop in Dublin, and there was no comparison.

At midday on Saturday, Ivan said, 'You get off now, Tamara. Enjoy the weekend and we'll see you again on Monday.'

Tamara had butterflies in her tummy and couldn't wait to see Kit. Unfortunately, the hole in the sole of her boot had worsened and she was tempted to go shoeless. But she had put aside her gypsy ways, and the last thing she wanted was to draw attention to herself. Back in her room, she warmed a pan of water, but as soon as she put her foot into the warm water it stung, and she winced. She rubbed on some ointment and covered it with a piece of lint. Then she cut round the lid of the cardboard box she kept her gypsy jewellery in and pushed it inside her boot, hoping it would hold until she got back, then she spit on the toes to make them shine.

She changed into a black twill skirt and a long sleeve white blouse with a Peter Pan collar. She brushed out her hair and it bounced onto her shoulders. Then she made herself as attractive as she could by spreading a light coating of red rouge across her full lips.

Outside, she looked up at an overcast sky and prayed the rain would keep off until she got there. Arriving with her hair wet and looking like a frizz of rats' tails wasn't the look she intended. She walked to the bottom of Moor Street and out onto Charing Cross Road. The traffic was chaotic with honking horns, snorting frustrated horses, and irate drivers yelling at one another to get a move on. It made her head ache and she was glad she was on foot.

It took her a while, but she found her way there with no trouble. As she approached the circus, her butterflies were doing a somersault. The site was almost empty. This was how it had looked when they had arrived here just before Christmas.

It was unusually quiet. A log smouldered on the campfire and the realisation that the circus had gone sent her previously high spirits plummeting. She walked further into the camp when she caught sight of the caravan Mr. Billy had given her to live in. It brought a lump to her throat. At the far end of the camp, two men were doing repairs. She didn't recognise either of them. As she came closer, one of them downed tools and looked around at her. 'What's ta do, lass?'

'Can you tell me where the circus has gone?'

'It's moved south.'

'Where?'

'Brighton,' he said, continuing to hammer nails into a gate-legged table.

'When did they leave?'

'You ask a lot of questions,' the other man said, lifting a door from its hinges.

'I'm sorry. I'm looking for Kit Trevelyan. Has he gone, too?' It was a stupid question, but she half hoped that he was still here.

'We're paid to work. There's no one else here right now.'

Tamara nodded and turned to go, tears gathering in her eyes. Why, oh why hadn't she gone back sooner? Brighton! She had no idea where that even was. Her hopes of finding Kit and telling him the truth were slipping out of her reach.

She recalled little of her journey back to Moor Street; her mind distraught. In her room, she threw off her coat, kicked off her boots, and flung herself down onto her bed and wept.

When she finally pulled herself together, it was five o'clock and still light outside. She made herself some tea, milked and sugared it, and ate one of the muffins Beth had given her. She still had the rest of the weekend to sort something out. How far could Brighton be, anyway? Shrugging back into her coat and pulling on her boots, she made her way to the church on Maiden Lane. Father Malone was bound to know how far Brighton was. He knew most things.

The church was open and she went inside and knelt down in one of the pews. There was a queue for Saturday evening confession. It was a lovely church with many statues, and she prayed to them all to help her find Kit.

An hour later, the priest looked surprised to see her.

'Did you want to confess, my child?'

'No, Father. Can I have a word?'

'Why, of course.' He sat down in the pew next to her. 'Are things not working out at Ivan's then?' He frowned.

'Oh, yes, it's grand, Father.' Lowering her head, she spoke in whispers. 'This afternoon I went to see Kit, but the circus was gone.'

'Gone! Gone where, child?'

'The circus has gone travelling again.' She sighed. 'It's my own fault, Father. I should have gone back sooner.' A sob caught in her throat. 'My foolish pride, I guess. I wanted to be able to say I had a job and somewhere to live. I didn't want anyone to feel sorry for me.' She glanced up. 'Now, I'll probably never see him again.' Tears dropped onto her hands, which were folded in her lap.

'Do you know where they've gone?'

'Brighton! Is it far?'

'Near on 50 miles from here, and I doubt you'd get there and back in time for work on Monday morning.' He chewed his bottom lip. 'Do you know when they left?'

Tamara shook her head. 'The camp fire was still smouldering.'

'But that doesn't necessarily mean...'

'Oh, I know. What am I going to do, Father?'

'Look, I could let you have the pony and trap, but...' he sighed, shaking his head. 'I'd feel responsible if any harm came to you.'

'I've travelled alone before. Sure, I'll be grand, Father.'

'That might well be true, but no. What you need to do, child, is wait and think things through, then on Friday, when you finish work, catch the train to Brighton.'

'A whole week. I'm not...'

'Look, you'll have time to organise yourself. Rushing off in the heat of the moment won't solve anything.'

She glanced up at him. 'I'm sorry, Father Malone. You must think me very irresponsible.'

'Indeed, I don't. Love can do strange things to us all. Sure, I can feel your disappointment. Now, say a prayer for guidance, then come back in a few days and let me know what you plan to do.' Smiling, he walked away and left her to her thoughts. Father Malone was right; it would be foolhardy to race off with no idea where in Brighton Kit was.

That night, as she lay in bed going over the day's happenings, she thought about calling on Flory, who lived nearby in Covent Garden. She was bound to know when the circus had left. In a happier frame of mind, Tamara drifted off to sleep.

CHAPTER FORTY-FOUR

She could hear the bells ringing out all over London, and she felt bad about not going to church, but what she had in mind was more important. With renewed hope, she made her way through the streets of Covent Garden. Everywhere was quiet and it felt strange to see the wide open space of Covent Garden without a hawker. Flory lived on Flora Street, and Tamara knew nothing about her religious habits, but hoped she was at home. One of the things she liked about living in London, was that no one took a blind bit of notice whether you went to church or not.

It did not take her long to find Flory's house. The curtains were still drawn and Tamara hesitated about knocking. Perhaps her husband, if she had one, would not be too pleased to find a girl standing on the doorstep at nine o'clock on a Sunday morning. The street was deserted and Tamara wished she had not come so early. Her hand hovered over the knocker when someone drew the curtains. It gave her courage to lift the knocker.

Flory opened the door. Tamara knew by the way she glared that she, too, believed her to be a thief. 'Oh, it's you, is it? I wondered how long it would tek ye. Circus people have long memories, gel.'

'Look, Flory, can I come in?' Tamara asked, as the neighbours' doors opened either side.

'Aye. But, I haven't got all day.' She walked ahead into the middle room and stood with her arms folded. There was a smell of fried sausages coming from the kitchen. The tick of the clock on the mantle appeared loud.

Tamara wasn't invited to sit. 'Flory, I'm looking for Kit,' she explained. 'Do you know how I can contact him?'

'It depends. That young man is a respectable chap and why he'd want to burden himself with the likes of you is beyond me,' the woman snapped.

'I didn't steal from Mr. Billy.'

'Will ye shut yer gobs down there and let a working man get some kip!'

Flory shook her head, then reached up to the mantelshelf and plucked a letter from behind one of the floral vases. She shoved the letter towards Tamara. 'Kit left it here before the circus moved to Brighton.'

Tamara clutched the letter in her hand as Flory ushered her down the hall towards the door. 'Thanks, Flory.' The woman clicked her tongue and closed the door.

Tamara ran down the street as if her legs had wings. She wasn't worried about what Flory thought, she had a letter from Kit with her name across the front. She kept stopping to look at it, and as soon as she got through the door she rushed upstairs to her room, jumped onto her bed, and ripped open the letter.

P.O. Box number 930
Circus Street
Brighton
February 1901

My dearest Tamara,
I have no idea where you are, or what has happened
to you. I suspect some form of foul play, which is one
of the reasons I went to the Peelers but they were less
than helpful. The other is, I can't get you out of my
head.
If you ever get to read this, reply to the above box
number, even to say you want nothing more to do with
me.
Kit x

When she had finished reading the letter, she
read it over again. 'Oh, Kit,' she cried, dancing
around the small room, tears running down her
face. It was now the end of March and she had
not felt this happy since the last time she had
been in his company, just before Christmas.

He had not said he loved her, but he couldn't get
her out of his head, whatever that meant. She
hoped it was good. She opened the chest of
drawers by the side of her bed, but then remembered that she had used up the last page of her
writing pad when she had written to Meg. 'Drat!'
she said aloud. As it was Sunday, she would have
to wait until the following morning to buy some
more.

She pulled on her boots, pushed her arms into
her warm coat, then secured her little black
velvet Sunday hat on top of her head and went

293

out. There was nowhere open and the traffic was lighter. In her excitement to get to the circus yesterday, she had completely forgotten to buy food. She was so full of the possibility of seeing Kit again that she decided to go to the presbytery and tell Father Malone about the letter. He was the only person she could talk to.

When she arrived, midday mass was just starting and she slipped quietly into the end pew. After the hour-long service, she made her way up the middle of the church. Miss O'Keefe was kneeling in the front pew and looked up at Tamara, surprise registered on her face. Tamara nodded and genuflected in front of the Tabernacle. Other people were on their way into the sacristy to talk to Father Malone, so she held back. Instead, she went over to the statue of Mary, where many candles burned brightly. She popped a penny into the money box and held a candle to one of the flames.

She had so many things to be grateful about. She had a job and somewhere to live, and she had received word from the man she loved. She knelt to pray and, when she turned round, Miss O'Keefe had gone. As the church cleared, Tamara glanced around the door of the sacristy. Father Malone had changed into his cassock and was bidding farewell to the clerk when he turned and saw Tamara. 'Tamara! Come in. Nothing wrong is there?'

'Oh no, Father. I've had news from Kit.'

His eyebrows went up. 'How did that happen?'

She told him about Flory and even let him read the note.

'Well, what are you waiting for?' He laughed. 'This young man will be expecting a reply, and the sooner the better.'

'I know, Father, but all the shops are closed and I've run out of writing paper.'

'Well, you've come to the right place.' He opened a drawer and handed her some notepaper and an envelope.

'Thank you. I'll repay you.'

'You'll do no such thing. Now, if you'd like to come across to the house, you can use my study to write your letter.' He gestured towards the presbytery, locking the sacristy door behind him. 'Why not stay and have Sunday dinner with us?' he offered.

'That's very kind of you, Father, but I don't want to impose. I just wanted to let you know about Kit.' She held up the sheets of writing paper. 'And thanks for this. I'll go back to my room and write it there.' As much as she would have liked to stay to dinner, Tamara could not bear the looks she was sure Miss O'Keefe would give her if she did.

'Well, if you're sure,' he said. 'Good luck with the letter.' He walked with her to the church door, telling her to come and see him again the following week.

Back in her room, Tamara warmed up soup she had left over from the previous day. She ate that along with a slice of stale bread, before embarking on her letter to Kit. She knew just what she wanted to say, but she kept making mistakes and having to start again.

Dear Kit,

How happy I was to get your letter from Flory. I had no way of letting you know what happened to stop me meeting you, and I cannot write it all down in a letter as I need to see you face-to-face.

I am working in a small knitwear business on the Charing Cross Road, and I have rented a room at the above address in Moor Street. If I'm still in your head, I hope that means you think of me.

When can we meet? There's so much I need to explain. Please write as soon as you can. I can't wait to hear from you.

Tamara x

She licked the envelope and copied the box number address on the front. Then she put her last penny stamp on the top right hand corner and went out to the postbox. She kissed the envelope, leaving a smudge of red lipstick, then posted it, noting that there was no collection until morning.

That night she slept with Kit's letter under her pillow.

CHAPTER FORTY-FIVE

Two weeks after his admittance to hospital, the doctor told Travis the results of his tests. In spite of demanding to know the truth, he raged in disbelief. He called the doctor an incompetent fool. 'Get me someone who knows what they're talking about!'

'He'll tell you exactly the same as I have. Now, if you'll calm down, I'll get nurse here,' he glanced round to where the nurse was attending to a man in the bed next to Travis, 'to give you something to ease your discomfort.' He walked away towards the back of the ward.

The nurse turned to Travis, who was cursing a God that he had earlier professed no belief in, as well as the gypsies, whom he believed had poisoned him with rabbit stew. He was becoming delirious again and she placed a clean cloth into a basin of tepid water next to the bed and placed it across his forehead. Aware that something terrible was happening to him, his mind raced. He was not ready to die.

As he flitted in and out of consciousness, he saw Tamara's face before him and reached out to touch her. He hoped she was still alive. He felt a strong urge to confess and ask for forgiveness. In his delirious state of mind, he became frightened of death. He knew few who would cry over his coffin. There would be no one to miss him. He imagined himself burning in Hell fire for all eternity. He heard himself scream as the flames licked over his body. He would do anything to be rid of this torment.

He would make his peace with Tamara, tell her he was sorry for the way he had treated her. He needed her forgiveness. He had watched men on this ward die, crying out for forgiveness and begging for a priest. He swore he would never do that, but he wanted to see Tamara.

'Nurse, nurse,' he called.

'I'm here, Mr. Travis.' She wrung out the cloth

and again placed it across his brow. 'You've been hallucinating again.' She wiped the sweat from his brow and, placing her arm around his thin shoulders, raised his head from the pillow and put a drink to his mouth.

He clasped her wrist. 'When the gypsy Jono comes in, tell him I want to talk,' he gasped between breaths.

'Are you sure you wouldn't rather talk to a priest?'

Travis ignored the question. 'Get on to my solicitor.' He mumbled the man's name. 'Tell ... him ... to come straight away.'

'I'll do what I can.' She rested his head gently back onto the pillow and went away.

It was late afternoon when Travis's solicitor arrived at his bedside. Travis glared at him as if he had no idea who he was. Then he closed his eyes.

'Jake, it's Jerry. Good God, man, what's happened to you?'

Travis blinked and his eyes opened a wedge. 'Jerry, is that you?'

'Sure, Jake. Why have you asked me to come here? What's the matter with you? Are you contagious?'

Travis shook his head. 'I'm dying.'

The solicitor glanced towards the nurse. She nodded and pulled a screen around the bed for privacy. The solicitor leant into the bed so that he could catch every word Travis uttered. 'What is it you'd like me to do, Jake?'

'I want to make a will. That damned brother of mine mustn't get a penny of my wealth.' His voice trailed off as if he was saving up the energy to speak again. Minutes later, when he had finished explaining his wishes, Jake Travis slumped back onto his pillow. The solicitor sat quietly writing down everything Travis had said. When he had finished writing, he looked into Travis's eyes.

'Are you sure about this, Jake? It's quite unusual.'

Nodding, Travis grasped the pen from his hand and signed his signature. 'It's done. Can he contest it?'

'He can try.'

The exertion had left Travis exhausted, but he felt a weight lift from his mind. When Jono arrived that evening, he informed the sister in charge that this was his last visit. 'I've done all I want to for this man.'

'I'm sorry to hear that, Mr. Redmond. Mr. Travis is a dying man.'

'He's an evil man,' Jono said. 'May he rot in Hell. He kidnapped my daughter and kept her prisoner.'

'Please keep your voice down, or I won't allow you onto the ward.'

'Suits me,' Jono said, turning to go.

'Have you no pity?'

Jono narrowed his eyes and, sighing, he shook his head. These sisters were all about forgiveness, but how could he...? 'Oh, all right then. Let this be the last time,' he said, and followed the nurse down the line of beds.

'You've got a visitor, Mr. Travis,' she said, shaking him gently awake.

Jono felt nothing for the man lying before him.

He cared even less for his feeble and miserable attempts of contrition for his treatment of Tamara. 'You can burn in Hell fire before she'll forgive you,' Jono told him. 'And if your brother comes throwing his weight around, we'll be ready for him.'

Travis's mouth twisted into a strange grin. 'You'll have no worries on that score.'

Jono was about to leave, when Travis's eyes pleaded with him. 'Wait,' he gasped. 'I know who Tamara's mo...'

'What are you trying to say?' Jono pulled a chair closer to the bed and glanced across at the sister.

'Mr. Travis has been hallucinating,' she said.

Travis raised his head from the pillow. Then he fell back and took his last mournful breath. The sister rushed to his side to pray. Jono stood up, shook his head, and walked out of the ward.

Back in Galway, Jono gathered the gypsies together to tell them the news of Travis's death. 'We're not out the woods yet. The bastard has a brother who, for all we know, could be just as brutal. What we must do straight away is to fence off our property. I'm determined to protect all that is ours. I want four of ye constantly on guard. We'll take it in turns. This time the Travis's are not going to win.'

CHAPTER FORTY-SIX

Under Beth's guidance, Tamara's knitting skills improved. Her stitches were tighter and she hardly dropped any. She enjoyed the work and Beth was like a mother hen around her. However, there were times when Beth's constant chatter about the price of wool and how she had to ask Ivan to change suppliers to keep the price down, made Tamara's head ache. This morning was like that; all she wanted to do was ponder why she hadn't had a reply from Kit.

'You must stay for supper tonight,' Beth offered. 'We have plenty of mutton stew, dear.' She smiled. 'I'm a bit concerned that you are not looking after yourself in that room of yours.'

'I'm fine, Beth, really.' The thought of eating mutton stew was more than she could stomach right now. Two weeks had passed without a word from Kit, and she could not eat another crumb until she knew why he had ignored her letter. Each day during her lunch break, she had hurried back to her lodgings in hope of seeing a letter on the hall table, only to be disappointed.

Now she wondered if she had read too much into his letter, and she felt sure he must have changed his mind. What else could she think? How foolish of her to assume that someone like Kit would wait for her, when there were other girls at the circus, and the beautiful Zeema carrying a torch for him. Kit had been the main reason she had come back here. Now she had no reason to stay.

For the first time, she was beginning to realise what a lonely, frightening place London was with no one to love. Sitting in her room night after night isolated her. She even missed the gypsy camp with dancing and singing round the fire on winter nights. She would put up with anything if she knew that one day she and Kit would be together. There was nothing back in Ireland for her, either, and Jake Travis would be waiting for her should she ever return.

After another night of feeling sorry for herself, Tamara woke late with red eyes. When she apologised to Beth for her lateness, the woman immediately made her a cup of tea.

'You know, Tamara, if we only had more rooms you could stay with us.'

'Oh, that's kind of you, Beth, but don't worry, I'll be fine.'

Sighing, Beth placed a basket of wool on Tamara's lap. When Tamara saw the pile of knitting that almost tripped her up on the floor, she set to. One thing she would never do was to take advantage of this kind, generous couple who had taken her under their wing.

'Ah, I thought I could smell tea.' Ivan popped his head round the door. Smiling, Beth went to make him one.

'Tamara, I have an urgent delivery today.' He sat down. 'That order I told you about for Oxford Street. It's amounted to two large boxes.'

'I remember.'

'Would you like to make the delivery in the pony and trap?'

It was just what she needed to clear her head. 'I'd be happy to, Ivan.' She stood up.

'Well, you know where Dobie is stabled. Do you think you'll be okay on your own?'

She nodded.

'Right then,' he said, as Beth walked in holding a small tray with tea and biscuits.

'Where are you going, dear?' She glanced at Tamara, who was already pulling on her coat.

'Tamara's going to deliver that consignment of jumpers.' Smiling, he broke a biscuit in half and crunched it in his mouth. 'I'll have the boxes in the doorway by the time you stop outside.'

In spite of the hole in the sole of one of her boots, Tamara walked the short distance to the livery. Ivan had told her, on their way to Portsmouth, how costly it was to keep Dobie stabled in the city, but he had no option if he wanted to run his business from here.

Later, when she got stuck in a traffic jam on the corner of Oxford Street, she hoped it wouldn't be for long. She'd read recently that traffic on The Strand had been held up for an hour because a horse had gone lame. She sat talking to Dobie and watched pedestrians taking advantage of the situation by darting in between carriages, horse trams and wagons.

As cabbies became impatient, shouting at one another, Tamara stood up and craned her neck to see what was going on up ahead. That was when she saw him, stepping from a hansom cab with a woman, both wearing black. They walked up the street facing her until they turned into a doorway on Oxford Street. He had the same proud stance, an air of importance about his demeanour. He wore a black suit and stiff white collar and a top hat. His knee-length black coat swung open and the older woman had her arm linked through his. No, there was no mistaking Captain Fitzroy, with his white hair sprouting from the sides of his face.

If only she had been on foot, she could have seen where they went, maybe even had a chance to speak to him. She cursed the missed opportunity. The traffic began to move forward and Tamara urged Dobie on, and halfway along Oxford Street, she found the shop for her delivery. She pulled up close to the kerb and the shop assistant helped her carry the boxes inside the shop, where she handed over the handwritten invoice and obtained a signature.

At the end of the week when Ivan handed Tamara her wages, he told her that he was thinking of taking on another woman: a presser. 'What do you think?' he asked.

'Won't that delay orders?'

'Not if the woman is experienced. It will still be less to pay her than what the dye works are charging me.'

'Well then, it's worth a try,' Tamara said, and Beth nodded in agreement.

On Saturday morning, Tamara tried to put Kit to the back of her mind as she made her way to Petticoat Lane in search of reasonably priced footwear. Now she had started wearing shoes, she wondered how she could have gone without them for so long. Spring was just around the corner and, after sending her last payment to Meg, she had a few shillings left to spend on herself. Today she was looking forward to throwing off her old boots and placing her feet into something light and comfortable.

These days she looked nothing like the gypsy girl who had run away from Galway over six months ago. She thought herself to be just as fashionably dressed as any working class girl she passed on the streets of London.

Since discovering she was no longer of gypsy blood, she found her fear of Jake Travis had lessened. He apparently wanted to marry a gypsy. Now her dearest wish was to find her birth mother. Her plans to come clean and tell Kit everything about her past had backfired, but with or without him she was determined to discover her true parentage.

Pondering these thoughts, she browsed the market stalls. She tried on a pair of suede court shoes, priced at two shillings. Then she changed her mind and settled for a black leather pair with scratches around the toes. She handed over a shilling, knowing that she could polish them to look new again. For another one and sixpence she picked up a grey two-piece suit; the jacket had a black velvet collar and hip pockets, and it fitted her waist perfectly and came down over her curvaceous hips. The skirt came to her ankles. After collecting a few groceries on the way, she went home happy.

The following week, Beth and Tamara were busy knitting ribs and cuffs for a special delivery, when Ivan made a surprise announcement. 'Tamara, I have three tickets for the theatre this Saturday, and one is for you. I hope you are not doing anything that evening.'

She had not been anywhere since arriving in London and the idea of a trip to the theatre excited her. 'Are you sure you want me to come along?'

'We'd love to have you come along with us, Tamara,' Beth said, smiling. 'Treat it as a birthday present.'

'Thank you. I'd love to come.' And she smiled properly for the first time in weeks.

CHAPTER FORTY-SEVEN

On the evening of the concert, Tamara could hardly contain herself. When she was dressed, she piled her hair on top of her head with hair grips. She finished sewing a purple feather which she had picked up at the market, onto the side of her little black hat with a narrow brim. She then secured it on her head and slipped her feet into her black shoes. Comfortable in her new two-piece and white blouse, she picked up her bag and wished she had bought herself some gloves. When she heard Ivan pull up outside, she locked the door and hurried downstairs and opened the front door.

'You look lovely,' Beth said.

Smiling, Tamara stepped up into the trap next to the other woman. Ivan jerked the reins and Dobie trotted off. The city streets were still busy with trams and carriages, but there was no daytime delivery traffic to hold them up.

Inside, the theatre was ablaze with lights and atmosphere, and from the moment the curtain went up Tamara's eyes were fixed on the stage. She enjoyed the variety of artistes and she sang along when she knew the songs. At the interval, Ivan said he would try to get them a programme.

'I'll go,' Tamara said, getting to her feet. 'I want to have a look around.'

She had never been inside a theatre before and was interested in seeing everything. She walked down the elegant staircase, glancing at the portraits of artistes like Marie Lloyd, Lillie Langtry and Harry Lauder on the staircase wall. They all looked so glamorous. She joined the queue for a programme, but the man in front bought the last one.

'Oh,' he said, turning to her. 'You take it.'

'Are you sure?' She offered him two pence, but he waved it away.

'Enjoy the rest of the show,' he said.

As he turned and walked away, Tamara held her breath. Was it possible? She lowered her eyes, aware that she was staring as he placed his hand on a woman's arm. Tamara's heart thumped. How could she let him disappear without saying something? The foyer now packed and noisy, she made her way across to where he was standing talking to his companion. Gripping the programme in her hand, she stood before him. He frowned and raised his top hat.

'Captain Fitzroy, sir,' she said.

She could see he was struggling to remember her. 'Do I know you, young lady?'

'I'm the girl who stowed away on your ship last year. I ... I...'

'Well, well. Are you really the same lass?' he chuckled. 'I'm delighted to see that you survived.'

'Only because of you, Captain.'

'Are you...?'

'I'm here with my employers, Ivan and Beth Brooks, from Charing Cross.'

He glanced towards his companion, who raised her eyes. 'Well,' he shook his head. 'I'm delighted to meet you again and in such pleasant surroundings, Miss...'

'Tamara Redmond.'

'Ah yes, of course.' He smiled. 'The unforgettable Tamara.' He shook her hand, then raised his hat. 'Well, Miss Redmond, I'll bid you goodbye.'

Tamara turned to go, their meeting all too brief. She glanced back over her shoulder, but he had mingled with the crowd now making their way back into the theatre.

When Tamara sat down again next to Beth, she could feel the flush of heat cover her face and hoped that the other woman had not noticed. She was thrilled at meeting the captain again, and at the theatre of all places. 'I'm sorry I was so long,' she said, glancing towards Beth and passing her the programme.

'You did well to get one, dear,' Beth whispered,

308

as the curtain rose.

For the whole of the second half, Tamara found it hard to concentrate, her mind going over what had transpired between her and Captain Fitzroy just moments earlier. How could she tell Beth and Ivan without telling them everything? Would they still want her to work for them once they discovered she had stowed away on a ship without permission and ended up in a cell in Liverpool?

She wanted to see him again. His kindness had overwhelmed her, and she had seen it again in his eyes tonight. How could she let this opportunity go by without trying to speak to him again? When the show finished, she made an excuse about needing the powder room and went downstairs to the foyer. The patrons piled out from the downstairs tiered seats and the foyer was just a sea of heads. From her vantage point on the staircase, she could see his tall figure escorting the woman on his arm out through the main doors. 'Fiddlesticks,' she murmured, wishing she had come down sooner. When Beth and Ivan joined her in the foyer, she thanked them for a wonderful evening.

'So pleased you enjoyed it all, my dear,' Beth said.

'We must do it again soon,' Ivan agreed, taking his wife's arm.

'But the evening's not over yet,' Beth insisted. 'Tamara can have some of my homemade toffee cake and a warm drink before you take her home, Ivan.'

Tamara had given up hope of hearing from Kit, when a few days later, she picked up the post and spotted a letter for her in Jono's handwriting. She went into the small scullery, made herself a cup of tea, and took it with her to her room. She removed her coat and curled up on the bed to read the letter.

It was short and to the point. *Jake Travis is dead!* There was no detail. *Come home whenever you like. The bastard's dead.* The letter was signed Da.

She read it again. Jake Travis dead! Could it be true? She felt nothing at hearing the news, just relief. Jono was not one for writing letters, and Ola couldn't write. Why hadn't he told her more, like how Travis had died? Instead, she was left with this uncertainty. Had Jono killed him? The thought numbed her. What was she to think? She had hated Travis for a long time. He had been the cause of her missed date with Kit; the reason she was here in London, feeling lonelier than she had felt her entire life.

She would stay until the end of the week, then explain herself as best she could to Ivan and Beth, say goodbye to Father Malone, and catch the boat back to Cork.

CHAPTER FORTY-EIGHT

Kit sat up in his hospital bed, a newspaper open in front of him. He was reading about the Irish Nationalists being ejected from the House of Commons. His concentration adrift, he was hardly aware of the other men around him; some, the nurse had pointed out, much worse off than him. But it made little difference to how he felt.

His career in tatters, he could think of nothing else. Self-pity was something he had never indulged in, but he found his situation difficult to come to terms with. Why now, when Tamara had come back into his life and he had declared his feelings for her? Hearing from her had delighted him, and he had looked forward to seeing her. Once she knew about his accident, how would he know her feelings were not borne out of pity?

He lay back on his pillow and closed his eyes. Why, he asked himself one hundred times, hadn't he checked the safety net? Billy said that he had not been concentrating that morning, and maybe he was right. Just when he'd thought he would never see Tamara again, he had received a letter that made him yearn for her. His mind had strayed for a second, culminating in his disastrous fall – hitting the side of the net that had damaged his right shoulder, rendering him disabled. What use was he to any woman now? He couldn't use his right hand, and he couldn't be bothered to try using his left.

The doctor had given it to him straight, his life as a trapeze artiste was over. How could he tell Tamara? She would not want to spend the rest of her life tied to a useless circus has-been. He couldn't even write her a letter. And who could he trust to help him? He was not ready to talk about his injury. A sullen expression crossed his face as the door swung open onto the ward and Mr. Billy walked in.

'Well, how are you feeling today?'

Kit sighed.

'What's happened? Has the doctor been to see you? What had he to say?' Billy sat down on the chair next to Kit's bed and removed his hat.

'It's not good news, Billy. My career in the circus is over.'

Billy placed his elbows on his knees and lowered his face into his hands. When he looked up again, he said, 'We'll get a second opinion. Don't worry about the money.'

'And have my arm amputated? No thanks.'

'It's early days, Kit.' Billy pulled his chair closer to the bed. 'Bones heal and in time you'll get the use of your arm back.'

'And pigs might fly.' Kit punched his pillow angrily with his good hand and shifted his body up in the bed.

'This isn't like you to be so despondent.'

'I'm sorry, Billy, but it's so frustrating.'

'I've brought you some bits. Let me know if there's anything else you need.'

Kit nodded. He was grateful Billy found the time to visit as often as he did. Billy and Nelly were the only family he had, and Nick was God-knows-where. Not that he wanted to see that creep around him in his vulnerable state.

He felt partly responsible that Billy had been forced to cancel part of the show. 'What plans do you have to keep the circus open, Billy?'

'It's dying on its feet, Kit, with Nick swanning off, and you lying here injured.' The older man spread his hands despondently.

'I'm sorry, Billy.'

'Accidents happen, lad. Just you stay positive and get back on your feet.'

CHAPTER FORTY-NINE

Tamara sat next to Ivan at the knitting machine, the cones twirling round so fast she wondered which one would run out first. She had learned so much from Ivan, and enjoyed working for the old couple. She sighed. It was not going to be easy to explain why she needed to return to Ireland. Just as Beth walked in with a tray of tea and biscuits, there was a knock on the side door. She placed the tray down next to them.

'It might be that consignment of dyed jerseys I'm waiting for,' Ivan said, getting up from the knitting machine and going to the door.

'I'm sorry to disturb you,' the man said. 'But I'm looking for a young lady by the name of Tamara Redmond. I believe she might work here.'

Hearing his Scottish voice, Tamara hurried to

the door. 'Captain Fitzroy! How did you find me?'

'Please, please, come in,' Beth said.

'You know this gentleman?' Ivan stood to one side.

'Yes, I do.' She smiled. 'Our paths crossed on my first voyage across the sea.'

'Look, I'm holding up business.' He glanced at the machine which was still running, then he looked at Tamara. 'Would you do me the honour of having dinner with me this evening?'

'Yes, I'd love to.'

'Good. I'll pick you up at eight.' He smiled. 'You live here then?' He looked around the work room.

'No, but here will be fine.'

He raised his hat, shook Ivan and Beth's hands, and left.

Ivan appeared subdued after the man left. 'Is everything all right?' Tamara asked. 'You didn't mind me asking the captain to pick me up here, did you?'

'Why, of course not! You must be cautious in giving out your address. He appears to be a man of principles, but isn't he a bit old for you, Tamara?'

'Oh,' she laughed, as Beth went to fetch a teaspoon and placed it on the saucer before passing her husband a cup of tea. 'It's not what you think.'

'What isn't?' Beth said.

'Captain Fitzroy is an old friend. I bumped into him at the theatre the other night, during the interval.'

'You never said.' Beth sat next to Tamara with

her tea.

'No, it was very brief.'

'He's still a stranger,' Ivan said, draining his cup and moving across to the machine.

'I'll explain it all to you later before I leave with him this evening.'

Her answer seemed to puzzle them more. Beth fidgeted with her wedding ring and Ivan began replacing unnecessary spools of wool onto the knitting machine. She owed them an explanation; they had been so good to her, treating her like a daughter. They had never pried or asked her any questions about how, or why, she had come to live in London. They were such uncomplicated people and now she felt forced to tell them everything.

Tamara worked hard for the remainder of the day until the deliveries were neatly boxed and ready for Ivan to deliver the following morning. And there had been no more mention of the captain. She had completely forgotten about the letter from Jono and her plan to return to Ireland. It could wait until tomorrow.

At six o'clock Tamara shrugged into her coat, curious and excited about seeing the captain later. She wanted to know more about him and the woman he escorted to the theatre the other night. She glanced across at Beth, who was folding her knitting and pricking the ball of grey wool with the knitting pins.

'I need to go and get ready, but I'll be back well before the captain arrives.'

'I gather you won't want to eat with us tonight, Tamara, and spoil your appetite?'

315

Tamara shook her head, patted Beth's hand, and left.

As she weaved her way through the rush hour traffic, she wondered how Ivan and Beth would react if they knew she had been a stowaway on the captain's ship. Worse still, that she had been locked up in a cell in Liverpool. Telling them would serve no purpose and possibly taint their feelings towards her. She didn't want that.

In her room, she discarded her working dress, and then she poured water into the enamel basin and washed with a new bar of Lux. She pressed it to her nose and whiffed the scent. Letting her hair loose, she shook out bits of wool and fluff with her hands. Then bending her head forward, she brushed it several times until it sprung to life. She put on a fresh white blouse and slipped into her grey two-piece with its elongated jacket. Lastly, she placed her feet into her shoes, and coloured her lips red. Most of the young women were wearing rouge, but she never discussed fashion with Beth, who never coloured her lips or wore face powder.

She looked into the mirror on the inside door of her wardrobe and fiddled about with her hair, then she fastened her hat to the top of her head. She sat on her bed for a few moments to consider how much of her past life she was going to reveal to Ivan and Beth. Although Beth was a formidable woman, telling her about Jake Travis might be a step too far.

They only needed to know how she had met the captain, and that was all she planned to tell them; for now, anyway.

When Tamara got back, the smell of stew and dumplings wafted into the knitting room-cum-parlour, where she found Ivan and Beth relaxing on the sofa reading the evening newspapers. Smiling, Tamara sat down opposite them.

Ivan folded his newspaper. There was still half an hour before the captain called; enough time for them to talk.

'You look very lovely, dear,' Beth said, as Tamara sat down next to her.

'Thank you, Beth, and please don't worry. You've no need to.'

'Of course not, dear. It's your business.' She glanced towards Ivan.

'What Beth says is true, Tamara, but I don't understand why you would choose to go out with a man old enough to be your father.'

Tamara took a deep breath, then she told them how she had escaped an arranged marriage back in Ireland and how the captain had helped her, leaving out the rest. Ivan sat forward, placing his head in his hands and Beth went across and hugged her. 'You poor, poor dear,' she said.

Ivan lifted his head. 'Please don't feel that you owe this man any gratitude, Tamara. He did what any decent man would have done in the circumstances.'

'I doubt that,' she said. There was a knock on the back door and Tamara stood up, relieved to get away from the tension hanging in the room. 'I'll be fine,' she said. 'I'll see you both tomorrow.'

The March weather was blustery, and Tamara

317

had to hold onto her hat as the captain took her hand and she stepped up into the carriage. She sat with her back to the cab driver, inhaling the smell of the leather-upholstered seats. The captain sat opposite her. She recalled that when she had been destitute on the streets of Liverpool, she had wished to ride in a carriage like this. Nevertheless, and in spite of everything, here she was riding in a hackneyed cab with the captain on whose ship she had been a stowaway. It all seemed like a lovely dream.

She smiled as the carriage pulled away from the curb. And, glancing up, she glimpsed Ivan and Beth looking through their bedroom window. She felt bad that her dinner date with the captain was causing them anxiety.

'I suppose you're wondering why I have asked you to dine with me, Miss Redmond?'

'Well, actually, I'm glad you did, because I have wanted to thank you for your kindness towards me last year. It got me out of a few scrapes.'

'Well, I'm pleased, lassie. I'm sorry I could not have done more, but you appear to have done well for yourself and outrun that blackguard. You never did tell me his name.' They were skirting Covent Garden and, in spite of it being evening, some of the narrow streets were still congested.

'It doesn't matter now,' she said matter-of-factly. 'He's dead.'

He glanced across at her. 'Oh. And how do you feel about that?'

'Good, Captain. His death has released me and given me back my life.' She glanced down at her hands. He would probably think her heartless.

The driver reined in the horse as they came to a junction. 'London traffic.' The captain shook his head and craned his neck through the window to see what the hold-up was. Young boys and some women were running between carriages to sell newspapers. 'This practice should be stopped before someone gets killed.' He tapped the hood of the cab for the driver to get a move on in spite of the congested traffic.

'Perhaps Shanks's pony is best,' she smiled.

He frowned.

'On foot.'

He laughed aloud. 'Would you have preferred that?'

'And miss this treat? Oh no.' She shook her head as the cab moved on again along The Strand then turned off towards Maiden Lane and pulled up outside Rules restaurant, the same one she had passed last year when she ran into the church for sanctuary. She smiled inwardly and wondered what Father Malone would say if he saw her now.

Tamara stepped from the carriage as if she was a woman of means. The concierge opened the door to them and a waiter guided them to a table. The restaurant was busy. The tables were covered in pristine white cotton tablecloths and adorned with sparkling glasses and cutlery. Red and white wall lamps were in contrast with the black and white floor tiles. The waiter seated them both on dark wooden, round-backed chairs and Tamara, looking a little bewildered, glanced around her and then down at the row of cutlery in front of her.

The captain raised his eyebrows. 'Don't worry, lass. Work from the right in.'

Relieved, she smiled. Music befitting the clientele played in the background, and the waiter brought them each a menu and spread a napkin across her lap. It felt good to be treated as if she was someone special, and she felt a flush to her face.

At least the menu was in English and the restaurant appeared to specialise in game and grouse. Tamara was familiar with both, as her gypsy father hunted for game. She asked for rabbit while the captain opted for game pie.

'Do you drink wine, Tamara?'

'Yes, that would be nice, thank you.'

The waiter poured the house wine into their glasses and she lifted the glass to her lips. 'This is very nice, Captain Fitzroy.'

'You can drop the captain, and call me Jock.' He glanced across at her. 'No one calls me captain, except when I'm on board the *Maryanne*.'

She nodded. 'Will you be in London long?'

He cleared his throat. 'I came to attend my brother-in-law's funeral.' He fingered the pointed tip of his beard. 'I'm returning to Scotland tomorrow.'

'I'm sorry to hear that.'

'That's life, lass. That was my sister I was with the other night. I thought the theatre might cheer her up, but I think it was a wee bit soon.'

'Your wife must get lonely when you are away at sea,' she asked boldly.

He placed an oyster into his mouth, and chewed it before answering. 'I never married.' He

320

placed both elbows on the table, paused and glanced down. 'The woman I loved died many years ago, and for some reason, you remind me so much of her.'

'Really?' Would that be the reason he had helped her back in Liverpool? Their meal arrived and the smell of rabbit stew with dumplings revived her appetite. 'Umm, this smells delicious,' she said.

'Well, eat up, lassie, while it's nice and hot.' He hooked a piece of game pie onto his fork and placed it into his mouth.

When they'd almost finished their meal, he glanced across at her and smiled. 'Tell me about yourself, Tamara. How did you end up in London?'

She finished a spoonful of rabbit stew. 'It's a long story.'

'Well, the last time I saw you, you were in a very bad place. And I wish I could have done more to help you.'

'You did help me. You got me out of that terrible cell. I joined a circus in Liverpool and it took me here.'

'Amazing! Are you happy where you are working now?'

'Yes, I think so. I appreciate what Ivan and Beth have done for me.'

'Och sure,' he said, as the waiter carried across their desserts. 'These look good.'

After apple pie and custard, Tamara felt fuller than she had in months. Just as she thought that she couldn't eat another bite, the captain insisted that she have coffee with him. The waiter brought the drinks in small white cups and Tamara sat back in her chair, holding her stomach.

'That was really delicious. Thank you,' she said.

'Good.' He looked pleased. 'I'm glad it was to your liking.' He leaned back in his chair and undid the buttons of his waistcoat. 'Tamara, do you have a beau?'

She felt herself blush. 'Well, I thought I had, but he hasn't answered my letter.'

'Well, he's a fool.' He smiled. 'I'm afraid I have my reasons for asking you to dine with me this evening.'

Tamara raised her eyes. 'Oh!' She wasn't sure what to say, or think.

'I'm leaving London tomorrow evening.' He sat forward. 'There is something that has troubled me ever since I first set eyes on you. I never did marry, but...' He paused. 'Do you mind if I smoke?'

Tamara shook her head. She felt uneasy, wondering what he was going to say and how she was going to respond if this carried on the way she feared it might.

His pipe lit, the captain took two puffs then sighed. 'I was in love once, with a beautiful woman. Unfortunately, she was already married.' He paused. 'Would you like to see a picture of her?'

Tamara placed her hands on the table. 'Yes, please. Yes, I would.'

He unzipped part of his wallet and produced a small photo, glancing affectionately at it before passing it to Tamara. 'Do you see any likeness?'

At first she did not see what he meant, as the black and white photo had a crease running through the centre. She took a closer look, and placed her hand to her throat. She looked up, unsure what to say. 'Her eyes, or perhaps her hair. She is very beautiful.' But Tamara saw much more than that.

He looked down at his hands. 'She was indeed beautiful. It was almost déjà vu when I encountered you on my ship, young lady.'

'I'm sorry.'

'No, lass. She's been gone a long time.' He retrieved the photo and carefully placed it back inside his wallet. 'The first time I saw her, she was sitting on a rock near the bay in Galway. She reminded me of a mermaid, with her long hair cascading over her shoulders. We got talking and as we grew to know each other, she finally confided in me about her unhappy marriage.' He sighed. 'I fell in love with her; couldn't help myself. I'd never met anyone like her before.'

'How did she die?'

'We corresponded for a while and then she asked me not to contact her again, because if her husband found out he'd kill her. I respected her wishes, but found I couldn't keep away. Then I had a large consignment to ship over to Holland and Denmark. I was away for months. When I returned, I came looking for her only to discover that she had died in childbirth and her husband – a man by the name of Bruce Travis – had sold up and gone to live abroad.'

Tamara couldn't stop shaking, and tears filled her eyes. Dear God! She didn't want to believe it. If this woman was her mother, she did not want her to be dead. Worst of all was the thought that

Bruce Travis could be her father. She stood up.

'Oh, lass. What is it? I've made you sad. I'm so sorry.' He opened his wallet as the waiter came across with the bill. 'Keep the change.' He turned to help Tamara with her jacket.

Outside, he hailed a carriage. The March winds were much lighter as he helped her into the cab. 'You're shaking.' He placed his overcoat around her shoulders and handed her his handkerchief.

'Thank you.' She blew her nose and then raised her eyes, turning round to look at him. 'I think I know who the lady was.'

'Och, you do?'

'What was her name?'

'Catherine. Lady Catherine Greystones.'

'Catherine!' Her heart thumped and her hand rushed to her face. The captain rapped on the roof of the cab and they rode in silence until it stopped outside the address in Moor Street she had given him. 'Could you wait here a moment, please?' she asked.

'Of course.' He stepped from the carriage and held the door. He told the cabby to wait and he would pay him for his time, as Tamara hurried upstairs to her room. It was too much of a coincidence. If the captain's Catherine was her mother, she wanted this wonderful man to be her father, but the chances were she was the daughter of a Travis.

She lit the oil lamp on the mantelpiece and recovered her mother's letter from its secret place at the bottom of the wardrobe. Then she hurried back down. The captain was standing on the pavement underneath the streetlamp. Tamara handed

324

him the letter.

'Please, read this.'

She watched a mixture of emotions flash across his face. 'Where...? How did you come by this?'

'My gypsy parents gave it to me. Is it the same woman?'

'This is Catherine's handwriting. I had no idea she was with child.' He ran his hand over his forehead and along his bearded face, before handing her back the letter. She folded it almost reverently, careful not to rip it, and put it inside her bag.

'If this was my mother...' a sob caught in her throat. He placed his arm around her shoulders and it felt warm and comforting. 'Please, please tell me Bruce Travis is not my father.'

'My beautiful child. That man was impotent, which is why I was so upset to hear the circumstances of her death. Therefore, I am your father.'

CHAPTER FIFTY

Kit was back at the circus, his arm in a sling. He had been encouraged when the doctor told him that in time he would get back the use of his arm and shoulder. Nelly came into his wagon to bring him breakfast of bacon and scrambled eggs. The smell of the delicious breakfast reminded him of what he missed while in hospital.

'That looks lovely, Nelly.'

Smiling, she placed the tray on the table in

front of him and he could smell the familiar whiff of her piped tobacco. She moved away and sat down facing him as he picked up the fork with his left hand and began to eat.

'Have you given any thought to what you're going to do?'

He shook his head sadly. 'I've done nothing else, Nelly.'

'Billy will find something to keep you working. He won't want to lose you.'

He mopped the sides of the plate with bread, and pushed it aside. 'That was nice. Thanks for bringing it across, Nellie. I suppose I'll have to face everyone eventually. But ... if I can't go back on the trapeze, I...' He sighed.

'Don't make any rash decisions, Kit. It's early days.'

Kit stood up and looked through the half open door. 'Nelly, can you do me a huge favour?'

'Anything, lad, anything.'

'Will you write a letter to Tamara for me?'

It was the older woman's turn to sigh. 'Are you sure this is what you want?'

'Will you write the letter?'

She nodded, but he could tell that she would have preferred not to. He knew what she was thinking, too, that Tamara might shun him because of his injury. But he hoped he knew her better than that. He handed Nelly a pen and paper and a small bottle of ink.

'You know I'm not the best with words or writin' for that matter,' she said, pulling the chair closer to the table.

'Don't worry. I'll tell you what to put.'

'I can't spell neither.'

'Please, Nelly, just try.'

When the letter was finished, it was simply a string of words strung together like a frayed piece of rope with no spaces between the words, and he hoped that Tamara would be able to decipher his message.

Addressing the envelope was hard work. It looked as if a three-year-old had written it. Nevertheless, he was grateful to Nelly. He walked to the nearby post office, bought a stamp, and posted it. Afterwards, he wondered if he should have warned Tamara what to expect, but it was too late now. At least this way, he supposed, he would see her reaction first hand.

After work on Saturday morning, the sun shone as Tamara walked to Maiden Lane to talk with Father Malone. Rather than face Miss O'Keefe's disapproving scowl, she waited for him in the church until he had finished hearing confessions.

'It's nice to see you,' he murmured. 'If you've come in for some quiet contemplation, I'll leave you in peace.' A few people were saying the rosary, she could make out the sound of clicking rosary beads as they turned them round in their fingers.

'Oh no, Father,' she whispered. 'I was hoping you might have time for a chat.'

'Come through.' He removed his scapular, kissing it, and hung it up in the vestry. He walked ahead of her towards the presbytery.

She could hear the sound of crockery coming

from the kitchen. 'I won't keep you long.'

'Take as much time as you need, child,' he said, closing the study door behind him. 'It's a glorious morn, to be sure. Let me take your coat.' She removed it and he placed it across a chair. 'Sit yourself down,' he gestured, then sat in a chair opposite her. 'I'm all yours.' One of the things she liked about Father Malone was that he listened to her when she had no one else to confide in.

Tamara relaxed back into the chair and poured out everything that had happened in the two weeks since she had last spoken to him.

'Well now, that's a lot to take in, child. It must have come as a shock. Are you happy that the captain might be your father?'

'Oh yes, Father, he's a wonderful man. I can see why my mother was attracted to him.'

The priest stroked his chin. 'Do you think you'll hear more from Captain Fitzroy?'

'I do. He's given me his address in Scotland and his sister's address here in London in case I need anything.'

'How do you feel now that Jake Travis has died?'

'God forgive me, Father, I feel nothing but relief. I'd be happier if I knew Jono had no involvement in his death, though.' She pushed a lock of her hair behind her ear.

'Yes, I see. Write straight away to your gypsy parents and find out. I wouldn't go rushing over there just yet. All we can do now is to pray for the man's soul.' He stood up. 'You'll take some tea?'

'I don't want to be any trouble.'

'It's no trouble, I can assure you.'

He went off to the kitchen and she heard a mumbling of voices before he returned and sat down. 'The captain could be rather influential in your life now.'

'Yes, and it feels rather strange to discover my father is a sea captain.' She lowered her eyes sadly. 'I was rather hoping to find my mother alive.'

'Umm ... but you know she loved you.'

As she glanced up, the housekeeper was carrying in a tray of tea and biscuits. She placed it down on the desk. 'Thank you, Miss O'Keefe.'

The woman nodded towards Tamara and left, but there was no mistaking her hostility.

'She still doesn't like me.'

'Oh, take no notice. It's how she is. God help us!' As they drank their tea, Father Malone asked, 'I take it you've not heard from Kit.'

Tamara shook her head. 'I don't know what to do, Father.'

'If you feel you know his character well enough, then you must find out why he hasn't replied, no matter how painful it might be.' He placed his cup back on the tray. 'Have you tried calling on this woman Flory again?'

Tamara finished her tea and placed the cup back gently on the saucer. 'Why would he send a letter to Flory when he has my address?'

'He may not have received your letter. It's always a possibility.'

A glimmer of hope lit up Tamara's eyes.

When Tamara left the priest's house, she went straight to Flory's house. She dreaded knocking in case the woman's husband bawled her out, but

329

her shoulders relaxed a little when Flory herself opened the door. 'And what do you want?'

'I'm sorry to bother you, Flory. Have you heard anything from Kit lately?'

Flory came out onto the pavement and pulled the door behind her. 'You haven't heard from him, then?'

Tamara shook her head. 'I'm going out of my mind with worry. If you know anything at all, please tell me.'

The older woman folded her arms. 'Do ye love 'im?'

'Well, of course I do. We both... I thought he loved me, too, but he hasn't replied to the letter I sent him weeks ago.'

'Look, what I heard might not be true, so don't go takin' it as gospel.'

'What is it?' Her heart raced. 'Tell me, Flory?'

'He's been injured.'

'Injured! How? What happened?'

'I know no more than that.'

'Who told you?'

'Mr. Billy wrote a while back and said they might be back in Covent Garden sooner because Kit had had an accident. That's all I know.'

Tamara was stunned. She turned away, tears filling her eyes. Flory went back inside and Tamara ran down the street as passersby stared curiously after her.

CHAPTER FIFTY-ONE

That night, Tamara tossed and turned, her mind full of unanswered questions. Her eyes red from crying, she chided herself for not trusting Kit more. She should have guessed that something had kept him away. What kind of injury did he have? Her mind fogged with the worst possible scenario. Had Nick somehow injured him in a fight? It must be serious if Mr. Billy was bringing the circus home.

When the light of dawn seeped in through the thin curtains, Tamara got out of bed, went downstairs and made a cup of tea. She got ready for work, and by the time she was on her way out the front door, her mind was made up. She would go to Brighton and see Kit for herself. It was the only way to put her mind at rest.

As soon as she arrived at the knitting factory, Beth gave her a curious look.

'Are you all right, dear? Did everything go well with your escort on Friday?'

'I had a wonderful time, thanks, Beth.' She removed her coat and hung it up on the back of the door.

Ivan walked in. 'There you are Tamara. Come, I want to show you a new yarn that has just come on the market.'

It wasn't until they had a tea break that Tamara could tell Beth about the captain.

'I'm pleased you enjoyed your evening out, my dear. Will you be seeing him again?'

'Yes. I hope so.'

Ivan placed his cup down on the table next to where he was working, and turned round. 'Is that wise?'

'He's gone back to Scotland.'

She saw Ivan's face relax, and she realised he was just as concerned as Beth. She didn't blame them; after all, they only knew half the story. Ivan had been involved in her escape last year and she suspected he felt responsible for her, but this wasn't the time to start telling them intimate details of her life. She was worried sick about Kit and she still needed to come to terms with the discovery that Captain Fitzroy was her father.

For the remainder of the morning, orders piled in and they could hardly keep up. Ivan said he was trying out a woman presser that afternoon, and if she proved satisfactory, he was going to employ her now that the business was doing well.

At lunchtime, Tamara went out for some fresh air. She found it hard to concentrate. She bought a newspaper and some fruit to take back to her room and was surprised to find a letter for her lying on the hall floor. At first she thought the obscure writing on the envelope might be Ola's, as the woman could hardly write her own name.

With shaking fingers, she tore open the envelope and pulled out the letter. It was only a couple of lines, but was so badly written that it took Tamara a few minutes to make it out. Finally, she got a piece of paper out and wrote all the letters down in a straight line, and came up with:

I'm comin' to see you on Friday. Meet me at the station. My train gets in at 6 o'clock

Kit

There were no sign of affection, not even a kiss. Was he coming to tell her he didn't love her any more? What else could she make of it? In spite of her doubts, she danced round and round the small room, her skirt swinging outwards as if she was dancing around the gypsy campfire, then she fell onto her bed, hugging the scribbled note to her.

The note had obviously been written by someone other than Kit, which raised more questions. Why hadn't he written it himself? Why hadn't Mr. Billy, who had a good command of the English language, written it for him? Whoever it was could neither write nor spell. Still, she refused to let anything bother her now. In four days' time she would see Kit.

She folded the note and pushed it inside her bag, then ate some of the fruit, tidied her room, and made her way back to work. As she meandered her way along the busy pavements, she thought about Kit's injury. It obviously wasn't so bad as to stop him travelling. Whatever it was, she would nurse him back to health and let him know that her love was his forever.

Beth was the first to notice Tamara's happy frame of mind that afternoon as she wound up the skeins of wool. 'You've had some good news, Tamara?'

Tamara was surprised at how well this woman could read her. 'Yes, I've had a letter from Kit. He works at the circus. He's coming to see me on Friday.'

'A circus! How exciting. What does he do?'

'He's a trapeze act. And he's very good.'

'Well, perhaps we'll get to meet him.'

Tamara smiled. 'Yes, I hope so.'

The new woman Ivan was trying out for the job of presser looked over at Tamara. 'Them circus people can be dodgy. I'd watch me step if I were you.'

Tamara did not reply. The woman, a typical Eastender, had a large family to feed. Taking her on would change nothing except increase Tamara's workload. She was an untidy woman, leaving bits of work down everywhere she went and losing collars and cuffs.

Already Tamara had had to pick up after her and keep track of the number of garments she pressed, as she couldn't count. But it would be Ivan's decision on whether to take her on or not. And now that Tamara had seeing Kit to look forward to, nothing could upset her.

On Friday, she bought a pair of silk stockings from the market, and asked Ivan for Saturday morning off. He pursed his lips.

'I'll make the time up next week,' she promised. After a pause, he agreed.

Later, when he paid her wages, he wished her a nice weekend.

Tamara was at sixes and sevens as she got ready. She kept looking at the small red clock on the table by the side of her bed. She had made sure to wind it up the previous night before she went to sleep.

She checked the line at the back of her stockings, then slipped her feet into her shoes and set out to walk the short distance to the train station. Her hair tumbled loose around her shoulders. The evening had turned cool, and she wore her new skirt and jacket with a fresh cream blouse. She hoped Kit would like the new Tamara. It had been months since they last met and her feelings for him had not waned; indeed, the thought of never seeing him again filled her with despair.

As she neared the station, her heartbeat quickened. She wondered how serious Kit's injuries were. Would he have changed? Would he still feel the same way about her? So many questions ran round in her head and could only be answered once Kit stepped from the train.

The station was noisy and smoky, with steam hissing from engines waiting to depart and other trains pulling in. She enquired about which platform the Brighton train would arrive at.

'We're not sure yet, miss,' the porter told her. 'There's been a slight delay.'

'A delay,' she repeated. 'Has something happened?'

'Oh no, miss. It's not unusual. Don't worry. You'll hear the announcement.'

Tamara nodded, then sat down on one of the wooden seats. It was colder inside the station and she buttoned her jacket and pulled up the collar. She was biting her nails when the train puffed into the station and hissed to a stop.

Tamara stood back as people around her rushed forward to greet passengers. Then she saw him step onto the platform, a small bag strapped to his back, his right arm wrapped in a triangular bandage in the form of a sling. His dark wavy hair fell across his forehead and he was clean-shaven, apart from a neat thin moustache. She watched him glance down the platform and then wave to her.

Tamara stood and rushed towards him. Over-whelmed, she placed her arms around his neck and kissed him. It seemed the most natural thing in the world for her to do, as everyone around them was doing the same. Then she drew back. 'I'm sorry.'

'Don't be. I've missed you, too. You look different. I like your outfit.'

Her concerned eyes searched his face. 'What happened to you?'

He held his hand close to his chest and his fingers curled into a fist as he guided her towards a seat. 'I hit the side of the net and bounced onto the floor, permanently injuring my shoulder.' He was watching her closely.

'Oh, Kit, that's terrible. I'll take care of you. I've missed you so much.' She looked into his eyes and saw tears before he turned away.

'Come on,' he said. 'Let's find somewhere private to talk. I've something important I want to discuss with you.'

CHAPTER FIFTY-TWO

The lights of the city were bright as they came out of the dimly-lit station, the smell of steam lingering on their clothes. They walked in silence, back towards Covent Garden, her arm linked through his good one. The roar of the traffic made her head ache and each alehouse they passed was full of rowdy drinkers.

'How's Mr. Billy keeping?' she asked.

'It's nice that you should ask.' He shrugged. 'He's a broken man, Tamara. But then,' he sighed, 'he's not the only one.'

She leant in close to him. 'What do you mean, Kit?'

'I'll explain later, but first, I've got some news you'll be interested to hear.' He stopped walking and turned towards her. 'The missing money has been found. No prizes for guessing who the culprit or culprits were.'

'I knew it. So where was it?' Anger flared in her eyes.

Kit pulled her into a doorway while he related the rest of the story.

'Oh, Kit. I knew it was Nick, but how could Zeema be part of it? Is she still at the circus? I'd like to go and give her a piece of my mind.'

He shook his head. 'Billy threw them both out, but he has since relented and allowed Nick back. He's living with the woman who had his baby, the same one you saw him with. Nick just used Zeema, the way he does anyone foolish enough to trust him.'

Holding her with his good arm, he kissed her lightly on the lips and she responded. 'I never believed you'd taken that money, Tamara.'

She lowered her head. Talking about it brought back bad memories she'd rather forget, but one question still niggled her. 'Why hasn't Mr. Billy written me an apology?'

'He wanted to, but at that time we didn't know where you were. Forget about them. This weekend is about us. I can't tell you how good it is to see you. I thought I'd lost you forever.'

She gave a little shiver and Kit pulled up the collar of her jacket. 'Look, it's cold standing about,' he said. 'I think I know where we can go.' They walked on, his arm around her.

'I've arranged to stay at Flory's tonight,' Kit said.

'Oh.' She should have guessed that Flory would know he was coming.

'Perhaps we could go there now. At least we'd be warm.'

'Is there nowhere else?'

'It's gone seven and you know how noisy inns can get on a Friday night.'

She nodded. They had so much to talk about, but she wasn't happy doing it at Flory's.

He took hold of her hand. 'What are you thinking?'

'Oh, how wonderful it is to see you again.'

When they arrived, Tamara hoped Flory would at

least be civil towards her. She greeted Kit like a long lost son. 'It's good to see ye, Kit, come in.' She nodded towards Tamara, and closed the door behind them.

'I hope you don't mind me arriving early,' he apologised. 'We needed somewhere to talk.'

She opened a door along the hallway. 'The oul fella's at work and the kids are asleep, so you'll not be disturbed. I'll go and put the kettle on.' She closed the door behind her.

The room was tidy and Flory's knitting lay in the armchair. They had obviously interrupted her relaxing time.

Tamara and Kit sat down together on the sofa underneath the window. Flory brought in tea and homemade fruitcake and, after a long chat with Kit about his injury, she left them alone. When they had finished, Tamara moved the cups aside and swallowed the lump forming in her throat.

'Kit, I'm sorry I let you down at Christmas, but it wasn't my fault... I...'

He turned towards her. 'Tamara, I don't know where you've been or what happened the night you disappeared.' She made to reply but he placed his fingers across her lips. 'It matters not one iota. You're here now.' He swallowed. 'I love you, and it makes what I've got to say all the more painful.'

'What are you talking about?' Her heart was pounding.

He looked into her eyes, but she looked away, frightened of what he was about to say. 'Look at me, Tamara. I'm not the man I once was. I can't let you waste your life on someone like me, I

339

can't...' He paused and swallowed. As she raised her hand and gently stroked his face, he took her hand and held it in his. 'I can never work again, not as a trapeze artiste. And I don't know anything else.'

'Please, please don't talk like that, Kit. If you love me, we can work it out. Please don't give up.'

'I'm sorry, Tamara. It's because I love you that I must do this.'

She stood up and folded her arms. 'So, you've come all this way, to tell me this?' A sob caught the back of her throat. 'No, Kit, no.'

'You don't understand. I may never work again.'

'Oh no,' she cried. 'Perhaps you won't work in the circus, but there are other kinds of work you can do as your arm gets stronger.'

'Tamara, listen.' He drew her back down next to him. 'What kind of life would you have married to an invalid? You'll soon find someone else who can give you the things you deserve.'

'Aye! Someone I don't love. I want you and that's an end to it.' She moved apart from him, a defiant expression on her face. Neither of them spoke for a few seconds. Kit sighed and leant forward, his head in his hands.

Tamara placed her hand on his shoulder. 'Are you saying you don't love me? Because that is the only reason I'd let you go.'

'It's not about that, Tamara.'

'Should I not have some say in this?'

He shook his head. 'Of course, but you're young and you don't know what this might mean in the future.'

'I used to think I could see into the future, but

340

no one can, Kit, and I want to spend mine with you.'

Flory tapped on the door and walked in. She fluffed up the cushion in the armchair and rolled up her knitting. 'Have you seen the time, Kit? Tamara needs to be getting back.'

CHAPTER FIFTY-THREE

The next morning, when Tamara walked through the mahogany glass doors of Twining's teashop on The Strand, Kit was waiting. He stood up and she walked towards him. As he kissed her cheek, and she inhaled the masculine scent of him, she realised that she could not have loved him more.

Over tea and cakes at a small table in a quiet corner of the tearoom, they talked of many things. She told him about her job at the knitwear factory, and about Beth and Ivan. Finally, she discussed everything openly with Kit, including her constant fear of Jake Travis, and her discovery that she no longer belonged to the gypsy clan. During the telling, she paused many times and Kit reached out and touched her hand. She saw him grit his teeth and flex the knuckles of his good hand.

'You've been through so much. I could have helped if you'd told me some of this earlier.'

'I couldn't involve you then.'

'I'm so proud of you, Tamara. In spite of everything that's happened, you have managed to make something of your life. When I've gone back, I want you to think carefully about what I said last night.'

'I won't change my mind.'

Kit shook his head and squeezed her hand. 'Stubborn as ever, but I love you for all that. Doctors cost money, Tamara.'

'But you can't shrug it off, Kit. You must see a specialist.' She licked the cream from around her lips and sat back in her chair.

'Oh, I almost forgot. I've got something belonging to you.' He opened his pack and passed a small bundle over to her.

'My cloak! I don't believe it.' She held it close. 'I thought he'd burned it with the rest of my things. But how? Where?'

'I went to Tom Murray's looking for you, and when he said he knew nothing about your disappearance, I didn't believe him and insisted on going upstairs. I knew you would never leave it behind. With hindsight, I wish I had gone to the police. I'm sorry I didn't do more.'

Tamara touched his hand. 'It doesn't matter now.'

He cupped her hand in his. 'What is your father like?'

'He's wonderful, Kit. I'm so thrilled to have found him.'

'Perhaps he will tell you more about what your mother was like.'

She nodded. 'I'm sure he will.'

Kit glanced at his watch. 'My train leaves in half an hour.' He called the waitress and paid the bill.

'Must you go? Surely if the circus is coming

back, you could stay here.'

'I can't, Tamara. I owe so much to Billy.'

She lowered her head. She still found it hard to forgive the man who had thrown her out on that winter's night.

'Don't be sad.' He raised her chin. 'I'll be back in a couple of weeks. Come and see me off.' He helped her on with her jacket and they left the teashop.

The station was a hive of activity with porters humping sacks and crates onto trains. Tamara and Kit stood close together in a warm embrace, surrounded by passengers waiting to board. 'You'll write, even if I can't write back?' he urged. 'Promise!'

'I will.' Tears wet her lashes as they kissed. Carriage doors banged and shut and, at the shrill of the whistle, they pulled apart and Kit quickly stepped onto the train. Tamara ran along the platform waving until the train was out of sight.

The night before the circus arrived, it rained heavily. Tamara could hear the pitter-patter against her window, and it continued all morning as she waited on the corner near to The Strand with a few brave souls to watch the circus come back home. She wore a yellow waterproof coat which she had borrowed from Beth, and a matching bonnet tied underneath her chin. By the time the parade of soggy caravans arrived, rain was dripping down her face and onto her hair.

Tamara ran alongside Kit's trailer until the train of trailers stopped at the junction. His door

343

opened and he helped Tamara inside the wagon, laughing when he saw her attire.

'Lovely weather for ducks,' he laughed. He helped her out of her wet coat and hung it up on the hook where it dripped onto the floor. He handed her a towel. 'I never expected you to stand about in the rain.'

'I couldn't wait to see you.'

'Me neither.' He kissed her hungrily, burying his face in her hair, inhaling its scent mingled with rain.

'How is your arm?'

'Much the same.' He shrugged.

The trailer rocked and they fell onto the small bunk laughing. He kissed her again and she wrapped her arms around him. A loud cheer went up outside and Kit pulled her to her feet. 'We're home, and I'm starving.'

'Do you think anyone will object to me being here?' She was a little nervous at seeing some of the circus folks again.

'You've nought to be ashamed of. They should apologise to you.'

She wasn't sure how she felt about seeing Mr. Billy, but if he was kindly towards her, she would try and put the past behind her.

It wasn't long before everyone was gathered inside the food tent, where the smell of hot broth was welcome after the long journey. Nelly was in charge of the proceedings and made sure everyone got a fair helping. Kit and Tamara were about to tuck in when Tamara saw Mr. Billy walking towards them. She stood up and swallowed. The last time she had seen him, he had looked at her with contempt. Now he had a smile on his face.

'Hello, Tamara,' he said, raising his hat. 'I hope you don't mind me being here.'

'Well, of course not. I'm delighted you bothered to come, after the way I treated you. I should never have tossed you out like that. It was wrong. Can you forgive an old fool?'

Tamara still felt the sting when she remembered the way she had been forced to walk the dark streets, frightened for her life. 'Why didn't you believe me?'

'I'm sorry. I never dreamt that Nick would...' His voice trailed off sadly. 'I hope in time you'll let me make it up to you.' Tamara stayed silent. 'Sit down,' he said. 'Don't let your food go cold.' He sat opposite them as they ate their soup. He glanced at her smart clothes. 'You look well. Have you found work?'

She brushed her hand over her damp hair. 'I work for a family-run knitwear business on Charing Cross.'

'Umm. I didn't have you down as a factory girl.'

'Why? Because you think gypsies can't be trusted?' Tamara bristled.

'I didn't mean it that way, girl. You've got fire in your belly.' He looked at Kit. 'I knew that the first time I set eyes on her.' Mr. Billy stood up and popped his hat on. 'I misjudged you. In more ways than one, it seems.'

Tamara managed a watery smile.

'Is Pablo still around?' Tamara asked Kit as they left the food tent.

'Yes, he's around somewhere. When he heard you were coming, he ran into hiding. I told him you'd forgiven him, but he shook his head.'

'Let's go and see him.' She grabbed his hand and they walked down to the stables where they found Pablo swilling out the pony stable. He cowered when he saw Tamara.

'It's all right,' Kit said. 'Tamara's not angry. Come out. Come and shake hands.'

Pablo dropped the bucket and slithered out into the light, his head bent and his arms swinging by his side. Tamara placed her hand on his shoulder. 'Don't be scared. It's all right now.'

'Me, bad person. Zeema said you bad person. Me sorry.'

They both laughed. 'You're not a bad person, Pablo.'

'The bad people are gone,' Kit told him.

The man rubbed his hand down the side of his pants and offered it to Tamara, and she shook it firmly. He gave her a weak smile, picked up the bucket and hurried away.

'Poor little man,' Tamara said, as they strolled around the site. 'Nick and Zeema played on his childish sense.'

Kit guided her back towards the tents. 'It's not the same any more. I've not practised in weeks. My life in the circus is over.'

'Perhaps a couple of weeks off will inspire Mr. Billy with new ideas. And at the same time give you time to heal,' she suggested.

They sat down on the grass. 'You don't understand. You mustn't get your hopes up.'

'I'm an optimist by nature, Kit, and you must

be, too. Oh, I almost forgot.'

'What?'

'Beth and Ivan have arranged for us to have dinner with them one evening next week. Do you mind?'

'I'm looking forward to meeting them.'

'There's one other person I'd like you to meet before that. He's been a dear friend to me and saved my life.'

'You mean Father Malone?' He pursed his lips. 'He won't try to convert me, will he?'

Tamara laughed. 'No. But his housekeeper, Miss O'Keefe, might if she gets a chance.'

CHAPTER FIFTY-FOUR

After their visit to Father Malone, Tamara and Kit walked in silence along Maiden Lane, away from the hustle and bustle of the street hawkers. Had Kit taken Father Malone's suggestion of a second opinion as interference?

'What are you thinking?' Tamara broke the silence.

Kit paused on the corner and glanced down at her. 'I thought you said my injury didn't matter to you.'

'Of course it matters, but not in the way you think.' She raised her voice. 'If you won't at least try, then you're not the man I thought you were, Kit Trevelyan.' She stormed ahead until he caught up with her and placed his left hand on her arm.

347

'There's nothing anyone can do. Don't you see that?' He sighed. 'Besides, I've already seen two doctors in Brighton. I don't want you disappointed like I was.'

'Don't you think it's worth a try?' Her eyes pooled. 'Oh, Kit. I just want you to get the best possible treatment. Please, give Father Malone's suggestion a try.'

When Kit explained how the accident had happened, the first thing the specialist did was to remove Kit's sling. 'Let's take a look,' he said. 'How long ago since you fell?'

'Five weeks.'

Mr. Simpson placed both his hands on Kit's arm. 'Try and straighten it for me.'

Kit winced, but managed to uncurl his arm so it looked like a hook. 'That's good,' said the specialist. He took Kit's hand – the fingers curled inwards – and gently turned it so that the palm side faced upwards. 'Have you had an x-ray?'

'I don't think so.'

Tamara frowned. 'What's one of them?'

'It detects broken bones, even small ones.' The specialist smiled. 'The damage to your shoulder,' he sighed, 'is more serious. But, before I do any more, I want you to have your hand and wrist x-rayed.' He scribbled something down on a notepad. 'Be prepared for a long wait and then make another appointment to see me.'

He opened the door and looked back to see Kit pick up the sling. 'I wouldn't bother with that for now,' Mr. Simpson smiled, then led them out of the room towards his receptionist.

The x-ray showed that Kit did, in fact, have two broken bones in his hand and wrist. 'The bone in your hand will heal by itself, providing you don't put too much pressure on it, but your wrist will need to be plastered.' The hospital doctor smiled. 'Nurse here will take care of you.'

Kit was pleased that Tamara had insisted on another opinion. He was already moving his arm better, in spite of the heavy plaster weighing it down. When the plaster was finally removed, he made another visit to the specialist. Mr. Simpson explained how important it was for Kit to exercise his arm and hand with gentle circular movements.

'Will I be able to use it as before?' Kit wanted to know.

'Raise your right arm.'

Kit raised it as far as he could.

'Can you wiggle your fingers? Good. You've made good progress, young man. The damage to your shoulder is more permanent, I'm afraid.' He sighed. 'If you follow my instructions, you'll gradually gain more strength in your right arm.'

Father Malone was delighted to hear the good news when they called back to see him. 'I dare say you won't be swinging from a trapeze again, but you have other talents, I'm sure. Have you given any thought to what you might do?'

Kit pursed his lips. 'I'm looking to the future, and I'll take any kind of work that comes along.'

The priest laughed. 'You won't go wrong with that kind of attitude.'

Kit hugged Tamara close. 'Well, I've got Tamara

349

back and that's incentive enough.'

'I'll expect an invitation to the wedding, so.' The priest winked at Tamara.

Kit cleared his throat. 'I ... I'm not sure I...'

'That's okay,' the priest laughed. 'It's entirely your choice where you marry, as long as you make an honest woman of her.'

Tamara wasn't at all surprised when Kit hit it off with Ivan. The two men became engrossed in conversation from the word go. Kit was very interested in seeing the knitting machine that Tamara had told him so much about, while she laughed and chatted with Beth and helped her carry the feast to the table. Beth's Sunday roast dinner was one of the best Kit had tasted. After they had eaten, he confided, 'I enjoy Nelly and Flory's cooking, but this has surpassed them both.'

Beth beamed with delight.

That afternoon, they walked back hand-in-hand to Trafalgar Square. 'I like the hushed quietness of Sundays, don't you?' Kit said.

'Less traffic, I suppose.'

They sat by the fountain. A few families were walking around enjoying the sunshine, and they watched a young couple toss coins into the water.

'Wonder what they've wished for,' Tamara mused.

Kit smiled. 'Umm. They look far too young for grown-up wishes.'

'Oh, I don't think so,' Tamara said.

'That's because you, too, are so young.'

'And you're an old man, I suppose,' she laughed.

He turned towards her and placed his arm around her shoulder. 'My twenty-five years slip away when I'm with you.' He reached into his pocket. 'I have something for you.'

'You have. What is it?'

He took a small square box from his pocket. 'I've been nursing this all day, waiting for the right moment.' He placed it on her knee, then removed his arm from around her shoulder while she opened it.

Her eyes widened. 'Kit. Is this an engagement ring?' She lifted it from its white cushion. 'It's beautiful.' Tears welled in her eyes.

'I want us to get married, but not yet.' He took the ring from her and placed it onto her finger. The solitaire was a perfect fit. 'Will you marry me?'

'Oh, yes. I love you, Kit.' Their kiss was passionate and when Tamara pulled away, she felt a flush colour her face.

That evening, Tamara showed off her engagement ring to the circus company. Mr. Billy insisted that she stay in one of the vacant wagons.

'Are you sure you want me to stay?'

'Please. Stay as long as you wish,' he said. 'Why not borrow the small cart and collect your stuff tonight?'

It was nice to be back at the circus with Kit, people she knew and, of course, the animals. It made her all the more aware of how lonely she had been in the room at Moor Street. The following day, she went back to the house and placed a letter, with the key inside for the property owner, on the hall table.

Two letters addressed to Tamara lay on the floor, and she picked them up and left, closing the door behind her. Outside on the pavement, she glanced at the letters. One was a long white envelope addressed in a good hand, and the other a small brown envelope with Meg's scrawl across the front. Dodging traffic, she crossed the road and hurried inside a teashop. She found an empty table, ordered tea and a bun, then opened Meg's letter. It simply said:

Tamara why ye staying away? Ye've paid your debt to me in full. That blackguard is dead. Come 'ome where ye belong.
Meg

A small sprig of shamrock between the folds of paper made her smile. She placed it back in her bag. St. Patrick's Day was over, but it was nice to get a reminder just the same.

She sipped her tea and finished her bun, brushing the crumbs from her blouse. She looked again at the official-looking letter, turning it round between her fingers, a little scared to open it. It bore an Irish postmark. Whom did she know of importance in Ireland? Sighing, she pulled it open.

Her eyes widened as she scanned the letter from a solicitor in Galway. He wanted to see her in his office as soon as she could make arrangements. Then she would hear something to her advantage; it was signed, Jerry Monroe. A little dazed, Tamara leaned back in her chair.

What could it mean? She had never been to a solicitor in her life. Her father, Jono, had a few years ago when he was accused of stealing two horses. Nothing had come of it. Whatever the solicitor wanted to see her about was a complete mystery.

Kit was waiting outside her work. Delighted to see him, she was about to show him the solicitor's letter when he smiled and took hold of her hand. 'I've something to tell you.' He walked so fast that Tamara had to run to keep up with his long strides.

'What's the hurry?' He slowed down so they could weave their way across the busy Charing Cross Road, bustling with traffic. Catching her breath, she said, 'Tell me your news.'

'I've got a job.'

'Really! Where?'

'Let's go in here. It's not too busy yet.' He ushered her inside an inn. 'Lemon and soda okay?'

'Lovely,' she nodded.

She removed her coat and sat down on a bench with her back to the window. Kit sat opposite her. The table between them was covered in wet ring marks and scratches.

'Well, come on,' Tamara said. 'Tell me more.'

'It's at the Lazy Man's Gym in Peckham. As soon as I saw the advert, I went straight over there.' He smiled. 'I had a chat with the manager and got the job.'

'That's wonderful news, Kit. What will you have to do?'

'As a training instructor, it'll be my job to

encourage men to come along and do exercises. The chap is retiring and they need me to start as soon as possible.' He smiled. 'It's just what I need to build up my muscles.'

'Oh, Kit. I know how much it means to you.'

The bartender came across with their drinks. His hands shook and the drinks slopped onto the table and the floor. Tamara sat back and Kit gave him an angry stare.

'Ah, sure I filled them too full,' he cackled. 'I won't charge ye any more.' He took a grubby rag from his trouser pocket, wiped the table, and went back to the bar.

'Can you understand what that was all about?'

Tamara shook her head. 'Sounds like something old Paddar, at the fish market, would say.'

They sipped their drinks, then Kit reached for her hand. 'I want to marry you as soon as I can support you.' He leaned in closer. 'Will you wait? You won't get impatient, will you?'

Tamara couldn't resist teasing him. 'How long for?' She took another sip of her drink.

'It could take months.'

'Months!'

'Is that too long?' He looked worried.

She smiled. 'Of course, it's not. I love you, Kit Trevelyan. Don't you know that yet?' He squeezed her hand.

'By the way, I got this letter in the post today.' She passed it across to him. 'What do you suppose it's all about?'

Kit read it and frowned. 'You've no idea, then?'

'No. You don't think I'm in some kind of trouble, do you?' She placed her hands underneath her chin. The inn was getting busy and Tamara wrinkled her nose at the smell of tobacco and spilled beer.

'No. I don't think you're in any trouble, Tamara. But solicitors don't write letters like this unless it's important.' He took her hand, then he sighed and played with the ring on her finger.

'What is it?'

'It's just... Oh, damn it. I don't want you to leave me again. I can't go to Ireland with you. Not now, and miss this job opportunity.'

'Well, of course. But you think I should go?'

'No! Yes, I suppose so.' He nodded. 'As it's from a solicitor, you'll have to go over there and find out what it's all about.'

Two women walked in and draped themselves across the bar while men reached out, grabbing and touching them. It made Tamara mindful of how her life might have gone had she not met and fell in love with Kit. An unsavoury drunk slithered onto the bench next to Tamara, sliding his arm around her.

'Get off.'

Kit was on his feet. 'Get your filthy hands off her.'

'Ye mingy devil. I don't mind taking me turn.'

Tamara inched from the bench and stood up. She could see Kit's eyes flare and, in spite of his injured arm, he was about to punch the man. 'He's not worth it, Kit,' she said, picking up her coat.

Kit placed his arm around her. 'Let's get out of here before I burst a blood vessel.'

CHAPTER FIFTY-FIVE

Tamara decided to bide her time before speaking to Ivan. Business was picking up and they were run off their feet. She hated having to ask for time off, especially as she had only been working for them a few months. As soon as she had a break, she showed him the solicitor's letter and waited while he digested the content.

Ivan rubbed his chin. 'I guess it must be important. Have you heard from your family recently?'

'Yes, they're grand. I had a letter the other day.' She frowned. 'I suppose I should go.'

'Well, of course you must. Aren't you curious?'

'Well, yes. I'm more puzzled.'

Folding the letter, he handed it back. 'How will you get to Portsmouth?'

'I'll catch a train.'

He glanced round at the mountain of work. 'I dare say we'll cope, but hurry back.'

'I really wish I was coming with you,' Kit told her, as they stood in the train station. 'Will you be all right on your own?'

Tamara laughed. 'Are you coddin'?'

'Well, of course.' He pulled her close. 'I'll miss you. Promise me you won't stay longer than you have to.'

She nodded. 'Promise. I'll miss you, too, and

356

I'll think about you all the time.' He lifted her case into the carriage and took her in his arms. His kisses were passionate and urgent and left her wanting more.

As the train puffed out of the station, Kit threw her a kiss and she waved until steam clouded her vision. Turning her face away, she felt a sob catch the back of her throat and she cursed the letter that had parted them once more.

There had been no time to inform her gypsy parents, so her visit would come as a surprise. It was early evening when she got there, and she sensed a peaceful mood surrounding the camp. She could see the glow of the fires, and the smell of cooked rabbit and hare. She smiled to hear the women chanting as they went about their chores. It had been years since she last remembered such a happy atmosphere, and she knew why.

Ola came down the steps of her wagon, carrying a bowl of soapy water. She threw it onto the grass at the side of the caravan. She looked towards the track when she saw Tamara. She dropped the basin and ran towards her with open arms, folding her in a warm embrace. 'I knew you'd come back.' She held her at arm's length and looked down at her modern clothes. 'You're not one of us any more.'

'Don't start that malarkey, Ma.'

Small children ran around her, laughing and calling her by her name. Women stoking their individual fires gave her a wave. She had not received such a welcome since she first ran off. 'Let's get inside, Ma. I'll tell you everything over a cup of tea. I'm parched.'

Once inside, she could smell Ola's cooking of rabbit stew and dumplings. Her mother stoked the small stove and turned towards her. 'Jono's down the field doing a bit of digging and planting vegetables. Now that bugger is dead, we are free to plant what we like.' She put some cups and plates on the table before her eyes rested on Tamara's ring.

'What's that on yer finger?'

'I'm getting married, Ma.'

Ola sat down. 'Is that why ye's come back? Glory be to God! Are ye in family way?'

'No.' Tamara stood up and glared at Ola. 'I'm not a slut. Why are you ready to believe the worst of me?'

'Sit down, will ye. Still hot-tempered, I see. We've not seen hide nor hare of ye for months and then ye turn up out the blue, a ring on yer finger and no feller with ye. What am I to think?'

'Well, don't,' Tamara snapped. She slipped off her coat and drunk the tea and bit into the oat cakes in front of her.

Ola glanced at the ornamental clock on top of the small cupboard. 'Jono will be here in a minute. The childer will have run to tell him.'

'What did Travis die of then?' Tamara finished her cake and Ola put out some more.

'A rake went through his hand and poisoned him. Good riddance to the bastard is all I can say. We're all free of him now.'

Tamara nodded. 'Umm. Did his brother attend his funeral?'

'No. Lives in Spain, don't he? It's not likely we'll hear from 'im. So, what brings ye 'ere?' Ola pulled her shawl closer across her chest.

Just then, Jono stepped into the wagon. 'Ah, yer back then?' He placed his hands, dirty from the soil, into a basin of cold water and scrubbed them before drying them on a discoloured towel and kissing Tamara's cheek. 'How's things in your neck o' the woods then?' He sat down for the meal Ola had placed in front of him. 'Why'd ye go off again without a word? Ye'll have to stop doing that.'

'Yeah, well, I'm here now. I got a letter from a solicitor, Jerry Munroe, the one beyond in the Claddagh village. That's why I've come back.'

The smell of food Ola placed on the table was too strong to resist. While they ate their meal, Tamara took out the letter and read it aloud.

'What the bloody hell's it all about then?' Jono garbled, and pulled a piece of gristle from his mouth. 'Read it again, Tamara?'

'Have ye been up to no good? Look at the way yer dressed,' Ola said.

'Oh, be quiet woman,' Jono said. 'How can anything she's done in England be linked to a solicitor here?'

Tamara stood up. 'I've not come here to argue, or to talk about my clothes. I'm off over there now to find out for myself.'

'I'll come with ye.' Jono got to his feet.

'No, I'll go alone.'

CHAPTER FIFTY-SIX

The solicitor operated from the front room of a two-storey cottage on Main Street. Tamara knocked and entered. The office was dismal and little light came in through the tiny window.

The man turned up the wick on the lamp. His desk swamped the room, and a giant map of Ireland was pinned on the wall behind him. He beckoned with his pointed nose for her to sit and glared at her over his half-mooned spectacles. 'How can I be of assistance?'

It was obvious he had no idea who she was and she fumbled in her bag for the letter, placing it down in front of him. The smell of tobacco from a smouldering pipe lying across the ashtray, assailed her nostrils. He shifted in his chair, sniffed, and then blew his nose loudly into a red handkerchief and returned it to his pocket.

'What's it all about?' she asked, becoming impatient with the man. 'I hope I haven't come on a wild hare chase.'

'Oh,' he said, and glanced down at the letter. 'Yes, yes, of course. You must be Miss Redmond. Do you have any idea why you're here?'

'Well, if I had, I wouldn't be asking.' Tamara was tired after her long journey across the sea. 'If I'm in any trouble, you'd better tell me and get it over with.'

'Oh, no, no, no. You're...'

The telephone rang, and the solicitor answered it. 'Later,' he said. 'I'll see to it.' He replaced the receiver and gave Tamara a lopsided smile.

She let out an audible sigh. 'So why am I here?'

He pulled open a drawer in his filing cabinet and rummaged through his files, then plucked out a long white envelope and swivelled back to face her. He placed the envelope on his desk and ran his fingers along the edge of his stubble. 'How old are you, Miss Redmond?'

'Why? What's that got to do with anything?'

'You're a very impatient young woman. I know little, if anything about you, Miss Redmond. But the person who wrote this,' he held up the letter, 'certainly does.'

Tamara stood up, straightened her shoulders, and cocked her head. 'What do you mean? What person?'

'Please, please. Sit down.'

Sitting, she narrowed her eyes. 'Is that letter for me?'

'Yes, it is, and you'll have it when I explain a few important things to you.' She fiddled with the strap of her bag. 'You still haven't told me what I've done and why I'm here.'

'You, my dear young woman, are about to become a landowner.' The words appeared to choke in his throat.

Tamara was speechless. What was he saying? Had Meg died? If that were so, it would account for the delay in the letter with the shamrock. Why had Jono not mentioned it?

'You're shocked, I'm sure,' the solicitor continued. 'I must say, it took me by surprise, but a person's last will and testament must be carried out no matter how bizarre it might sound.'

'Who is it? Why would..? Please tell me.'

'Mr. Jake Travis.'

Tamara's eyes widened. She stood up and turned her face towards the window so he could not see the revulsion she felt at hearing who her benefactor was.

'I've been solicitor to Mr. Travis for a long time. He confided in me. I know how distressed he felt when you jilted him.'

She swung back round. '*Jilted!* I never agreed to marry him in the first place.'

There was a knock on the door and a woman, her hair tightly scraped back, popped her head round. 'Is everything okay, Jerry?'

'Yes, dear,' he smiled. 'See I'm not disturbed for the next half hour.' She promptly closed the door.

He leaned back in his chair. 'As I've said, Mr. Travis took me into his confidence, and not only about his business affairs. I feel that I should warn you of the consequences of your good fortune.' He rubbed his hands together. 'Should you, of course, decide to honour Mr. Travis's last wishes.'

Tamara sat back down. 'Are you saying I don't have to take it, or that I shouldn't?'

'The decision is yours, Miss Redmond.'

'Why shouldn't I, after the way he treated me. I hated the man, and I believe the feeling was mutual.'

'Well, you're entitled to your opinion, Miss

362

Redmond. He left you comfortable.' The solicitor watched her reaction over the rim of his specs.

'Why in God's name would he do that? What's the catch?'

'Jake Travis was a shrewd man and, as you know, he never did anything unless for gain. He left the bulk of his estate to the Dublin hospital that looked after him in his last weeks. He also has a brother, Bruce; a brother he hated more than the devil himself. He is a brutish man who treated his wife shamefully. To spite him, Jake left you his land. Lock, stock and barrel.' He paused, allowing her to absorb what he had just told her.

Tears sprung to her eyes. 'I hope you won't think me too blunt, Miss Redmond.' The man sat forward. 'He wanted to marry you, that bit is true.' He shifted in his seat then looked straight at her. 'He wanted to avenge his brother, Bruce, by marrying the illegitimate daughter of Lady Greystones.'

Tamara didn't speak.

The solicitor continued. 'An arrogant cuss of a man, if ever there was one.' He took out his handkerchief again and blew his nose.

The news of her parentage had not come as a complete shock to Tamara, thanks to her father, the captain.

'How do I know I can trust what you say?' she asked.

'I'm a solicitor, Miss Redmond, with a reputation to uphold. It was a closely guarded secret.'

'And no one knew?'

'The Travis's had ways of silencing tongues. Most folks assumed the child was her husband's, others say different. Catherine Greystones died shortly after giving birth to you.'

Saliva increased in her throat and her hand rushed to her mouth.

'This is upsetting, Miss Redmond, but the reason I am telling you all this is that there is every possibility that Jake's brother, who lives in Spain, will contest the will. You and the hospital trust might have a fight on your hands.'

She crossed her arms. 'I don't want anything of his.'

'Don't be hasty, Miss Redmond.' The solicitor opened the drawer in his desk, took out a glass, then poured a little water and handed it to her. She sipped it.

'All this land marked out here, thirty acres,' he stood up and pointed to the map, 'is yours. It includes his Connemara farm, horses and stock. You don't have to make a decision right now.' He sat back down, leaned his arms on his desk and linked his bony fingers. 'But I can advise you on how to invest it.'

Tamara wasn't listening, she was more concerned that even from beyond the grave, Jake Travis was continuing to torment her. She ran her hands distractedly through her flowing red hair.

'I need to think about all this, Mr. Munroe.'

'Yes, yes, of course, Miss Redmond.'

Tamara walked back to the gypsy camp in a daze, hardly noticing anyone or anything in her wake.

She could hear the workers in the fields beyond, the sounds of the different implements digging the soil and breaking up the clumps of fertile clay. Workers were busy, heads bent over the freshly dug ground, sowing and reaping their small plot of land. Things had changed for the better since Travis's death; something she never thought she would see.

The wagon was empty when she went inside. Ola and Jono were in the fields. Jake Travis had kept them from growing potatoes and vegetables on the land, so they were making up for it now.

Thoughts of her mother's connection with the Travis family infuriated her. She was the victim of this whole web of deceit. The long white envelope with her name written across the front was inside her bag. She sat down in Ola's rocking chair and then, with trembling fingers, she opened it.

Dearest Tamara,
Your first reaction will be to rip my letter to shreds. Please don't.

I'm dying as I write this. I knew the day Jono brought me to hospital I would not be coming out. I need your forgiveness. In spite of everything, I am frightened of dying. Please visit my graveside sometime and say you forgive the terrible crimes I committed against you. I desired and wanted you for selfish reasons.

You are probably not aware that those two gypsies are not your parents. I was in love with your mother, but she chose to marry him, my so-called brother. I knew he wouldn't make her happy and I would have done anything for her. When I first came across you at the gypsy camp, you were ten years old. I had only seen that kind of beauty once. I knew who you were and set out to marry you. I wanted you at all costs, if only to vent revenge on my brother. I hate him. I know what you're thinking. I'm a bitter old man... God forgive me, but, for all that, Tamara, you are a beautiful young woman as your mother was.

I am being honest for the first time in many years. Promise me Bruce won't get his hands on any of my land. You have as much reason as I had to hate him for the way he treated Catherine. Distribute the land as you wish, as long as that scoundrel doesn't get a sod.

Fight him if he contests the will.
Pray for my soul,
Jake

Tamara read it again in total disbelief and then, unable to bear the pain tearing through her, screamed out, 'How dare he? How dare he ask for my forgiveness?'

When Ola came back to make bread for her husband's lunch, she found Tamara staring into space, the letter crumpled on the floor.

'Sweet Jesus, Tamara, what's the matter? What did the solicitor want?' She picked up the letter, straightened it out and struggled to make sense of it before running back outside for Jono.

'We're sorry about your mother, Tamara.' Jona glanced down at the letter again. 'We had no idea the bounder knew all along, did we, Ola?'

She turned round from the stove. 'We'd never a gone along with his plan to marry ye, had we known.' Ola placed her arm around Tamara's shoulder. 'Try and eat something. Ye'll waste away.'

Tamara pushed the porridge aside. 'To think my mother was married to his brother.' She shook her head. 'I can't bear it.'

'Don't be maudlin, Tamara. It's past now.' Jono spread his arms. 'Travis was worth a queer penny, and he's left ye all that land. Do you realise what this means? Ye're a rich woman. We're all rich.'

'Don't you see anything but money? Jake Travis knew who I was all along, and yet he imprisoned me, tried to rape me, and claimed he loved my mother.' She stormed from the wagon and, quickening her pace, she ran, scattering the chickens, as if she was running a race. She climbed the gate and fled across the fields, her face wet with her tears. She took short cut she had often used to reach the sandy cove when she was lonely. Seagulls squawked and flew above her. The wind blew at her hair and cut through her clothes, as she scrambled onto a rock and looked out towards the ocean.

'Oh, Kit,' she cried. 'What am I to do?'

When she returned some time later, fires burned brightly all round the camp. Fiddles were tuned and tambourines clashed while gypsy children danced round in circles.

'This is all for you, Tamara,' Ola said.

'Come and dance, Tamara,' Jono called. 'It's like old times.'

She waved and gave them a watery smile before going inside the wagon. She threw her belongings into her case and slipped away into the night.

CHAPTER FIFTY-SEVEN

It was late when Tamara, her eyes red, stepped from the train in London. She spent her last shilling on a cab to the circus, then went to her wagon and slept.

Next morning, as she was on her way to the water pump, Kit spotted her and called out, 'Tamara. When did you get back?' He took the basin from her and hugged her. 'I've missed you so much.'

The rest of the crew caught sight of them kissing and began to whistle and hoot. Kit pulled her behind one of the wagons. 'How did it go, then? Tell me.' He held her at arm's length. 'Something's upset you.'

'I'm grand,' she replied. 'How are things here?'

'Billy's selling up. An old buddy of his is taking the circus off his hands. The animals are being shipped out today.'

'That's sad. How's he taking it?' It was good to talk about someone else's problems.

'Well, I think he's had enough. He's given the best years of his life to the business, but it's time he took a rest.' He drew her to him. 'You still haven't told me what's upset you?'

'I'll tell you tonight. I have to get ready for work.'

'Sounds ominous!'

Her eyes pooled. 'I can't talk about it now, Kit, I have to go.'

'Okay!' He released his hands from around her waist, but she could feel his eyes upon her as she retrieved her basin and continued towards the water tap.

Ivan and Beth were pleased to see her back so soon. 'It wasn't anything serious I hope,' Ivan said, looking at her downcast face.

'No, nothing serious.'

'Do you want to talk about it?'

'No. I'm grand thanks.' She stood next to the knitting machine and began winding the wool onto the spools.

'I didn't mean to pry.'

She nodded, sat down on the bench seat and started up the machine. 'How are ye getting on with the new machine, Ivan?'

'Slow!' He laughed, lightening the mood. 'I'm just getting the hang of it. This order is taking me longer. Bright colours, fully fashioned garments,' he sighed. 'What next?' He busied himself concentrating on the spinning yarns, and Tamara was glad to be left to her own thoughts.

Beth came in from the other room where she was supervising the older woman folding and boxing finished garments. 'Oh, Tamara, you're back. I trust everything went well for you in Ireland. When did you get back?'

'Last night.' Her foot pressed the pedal sooner than she expected and the noise of two machines drowned her reply. Smiling, Beth nodded and left. There was plenty of work to concentrate on and Tamara was glad of the distraction.

Every now and then, the name Catherine Greystones came into her mind. If only her mother had lived. By the end of the day, her head ached. The only person who could put her mind at rest regarding her mother was Captain Fitzroy, and now she had every reason to get in touch with him.

That afternoon, Kit asked Nelly if she would make up a picnic for two. He washed his hair and it fell in dark waves around his face. It was the last day of March and a sunny evening when he walked towards Charing Cross. He wore a grey jacket with a white shirt open at the neck. A canvas bag hung across his shoulder, at odds with the city men in bowler hats, leaving their offices for home.

He hoped to find Tamara in better form. He had never known her to let anything upset her for long. Perhaps she was still tired after her sea journey. Or had something happened in Ireland? Had her gypsy parents tried to marry her off to someone again? It would not surprise him. She was so beautiful and those flowing red locks were sure to attract admirers. The sooner he married her, the better. Now he had found her again, he did not intend to let her slip through his fingers a second time.

When Tamara came out and saw him lolling

against the shop window, she smiled and slipped her arm through his. 'Hello, Kit. You're a sight for sore eyes. Do I need to go back and change?'

'You look lovely to me as you are.' He smiled down at her. 'Have you had a good day?'

She shrugged. 'What have you got there?'

'A picnic! It's such a nice evening.' He glanced up at the sky, clouds shading the last of the evening's sunshine. 'I thought we could go on the common, have a bite to eat, and you can tell me everything that happened in Ireland.'

She squeezed his arm and nodded, and they walked on towards the common, her head lolling on his shoulder. It was nearly six and the common was free of people, apart from a couple of boys playing with a ball. They found a bench and sat down. Kit made sure that Tamara ate some bread and cheese and drank a beaker of lemon soda, before pressing her for answers.

An hour later, the sky had darkened and Tamara's face was wet with tears. Kit wiped them away with his fingertips. 'I should have gone with you. It's bound to have been a shock.' He placed his arm around her. 'I could have come if I'd known you were coming back so soon!'

'It's all right.'

'Why'd he not tell you that in the letter? Why drag you over there to humiliate you like that?' Tamara lowered her gaze. 'What is it? Is there something you haven't told me?' He released his arm, held both her hands and turned to face her. She looked up at him, her big eyes filling with tears again. 'Is it that bad?'

'Jake Travis left me his land, every last acre, just to spite the brother he hated even more than he hated me.'

Kit didn't speak. She stood up, crumbs falling from her coat. 'I don't want anything of his. His brother is bound to come after me and I won't be hounded by that family again.'

Kit stood next to her, his arm around her. 'Tamara, shush, darling.' He rocked her in his arms. 'I wouldn't blame you if you kept it. God knows you deserve it, but I can't take a penny of it. When we're married, I'll keep my wife. It certainly won't be on another man's brass; illegal or otherwise.'

'What shall I do, Kit?'

'Have you told any of this to Ola, and Jono?'

'Yes, they know everything and they're celebrating already. They've no idea how I feel.' She pressed him to sit. 'Take a look at this letter left with the solicitor. It will help you understand.'

Tamara fidgeted with the strap of her bag and watched Kit's face change from one kind of emotion to another. 'The bloody coward,' he said. 'He thinks he can clear his conscience by lavishing his wealth on you to avenge his brother. He was one sick bastard.' He shook his head and pulled her close. 'No wonder you've been distracted, darling. All I can say is that it's a good job he's dead, or I'd strangle him and willingly go to prison.'

'Please don't say that, Kit.'

He lifted her face and kissed her, then again with passion. Tamara wrapped her arms around his neck. Entwined in each other's arms, nothing appeared to matter, until a dog scavenging for food nosed its way into Kit's bag and broke the spell.

'Come on.' Kit pulled her to her feet. 'Let's go home.' He kissed the top of her head. 'Whatever you decide to do, I'll back you, just so long as you understand how I feel.'

CHAPTER FIFTY-EIGHT

Kit had never thought of Tamara as a true gypsy. Yet, she had many of the Romany ways and a fiery temper to match, inherited from the people who had brought her up. But she was without a mean streak in her body. Her beauty, slim figure, hair he loved to bury his face in, and the way her eyes flashed when she was angry, could melt his heart at any given moment. Her blistered hands showed she had worked hard in her seventeen years, and he loved her more than he had any other woman.

Kit was pleased that Captain Fitzroy was Tamara's biological father. The alternative would be too much for her to bear. That weekend, they went for a long walk in Hyde Park, where they discussed their future. He agreed with how she planned to dispose of Travis's land.

'You mustn't do this for me, Tamara. It must be what you want.'

'All I want is your love, Kit, and to be around horses again. How would you feel if I kept the horse farm?' Her eyes moved over his face.

'What makes you think it's a legitimate business?'

'I don't,' she sighed. 'I've written to the solicitor to ask.'

'Will you still want to keep it if you find out he got it through dishonest means, like the rest of his businesses?'

They sat on a park bench, Tamara glancing at her hands, twisting them in her lap. 'I don't know. Some of Travis's horses are rare breeds. I can't let them be sold to just anyone, especially anyone who might ill-treat them.'

'Oh, love. I feel I'm stopping you from doing what you really want, and...'

'No, you're not. Let's wait and see what Munroe comes back with.' When she placed her arms around his neck, her kiss aroused his passion and he found it difficult not to take their lovemaking further. In spite of Tamara tempting him, he knew she wanted to wait.

A few days later, a letter arrived from Munroe asking if she could arrange to come over again. There were things to discuss about the farm and her signature was needed to dispose of the inherited land as she wished. He would be happy to help in his capacity as solicitor if she was unsure about anything.

She did not expect to be letting Ivan down again so soon, but she had no alternative than to go over to Ireland again.

'You've just got back and we have so many orders to fill.'

374

'I'm sorry, Ivan. I wouldn't ask, only this is important.'

Beth gave her a curious look. 'What is it, Tamara? Is there anything we can help with?'

'No, thank you, Beth. Perhaps it might be best if I handed in my notice, I've not been reliable lately.'

'Oh no. I won't hear of it.' Ivan had already gone back to his machine and the noise drowned their voices.

'I'm sorry, Beth. I'm going this evening.' It would take her too long to explain and it wasn't the right time while they were all so busy. Time enough for that once she got back.

Later that evening, Tamara and Kit were in their respective wagons, packing. Kit had asked for a few more days before starting work. Although they were not too happy, his new employers had agreed to wait for him.

He had never been to Ireland, and was looking forward to seeing where his grandfather and great-grandfather had lived and died during the great famine. Tamara packed her small case, taking only what she needed. She wore a sky blue ankle-length skirt. It went well with her white lacy blouse. Over that she wore a black jacket that came down over her hips and nipped her small waist. She slipped her feet into black leather boots and laced them up. Her red hair tumbled around her shoulders as she closed the wagon door behind her.

Kit was sitting on the steps of his wagon, his hands resting on his knees, his black curly hair falling across his face and a large haversack on the ground next to him. He glanced up and smiled when he heard Tamara approach. He stood up and brushed back his hair, revealing his rugged looks. He had on a thick woollen coat and a red scarf wrapped round his neck.

As he strode towards her, Tamara felt her pulse race. 'Ready, darling?'

'You bet.' She felt excited to be going back to Ireland, this time with Kit. He placed his free arm around her waist and kissed her.

Nelly called out to them, waving one of her knitted shawls. 'You'll need this on the boat.' She placed the multicoloured knitted shawl across Tamara's shoulders. 'Thanks, Nelly.'

'Off you go, the pair of ye. Have a good journey.'

When the ship docked in Cork, Kit wanted to start exploring until Tamara reminded him that they only had a few days to sort out important issues before they could relax.

They hitched their way to Galway. It was an opportunity for Kit to see parts of the countryside and already he was falling in love with the place.

'I never realised the landscape here was so beautiful, Tamara. I can't wait to see Connemara.'

Tamara smiled and snuggled up to him on the back of the hay cart, where she told him of her dream to work with horses again.

'I love horses, too, Tamara, you know that, but...'

'Please, Kit. Don't say no just yet. Wait until we've looked at it together.' She knew that once she saw the horses again, it would be hard to let them go. She had seen Jake Travis buying horses from shady characters in London, but somehow she felt she could overlook that as long as it did not cause a rift between her and Kit.

'No harm in taking a look, I guess.' Then sighing, he said, 'What I said before still stands. It has to be your decision, Tamara.'

They approached the town of Galway, busy with hawkers and market traders. Tamara called out to the farmer to drop them in Main Street. They jumped down from the back of the cart and brushed straw from their clothes. Kit plucked a stalk from Tamara's hair. Waving their thanks to the farmer, they made their way towards Jerry Munroe's office.

'Oh. Do come in.' They followed him into the small office and closed the door behind them. Jerry positioned himself behind the desk and glanced up at Kit, who stood with his back to the door while Tamara took the chair. 'I've not tied everything up yet, Miss Redmond.' His gaze lingered on Kit. 'There's still time to change your mind if you want to keep the land.'

'I won't change my mind. I'd like this over and done with as quickly as possible,' Tamara said. She turned toward Kit. 'This is my fiancé, Kit Trevelyan.'

Munroe nodded and cleared his throat, then leaned forward and placed some prepared papers in front of her. 'This states that all the land you specified will go to Jono and Ola Redmond, along with the land they live on, plus the adjacent two acres of arable land.' He handed her a pen and pointed to where he wanted her to sign. 'You will, of course, have copies of these in due course.'

Tamara glanced round at Kit, but his eyes were cast down towards the floor and she wondered what he was thinking. She could see he was not going to be dragged into this.

'Your wishes regarding your mother's name will happen in due course, Miss Redmond. You asked me about the farm. It's on prime land and will fetch a good price with those rare breeds and stock, should you decide to sell.'

Tamara nodded. 'Do you know how he came by it?'

'Yes, indeed.' He coughed and cleared his throat. 'The farm originally belonged to Catherine Greystones.'

'My mother owned the farm?' Tamara's eyes widened. 'Why didn't you say this earlier?'

'I ... well ... if you'll let me finish.' He leaned back in his chair and twirled his pencil between his fingers. 'Lady Greystones sold it to Jake Travis, because her husband didn't want her spending endless hours with her horses.'

'My mother liked horses?'

'Yes, I believe she was a keen horsewoman.'

'So,' Kit intervened, 'this Travis guy bought the farm legally from Tamara's mother?'

'Yes indeed, from what I've been given to understand.' The solicitor shifted in his chair. 'I didn't handle the deal, you understand. It could well have been a private exchange between the two.'

'Can we see the farm?' Tamara was on her feet.

'It's yours, Miss Redmond. I'd recommend you take a look around. It is a lovely spot, off the beaten track, close to Maam's Cross. The old sign is still there; Jake never changed the name. His head groom is a local man, called O'Leary.'

'Thank you.' Her eyes were bright with excitement. 'Shall we go up there tomorrow, Kit? Jono will loan us a couple of mares.'

Kit nodded. 'Just as a matter of interest,' he said. 'What will happen to Travis's offshore businesses?'

'All his overseas businesses will close down. According to his will, he had no wish for them to continue running after his death. Once you let me know your intentions regarding the farm, Miss Redmond, I'll have everything drawn up for you to sign in a couple of days.' He smiled and shook both their hands as they left.

CHAPTER FIFTY-NINE

Tamara squeezed Kit's hand as they stepped inside Jono and Ola's wagon. Kit glanced around. The small interior was spick and span, and the table was set for their meal.

'I've made ye some soup and fresh oat cakes, so sit yourselves down before it goes cold.' Ola pulled over a chair for Kit.

'Thanks. It smells good.' He smiled across at Tamara.

'Well,' Ola said, sitting down. 'How'd yeas get

on? Did he leave much?'

Tamara sipped her soup. 'Where's Jono? I thought he'd be here.'

'What's the matter? Can't ye tell me?'

Tamara moved her soup bowl aside. 'I'd rather wait until he gets here.'

'Well, he's up in the top field planting. He'll be down when his belly rumbles.' Ola directed her gaze at Kit. 'Well, young feller. What clan do you belong to then?'

Kit looked up. 'I'm afraid I don't belong to any clan.' He raised an eyebrow at Tamara.

Ola, straightening her shoulders, removed the empty dishes and placed them into a small bowl for washing. 'So, you're hitching up to a Gorgia. I hope ye know what you're doin'.'

'I am a Gorgia. Have you forgotten who my real mother was?'

'Aye, that may well as be, but ye were raised in the gypsy ways, Tamara. You know nothing else.' She turned and glared at Kit.

Tamara jumped up. 'Oh, but I do, Ola. I've never fit in and now I know why.' She reached for Kit's hand. 'Why don't you like Kit? He's a good man, the best.'

'He has the good looks of a Roma, but he's still not one of us.' She spat into the fire and sat down again.

Kit felt he had to defend himself to this strange individual. 'No, I'm not a gypsy, Mrs. Redmond, I'm my own man. I love Tamara and I believe she loves me. If need be, I would protect her with my life.'

'Aye, well, see that you do.' She continued to

keep busy.

Tamara smiled across at Kit. At least the woman had brought her up and not abandoned her to the workhouse; Kit was grateful to Ola for that. Now he wondered how Ola and Jono would react to the news that Tamara was about to hand over her inherited land to them.

Jono arrived and washed at the tap outside before coming inside. 'Ah, so, this is the bold Kit.' He shook his hand and sat down to his meal.

Kit smiled. 'Nice to meet you, Jono. Tamara's told me a lot about you.'

'She has, has she?' He supped his soup, then looked up at Tamara. 'Well, you're a wealthy woman now.'

Ola glanced up from the stove, listening, as Jono sat back in his chair. 'What do ye plan to do with all that land?'

'Oh, I've got plans,' she smiled. 'That's not to say his brother won't contest it.' She moved closer to Jono. 'But you'll have to deal with it.' She passed him the signed land deeds. 'I've signed all the land he left me over to you and Ola.'

'What are ye blabbing about?'

'It's yours, and I hope you'll continue living without worry for the rest of your lives.'

Ola came and sat by them. 'But ye can't do that, love. I thought ye wanted to get married.'

'Ola's right,' Jono said. 'We can't keep it all.' He looked at Kit. 'Did you know about this?'

'It's Tamara's choice.'

'It was never my intention to take anything be-

381

longing to that man,' she explained. 'He left me something I can be really proud of. The only thing I want is the farm that once belonged to my mother.'

Ola had tears in her eyes. 'Does that mean you might come back here to live?'

'We've not decided anything yet. We're going over to see the farm tomorrow.'

She took the dishes to the washbasin and began to wash up.

Jono scratched his head. 'Are you sure you want to give it all away, Tamara?'

Tamara glanced towards Kit. 'We've got plans of our own.'

'I'll support my own wife when we're married,' Kit told them.

Jono stood up and kissed her, then offered his hand to Kit again. 'I can see you're not one of us, lad. A Roma would never be too proud to take land or money, no matter how they came by it.' He smiled. 'All I ask is ye treat her right.'

'I intend to, Jono. Never fear.' Kit glanced towards Ola.

'Yeah, well, ye seem to have tamed her wild ways.' Then she cried. 'My Tamara, soon to be wed. It's not five minutes since ye were knee-high to a blade of grass.'

Tamara wrapped her in a hug.

CHAPTER SIXTY

Tamara and Kit rode towards Connemara. Ola had packed them a parcel of food to eat on the way. Excited at the prospect of owning something that had once belonged to her mother, Tamara could not hide the thrill of knowing their mutual love of horses had nothing at all to do with her gypsy upbringing.

Kit appeared preoccupied and she guessed he had some misgivings running through his head. She left him to mull things over without interruption. The day had turned warm and the sun was shining, and after a while they stopped.

'God! This is an amazing view,' said Kit. 'Shall we stop here awhile?'

She dismounted. 'Yes. I'd forgotten how beautiful it is.'

They walked away from the track into a nearby field, where Kit tied both animals to an oak tree and sat down. He undid the flask and the food parcel. Then he patted the grass for her to sit next to him and they shared the flagon of cold tea between them and bit into their egg bread. The scene around them was calm and peaceful, with sheep grazing in the distance. Tamara lay back on the grass, her hands behind her head. She could hear the nearby stream trickling over the stones.

'Kit,' she said eventually. 'What are you thinking?'

'Oh, just how lucky I am to have found you and how much I love you.'

She smiled and he leaned across to kiss her lips. Tamara put her arms around his neck and looked at him with big eyes. 'Do you like Ireland?'

'I've not felt this relaxed in a long time.'

Tamara glanced up at the rugged, handsome features of the man she loved, and her hand reached behind his head, her fingers roaming through his curly black hair. She let her free hand travel across his muscular chest. She knew exactly what she was doing. She had loved this man for months, and this was a rare occasion to be alone with him.

It was quiet, apart from the birds twittering and the distant hum of a tractor. She kissed his mouth, her mass of red curls covering his face. He wrapped his arms around her tightly, burying his face in the warmth and tenderness of her body so close to his. He kissed her several times and then with such passion, crushing her to him. She felt his hands touch her in places he had not gone before, and her feelings were so strong that she did not want him to stop.

Suddenly they heard the yelling of an irate farmer, who waved his stick at them from the brow of the hill, forcing them to scramble to their feet, untie their horses, and flee back to the track.

'Were we on private land?'

'Probably,' she giggled.

A few hours later, Tamara and Kit stood wide-eyed by the gate of the farm, taking in the enormity of the place. A wooden fence, heightened by thick wire, enclosed the area. A weather-beaten sign swayed lightly in the breeze and Tamara's breath almost caught in her throat as she read aloud, Greystones Farm. From the gateway, she got that familiar smell of horses. Six brood mares frolicked in the field, making her laugh.

'Isn't this wonderful, Kit? Her eyes danced.

Kit nodded, holding tightly to Jono's two mares, which were snorting and straining for freedom. As Kit took in the panoramic view before them, with the Connemara hills as a backdrop, she could tell he felt the same way.

'So, we had better take a look around.' Kit unbolted the wooden gate, closing it behind them, and walked along a gravelled pathway. It was quiet apart from the horses hooves crunching the small stones. To the right, a well-maintained, whitewashed, stone-built cottage was an attractive sight, apart from a neglected rose bush underneath both windows.

They came to an open square yard with stables on both sides. Farm smells and the odour of manure grew stronger. Two older outbuildings ran alongside the newly-built barn next to a lopsided hay barn, housing the last of the winter hay.

There appeared to be no one about until a gangly youth with a sour expression, his wellingtons covered in horse excrement, came up behind them.

'We don't buy gypsy horses. Market at Maam's Cross was yesterday.'

'We're here to see whoever's in charge,' Tamara said, ignoring his remark.

385

'Who's asking?' The youth ran his eyes over Tamara.

'I am.' Kit stepped forward, giving the youth a stare of authority.

The lad coughed and shuffled his feet. 'Over there,' he pointed towards one of the barns that ran alongside the hayloft.

Kit handed him the reins. 'Feed and water these animals,' he said. Then he took Tamara's hand and they strode towards the smell of burning metal, and the sound of a horse being shod.

'Mr. O'Leary.'

The man glanced up, holding a horseshoe in his hand. He wore a check shirt with the sleeves rolled up to his elbow, and his ginger hair showed beneath his brown cap.

'We'd like to talk to you, but I can see you're busy,' Tamara said, with one eye on the agitated black stallion. It snorted and flared its nostrils, its eyes wide.

'Well, sure, if ye can give us a minute,' he said, turning back to the reluctant mount. 'Come on now, boy. That's enough messin'. You'll feel better when this is done.' The horse kicked out with its hind legs, knocking over a galvanised bucket, sending it clattering across the stable.

Tamara stepped in to offer her help. 'Hoy boy, steady now.' She came closer, gently moving her hand along the animal's back until it whinnied and shook its long mane. Kit held the halter. Tamara murmured words into the horse's ear that only the animal appeared to understand, and the job was done.

'You're good with horses, then,' O'Leary said,

386

and Kit loosened the halter, handing it back.

O'Leary led the stallion across the yard towards the field, while Tamara and Kit followed. He slapped the animal's rear to drive him into the paddock and secured the gate, watching as the stallion kicked up its heels churning the turf. Turning to Kit, O'Leary said. 'If you're looking for Mr. Travis, you're about two months too late.'

'We're here to talk to you, about the farm,' Tamara said.

'To me? Well, sure what can I do for ye?'

'I'm the new owner, and this is Kit Trevelyan, my fiancé.' She glanced up at Kit. He raised an eyebrow, but a smile creased his face.

'Oh!' O'Leary wiped his hands down his trousers and shook hers. 'Have ye any proof of this? After all, you could be anyone.'

'Why, yes.' She showed him the documents folded in the pocket of her jacket.

Satisfied with what he saw, O'Leary said, 'I'm relieved to meet ye. Look, why don't we go into the office and I'll put the kettle on, or perhaps you'd prefer some lemonade?'

'Tea sounds like a good idea,' Kit said.

Tamara placed her hands around the mug of hot tea. 'Who lives in the cottage?'

'Well, sure Mr. Travis when he was here. No one's been inside since he locked up on his last visit.'

'Oh,' Tamara said. 'So we can't see inside?'

'Well, as you're the new owner, Miss, you can always have new locks fitted.'

'How have you managed to keep the place running?'

'It's not been easy. In fact, I can't manage another week on me own, like.'

Kit stood by the window, his thumbs hooked into the pockets of his trousers. 'We're grateful to you for holding the place together, O'Leary.'

'Sure, I couldn't walk away and leave these beautiful animals to fend for themselves.' He pursed his lips. 'Though, can't say the same for the rest of Travis's staff.' He told them how three of the men, with families to rear, had walked out. He only lived down the road, and the youth they met when they arrived was a neighbour's lad who worked for a shillin' a week.

'Thanks for your loyalty, Mr. O'Leary,' Tamara said. 'We'll make sure you get the wages you're owed.'

'Well, it's not just a matter of wages, Miss. I'm out of pocket keeping the feed bins filled. And if it weren't for the lad, the place would be left unguarded when I have to go and fetch the feeds in the cart.' He shook his head. 'I was sorry to hear of Mr. Travis's passing. Sure, he wasn't much older than meself. We thought he'd gone off on one of his jaunts, as he so often did, until the wife read of his death in the local newspaper.'

Tamara nodded.

O'Leary drained his mug. 'Stocks are dangerously low. Are ye going to keep the place going, Miss?'

'Yes, I'm hoping to.'

'Will ye still be needin' a foreman, like?'

'You bet.' She looked up at Kit.

'Okay.' Kit intervened. 'Make a detailed list of what you're owed. I'm assuming you kept invoices and receipts?'

'Oh, bedad I did.'

'Hire a couple of local men to help out, and we'll be back before we return to England to see how you're getting on.' Kit handed O'Leary sufficient cash.

'You're going back to England, then?'

'Miss Greystones only heard she'd inherited the farm days ago. We both work in London, so we have to go back.'

'Greystones? You're related to the Greystones family? I might have guessed,' he said, 'the way you handled that stallion.'

'We're delighted you're staying on,' Tamara interjected.

'Yes, as long as there's the money to keep the place running.'

'There will be,' Kit assured him.

Tamara had to resist the urge to throw her arms around Kit and kiss him. O'Leary untied the filly next for shoeing. 'Well, I'm glad to see that the farm will be in capable hands again.'

'As I said,' Kit told him, 'we just have a few things to tie up in London.'

They bid O'Leary farewell, and when they reached the yard, the youth brought their horses to them. They set off back the way they came, taking in the beauty around Maam's Cross, with spectacular views alongside a range of mountains that seemed to enclose them.

CHAPTER SIXTY-ONE

Two days later, with everything tied up at the solicitors, Tamara and Kit were on their way back to London. Kit was eager to explain to the manager of the Lazy Man's Gym that he wouldn't need the job after all. Tamara was just pleased to be away from the confines of her gypsy parents, where Ola talked non-stop about the money she could make.

Tamara had more than the inheritance on her mind. Consumed with the horse farm, and the fact she would soon be a married woman with a husband to care for, not to mention the responsibilities of running their own business, she could hardly breathe at times with excitement.

Before the ship docked in Southport, Kit took Tamara's small hand in his. 'Tamara, I want to ask you something, and I want you to be truthful,' he said. 'You've given up a lot for me. I need to be sure you won't regret it.'

'That land was never really mine, Kit. Jono and Ola will sell it and make a lot of money. They deserve it after what they've had to put up with.'

He pulled her to him. 'I want you to know how much I love you. And I'll see that you never want for anything.' As people jostled around them, they picked up their luggage and joined the queue to disembark.

The following morning, Kit rose early and dressed in his best suit, a grey serge fleck. Unaccustomed to tight-fitting shirt collars, he chose a white cravat from his collection of neckties and secured it round his neck. He checked his pockets, making sure he had the right credentials. As he walked toward the town, he recited in his head what he would say to the bank manager. He had gone to the bank with Billy on a couple of occasions in the past, and the manager had appeared austere and unapproachable.

The town was busy and noisy and he felt a little out of his depth when he passed men in their fine suits, stiff collars and bowler hats. Clearing his throat, he straightened his shoulders and went into the bank. It had just gone nine and the building was quiet. He stood in front of the tall polished mahogany counter and asked if he could speak to the manager.

'Have you an appointment?' The black dress and neat white collar the woman wore did nothing to alleviate the severity of her glare.

Kit shook his head. 'No, but I must see him today.'

'Mr. McBride is busy, but if you'd care to take a seat, I'll see if he can fit you in. It's usual to make an appointment first.'

'I'm sorry...'

Before he finished speaking, the woman had turned towards another customer. Kit went and sat down. He looked up at the tall ceiling and down at the shiny black and white tiled floor. How long would he have to wait? The quietness unnerved him and he coughed to relieve a tickle at the back of his throat.

He already had an account at the bank with substantial funds, and he hoped the manager would see him as trustworthy. True, he had not invested any money in the past couple of months, and he hoped he wouldn't have to explain. Now he wanted to marry the woman he loved and he wanted to give her the wedding present of her dreams.

The imposing interior of the bank made his stomach contract. The thought of failure worried him. He listened to how other men conducted themselves inside the bank, and how they were treated. They said, 'Good morning, Miss', and raised their hats. In return, they were rewarded with a smile, which was more than he had got.

When at last the door opened on his right and a well-dressed man came out, the haughty woman behind the counter replaced the phone and nodded towards Kit. 'Mr. McBride can see you now.'

Kit reciprocated with a nod and went inside, closing the heavy door behind him. An expanse of oak panelled walls surrounded him, and the stout man looked older than he remembered.

'Take a seat,' he said, continuing to write. A few seconds later, he looked up. 'I don't appear to have your name.'

'Trevelyan.'

'What brings you to my bank, Mr. Trevelyan?'

He began to fidget with his hands. 'I'm after a bank loan, somewhere in the region of two thousand guineas.'

McBride's eyes widened over the rim of his specs. 'That's quite a large loan, Mr. Trevelyan. I'd much prefer you were here to deposit a large amount into my bank.' He pushed his glasses further up on the bridge of his nose.

Kit swallowed. 'I do have an account, Mr. McBride.'

'I see. Let me get out your details.' He reached across to his filing cabinet. He flicked through until he found a thin folder, plucked it out and swivelled back to face Kit, glancing down the entries. Then he placed his elbows on the desk. 'You've got substantial funds here, Mr. Trevelyan. Why do you need a loan?'

His heartbeat quickened. 'I'm getting married and I want the money to finance a horse farm in Ireland.'

McBride stroked his wispy sideburns. 'I see. When were you thinking of going there?'

'As soon as possible.'

'What can you offer as collateral?'

Kit felt his shoulders relax. 'I was hoping my savings would act as security.' He leaned forward in his chair. 'You see, once we take over the farm, we intend to increase profits.'

'Is it a going concern?'

'Oh, yes. The previous owner died and left the farm, horses and stock to my future wife.'

Kit took out a financial sheet with a detailed progress sheet for the past few years. 'I can't promise we'll double that figure by next year, but I'm confident we'll increase it. And once I've repaid the loan, I'll continue to invest in your bank. I can't say fairer than that.'

'Umm.' McBride nodded, pursing his lips. He glanced up at the clock. 'Look, give me a day to look over the figures. If you make an appointment for the same time tomorrow, I'll give you my answer then.'

Tamara walked along Charing Cross Road, glancing in the shop windows on the way to her employers. She hoped they would be pleased with her news, but just the same she felt sad to be leaving. Ivan and Beth were two people she would miss. She had never told them about Jake Travis, but now she felt she owed them an explanation for her weird behaviour lately.

It was lunchtime when Tamara walked in. Beth's eyes widened.

'Tamara. How nice to see you. Is everything all right now?' She lifted her skeins of wool so Tamara could sit down.

'We got back early.' She perched next to Beth. 'I don't want to take up too much of your lunch hour, Beth, but there are things I need to explain.' She could hear the constant thump of the flat iron as the presser worked on a nearby bench. The woman stopped for a minute and looked across at Tamara before carrying on.

Beth leaned in close. 'She's on a piece rate.'

Tamara nodded and smiled. Ivan came in carrying a cardboard box and placed it down on the floor. 'Where did you come from? Are you staying?'

'No, I'm not, Ivan. Can we talk in private?'

'Can't it wait?' He checked the label on the box.

'I'm sorry. It won't take long.'

Beth led the way towards the kitchen and Ivan closed the door behind them. 'What's all this about?' he asked. 'We can't carry on in this way, Tamara.'

The three sat round the table. 'I know and I'm sorry, but I have to give you my notice. I'm getting married.'

Beth said, 'Is it true?'

'Yes, I'm getting married. I've been left a farm in Ireland with land and a cottage attached.'

Shock registered on Ivan's face. 'Well, I'm delighted to hear of your good fortune, Tamara, but we'll be right sorry to lose you.'

Beth knitted her fingers and twirled one thumb over the other. 'I gather you're marrying that nice young man, Kit.'

Smiling, Tamara nodded.

Ivan, showing more interest now, leaned his elbows on the table. 'What kind of farm is it, Tamara? Farming is hard work. Has Kit any experience?'

'It's a horse farm, Ivan, and it once belonged to my mother; my real mother.' She told them a brief history of her life and hoped they would not think any the less of her.

'Oh, Tamara.' Beth stood up and hugged her. 'Thank you for sharing that with us. We never realised. I'm sorry about your mother, but you have Kit now, and we'll always be here if you ever decide to come back for a visit.'

Ivan patted her shoulder. 'I always thought there was more to you, Tamara. So, you're really the daughter of Lady Greystones? What a turn-around. Will you be taking her name? Not that it matters, you getting married an' all.' He ran his hand over his face. 'It must have been a shock.'

'Yes, it was. It still feels strange.'

Beth wiped a tear from her cheek. 'I couldn't be more pleased for you. And to think Captain Fitzroy is your real father.'

'I'm sorry I couldn't be honest with you both before, but I wasn't really sure of anything until recently.' She sighed. 'You've been like a mother and a father to me. You helped me when I was down, without asking any questions. I'll never forget you.' She felt a lump form in her throat.

Ivan poured himself tea from the pot. 'It's been a pleasure.'

She choked back tears and stood up. 'I've taken up enough of your time. I'll let you know our plans, but please just make sure you're at my wedding.'

'Wild horses won't keep us away.'

CHAPTER SIXTY-TWO

Tamara spent the morning writing letters. In spite of her careful efforts, she found herself making one mistake after another. She bought herself a dictionary and wanted to make a good impression by writing her words correctly. She tried to keep all her letters the same size and, after three attempts, she finally finished the two letters.

One she addressed to her father, Captain Fitzroy, in Aberdeen, and the other to his sister, Mrs. Miriam Tranter, in Finchley. The letters explained she was to be married soon and hoped they would be free to attend her wedding. She had planned to call on Miriam, but the last few weeks had flown past in a whirlwind of excitement, and there just had not been time. With the important letters out of the way, she wrote a similar letter to Jono and Ola.

She stood up, stretched her slender shoulders, and bent her head to look into the small mirror that hung above the chest of drawers. She ran her fingers through her untamed mass of curls and pinched her cheeks, reminding herself that a few early nights would not go amiss, if she wanted to look her best for her wedding day. To have her real father give her away was her dearest wish. Just thinking about it sent a frisson of excitement through her, and she wrapped her arms around herself and danced happily round the small wagon.

She slid open the cupboard door and looked along the line of clothes hanging there. Her life had changed almost overnight. She had enough clothes – old and new to last her months. The horse farm would make them both rich, she was sure of it.

She was about to slip off her nightdress when she recognised the soft rap on her door, and Kit stood there smiling up at her. 'Oh, I'm sorry. Aren't you dressed yet? I couldn't wait to tell you the good news.'

'Come in. What is it?'

'The bank has agreed to loan me two thousand guineas on the strength of my savings, so we can get married as soon as you like.' He hugged her, lifting her off her feet.

'Oh, Kit, that's wonderful.' She reached up and kissed him. 'I'll go and see Father Malone today.'

'You're sure you want a church wedding?'

She nodded. 'Is that okay with you?'

'Nothing too grand, mind.' He pulled her close, kissing her until she responded. The thin strap of her nightgown slipped off her shoulder, revealing the swell of her breast. He kissed her delicate skin. 'Oh, Tamara,' he murmured, his kisses passionate.

'Kit, oh Kit.' She wanted him just as much, but with the sudden knock on the wagon door, she pushed him from her and covered her exposed breast. She pulled a shawl around her shoulders before opening the door.

Nelly stood on the bottom step looking up at her. 'Billy wants ta see Kit. Nick's 'ome.'

Kit moved in front of Tamara. 'What is it, Nelly?'

'I don't know, but Nick's 'ome.'

'How long?'

She shook her head. 'Billy's in the small tent. I sure as God hope you can cheer 'im up, 'cause I can't.' She walked away.

This was bad timing on Nick's part, but why should that surprise Tamara? The man was trouble. She touched Kit's arm. 'Be careful.' She reached up and kissed him. 'Don't let him rile you. I'll get dressed and follow you over.'

Billy sat alone. He looked up when he heard Kit and beckoned him to sit down.

'Is it true Nick's back?' Kit sat down opposite him, and saw the worried look that creased Billy's face.

'He arrived in the middle of the night, and with the kid in tow. They're both sleeping in the spare caravan.' He sighed. 'Can you believe he brought the child with him?'

'Did he say why?'

Billy shook his head. 'Just that he'd talk later when he'd had some sleep.'

'What will you do?' Kit reached across and placed his hand reassuringly on Billy's shoulder. 'Is he hoping for work? Doesn't he know the circus is dissolved?'

'Don't worry, lad. I'll think of something.' He puffed his pipe. 'You still haven't told me why you changed your mind about that job at the gym.'

Kit wasn't sure this was the time to tell Billy he was going to work and live in Ireland. But the older man had to know sooner or later. They both looked up as Tamara walked into the tent, wearing a full skirt in a green floral design and a green blouse. Her hair was scraped back from her face.

'Hello,' she said quietly, sitting down next to Kit. 'Is everything all right, Mr. Billy? Where's Nick?'

'Sleeping,' Kit told her.

Billy pressed a wedge of tobacco into his pipe. 'I'm anxious about the child.'

'He's got a child with him?' Tamara's eyes widened.

Billy nodded. 'We'll know more when he wakes up.' He looked towards Tamara. 'If you'd like some Rosie Lee, there's still some in the pot.'

She declined and leant across the table. 'Where's the child's mother?'

'It looks like she's scarpered and left him with the kid.'

'How was Nick?' Kit asked.

'Subdued. Troubled, I'd say. It could be to do with the child.' Billy picked up his hat and got up to leave, but Kit pressed him to sit back down.

'We have some news, Billy. And we can't put it off.'

'You're getting married and about time, too,' Billy laughed.

Tamara moved closer to Kit and he placed his arm around her shoulder. 'We have some great news, Mr. Billy.'

Billy leant his elbows on the table. 'Go on.' When they had finished telling him about the horse farm and how they were both going to run it together after they were married, Billy was astounded but delighted for them. 'Holy Moly! What a stroke of luck. When are you going?'

'Just as soon as we can get someone to marry us.' Kit turned and winked at Tamara.

'There will always be room on the farm for you, Mr. Billy, if you want it,' she offered.

'After the shabby way I treated you, you'd do that for me?' he swallowed.

'That's as good as buried. You gave me a job when everyone else rejected me for being a gypsy.'

He reached across and touched her arm. 'You're a fine lady.' He shook his head and looked at Kit.

'You've got a real good 'n there.'

Kit nodded and squeezed Tamara's waist. 'Don't I know it.'

'I've always wanted to see Ireland,' the older man said, tears welling in his eyes. 'But I doubt I'll be going anywhere now that Nick is back with my grandchild.' He came round the table and gathered them both to him in a bear hug.

Tamara went with her post on the way to Corpus Christi. Even though she had not attended any of the services there, she had decided to ask Father Malone to marry them. As she walked inside, a few women with shawls covering their heads knelt in prayer in front of the altar where the exposition of the Blessed Sacrament was taking place. She had seen this once before when her grandmother Lena, had taken her to Galway Cathedral.

She followed what others were doing and went down on both knees in front of the Monstrance, before she stepped into a pew towards the back of the church. A peaceful ambience cloaked her, and she looked up at the crescent-shaped gold container holding the small white host in an upright position. It reminded her of the sun's rays.

She knelt and said the prayers she could remember, then sat back and looked around her. On the night she took refuge here, she had hardly noticed how lovely the church was. Now she had time to take in her surroundings – candles burning on the main altar, the Lady Chapel on one side, and the Sacred Heart Chapel on the other.

She imagined Kit standing next to her on the altar steps and it made her heart flutter. Her gypsy parents would expect her to have a gypsy wedding in Ireland, with celebrations that went on for days. She would hate that and so would Kit. Ola and Jono never travelled out of Ireland and she guessed they would not do so now. They would be busy selling land and making money. She sighed. Sitting here thinking would get her nowhere. It was time for her to go and speak to Father Malone.

CHAPTER SIXTY-THREE

Tamara knocked and popped her head round the vestry door. The priest was pinning a list of names on the wall. He turned round when he saw her.

'Tamara. What brings you back so soon? I thought you were still in Ireland.'

'We got things sorted sooner than we expected, Father.'

'You're looking pleased with yourself. I guess things are going well with yourself and Kit?'

'Well, yes. Yes, they are.' She pushed a lock of hair from her face. 'Are you busy, Father?'

He placed the rest of the pins back into a tin. 'I've an hour before Benediction. Come across to the house and I'll make us some tea. Miss O'Keefe's at the market.'

In the kitchen, he gestured for her to sit at the

table while he boiled the kettle on the hob. It seemed strange to see the priest making his own tea. 'Shall I make it, Father?'

'You're surprised I can make tea, aren't you? I can also boil an egg and toast bread,' he told her, placing cups onto saucers. 'But I'm afraid that's as far as it goes.' He chuckled. 'I would no doubt starve, left on my own.' He wet the pot and brewed the tea, then placed everything on a tray and took it across to the table. 'Here we are.'

He passed her a cup, leaving her to milk and sugar her own, then sat down opposite her.

'May I say, you look well. It must have something to do with the Irish air.'

'I'm in love, Father, and we want to get married.' She smiled.

'Well, that's only natural. How can I help?'

'Will you marry us, here, in Corpus Christi?'

He did not answer straight away, but stroked his face thoughtfully. 'How does Kit intend to support a wife, with no job?'

'That's what I came to tell you.' She sipped her tea and then rested her hand underneath her chin, one elbow on the table. 'I've inherited my mother's horse farm in Connemara. Kit and I are going to work it and live there.'

'Well, sure, that's wonderful news, child. When are you going?'

'After you've married us, Father.' Excitement widened her eyes.

'But I can't marry you, my child. You should know that!' He looked sad.

'But why?'

'From what I've observed, neither of you are

403

practised in the faith.' He cleared his throat. 'Have you been baptised?'

'I don't know, Father.' Disappointed, she sighed and pressed her back to the chair.

'Look, I can't marry you unless you can prove by means of a baptismal certificate that you were baptised into the Church of God. You understand, don't you?'

Tamara nodded. 'What can we do?'

'Has Kit been baptised?'

She shrugged. 'I don't think so, Father.'

'And you don't know that you are, either. What a strange state of affairs.' He scratched his forehead.

Tamara stood up, her hopes dashed. She placed the crockery onto the tray and took it to the sink. She was about to wash the cups when Father Malone said, 'Leave them. Miss O'Keefe will do them when she gets back. Come and sit back down.'

She sat slowly back onto the chair, and he reached over to pat her hand. 'I'll check the church records in Galway for you, child. That way, we will both know for sure.'

'Thanks, Father Malone. Sure, that would be grand. Will it take long?'

He stood up. 'I have to get ready for Benediction. Come back and see me tomorrow and bring that young man with you.'

After her discussion with Father Malone, Tamara did not have the heart to shop for her trousseau so went straight back to her wagon. Kit was nowhere about so she lay on her bed, still pondering on the priest's words. Back home, it was mostly the women who went to church and her granny Lena had taken her when she hadn't slunk off somewhere to play. She had taken it for granted that she had been baptised. If the priest refused to marry her, she would feel rejected.

That evening, Tamara told Kit about her talk with Father Malone.

'I only want to marry you, Tamara, not sign up for anything.'

'Don't be daft. It's nothing like that.'

'Well, I don't think I've been churched, because my mother died when I was three. Will it matter?'

'I don't know, Kit. It all seems so complicated. I'd set my heart on Father Malone marrying us. He wants us to come and see him together. Will you come? And will you ask Mr. Billy tonight if he knows anything about your baptism?'

'Yes, and yes.' He put a gentle finger under her chin and tilted her crestfallen face. 'Don't worry. We'll find a way, even if I have to obtain a special licence.'

By mid-morning the following day, Tamara and Kit were knocking on the presbytery door. As they waited, Kit took his certificate from his top pocket and held it in his hand. 'Billy was up half the night searching for this,' he said.

'Fingers crossed.' Tamara smiled.

Miss O'Keefe peered round the side of the door. 'Father Malone is busy. Is he expecting you?'

'Yes,' Tamara replied. The door inched open

enough for them to step inside.

'I don't like to disturb him. Wait here.' She glared at Tamara. Kit's eyes widened and Tamara smiled. She could smell the cardinal polish on the red tiles in the hallway, and everywhere was spotless. The woman worked hard for her keep, it was a pity she lacked the basic social graces.

'Father will see you now,' she said, pointing down the hall towards the study.

Tamara nodded and they went inside. The priest stood up. Smiling, he took both their hands in a warm handshake. 'Please, do be seated.'

Tamara began to fidget with her hands and Kit placed his over hers. 'I know how much you two want to marry,' the priest said. 'So I'll get to the point.' He looked towards Tamara. 'I rang all of the churches in Galway and found no trace of you ever being baptised.' Tamara's face paled. It was not what she had expected to hear and her heart sank. 'But what can we do?'

'Will the fact that I have mine help?' Kit cut in, handing his certificate to the priest.

'If you want to marry in the Anglican Church, this will probably help. You'd best go along and speak to them.' He handed it back. 'Look, let me explain. If one of you were a baptised Catholic, I could marry you, but not on the high altar, only in the Sacristy because it would be a mixed marriage. Can you understand?'

'No,' Kit said, frowning. 'Tamara has her heart set on us marrying here, and you won't marry us because of a silly piece of paper.'

'Not won't, son, can't. Canon Law forbids it. I

406

don't expect you, as a non-Catholic, to under-stand.'

Tamara lowered her head as tears welled in her eyes. This was all very complicated and she had no idea what it all meant.

'I'm sorry, child. I really am. Although you appear to have been brought up in some of the Catholic traditions, you are not a baptised Christian. Your gypsy parents sadly neglected their responsibilities. It's hardly your fault.'

'Is it like this in most churches?' Kit asked.

'I'm only concerned with this one.'

'There must be something you can do, Father,' Tamara said.

He tapped his fingers on his desk. 'I'd hate to see you go away unmarried. Would you be prepared to receive the sacrament of baptism, Tamara?'

'Yes, of course. What would I have to do?'

The priest stood up and went across to a table where he opened a large ledger with lots of entries.

'When can you do it, Father?' asked Kit.

'I could fit you in, say...' He ran his finger down the pages. 'Would this coming Saturday, after confessions, suit you?'

Tamara nodded and Kit squeezed her hand. 'Thanks, Father. Sure, that's grand.' She got to her feet, her eyes aglow with happiness. 'We'll be here.'

'How soon afterwards can we be married?' Kit asked. 'We're anxious to get back to Ireland.'

'Six months is normal.'

'What!' Kit and Tamara sat back down.

'But, in your case...' he paused. 'I've got half an

hour free next Tuesday morning. Is that soon enough?'

Kit smiled at Tamara. 'Thanks, Father Malone,' she said. 'That sounds wonderful.'

Kit and Tamara left the presbytery and walked along the pavement, his arm around her shoulder, both smiling happily. 'Can you believe that we will be husband and wife this time next week?' Tamara was glowing with excitement.

'I can't wait to put that wedding ring on your finger and call you, my wife, Mrs. Trevelyan.'

Tamara giggled. 'What's it like being baptised?' she asked Kit, as they hurried across the street to avoid a horse and cart full with cabbages on its way to the market.

'I don't know,' he laughed. 'I don't remember.'

Tamara laughed. 'Of course.' She paused on the pavement and looked up at him. 'Will my father get here in time, do you think?'

'Don't worry, he'll be here. It's my job to make you happy.'

'Oh, I am Kit. More than I've ever been.' She reached up and kissed him. And as people hurried back and forth around them, they stood on the pavement, lost in the passion of each other's embrace.

Newly-baptised Tamara Maryanne Greystones and Kit were married at the Church of Corpus Christi on a sunny day in May 1901. She looked radiant and happy in a long white satin dress that hugged her figure, and with matching white satin slippers. She wore pink and white flowers in her hair that tumbled in waves of curls around her

408

shoulders, and held a small bouquet.

Kit looked dashing in a grey suit, white shirt and silver grey cravat. He was wearing black patent leather, laced shoes. Father Malone met them at the entrance to the Sacristy and led them along with two witnesses – her father, Captain Fitzroy, and his sister, Miriam Tranter, into the small room at the side of the main altar.

Tamara's knees trembled. Kit, noticing her nervousness, murmured, 'You look like an angel.' It helped her to relax.

Tamara looked around the room, disappointed to see that it was like a dumping area for old chairs and discarded church materials. Then Father Malone unbolted a door to the left. She could see a winding staircase covered in red carpet. At the top was another little room with a balcony that overlooked the main altar. The table had a white linen cloth, and on top lay everything needed to marry them. Tamara couldn't help the tears that threatened. She could tell by Kit's face that he approved. From there she could see the altar and the whole of the church. It brought a lump to her throat.

'I thought this might be appropriate,' Father Malone smiled. Her father placed his arm around her shoulder and nodded his approval.

Kit and Tamara stood side-by-side looking towards the altar as they said their marriage vows. The other guests waited outside the church to congratulate the happy couple.

Out on the pavement, Mr. Billy took photographs of the newlyweds, and Tamara looked over her shoulder at the smiling face of her father,

Capt. Fitzroy standing next to her new aunt Miriam, with Nelly and Flory, Ivan and Beth behind them.

She looked at Kit.

'Isn't it wonderful, darling?'

Smiling, Kit squeezed her hand. It was a glorious day and Father Malone allowed them to change in the Sacristy then wished them all the happiness in the world before hurrying off to attend a sick parishioner.

The rest of the guests, happy and chattering together, walked with them to the station, helping with their luggage. It was then that Miriam took Tamara aside. 'Please keep in touch, Maryanne,' she said, and hugged her tightly. 'I like your young man and I hope you'll both be very happy.'

'Thank you, we will.'

'I knew that Jock was in love with Lady Catherine all those years ago. If she was half as beautiful as you are, my dear, I can't blame him.' Tamara hugged the woman again.

As each of the guests said their individual good-byes, Tamara's father held back and then, with tears in his eyes, he drew her to him. 'My beautiful wee daughter,' he said. He cleared his throat. 'Promise me you'll come and visit. Make sure your husband knows; and no more running away.'

Choking back tears, she held onto him longer than she had to. 'I promise,' she said, kissing his face through his facial hair. 'You're welcome to visit us at Greystones Farm. Don't forget.'

Waving, she boarded the train while Kit bundled

410

their luggage into the compartment. Tomorrow they would set sail for Ireland, the place she had run away from in desperation almost a year ago. This time, she knew without a doubt that with Kit by her side, she would never want to leave again.

The publishers hope that this book has given you enjoyable reading. Large Print Books are especially designed to be as easy to see and hold as possible. If you wish a complete list of our books please ask at your local library or write directly to:

Magna Large Print Books
Magna House, Long Preston,
Skipton, North Yorkshire.
BD23 4ND

This Large Print Book for the partially sighted, who cannot read normal print, is published under the auspices of

THE ULVERSCROFT FOUNDATION

THE ULVERSCROFT FOUNDATION

... we hope that you have enjoyed this Large Print Book. Please think for a moment about those people who have worse eyesight problems than you ... and are unable to even read or enjoy Large Print, without great difficulty.

You can help them by sending a donation, large or small to:

**The Ulverscroft Foundation,
1, The Green, Bradgate Road,
Anstey, Leicestershire, LE7 7FU,
England.**
or request a copy of our brochure for more details.

The Foundation will use all your help to assist those people who are handicapped by various sight problems and need special attention.

Thank you very much for your help.